D1271662

WINNER TAKE ALL

WINNER TAKE ALL

JEFF PATE

Harlan Publishing Company
Greensboro, North Carolina

Winner Take All is a work of fiction. Any references to real people, events, establishments, organizations, or locales are intended only to give the fiction a sense of reality and authenticity. Other names, characters, places, and incidents portrayed herein are either the product of the author's imagination or are used fictionally.

Harlan Publishing Company
5710 High Point Rd. PMB 280
Greensboro, NC 27407 USA.

Quotation from THE TEACHING OF REVERENCE FOR LIFE by Albert Schweitzer. Reprinted with the permission of Henry Holt and Company, LLC. Copyright © 1965 by Henry Holt and Company, LLC.

FIRST EDITION

Library of Congress Catalog Card Number: 99-97248

ISBN 0-9676528-0-4

First Printing: April, 2000

Author's note and acknowledgments

Obviously, the completion and publication of an author's first novel is quite an accomplishment—one that would not have been possible without the assistance and support of family and friends. While the list is too vast to include in its entirety, I succinctly acknowledge everyone's contribution to my work.

First, to my parents. Without them, I would not be on this Earth and would not have striven to accomplish my goal of completing this novel. Thank you not only for your gift of life, but for your support and encouragement throughout the entire process. My brother Kevin and sister Betsy and their families, thank you for being there. CK and the boys: only time will tell...I look forward to it.

Immense gratitude goes to the friends and associates who eagerly read the manuscript in its rawest form and who sincerely offered their helpful comments: Josephine Goodson; Lynette Hampton; Karen Welch; Jamie Knight and Lt. Larry Stroud, High Point Police Department.

Special thanks go to Chief Louis Quijas of the High Point Police Department; and to Officer Kris Britton of the High Point Police Department, whose computer skills kept life breathing into this project. I hope I can continue to call for advice.

The following professionals were of invaluable assistance in contributing to the story: Mark Nelson, Special Agent-in-Charge, North Carolina State Bureau of Investigation, Crime Laboratory, Molecular Genetics Unit; Mark McNeill, Detective, High Point Police Department, Persons Crimes Unit.

Additional thanks go out to my closest friends: Terry Green, Mike Fain, Mike McDade, Pete Kashubara, and last, but certainly not least, Jim and Pam Hackenberg. All of you endured my mood swings during this endeavor and it should go without saying, but, "Thanks."

Finally, to my editor, Sara Claytor. Without her relentless pursuit of perfection, this novel would not have been as good as it is.

An additional dedication must be made to my aunt, Helen Burleson. May you rest in peace and watch us from above. When all the people you have touched look into the sky, they will see your "light."

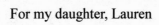

For my daughter, Lauren

"The essence of Goodness is: Preserve life, promote life, help life to achieve its highest destiny. The essence of Evil is: Destroy life, harm life, hamper the development of life."

—Dr. Albert Schweitzer, from
The Teaching of Reverence for Life

WINNER TAKE ALL

PROLOGUE

Wilmington, NC
July 31, 1996

T HE LIGHTS WERE LOW, almost off, and the glow of the flickering candles shadowed her face, giving the room an air of romantic anticipation. He stared at the woman seated next to him on the couch, the flame from the candles dancing in her eyes. Her name was Heather. As she sipped a glass of wine, he studied her elegant features. Her face was perfectly shaped, with full pouty lips, high cheek bones, and her nose was small, with a slight point. Her ash blonde hair was tucked delicately behind her ears, revealing the pink tone of blush makeup. She was tall and slender and the black dress she wore clung to every curve like it was another layer of her skin. The hem was scant and bared the smooth skin of her tanned legs while the collar unveiled her cleavage flaunting her ample breasts.

With her feet tucked under her, she leaned attentively like she was expecting great news; but only to listen to what *he* had to say. He imagined her nude, and the idea excited him greatly. Knowing the inevitable likelihood of sex, he wanted to savor the stimulation he experienced by watching her on the couch. She held the wine glass and slowly traced along its surface with her long fingers.

When she spoke, he followed her lips pronouncing every word and envisioned them pressed against his. The red lipstick she wore made her teeth look vividly white. She was flawless. Perfect in every way from her dainty ears down to her painted toes.

Pouring the wine into her glass, he thought about being close to her. He would kiss her soon. The right moment was approaching, and he knew she was receptive by the way she touched his arm and stroked her hair. But he wanted to see her move like she did hours before. A personal performance. Just for him. Not for the others in that *place*. All the hard dicks staring at her, believing she could be theirs.

"If they only knew," he muttered to himself.

He gave her the glass and looked deep into her brown eyes.

"Dance for me," he said softly.

"What?"

"Dance like you did for me before."

He stood, grasping her hands and swayed to the soft music playing on the stereo.

"You want me to dance? Oh, uh, I don't know."

"Please, you're so damned gorgeous," he said with his most convincing eyes. "I want you to dance for me."

A look of apprehension turned into poise as a seductive smile emerged on her face revealing her decision. Rising to her feet, she dragged the coffee table away from the couch and turned to the stereo in the entertainment center. He returned to the couch and watched her bend over to flip through the CD cases. The fabric of the dress wedged its way nicely in the crack of her ass, which launched a warm shrill of excitement through his body.

Heather straightened, holding a disc.

"Let's see, I think Alice In Chains will be good."

She inserted the disc and pushed the buttons on the player until she found the track she wanted. He recognized the song when it began. It was *Man in the Box*, a tune so familiar to him from all the "gentlemen's" clubs he had frequented. His mind silently kept time with the music, and he gave her a nod of approval. A heavy metal song with a seductive beat and hot guitar licks was the perfect recipe to make a sexy woman move.

With her back to him, her hips swayed seductively to the rhythm of the music. When she turned around to meet his gaze, it appeared she had been transformed somehow from a young school girl into an alluring woman with all the fire of the devil. Her eyes burned as she licked her lips, starting at the top. Then slowly, she moved her tongue to the bottom. Every enticing step she took, she danced, gracefully inching closer to him, their eyes locked in a trance, his arousal intensifying.

She stood over him, placed her hands on his shoulders and dropped her head, sweeping her hair onto his face. Its essence reminded him of honeysuckle blossoms. Her lips, so close he could feel her breath which smelled sweetly of wine. Teasing him, she pushed herself back and dropped to her knees and between his legs. With her hands on the top of his thighs, she pulled herself up into his chest again, tossing her hair in his face. He felt her breath again, hot and moist on his skin and the tickle of her lips brushing against his. As he watched her dance, his body surged hot with adrenaline.

She retreated again and flipped her hair, running her fingers through the silky mane. Her feet swiveled closer. Their eyes were frozen. She playfully lowered the strap from her shoulder partially exposing her left breast. She quickly spun, pulling the skirt up, and revealed the cheeks of her ass. The flame of desire engulfed him.

She faced him. Their gaze locked again as she massaged her breasts, then her hands fell between her legs. He reached for her and she twisted away with a teasing smile.

She used to do that. She'd look at me the same way this one was. Teasing me with that body. Oh, what a teasing whore.

Heather pulled up her hair, licking her lips, with each step, moving closer and closer.

She wants me to give it to her. She wants to see what kind of man I am.

His mouth watered and his chest pounded with excitement. He licked his lips, ready to close in. Touching his legs, her hands fell to his shoulders, and her hair crashed into his face. She sank to her knees, their eyes fixed on each other, filled with passion.

He leaned forward and their lips met. Two or three gentle kisses, and then their mouths opened. He grabbed her arms bringing her to her feet, and kissed her again, their tongues flickering, trying to find each other. The wine tasted sweeter coming from her mouth. The kissing grew more intense and he moved to her neck. Her breaths were deeper and more frequent as he licked and nibbled on her neck and ears. Feeling the pressure of her hands caressing his arms and shoulders, his lips returned to her mouth and a reunion with her tongue.

His heart was pounding. Her skin felt like it was on fire. He wanted her closer, and pressed his chest against her breasts, kissing her neck and shoulders. Her lips touched his neck, her tongue tickled his skin and produced a chill that shot through his body. His breaths were rapid. He inched his fingers under the dress and caressed her ass. She was wearing thong panties, and her skin was soft and smooth. He pulled her hips closer so she could feel the hardness of his crotch. She gasped and squeezed him tightly. His hands moved vigorously over her body, outside her thighs, across her face to her ears, and down her back.

He could not taste enough of her skin, trying to kiss every inch around her stunning face, neck and shoulders. Under the dress again, he glided his fingers along the satiny strip between her crack and felt the moist delight of the fabric covering her vagina. She was breathing harder, trembling, and she pulled his hips to hers. He moved his hands to her breasts and she moaned in ecstasy. She kissed him harder, her tongue hungrily moving inside his mouth, searching for his. He pulled up the skirt and skimmed his fingers inside the strap of the thong. She moaned and kissed him harder. Her hand now found his crotch, and she grabbed the tightness of his trousers. He groaned in pleasure.

In one motion, she pulled the dress over her head and tossed it on the floor. She wore a black satin bra and matching panties. Her breasts were ravishing. Although not large, they were exquisitely shaped. Bending over, he picked her off the floor and carried her into the bedroom, their lips still together, savoring the taste of her tongue. He placed her on the bed. As she lay on her back, he stood, mesmerized, focusing on her. Her breasts rose as she inhaled trying to catch her breath. The exchange of saliva from their kissing made her lips glisten in the light from the living room.

"You are so gorgeous," he whispered, leaning toward her, kissing her beautiful lips.

He was on top of her, and the weight of his body caused his erection to press directly on her crotch. She pulled him closer, thrusting her hips. He fondled her breasts and she brought her hands to his. She unhooked her bra and pulled it from her shoulders, placing it beside her. She caressed herself, stroking her nipples. Seeing that she was not afraid to please herself made him want her more. He reached for her hands and tried to imitate her movements. She took his hands and guided them, continuously moaning and thrashing her head back and forth in exuberant pleasure.

He raised himself and put his face between her breasts and embraced them against his cheeks, kissing and licking them, gently sucking the nipples, tasting the salt from her moist skin. She groaned with fervor and tugged on his hair, pulling his mouth closer to her chest.

His hands quickly returned between her legs, the dampness of the panties truly signifying her arousal. Her hand found his crotch and she ravenously pulled on the snap of his pants.

Impatiently, she helped him pull off his pants, falling in a puddle at the floor. She clutched his hardness, still covered by the boxer shorts and he moved his head back in pleasure. She pulled off his boxers, and took his penis in hand. Her head bowed and within seconds, he felt her lips touching him, then the warm moistness of her tongue. Unable to move he moaned with pleasure and grabbed the sheets below him. He stroked her hair away from her face and tucked it behind her ear.

He wanted to watch her. To see it in her mouth and know she was *his*.

She looked up at him. Their eyes met and she whispered, "I want you inside me."

As she mounted him, he watched her face. That lovely face with that mouth, and those lips. The lips which had, seconds before, been around his manhood. He entered her commencing a simultaneous "Ohhhhh!" from the heavenly warm sensation which surged through their bodies.

The heat of passion made his brow wet with sweat. He gently pushed further inside her. He wanted to go deeper, but it seemed endless. She swayed her hips and closed her eyes, appearing to savor all the euphoria. Her hands moved to her breasts again and she gently teased her nipples.

They rolled over and he lay atop her, still inside. The force of his strokes grew faster, and with more intensity.

"Harder!" she begged. "Do it harder!"

With all his energy, he plunged deeper. He felt her nails dig into his skin. His chest pounded. The breaths shorter. He saw the insatiable passion on her face as she hissed, "yesssss" repeatedly, in rhythmic time with his strokes.

She's ready for me to really give it to her now.

"Turn over," he whispered, and she obediently moved onto her stomach.

He entered her from behind, causing her to gasp, "Ohhh, my god!!!"

He slowly pushed inside her and she rose to her knees.

He spotted the bra next to him. He grabbed it, gliding it against his face, feeling the smooth fabric and remembering what beautiful breasts it once held. The speed of his strokes increased. She panted, "Oh yeah, oh yeah, ohhh."

He knew she was about to come and her voice grew louder with every thrust, shouting, "Oh my god, oh yeah, oh my god, oh yeah!"

Now, it's time to exercise my power. The fantasy has begun.

He slowly eased the bra under her chin, the straps coming together. He felt himself start to spasm. His body tensed.

With one quick snap, he pulled the straps, tightening them around her neck. Forcefully, he flexed his hips which pushed her to her stomach, his weight pinning her body to the bed. The stimulating effect of his orgasm increased the tension on the straps; she gasped once, then grabbed her throat. She gagged and tried to turn over. Still choking, her fingers clawed at the strap as she desperately struggled to release the pressure on her throat. But his strength and mass were too much to overcome. He continued to pull with all his energy as he relished in the immense power he possessed over her.

The involuntary contractions of the orgasm ended and still on top of her, he listened for any sign of life, feeling for any movement. He could feel his erection waning and her body—the body he so recently worshipped and caressed was lifeless. He rolled off the bed onto his feet, and flicked on the light. At the foot of the bed, he watched to see if she were still alive, if she were going to somehow awaken. Her mouth was open in a scream. Her fingers near her throat, frozen where they had unsuccessfully tried to loosen the constricting force of the garrote. The straps of the bra had fallen away from her neck exposing a thin red impression. He put his lips to her ear and whispered. "You were great."

He turned her over, marveling again at her beautiful face. Her eyes were open. Those eyes, once so lovely, were now lifeless and empty, like the eyes of a fish. He stepped to the bathroom and obtained a brush from a cabinet. With her head in his lap, he lovingly brushed her hair, looking into her dead eyes with every stroke. He propped her head on a pillow, stood and admired his work.

Satisfied, he stroked her hand. He whispered apologetically, "I'm sorry for being a little too rough. I thought you might like it that way. I hope we can get together again sometime."

He kissed her hand and then her lips, still warm and soft in her deathly state. He touched her cheek and slid his fingers across her lips. He tongued her ear as he whispered, "Sleep well, my dear."

1

A KILLER SMILED as he lay in his bed. Eyes wide open, he clasped his hands behind his head, fingers interlocked. Although his eyes were open, he could only see images inside his head. Memory of deeds done. Deeds of utmost importance and scope. The ultimate act of power. He reveled in it and its exhilaration wound its way through his veins like a flash of lightning. A cold breeze had found its way through the small opening in a window and tickled his skin beaded with sweat.

A newly acquired taste, killing was a thing he'd discovered he could be good at. Not everyone had the given "talent" for killing. Most people felt guilt or remorse if they killed the most insignificant living creature. Not him. He'd found himself to be quite a good killing machine.

But he wasn't a monster like some of them. He didn't go on giant sprees of death, sacrificing innocent people like those nuts out west. He didn't "go postal" and blast away all of his co-workers when he was having a bad day. No, he wasn't a monster—he was an artist.

It was an art the way he sucked his victims into his trap like bees to honey. Just like the one he'd done that night. The kill was fresh on his mind. So fresh he still smelled the scent of her perfume. Still smelled the fear—still smelled the intense power of watching her die. By his hand.

Only hours ago, the killer knew her body would soon be found. He dumped her like a piece of trash. That was what she was anyway— trash. Like the one before. And now that he'd tasted the sweet nectar of death, he knew there would be more. This teasing whore was just like her. Just like the rest of them. Showing off their bodies, teasing and moving like an alley cat, prowling seductively for all the "gentlemen's" pleasure.

"And what a pleasure it was!" he mused, with a toothy grin. "What a fucking pleasure!"

The killer's recollection caused the erection. The fantasy of it all—their eyes, the struggle. In fact, the ease of it all amazed and excited him. As he touched himself, he returned to his first love. The beginning. It was all her fault. He could love no one else like her; and what did she do? She tossed him away like he was the trash. For what? This was the only way he could be with her now. In spirit— in his fantasy.

The others had no relevance at all in his mind. They were simply tools to satisfy his fantasies of being with her. They were *her* to him. And what was good about them—he could kill her over and over again. That was good.

"Tomorrow will be a good day," he whispered to the moon outside his window.

Good because he was one step closer to achieving his quest for fame. His name would be splashed across the televisions and newspapers. And the stories would be about him. The killer closed his eyes and drifted off to sleep, knowing he would never be caught.

*   *   *

THE LEAVES RUSTLED as the deer crept to the edge of the pond. Motionless, its muzzle pointed to the sky, his nostrils flared searching the air for hostile scents. It was monstrous with a rack of antlers which resembled a large oak tree. Its majestic brown body shaded the white fur on his chest. Instinctively, his eyes scanned the area for predators. The pair of black dots atop his head met the hunter's glare, but clearly, didn't recognize him as anything but the tree he stood against. The brownish green bark of the pine tree blended perfectly with the camouflage outfit the hunter wore. The cold air was still; the hunter knew if he didn't move, the deer wouldn't detect his presence.

Hushed, he stood waiting for the deer to lower his head into the water. He inhaled, his heart pounding in anticipation of the kill. He cradled the rifle close to his chest, and could feel the wooden stock in his right hand, tensed, ready to raise it to his target some fifty yards away. His fingers inched toward the trigger guard.

Apparently satisfied with his current safety, the deer lowered his head to drink from the pond. Cautiously, the hunter raised his rifle and sighted the lens of the scope, placing the cross hairs directly behind the buck's shoulder. Holding his breath, he touched his finger on the trigger and in the distance he heard a phone ringing. In an instant, the image of the deer disappeared. The phone rang again. He awakened, dazed, and picked up the receiver next to his bed.

"Yeah," he mumbled into the receiver.

"Sheriff?" a man asked.

"Yeah, who's this?" he said lying on his side, his eyes still closed.

"Sheriff, it's Walton in dispatch. Are you all right?"

"What?" he groaned, trying to open his eyes.

His wife beside him turned over, pulling the blanket away.

"Sheriff, this is Walton in dispatch. We've got a problem. Lieutenant Tisdale asked for me to give you a call."

He was awake now.

"What's the matter?"

He looked at the alarm clock on the night stand, and it read 5:30 a.m.

"We found a body. Well, uh, some hunters found a body and Tisdale is out there and he wanted me to call you to let you know what they had."

"A body? Where?" he said, sitting upright.

"Ahoskie, sir. Over near the Potecasi Creek bridge, just off Highway 11 toward Murfreesboro."

"Ahoskie? Hmm, any idea who it is?"

"Don't know that, sir. Tisdale thought you might want to come out. It's, uh, I mean, the body's female. It's a woman they found."

"A woman, huh? Is he still out there?"

"Yes sir, he's out there with Deputy Lindsay. He also said something about calling out the SBI lab. He said I needed your permission to do that."

"Yeah, go ahead if Tisdale thinks he needs 'em. They gotta detective enroute?"

"Yes sir, they called out Raeford."

"Okay, you tell him I'm on my way, ya hear."

"Thanks, Sheriff. Oh, Sheriff?"

"Yeah."

"Sorry about waking ya up."

"Ahh, that's all right. I's just having the best dream any married man can have is all."

The sheriff hung up the phone and climbed lazily out of bed. He turned on the bathroom light and his wife spoke in a sleepy voice, "Why you up so early, Jacob?"

"Gotta go to work. Some hunters found a body in Ahoskie. One of the Lieutenants says I need to be out there."

"A body? Of who? Did they say who it was?" she asked as the pitch in her voice rose.

"No, just said it was a woman."

"A woman? Poor girl. Oh poor girl!"

Sheriff Jacob McAdoo was the first black sheriff in the small, rural county of Hertford, North Carolina. He had been sheriff for the past eight years, and after being elected to his third term in 1996, he decided it would probably be his last, for he had worked for the sheriff's department thirty-three years. A tall man with a large burly chest, McAdoo played linebacker for East Carolina, but chose a career in law enforcement instead of trying his luck in the NFL.

Until then, no extraordinary incidents had occurred while McAdoo was sheriff, other than a few homicides involving family or friends; or the occasional hunting accident which claimed the life of an avid deer hunter. For Sheriff McAdoo, it had been a relatively uneventful eight years as sheriff in Hertford County.

The sheriff stepped out his front door into the cold January morning. Standing on the porch, he took a deep breath of the smoky air emanating from the chimneys around. He exhaled and saw his breath blowing like steam from a leaky pipe. The grass was covered with a white powder of frost that crunched softly under his shoes as he walked toward his car. The sky was glittered with stars, and in the distance through the outline of trees, he saw the mounting light of the sun inching toward the horizon.

The overnight moisture had settled on the car and turned to frost, creating a frozen film on the windshield only a scraper or heat could remove. With the engine warming, he used a scraper and with each stoke of his massive arm, it shed a strip of the frozen crystals from the glass. McAdoo opened the door and sat in his brown Crown Victoria and decided the car had warmed sufficiently enough for his drive to Ahoskie. McAdoo lived in Winton, the county seat of Hertford, about a ten minute drive from where he was told the body was found.

The county of Hertford was situated in the northeast part of North Carolina; tucked in between the Chowan and Meherrin Rivers, and close to the Virginia border. Principally rural, the terrain was flat with thick forests of tall pines that enveloped acres of fields providing a perfect hunting ground for deer. In the fall and winter months, the entire northeast part of the state was saturated with deer hunters looking for their daily quarry.

A hunter himself, the sheriff knew what it was like to find a human body in the woods. On an hunting trip years ago, he had found the corpse of a hunter, the victim of an accidental gunshot to the head.

McAdoo drove along the winding country road and he thought about the dream he had before the phone rang. It was a dream a person enjoyed until it was interrupted, and once awake, would want quickly to go back to sleep and to the dream. His thoughts turned to the reason he was awakened from the dream that early Saturday morning. A rare morning when he allowed himself to sleep in past nine o'clock. He tried to picture the woman found and asked himself, "Who was she? How did she die? Was she from this area? Found by hunters?

"She was found near the bridge, they must've been getting an early start to their tree stand. A good location, right near the creek."

Just like his dream.

McAdoo saw the familiar red and white sign of Carolina Power, and turned the car north on NC Highway 11, accelerating toward his destination.

Of the three cities in Hertford County, Ahoskie was the largest with a population of about 4,500. It was a small, quiet farming community where strangers were scarce. The Potecasi Creek bridge wasn't within the city limits of Ahoskie, but in the rural part of the county which carried Ahoskie as its post office. That was the reason the sheriff's department instead of the city police was called about the body. In fact, the bridge was about half way between Ahoskie and Murfreesboro along Highway 11.

The bridge was in an area with few houses around, save one which sat behind some thick trees, occupied by "Old Doc Burton," McAdoo's family physician, but he knew that Burton was out of town, and he probably wouldn't have been any help anyway. He pretty much stuck to himself in that old house after his wife died eight years ago. McAdoo wondered on which side of the road the body had been found. Surely with it being found by hunters, it had to be the side opposite the house.

The Ford's engine hummed as he traveled down the dark, deserted highway, meeting only the headlights of an occasional car. McAdoo looked down at his speedometer and it read 80 mph. Startled at his speed, McAdoo reasoned he was distracted by the nature of his trip. The sheriff approached the bridge over the small tributary of the Meherrin River, distressed over what awaited him.

South of the bridge, and to the right of the road, McAdoo saw two marked Sheriff's Department patrol cars, their lights flashing, parked behind a pickup. A plain brown Ford, like his, undoubtedly belonging to Detective Raeford, was on the other shoulder facing him. He stopped behind one of the patrol cars and looked to his right where he saw in the twilight, the yellow crime scene tape in the shape of a square around the tall pine trees adjacent to the creek bed. McAdoo clutched his flashlight and got out of the car.

He looked down the hill and saw Lt. Tisdale at the edge of the trees. Deeper in the woods Raeford was shining a flashlight. At the shoulder, a uniformed deputy was talking to two men, one around sixty, the other, forty, both clad in camouflage suits with orange hats. He recognized both of them: Jimmy and Curtis Pruitt. Curtis was the father, and Jimmy was his son. "Good fellas," McAdoo said to himself.

Together, they ran a construction business in Murfreesboro. Both men were standing next to a patrol car and the deputy was writing in a notebook. The sheriff figured Jimmy and Curtis had found the body. Lt. Tisdale noticed the sheriff's presence, and started up the hill as McAdoo stepped down the wet grassy slope toward the yellow square.

Inside the perimeter of the yellow tape was the white form lying on the ground. From the distance, the body appeared to be nude, and McAdoo shook his head in disbelief. A mist hovered above the creek, the water rippling as it gently ran across its rocky surface. The woods smelled of pine and earth. Its floor, a combination of grassy weeds, pine needles, and dirt, was wet from the early morning frost.

Peering at the body, he pondered the discovery of the girl's corpse and how she came to her demise. As he stood, shaking his head, again in disbelief, Sheriff McAdoo had no idea the level of interest this case would eventually generate.

"Mornin', Sheriff." Tisdale said, an unlit cigar clenched in his teeth.

"Mornin', Tis. Whatcha got?"

"Well, the way they tell it, Jimmy and Curtis came out early to get to their stand before daybreak. They said they were coming down the hill here, ya know, using their flashlights and they saw this woman lying right there on the ground."

"Hmm, did they touch or move her?"

"Jimmy said Curtis went over to the girl and touched her; but she was cold as cucumber."

The sheriff looked at the body again.

"Any idea who she is?"

"Not a clue yet. Raeford's looking around for some clothes; but as of now, there's none to be found."

McAdoo looked through the dark trees and saw Raeford's distinguishable figure, holding a flashlight.

"You didn't find a purse or anything? No clothes?"

"Not a thing, so far's we can tell."

"How old's the girl?"

"Looks to be about twenty or so. Not much older."

McAdoo walked toward the body and Tisdale followed.

"Any idea how she died?"

"No. Can't really tell. We didn't see any blood or wounds, but she's lying on her side, and we haven't moved her yet."

"Wonderful," the sheriff said under his breath, stopping at the outer edge of the square.

Tisdale walked back up the hill and stopped to confer with the deputy. McAdoo looked down at the figure of the young woman lying in the grass beneath a large pine tree. He ducked under the crime scene tape, and shined his flashlight on the body. She was lying on her right side, in a fetal position on top of a blanket of pine needles and bark and looked like she was asleep; or worse, she could have been placed there by someone. Her dark brown hair, slightly below her shoulders, covered the side of her face, but her ear was visible and tattered with at least six earrings. She was thin, and looked young. McAdoo didn't want to disturb any evidence before the SBI crime lab arrived, thus, he went no further.

He directed the beam at her feet and saw the coloring of a tattoo on her left ankle. It was a dolphin about two inches long. Similar to the emblem of the Miami Dolphins football team, the dolphin was wearing a football helmet and outlined in aqua and shaded in orange. On the small of her back another tattoo, this one larger, of a sunset, its orange mass sunk into the blue ocean. McAdoo turned and stooped under the barrier and looked over to Raeford, using his flashlight in the woods.

"I think you'd better increase the area of the crime scene, if you think there might be evidence in these woods."

"Yeah, Sheriff. I thought of that, but, the Lieutenant said we don't have any more crime scene tape. Used all of it at the Christmas Parade."

McAdoo winced. Under his breath, his lips formed the silent words, "At the Christmas Parade! What the hell we runnin' down here. A sheriff's department or a damned parade committee?"

"Raeford! Get on out of those woods with that flashlight. It's almost light. Let's wait so we won't trample on anything important out here."

"Okay, Sheriff."

He climbed back up the hill.

"Tisdale!" McAdoo shouted, "did the SBI give an ETA?"

"They said they'd have to come from Greenville and it'd be about seven before anyone'd get here."

The Hertford County Sheriff's Department was a small agency operating in a rural area. They had people trained to process crime scenes and collect evidence, but on major cases, like a homicide where the killer was unknown, they relied on the State Bureau of Investigation's Mobile Crime Scene Lab to respond. The SBI had agents and specialists who were highly trained in crime scene investigation and evidence collection. They would videotape the crime scene in addition to taking 35mm photographs. Not that McAdoo lacked confidence in his own people; it was common practice to call the SBI on cases like this because they had the necessary equipment and skilled personnel available to respond to major incidents. And from what McAdoo had observed to that point, he knew it was a major incident, not the normal Hertford County murder.

Raeford followed McAdoo up the hill. Phil Raeford was a good detective. He was forty years old; but he looked like he was thirty. A short man, portly, with a flushed face who wore glasses that were too small for his head, Raeford had been a detective for three years and a deputy for thirteen.

"Raeford, did you talk to Jimmy and Curtis?" McAdoo asked, trying to step carefully up the wet slope.

"Yes, sir I did. Just said they came out to their tree stand and just come up on her."

"You see a car around anywhere?"

"No, sir. I came from Murfreesboro. Didn't see any cars parked on the road 'tween here and there."

"Well, I rode up eleven from my house and don't remember seeing anything."

"With no car around, it looks like this girl was dumped, Sheriff."

"It sure looks that way."

McAdoo blew on the gloves covering his hands.

"C'mon, let's warm up a bit."

They got into the sheriff's car and McAdoo turned up the fan. The heat caused Raeford's glasses fog, hiding his innocent eyes.

Raeford removed his clouded glasses and wiped them with a handkerchief.

"Sheriff, you think as young as she was, she may have been over to the Ramada last night?"

"It's possible. You recognize her?"

"No. Never seen her before. She's so young, Sheriff. What do you think happened?"

"No tellin'. But I think it might be a good place to start."

One thing McAdoo knew about homicide investigations was that the first twenty four hours were important to the resolution of the case because people's memories faded over time and witnesses left the area. The sooner he started asking questions, the more likely he was going to get reliable answers, ones which may point him in the direction of the killer.

He wondered if she had been at the lounge last night. If she had been approached by some drunk at the bar and politely rebuffed him when he tried to make a date. Angry over the rejection, he waited for her in the parking lot. Outside, he confronted her again, and becoming bothersome, she insulted him. The anger turned to rage and he grabbed her and forced her screaming into his car. Struggling to escape, she attacked him, which brought on the murderous assault. After realizing he killed her, he disrobed her, and dumped her body in the woods to make it look like she was raped.

The sheriff shook his head and said to himself, "No, not here."

The Ramada Inn, now called The Ahoskie Inn, was on Route 561, about five miles from the Potecasi Creek Bridge. On Friday and Saturday nights, the lounge of the Ahoskie Inn posed as a night club, offering dancing and drinking to anyone willing to pay the $3.00 cover charge. Friday was the night of their biggest crowd; and with the holidays gone, there was nothing else to do in the area but go there. Far from being a true nuisance, the lounge endured the occasional fights that erupted whenever alcohol was involved. The patronage, primarily residents of the area, were easy going, fun-loving people who rarely caused trouble.

He looked over to Raeford.

"As soon as we clear here, we get a picture of the girl and show it to the manager and bartenders of the lounge to see if they recognize her, and also to see if there were any problems there last night."

19

"Right, Sheriff."

"C'mon, let's go get some coffee while we wait for the SBI to get here."

The sheriff and Raeford drove to the Duck Thru station at the corner of Route 561 and Boone Farm Road to get coffee and a box of doughnuts for the others. The convenience store, which was next to the Ahoskie Inn, stayed open all night on weekends. In the store, the sheriff talked with the clerk and asked if she knew of any problems at the lounge the previous night. McAdoo came up empty when the clerk told him it was a slow night.

McAdoo drove out of the parking lot, looking at the hotel and thinking the lounge must have been somehow related to the death of the woman found. The sheriff knew it was the only source of trouble in that part of the county and it would be the first place he would look for information.

They passed by Roanoke-Chowan Community College, and through Union. All the time, McAdoo looked for a strange car. But none were found. It was dawn when McAdoo approached the bridge and saw a black mini-van on the shoulder of the road with "SBI Mobile Crime Laboratory" in white letters printed on its side.

"The SBI's here. Maybe we'll get some answers after getting a closer look at the body."

McAdoo parked the car behind the black van, and he looked down to where the body lay, and noticed Pruitt's truck was gone. He saw two people in dark coats with "SBI" in large gold letters on the back taking down the yellow tape which encircled the body. Tisdale was standing at the shoulder. He turned when McAdoo's car stopped and walked to the sheriff's door.

"What are they doing?" McAdoo asked Tisdale from inside the car.

Tisdale, the cigar still in his mouth, leaned in the driver's window. When he spoke, rancid smoke from the cigar drifted into McAdoo's face.

"They said they'd have to make a larger area for the crime scene."

McAdoo got out of the car and walked down the hill with Raeford next to him. The sheriff towered over Raeford when they were side by side. As they got closer, McAdoo noticed one of the agents was female. The female agent looked up and saw the sheriff coming and walked over to greet him.

"I'm Sheriff McAdoo. And this is Detective Raeford. I really appreciate ya'll coming out so quickly. It looks like we got us a good 'un here."

"Hi Sheriff, I'm Betsy Steelman," she said as she shook his hand.

McAdoo noticed her grip was firm and she pointed to her partner, who was extending more yellow tape.

"And this is Tom Moffitt."

He smiled and nodded.

"I got a preliminary from Deputy Lindsay, and he said two hunters found her this morning around five a.m. Since she's not wearing clothes, it's going to be hard to identify her."

She turned toward the body and gestured with her hands.

"We'll start with the video of the entire scene. Then we'll do the stills, okay? Did y'all find any evidence? I was told one of your detectives was out here searching for something."

"Yeah, he was looking, but he didn't find anything."

"All right, then. After we get the pictures, we'll have a look at the body. Did you call the medical examiner out? Do you know if he's going to come to the scene?"

Raeford answered, "Yeah, we called Dr. Allen. We told him to stand by until ya'll were through, so's he wouldn't have to wait too long."

"Good idea, I'll bet you're glad he'll even come out. A lot of them won't come out to a scene. They just wait to see them at the morgue."

"I'll get dispatch to call him and let him know it's okay to come," Raeford said, and walked to his car.

Steelman turned to McAdoo.

"Okay, look Sheriff, if there's something you'd like for us to do, let us know, okay? You know, it's your case, and we're just here to help you guys."

21

"I'll let you know. I don't know of anything special. Just the usual processing."

The sheriff was already impressed by Steelman. She was young, in her thirties; but seemed confident and self-assured. McAdoo could tell Steelman was from North Carolina. Her drawl was definitely from the eastern part of the state where the r's are pronounced like l's or w's. She was a short, stocky woman and pretty. Her curly brown hair was pulled into a pony tail that rested on the fur collar of her coat.

Moffitt had yet to say anything but Sheriff McAdoo was confident they would do a good job. Moffitt looked younger than his partner, and went about his task with an uncertainty in his movements. By their physical presence, McAdoo would have guessed Moffitt was in charge. But in spite of Moffitt's tall and muscular good looks, Steelman directed his movements, and the sheriff caught him rolling his eyes in response to her guidance, apparently in chauvinistic insolence.

The SBI agents went about their work video taping from every angle. After the video, they took the 35mm photographs. First, from a distance, then several close-up shots of the body. As McAdoo watched the agents work, it looked as though Steelman was walking through the procedures of crime scene processing with her younger partner. Her hands gestured as if she was giving instruction, and it was evident she was training a new agent.

After the photographs were taken, the two agents measured the location of the body relative to permanent objects. The results would later be used to construct a scaled drawing of the scene, essential for determining the exact position of the victim at the death site. Upon completion of the measurements, the body could be moved and examined for causes of death.

North Carolina law stated that the medical examiner must be notified of the death of any person resulting from violence, poisoning, accident, suicide or homicide. The law also required that the body at the scene of a death shall not be moved until authorized by the medical examiner. The medical examiner for the Hertford

County area, Dr. Stephen Allen, arrived shortly before the agents completed the measurements.

Dr. Allen was employed by the State of North Carolina as a medical examiner; even though he didn't perform autopsies on the deceased. His preliminary findings were forwarded to the pathologist performing the autopsy. Allen was a middle aged man of ordinary features. Topping his wiry frame, his thin salt and pepper hair was swept over to the side and he wore small reading glasses which drooped low on the bridge of his nose. Without much of a personality, Allen was stoic and to the point, but he knew his business and was reliable to respond to death scenes.

Dr. Allen knelt next to the body.

Making notes on a voice recorder, "The decedent appears to be a healthy white female, twenty to twenty five years of age, and is unclothed."

He grabbed her left arm, and moved it, testing the range of motion, "The body's in stage two rigor, and lividity is evident."

Allen turned her over to her back. Her eyes were open, and she had the look of death, with her mouth open and her face indented on the side she had lain. Moffitt snapped more photos. Allen lifted the woman's eyelids and assessed the victim's throat area which was discolored like a bruise.

"There is evidence of petechial hemorrhage in the eyelids and there appear to be contusions around the neck area; but the discoloration could be a result of lividity."

Dr. Allen examined the rest of her body. He sifted through her hair, and carefully inspected her hands. In his opinion, no other injuries were apparent.

The doctor stood and pulled off his rubber gloves. Sheriff McAdoo walked over to him.

"Well, Doctor, what do you think?"

He looked at the sheriff over his glasses.

"I think it's too early to make a definite conclusion; but from what I saw, I'd say she was strangled."

23

"Do you have a guess as to the time of death?"

"I don't know. It was pretty cold last night and bodies stay well preserved in cold temperatures. With rigor still set in, I would say she was killed no more than twenty-four hours ago. Do you have any idea who she is? She looked to be such a pretty girl."

"No, Doctor. Not yet."

"I sure hope you find out who she is. Poor girl. Good luck, Sheriff."

"Thanks, Doctor Allen."

"See that the body is taken to the hospital morgue. It'll be picked up for Chapel Hill later on today."

"Right."

It was almost 10 a.m. when the doctor left. McAdoo looked up at the sky to see a front of dark clouds moving into the area, giving rise to a possible storm. A gaggle of geese flew overhead and their incessant honking was nerve racking. There were hundreds of the birds, a mass of flapping wings and dull chatter migrating to warmer weather. It seemed to go on forever, but once the main part of the group passed, only the faint call from a straggler or two could be heard from above. Steelman walked up to the sheriff, her hands stuffed in the pockets of her jacket, and her nose and cheeks red from the cold.

"It looks like we're pretty much done here. We searched a pretty large area around her body and the creek, but couldn't find anything. The detective says he can't think of anything else."

"Yeah, well, oh, could you take some close-up Polaroid shots of her and those tattoos? We'll probably need 'em for an identification."

"Sure, Sheriff. Hey, Moffitt!" she shouted and turned in the direction of the body, cupping her hands over her mouth like a megaphone. "Take some close-ups of her face and the tattoos with the Polaroid so the sheriff can have 'em."

The black mini van from Jenkins Funeral Home had arrived to transport the body to the hospital morgue. The girl's body was wrapped in a sheet and then placed in a black vinyl bag with a long zipper. The three men hoisted the bag onto a stretcher and rolled it up the hill to the road. It wasn't an easy climb, and Raeford lost his footing, trying to push the load up the slippery bank. McAdoo watched the stretcher slide into the cargo area of the van and thought he'd missed something. It was an unfathomable feeling like they had neglected to do some important task, similar to the anxiety of leaving on a trip with the notion that someone forgot to turn off the stove. Maybe it was his own insecurity.

It had been a long time since he'd been involved in a homicide case where the killer was unknown and there were no witnesses. The "smoking gun" cases were easy. Commonly, the killer was a family member or friend who was still at the scene when the police arrived. The dilemma he faced was what they called in law enforcement a "whodunit?" Like a jigsaw puzzle with millions of pieces waiting to be assembled. When the parts of the puzzle fit together perfectly, they would be one step closer to finishing it.

The sheriff was concerned they may not have done enough; but he tried to persuade himself they had. Raeford was a competent detective; but he'd never been in charge of a homicide investigation like this when both victim and suspect were unknown. He frowned and shook his head, dismissing the sentiment. Perhaps he was over reacting; maybe it would turn out to be a relatively easy case.

"Who knows? One piece at a time."

Sheriff McAdoo stood at the edge of the road. Cars and trucks passed slowly, filled with hunters and others out early on a Saturday, curious of the spectacle of the sheriff's cars and crime lab van, and wondering what tragedy had brought them there. A car stopped in the road. McAdoo saw the necks bend as the two men tried to catch a glimpse at the gore. There was nothing gory about this case. It wasn't like the slasher movies where the unsuspecting victim was butchered and lay in a pool of blood.

Those things happened in real life, McAdoo knew, but not this one. This murder was uninteresting: no blood, no guts, no severed parts strewn about. But she was dead all the same, and death was real, and not like the sanitized version depicted on the screen. It wrenched his heart thinking about it.

"What a waste of precious life."

He waved harshly at the car, a signal their morbid curiosity was aggravating him. The motorist apparently saw the large man in the brown uniform advancing toward his car and quickly continued on his trip.

The agents put the last of their equipment into the van and closed the door. Steelman walked over to the sheriff as he stood thinking about the case.

"Sheriff," she said, and handed him three Polaroids: one of the victim's face, and one of each of the tattoos. "I guess that'll wrap it up on our end if you don't have anything else."

The sheriff flipped through the pictures of the girl.

"No, I guess that will do it."

"She sure was young, wasn't she?"

McAdoo looked at her.

"Yep, and pretty, too."

He shook his head.

"We don't get too many of these around here."

"Look, Sheriff, if you have any questions. Or, if you need some help with the case, I'm sure one of our agents would be glad to help you out."

"You're not agents? I thought ya'll were sworn agents."

"Oh no!" Steelman said with a surprised look on her face. "We're Crime Scene Specialists. We don't do any investigative work. Just work on crime scenes. Murders, arsons and stuff like that."

"Oh—"

"We've got this unit. The Investigative Support Unit. They work on homicides like this."

"Really? Not one of the regular field agents?"

"No, these guys are specialists. Trained by the FBI. They investigate murders of important people, like police officers and public officials. The SAC is supposed to be an expert profiler on crime scenes and murderers. He even worked in the FBI's Behavioral Science Unit profiling serial murderers and stuff like that."

"Damn, what's his name? Do you know him? Is he good?"

"No, I don't know him personally; but his name is Clark Hager. And yeah, I heard he was really good. The FBI even wanted him to come there to work with them full-time. That's how good they say he is."

The sheriff raised his eyebrows.

He mumbled to himself, "Hmm, we may need some help with this one. I might just give this guy a call."

"If you find out you've got no other leads, give them a call. They might be able to help you. Sheriff, it was good to meet you and good luck with the case."

He shook her hand again.

"Thanks for coming out. Ya'll were a big help."

Steelman walked toward the van. She stopped and turned around like she'd forgotten something.

"Oh, we'll have those pictures ready in a couple of weeks."

The sheriff nodded.

"Hey, Steelman! Where do they work out of? That special unit?"

"SBI Headquarters in Raleigh. Where else?"

She flashed a quick smile.

"Good luck."

McAdoo got into his car and Raeford joined him in the passenger seat.

"Raeford, we got us a tough one this time. You think you can handle it? Cause if you can't, I understand. We can get some help, ya know, from the SBI?"

"I'll be honest with ya, Sheriff, I've never worked a killing like this. We don't even know where it happened, or who she is. I don't have a problem at all with gettin' some help. I know when I'm in over my head."

"Good," McAdoo said, relieved. "I was hoping you'd see it that way. Too many times we let our pride get in the way of common sense, and then we end up fuckin' somethin' up that ain't even ours to fuck up. I'll make a call to Raleigh and see if we can't get some help from their people. In the meantime, we'll take these pictures over to the inn and see if anyone saw her there last night."

2

BILL MATLIN looked in the mirror as he tied his tie. It had been two weeks since he'd last done it, but it felt like it was only yesterday. A vacation was something Matlin had needed desperately, only to learn no matter how long he stayed away, the work would still be given to him while he was gone.

"That's the price you pay," he said to himself, "for being a detective. The job never ends and the killing never stops."

Fortunately for Matlin, he worked in a city which had a reasonably low murder rate. In 1995, there were only seven homicides reported in Wilmington, North Carolina, and all of them were solved.

With a population of around 55,000 people, Wilmington was a fairly safe medium-sized city, known more for its recent rise in popularity as the setting for big screen movies, like *Cape Fear*. The city was snuggled between the Cape Fear River and the Intercoastal waterway and a short drive to Wrightsville Beach. Barely a modest tourist attraction until recently, Wilmington's only source of interest for many years, was the memorial for the battleship *U.S.S. North Carolina*, which stood within sight as U.S. 421 crossed over the Cape Fear River. Presently, the city boasts a large Hollywood movie production studio and the increasingly popular UNC-Wilmington.

Matlin fastened the holster to his belt, slid the pistol into the leather carrier, and snapped it closed. During his time away, he didn't wear his gun once, and it felt heavy, pulling on his belt. He clipped his badge to the belt and tucked a pair of silver handcuffs in his waistband. Satisfied with the tie, he buttoned the top button of his shirt feeling the snug fit of the collar. The gorging accomplished over the Christmas holiday had taken its toll on Matlin's waistline, adding a few unwanted pounds to his frame. In the closet hung his sport coat; he slipped it on and after kissing his wife good-bye, he picked up his car keys and walked to the front door.

It was drizzling and unusually cold, even for early January. The street was dank, and the sky was gray with darker clouds coming in from the Atlantic signifying more rain was likely to come. As Matlin drove, he thought about the work that waited for him. The new cases he would investigate. And the old ones which lingered, waiting to be solved.

A five-month-old murder was foremost in his mind. It had baffled him and other members of his unit; it still remained unsolved. The murder of a young female college student in her apartment made big news in a city like Wilmington. Immense pressure was placed on the police to find the killer. The girl's parents, friends, and city officials pushed for its resolution, but most of the heat came from the media.

The print and television news were unrelenting. Along with the incessant badgering of investigators, they strove to leak any information which enthralled the public. They also paralleled their efforts with stern criticism of the detectives for keeping details close to their chest. The case endured not for the lack of effort, but for the failure of the detectives to identify the killer or determine a motive for it all. As Matlin watched the wipers sweep across his windshield, he remembered that night in early August.

Around 11 p.m. a resident of the College Oaks apartment complex on South College Street called the police to report a foul odor coming from the apartment building. The apartment complex was near the university and home to various people including several students who preferred to live off-campus. A patrolman arrived at the apartments, and described the odor not unlike the smell of spoiled trash. The officer determined the odor was emanating strongest from the door of Apartment "E" which was on the second floor of the building.

The officer asked neighbors about the apartment's occupant and was told a young woman, believed to be a student at UNC-W, lived there alone. The officer learned that her car, a white Mitsubishi Eclipse, was parked in front of the building.

After checking the license plate through the Division of Motor Vehicles, he discovered the Mitsubishi was registered to Heather Marie Kingston of the same address on College Street. Despite the routine appearance of the call, the officer, a twenty three year veteran, experienced a peculiar uneasiness about it. In the officer's opinion the odor was much too powerful to be spoiled trash, and smelled more like a dead animal, or worse, a dead person. At the officer's request, the maintenance man was summoned with a master key to open the door.

When the door opened, the officer related the odor became more intense and sickening. Upon entry, he found the decaying body of a woman lying in a bed.

Matlin was the detective on call that night. The phone rang just before midnight, interrupting the movie *Bridges of Madison County* he and his wife were enjoying. It was a feeling of dread whenever the phone rang at such a late hour. Being the parents of teenagers, a late night call was always taken with angst. After breathing a sigh of relief the phone call wasn't concerning his children, Matlin dressed and drove to the apartment complex, arriving there around 1 a.m.

It was a warm and muggy summer night, and thick clouds prevented the stars from shining. Dew had already started to settle and bead on the metal surfaces and windows of the cars parked in the parking lot. Matlin got out of his car and jotted a few notes on his legal pad about the time, weather, etc. He walked to the apartment building layered with brick below the grayish vinyl siding. The apartments on the ground floor had cement patios off a sliding glass door, and the units on top had wooden balconies decorated with iron railings.

The crime lab van was parked next to two squad cars in front of the building. A male officer was guarding the door of apartment "E" at the top of the stairs, and nodded to Matlin when he reached the summit.

"Is he inside?" he asked the officer.

"Yeah. In the bedroom," the officer answered, and wrote Matlin's name on his pad.

He entered the apartment, engulfed in the putrid odor of decay.

An oil painting hung on the wall above the living room fireplace—a picturesque lake with mountains and trees in the background. On the coffee table, an empty bottle of Beringer White Zinfandel wine rested between two crystal goblets. Another uniformed officer writing in a notebook and a crime lab technician were talking in the living room and looked up when Matlin entered the room.

"Hey, Matlin. How are you?" the officer asked.

"Good. What do you have?"

The officer walked him to the bedroom. The overhead light shone on her as she lay in the bed. A wooden four poster queen size bed with canopy was flanked by two night stands, and faced a chest and a long dresser with a mirror. The soft pink comforter covered the supine body to her chin. As he stepped closer, he could hear the buzzing of flies around the body. The eyes had been invaded by the insects and from the sockets, like little worms, wiggled the fly larvae commonly called maggots.

Her hair was blonde, neatly brushed, and she was wearing red lipstick, which shimmered in the light. Looking around the room he saw a photograph in a frame on the dresser. It looked like a prom picture with the victim wearing a blue sequined gown, standing in arm with a young man in a black tuxedo. Above their heads, was a glittered sign: "Senior Prom—1994". Matlin appreciated the attractiveness of the girl in the picture, and wondered what significance her male friend would have in this case.

He looked at the overhead light.

"Was that light on when you got here?"

"No," the officer answered, "all the lights were off."

"It may mean something if the lights were off. But it may not," Matlin mumbled. "All right, let's go ahead and do the processing before we move anything. We'll do the pictures first. Did someone notify the medical examiner?"

"Yeah, headquarters called him, and he said he wouldn't be coming, and to call Gray Transportation to take the body to the morgue."

"That's just great."

Matlin was frustrated. He believed the medical examiner should respond to all unattended deaths, especially homicide scenes. As far as he knew then, the case wasn't officially a homicide, and on the surface, it didn't appear to be one. But, Matlin had already seen some things that didn't make sense. She was in the bed lying completely straight, with her arms under the covers.

"She didn't die in her sleep," he concluded. "No one sleeps like that. Besides, who puts makeup on before they go to bed?"

Matlin went out in the hall to smoke a cigarette while the crime scene techs did their work. He took the opportunity to knock on the doors of the other occupants of the building.

Most of the neighbors to whom he talked couldn't provide any pertinent information about the girl. A lot of them were elderly and stayed to themselves. Matlin could only confirm that she was a college student and believed to work a job at night. The most helpful information was acquired from the resident of the apartment directly below the victim.

Lois Tanner lived in Apartment "A". Matlin asked her about the young woman living above her. The middle-aged blonde divorcee invited him in and the detective took a seat in a chair at a dinette table. Tanner lit a cigarette and sat opposite Matlin at the table.

"I really didn't know her at all, other than I think she went to UNC-W. I work during the day so I'm not at home, but she wasn't at home at night very often either."

"How do you know that?" he asked.

The woman pointed to the ceiling.

"Well, you can hear just about everything going on up there. Even footsteps, you know, when people walk hard."

She stomped her feet on the floor, "Boom—boom."

"Do you remember the last time you saw her, ma'am?"

She rubbed her chin and her eyes closed in thought.

"Hmm, I saw her," she whispered. "Was it Wednesday or Thursday?" She blurted out, "Oh, Wednesday about ten in the mornin'. That was the last time I *saw* her."

Matlin noticed her emphasis on the word saw.

"You say you saw her on Wednesday. But do you know if she was in the apartment after that?"

She smiled and puffed the cigarette.

"Oh yeah, I do."

"Well?"

The smoke escaped her mouth as she spoke.

"I heard her late the same night. I was up watching a movie 'cause Thursday's my day off, you know, and it was a little after midnight when I heard the music upstairs."

Matlin took a Marlboro from his pack and stuck it between his lips.

"Do you mind?" he asked.

Sucking on her cigarette, she shook her head and the smoke drifted from her nose.

He flicked the lighter and burned the end.

"Is that all you heard? Music?"

"No, the usual stuff. Footsteps and laughing, but..." she paused to drag the cigarette. "About an hour later the music got louder and I thought I was gonna have to go upstairs and say something..." she puffed again and smoke poured from her mouth. "But, you know, those college kids, they turn it up some. So, I just turned up my television set and kept on with the movie."

"When did the music stop?"

"Don't know. It was still going when they started."

Matlin wrinkled his brow.

"Started. Started what?"

The woman giggled and covered her mouth like a child.

"You know," she giggled again, covering her mouth. "You know, heavy breathing. Bed squeaking. You know? "

Matlin got the analogy.

"Oh, I get it. They were having sex. I see."

The woman giggled again and she looked like a child who had just said a word she wasn't supposed to.

"Well, after they stopped, I didn't hear anything else the rest of the night. I fell asleep before the movie was over."

"Did you hear a man's voice?"

The woman tilted her head to the side and pursed her lips.

"No, I don't recall hearing a man's voice. Just a woman's. You know, with all that 'ooing and ahhing' I said to myself, pa-leeease, *I* never had it so good."

He asked Ms. Tanner if she ever saw Heather with a man and she said she had not, but she told him two other college girls lived in the apartment across from her and could possibly tell him more. Matlin thanked her and went back upstairs to the apartment.

Matlin returned to the apartment and saw the crime lab technician vacuuming the floors around the bed and in the living room; and another lab tech, a female, had arrived to help the other, and was snapping 35mm shots of the body and the apartment.

Vacuum cleaners were used to collect microscopic evidence from the carpet or other objects, such as the bed, curtains, and floors.

After the vacuuming was finished, Matlin walked over every inch of the apartment with the lights on in search of evidence. The wineglasses and bottle on the table were dusted for fingerprints. Everything else appeared to be completely normal. Except for the usual dust and clutter, the apartment's condition was customary for a college student. The crime lab techs took measurements, and started a crime scene sketch. With the preliminary tasks completed, the victim's body was then scrutinized for possible causes of death.

Matlin cursed the fact the M.E. would not show, and it incensed him. He was an idealist when it came to homicide investigations. In a perfect world, not only did the homicide investigators respond to the crime scene, the medical examiner and a representative from the District Attorney's office would be mandated to participate in the investigation from its onset. Matlin had been involved in a number of murder cases, but he regarded himself a layman in establishing cause of death. In his opinion, it was essential for a physician with forensic training to respond to a death scene, where many questions could be answered. Matlin knew there was no sense in brooding over the situation. He could do only with what he had.

Matlin stood over the bed where the woman lay, flies still buzzing around her head. The stench was nauseating. He knew this was the worst part of the job, but she deserved for him to be professional. Holding his breath, he pulled back the covers and revealed her torso, which was unclothed. A swarm of flies sprang up from the body, causing Matlin to blow out his breath and step away leaving the comforter at her waist.

The detective regained his composure, inhaled deeply, and approached the body again. He removed the cover entirely, exposing her whole body. She was totally nude and slightly swollen. Matlin guessed she'd been dead a couple of days due to the swelling and the presence of maggots.

She was lying with her arms directly by her side; her legs were perfectly straight. The flies cleared, but still buzzed about the room.

"Open some of those windows," Matlin ordered, swiping at the flying pests.

Matlin noticed a tattoo on her left ankle. It was the logo of the University of North Carolina at Wilmington. A green and yellow bird, apparently a seahawk, with "UNCW Class of '98" inscribed underneath. Like a beacon, the thin red scrape around her neck immediately explained her fate.

"She was strangled," he said.

He pointed to her throat.

"Get a good close up of this." The camera clicked.

"Damn," one officer said. "She was so pretty. Who'd want to do something like that to her?"

Matlin looked closer at the ligature wounds on the woman's throat. The marks were thin, about a quarter-inch in diameter, and the edges of whatever was used had cut into her skin. He also noticed scratch marks perpendicular to the ligature marks. He pointed at them.

"She must've scratched herself as she was trying to release the pressure of whatever was choking her."

Matlin shook his head.

On her chest, slightly above her breasts, were several spots of dried liquid. Matlin wasn't sure, but the white crusty stain could only be one thing: semen. His entire body shuddered.

"Let's turn her over," Matlin said.

They turned her over, seeing no blood or wounds. All he could see were red patches in the skin made by blood which settled in the lower parts of the body after her heart stopped pumping.

Matlin hadn't seen any clothing the girl may have been wearing, and he pulled the entire comforter away from the bed. Nothing. Holding his breath, and swatting more flies, he went to his knees, and shined his flashlight under the bed. Nothing but gobs of dust clinging to the box spring.

"Where are her clothes?" he asked the officer.

"I didn't see any. Maybe she took them off."

Matlin looked around the room and walked into her closet. A hamper sat on the floor, and Matlin opened it, finding a pair of jeans, socks, a small shirt, bra, and a pair of panties.

"Those could be them," he whispered to himself.

Only the last person who saw her alive could confirm what she was wearing. He walked out of the closet.

"There's some clothes in the hamper," he told the lab tech.

"Better collect 'em. They might be what she was wearing."

The crime scene processing was complete, but Detective Matlin's job had just begun. Matlin dialed the cellular phone, called his lieutenant, and informed him he had a homicide. No details were discussed because he was on a cell phone, and he didn't want vital information broadcasted over the public airways. A good homicide detective never used the telephone at the crime scene, because he could learn important facts about the last number dialed by simply pressing the re-dial button on the telephone. Conceivably, the last person the victim called could have been who killed her.

The female lab tech was standing next to him as he talked to the lieutenant. She was holding some white cards with black fingerprint impressions on them. Seeing her standing in front of him, the detective concluded the conversation and disconnected the phone.

"Did you get some prints from the glasses and bottle?"

"Yeah, we lifted some good ones from one of the glasses, but there were no prints at all on the other one, or the bottle."

"Great," Matlin said to himself. "Now we have a killer who wipes off his fingerprints."

Matlin knew the killer must have known the victim to have been in her apartment listening to music and drinking wine. He remembered what the woman downstairs had told him about hearing people having sex that night.

"She must've been with her boyfriend or someone she was very friendly with."

He then recalled the picture on the dresser of the victim and a young man. Matlin walked into the room and looked at it. It was two years old, but he thought if she still had it on a dresser, he was still involved in her life.

Matlin heard voices of females outside talking to the officer at the door and he went out to see who it was. The officer was standing outside the apartment talking to two college-aged girls, an attractive redhead and a pretty brunette.

The redhead was talking to the officer.

"What's the matter? What's wrong with Heather?"

The officer looked at Matlin for an answer.

"Can I ask who you are, ma'am?" the detective asked.

"I'm Lisa. And this is Carol." The redhead said pointing to her friend. "We live here in apartment 'H'."

"I'm Detective Matlin with the police department."

He pointed to their door.

"Can we go inside and talk?"

The two girls entered the apartment and Matlin followed. They stopped in the living room. While the two girls sat on the couch, Matlin remained standing.

Carol spoke first.

"Detective, what's going on in Heather's apartment?"

"Did you know Heather well?"

"Yeah, uh, she's our friend. We go to school together and what did you mean by *did* you know her?"

Matlin saw the worried look on both of their faces.

"I'm sorry to tell you this, but," he took a deep breath. "Heather's been killed."

Both girls broke into tears and Carol grabbed Lisa's arm.

"Oh my God! There's no way. Are you sure?" Lisa asked.

"Yes we're sure."

"When? What happened?" Carol implored. "Who would do such a thing? Oh my God!" She continued to cry.

Lisa leaned her head on Carol's shoulder, her eyes and cheeks red from crying. Matlin moved to the bathroom and pulled some tissue from the dispenser and brought it back to the sobbing girls. They wiped their eyes and noses trying to compose themselves.

"How was she killed?" Lisa asked in between sobs.

"We don't really have many details right now. Can you tell me when the last time you saw her was?"

Carol answered, "The last time, uhh," she sniffled. "I think it was Tuesday night. She came over to borrow some laundry detergent. Yeah, it was about eight thirty or so."

"Are you sure it was Tuesday?"

"I'm positive it was Tuesday because Lisa and I had a test the next day, and we were studying for it when she asked to borrow the detergent. When did this happen?"

"We don't know right now. That's why it's important to know when the last time she was seen alive. Did she have a boyfriend?"

Lisa wiped her nose.

"Boyfriend? Josh! Where's Josh? Is he okay? Does he know yet?"

"Josh? Who's Josh? Is he her boyfriend?"

"Yes," Lisa answered. "Yes he is. They've been dating for a long time."

"How long have they been dating?" Matlin asked as he was scribbling on a legal pad.

They looked at each other and Lisa said, "Oh, they'd been dating for ever. She told me it had been since high school."

"What's his last name? Does he go to school here, too?"

"It's Gregory. Josh Gregory. He lives with a couple of his friends in an apartment on Clear Run Drive," Carol said.

"Do you know which one?"

"I think it's called Clear Run Apartments."

"Do you know his address?"

"No, not the address, but I know his phone number." She got up and went to her bedroom returning with an address book. "It's 673-4275."

Matlin wrote the number on his pad.

"Officer?" Carol asked. "How was she killed? Who would do such a thing?"

"We don't know yet. We'll have to wait until the autopsy. Do you know her parents?"

"No, we never met them, uh, but I don't think she was real close to them. You know, because of what she did." Lisa said.

"What she did? What do you mean? What did she do?"

Lisa looked surprised.

"Oh, I guess you haven't found that out yet, um, it's where she worked." They both looked at each other again reluctant to tell.

Matlin raised his eyebrows.

"Where she worked. What do you mean? Where did she work?"

"At the Doll House. She was a dancer. A—"

"A stripper." Carol finished.

Lisa turned to her, "Carol! An exotic dancer."

Carol rolled her eyes and she crossed her arms at her chest. "Same difference, Lisa."

"The Doll House, hmm. Did Josh know she worked there?"

"Oh yeah, he knew. She said they used to fight about it all the time. He hated the fact she worked there. But she worked there still. Said she made too much money to quit."

The information he had obtained from the girls furnished Matlin with the first true lead in the case, and potentially, the one needed to solve it. Matlin left the two girls' apartment and returned across the hall to get the picture of Heather and the young man. He returned with the picture and showed it to them.

"Is this Josh?"

Carol looked at the picture of the young man wearing the tuxedo, with the blonde hair, almost the same color as Heather's hair.

"Yes, that's Josh." Lisa nodded.

DMV listed Josh Gregory's address as 732 Clear Run Drive, Apartment B. After he was finished at the crime scene, Matlin drove to the Clear Run Apartment complex, believing he'd probably already solved the murder of Heather Kingston.

The detective had a person who knew the victim, they had an intimate relationship, and he learned from the girls they had quarreled lately over Heather's job as a topless dancer. Matlin imagined the two came back to her apartment and drank some wine and listened to some music. Then, they moved to the bedroom and had sex. After they were finished, Josh demanded she quit her job, and they argued. Josh, probably drunk, got angry, lost control and choked her. In a rage, he probably didn't realize he was killing her until it was too late, and he put her into bed like she was asleep, wiped his fingerprints from the wine glass, and left.

Matlin remembered the ligature marks on her throat.

"She wasn't strangled with the hands or an arm. She was choked with something else. Maybe this guy meant to kill her."

Matlin drifted back to reality and continued his journey through the cold rain, which had gotten stronger during his twenty-five minute drive. Perhaps he'd been mistaken in his assumption about Josh killing Heather. His mind drifted to the past again.

The day after Heather Kingston's body was found, Josh Gregory was located in Myrtle Beach, South Carolina, sixty miles south of Wilmington at a motel with a few of his college friends. Matlin brought him back to Wilmington where he was interrogated about his whereabouts from Wednesday night until he went to Myrtle Beach.

Shocked and grieved upon hearing of the death of his long-time girlfriend, Josh immediately lost control of his emotions. The questioning continued after he regained his composure, and Matlin learned Josh had an airtight alibi: his parents. Josh went to his hometown, Asheboro, NC on Tuesday night after he left his job as a waiter at Outback Steakhouse in Wilmington. Josh was depressed because he and Heather had broken up the weekend prior to July 31, and he wanted to get away from her. He didn't return to Wilmington, but went directly to Myrtle Beach on Friday, where he met his friends at the Ocean Drive Motel.

Both his parents and a slew of others confirmed his story, but the time between Asheboro and Myrtle Beach couldn't be accounted.

The trip was made alone and, feasibly, he could have diverted through Wilmington. Josh Gregory was interviewed for hours and continued to deny having anything to do with Heather's death. He was given a polygraph test and passed, which all but cleared him of suspicion. Matlin wasn't totally convinced of the boyfriend's innocence, but realized he would have to dig deeper to find out who killed this young woman.

The cause of death was no surprise. Ligature strangulation was listed under the heading. The autopsy report indicated in addition to the ligature marks on the neck area, there were vertical scratches on both sides of her throat about a centimeter from the top of the impression. Those marks were determined to have been made by the victim's fingernails, apparently, in a desperate struggle to loosen the constricting force. Indicating the victim had consumed alcohol the night she died, a blood test revealed an alcohol concentration of .07%.

The report showed no other injuries to the woman's body. Semen was found in and around the woman's vagina, and evidence of it was found on her chest and shoulder, where the stain was observed. A Sexual Assault Evidence Kit was used to collect the semen samples and other evidence. The rape kit was submitted to the SBI for DNA comparison to Josh Gregory after Matlin obtained a blood sample from him. Despite the seriousness of the case, the test results wouldn't be available for weeks, maybe a month. The DNA Analysis Unit was back-logged for months on other cases of equal importance. They had to complete those tests before getting to his. The wheels of justice turn very slowly.

This delay, however frustrating it was, gave Matlin time to conduct interviews of witnesses, and others. Matlin started with Heather's co-workers at the Doll House, and learned her last night at work was Wednesday, July 30, 1996, from 6 p.m. until 11:30 p.m. One dancer described a customer who was paying a lot of attention to Heather. Apparently, the man had been in the club two straight days before her last night at work and claimed to be a photographer for a magazine. Another girl, also a dancer, told the detective the same man had offered her a modeling contract, but when he saw Heather, he tried to monopolize her, and spent a lot of money for her to dance for him exclusively. Matlin learned other dancers remembered the man because he was spending a lot of money.

A cocktail waitress informed Matlin she remembered seeing the man leave about the same time Heather did the last night she worked. A description of the customer was taken, but it was very vague: a white male, about 25-30 years of age; six feet tall, or better; with a muscular build, and nicely dressed. Clean shaven, he had short dark wavy hair and exhibited an outgoing personality. No one knew the customer and had never seen him before he came in those three nights, but all whom Matlin interviewed concluded Heather had left with the man. Bill Matlin had nothing. And what they said, didn't seem to fit the lifestyle of Heather Kingston.

According to the numerous people who knew her, Heather didn't conform to the stigma of the stripper or exotic dancer. She truly lived the cliché so many dancers used as a reason for their vocation. The impoverished college student strenuously trying to pay for the expensive costs of higher education. The young woman was this and more. In addition to her honor roll status and membership in the National Honor Society, she was described as model student and daughter. Her character and promiscuity were questioned but, as a result, Matlin learned from Heather's closest friends, she had been sexually involved with only one person: Josh Gregory.

That fact contributed to the implausibility she would have brought a stranger back to her apartment for drinking and sex. It was her unblemished character and reputation which made it enormously difficult for the Wilmington Police Department to surface some motivation for the murder. With all of Heather's background information factual, the focus of the investigation could only be aimed at the boyfriend. A month after Heather's death, however, the DNA test results were returned and they didn't match Josh Gregory. The results of the DNA test officially cleared Gregory from the suspect list.

Matlin worried about the man seen leaving the club the same time Heather did. This "photographer" could have been the last person to see Heather alive and was possibly her killer. His next step was to check with all the other topless clubs in Wilmington to see if anyone fitting the description given had been there representing himself as a photographer. After checking all the clubs, Matlin learned nothing useful and was thrown back to where he'd started.

The murder was greatly publicized in the Wilmington area, with news broadcasts making pleas for help, but Matlin didn't receive any information that brought him closer to the identity of the killer. Matlin was frustrated. If Heather's boyfriend wasn't responsible, then it was definitely someone she knew and trusted.

Like a gopher, Matlin burrowed deeper into the life of Heather Kingston. In a period of several weeks, he interviewed more friends and acquaintances. To no avail, however, Matlin still had no killer, or any clue as to why it had happened.

In the first week of October, Matlin found out about a homicide investigation seminar sponsored by the State Bureau of Investigation in December to be held in Wilmington. The lecturer was Clark Hager, Special Agent-in-Charge of the SBI Investigative Support Unit. Matlin recognized Hager's name and decided he would attend the school.

Hager's reputation as an expert profiler of criminals was prevalent throughout the state. Similar to the FBI unit with the same name, the Investigative Support unit consisted of two highly trained agents who assisted in investigations, conducted crime scene analyses, offender profiles, and gave advice on interrogation strategies to investigators. Matlin was looking forward to meeting Hager and he was determined to talk to him about his puzzling case.

The Wilmington detective attended the three-day seminar, and wasn't merely impressed with Hager's knowledge and insight, but more by his personality and humility. An aura of superiority didn't permeate from Hager, giving the notion he considered his peers equals and deserved of respect. Closing a lecture, Hager, in fact, gave credit to the investigators of police and sheriff's departments for solving the cases. He described himself as a tool to be utilized, but hinted to his passion for investigation, and even admitted he would ask permission from local agencies to involve himself in an intriguing case.

Matlin was able to corner Hager during one of the breaks in the seminar and invited him to dinner with some of the other detectives. At the restaurant, Matlin described his mystifying murder.

Hager agreed it was an interesting case and recommended that Matlin send the entire file to the SBI to be profiled.

3

CLARK HAGER was sitting at a desk in his office when the telephone rang. He'd just sat down with a cup of coffee and begun to eat his usual breakfast of one cinnamon and raisin bagel. Hager and his partner, Lloyd Sheridan, alternated making the trip to Best Bagels In Town on their way to work each morning.

The phone continued to ring. Hager looked at the clock on the wall and it showed 7:55 a.m. On the fourth ring, he picked up the receiver, "State Bureau of Investigation, Agent Hager."

No response.

"Hmm, must have hung up. No patience." Hager said and sipped the coffee.

Several minutes later he heard a knock on the open door. Hager turned toward the door and saw his boss, Bob Maxwell, standing in the entrance. The Assistant Director of the SBI was holding a piece of yellow paper and wore a concerned look on his face.

"Hey, Bob. How's it going?" Hager mumbled, his mouth half full of bagel.

"Great, Clark. And you?"

"Just another day toward retirement. What's up?"

"Clark, have you and Lloyd got anything major going at the moment?"

"No, uh, not really, but I'm expecting a homicide case for profiling from Wilmington. Why?"

"Well, the Director got a call from a Sheriff McAdoo in Hertford County. It seems they've got an unidentified female dead over there and they'd like our assistance."

"Hertford County?" Hager asked knowing that was where his parents lived.

"Yeah, Hertford County. The woman they found was nude and the M.E. said she'd probably been strangled. They haven't been able to I.D. her yet."

"When did this happen?"

Maxwell looked at the piece of paper and it crinkled as he straightened it.

"Around five Saturday morning. From what his message said, the body had been dumped in a wooded area."

"Hmm," he whispered. "Strangled and found nude in the woods. Interesting. This case I'm expecting from Wilmington was a strangulation, too. A female college student about five months ago. But she was killed in her apartment, not dumped."

Hager drank from his cup again and recalled the detective from Wilmington describing his mysterious case over dinner a few weeks ago. He nodded his head and leaned back in the black leather swivel chair picturing a body found in the woods and then, a young woman dead in her bed. "Five months," he whispered again.

Maxwell handed the paper to Hager.

"Clark, if you have a moment this morning, give him a call and see what he's got. It might be a case where you can just give him some advice."

Maxwell turned and started for the door.

"Sure, I don't mind. You know, Bob, my mom and dad live in Hertford County. In Ahoskie actually."

"Really? Well, you might just get to go see them real soon, Clark." Maxwell walked out of the office.

What Hager told Maxwell was true. Clark Hager certainly didn't mind giving advice on any case; but murder cases were his specialty. Hager was a graduate of the FBI Academy in Quantico, Virginia, and served a year-long fellowship in the FBI's Behavioral Science Investigative Support Unit where he studied violent crimes and worked as a "profiler" of violent offenders. Hager also spent time in the Violent Criminal Apprehension Unit (VICAP) detecting similarities in unsolved violent crimes all over the country. For Hager, he'd found his calling. He'd been an SBI agent for ten years, but Hager had been in law enforcement for a total of twenty five.

Hager began his career as a police officer in Greensboro in 1973 after graduating from the University of North Carolina-Chapel Hill with a degree in Psychology. After several years on patrol, he was reassigned to the Criminal Investigation Division and worked as a detective in the Burglary Squad. His ability as a homicide investigator quickly caught the attention of the commander of the division when Hager assisted on a multiple murder of a prominent family. After being transferred to the Homicide Squad from Burglary, Hager realized he experienced a rush when he was called about a murder.

It was the formidable task of solving a case where, from the beginning, the killer was unknown, until the end, where a suspect was developed and found to be responsible. Like many of the most prominent FBI agents in the Investigative Support Unit, Hager tried to get into the mind of the killer, to imagine the thought processes and motivations of a person. Hager soon discovered he'd been doing what every homicide detective had been doing for years; but he did it better.

He seemed to have an uncanny genius in examining crime scenes and after careful thought, was able very accurately to reconstruct the incident as it had occurred. And this, without any formal training in crime scene evaluation. The young homicide detective, then 33, appeared to be destined for greater things, but not until tragedy struck his family did he think about the future of his career.

In early December of 1986, Hager's wife Kelly worked as a nurse in the Intensive Care Unit at Wesley Long Hospital in Greensboro. Kelly, a beautifully petite woman with short brown hair and eyes, was the object of Hager's deep love and devotion. College sweethearts, the two met at a fraternity party during their sophomore year and were inseparable from then on. In addition to being fortunate to have a wife whom he considered to be his best friend, Hager was also blessed with one of nature's greatest gifts: a daughter. Elizabeth Nicole Hager was born to them in 1977. The nine-year-old by herself was more than enough to handle, but both he and Kelly wanted a son to round out the modern-day family unit. For three years they had been eagerly trying to conceive, but to no avail.

Kelly was at the gynecologist's office for an examination and possibly an answer to their concerns why she'd not become pregnant. The examination proved to be, in one sense, a stroke of luck, but in another, a signal of despair. A Pap smear revealed the probability of cancerous cells in her cervix. A subsequent test was done, unfortunately, with the same results. Kelly had cervical cancer.

Both Hager and Kelly were completely devastated. A full hysterectomy removed the cancer. After the operation, Kelly underwent extensive radiation and chemotherapy treatments to prevent the cancer's spread to the rest of her body, something the doctor said would have been likely, had it not been caught at the time. But Kelly was still at risk.

Even though Kelly showed no physical symptoms, she was emotionally shattered. The dreams of her and Hager growing old together, hoping to watch their children graduate from college and get married were quickly eradicated. It would only be the three of them, and Hager was as satisfied as any man could be.

For about a month, both Hager and Kelly were sullen and despairing; but Kelly came to the realization she still had many years to live, and she determined herself she was going to make the best of a tragic situation and endure the treatments with a confidence they would stem the tide of the disease. Despite the eroding and draining effects of the chemotherapy, Kelly proved to be a fighter and kept a positive outlook on the future. Kelly's cheerfulness was as contagious as her affable personality and it gradually lifted her husband's spirits.

A month later, Hager was approached by an agent from the SBI about taking a job with the state. After fourteen years in Greensboro, Hager decided a move from the area might be beneficial to his family. He was subsequently hired by the State Bureau of Investigation early in 1987.

Hager completed the SBI training academy in Raleigh, and his initial assignment was in the western district of the state in Asheville. He packed up Kelly and Elizabeth and moved to the mountains. The Smoky Mountains provided beauty and serene surroundings, fresh air and open space to live, which turned out to be the perfect environment for Kelly's cancer remission. The ongoing treatments seemed to have halted the advance of the disease. Hager worked as a criminal agent where he conducted investigations and provided assistance to local departments.

After three years in Asheville, Hager had only investigated or been involved in three murder cases. Particularly, one case involved a serial killer who had murdered four people in three states, including two in North Carolina. Asked to assist on the interview with the killer, Hager was able to obtain not only a confession to the murder in Asheville; but the man also admitted to the strangling murder of a woman in High Point which subsequently led to the recovery of her body. Hager was recognized by the chiefs of police in Asheville and High Point, and letters of appreciation were written to the Director of the SBI in commendation of Hager's performance.

When the Director of the SBI called him to talk about the commendations, he told Hager the Governor was considering the formation of a special unit which modeled the FBI's elite Behavioral Science Investigative Support Unit and asked Hager if he would be interested in the assignment. Hager was thrilled, but knew the new job meant he and his family would have to move to Raleigh.

That evening, he talked it over with Kelly and Elizabeth, who was just about to begin her freshmen year of high school. Relieved and pleasantly surprised, his family was enthusiastic about the change and for his new assignment. Both Kelly and Elizabeth liked Asheville, but they perceived the city as boring, and the winters were too cold. Actually, the two were glad to be moving closer to the beach. Cary, a small suburban village about ten miles west of Raleigh, was selected to be their new home. They moved in a month.

When Hager accepted the new assignment, he was told he would be away for about a year, completing extensive training required for his new position.

Although worried about leaving his family during the week, Hager knew he would be coming home on weekends because of the close proximity of Cary to Quantico. With the fact that Kelly was apparently in complete health again, Hager felt the time away would serve as a way for she and Elizabeth to grow even closer, as they both were traumatized by the ordeal Kelly suffered with the cancer treatments.

From the moment Hager arrived at the FBI Academy, the agents and instructors recognized he possessed the intrinsic insight to profiling, and he was urged to apply for a job as an FBI agent. Even though Hager was flattered, he dismissed the notion because he'd already moved his family twice and wasn't going to put them through the ordeal again. Inasmuch as Hager enjoyed the profiling aspect of the job, he thrived on the actual investigation, which brought him much fulfillment. With the new assignment in Raleigh, he would be getting the best of both worlds, and thus, avoid having to travel frequently like the FBI agents.

Upon the completion of his training in Quantico, Hager excitedly returned to Cary for good. Hager's new position was to be the Special Agent-in-Charge of the SBI Investigative Support Unit, which consisted of Hager and one other agent. The unit's office was located in the complex which housed the SBI headquarters and the Highway Patrol Training Center in Garner, a small town just outside of Raleigh.

On his first day, Hager was introduced to his new partner, Lloyd Sheridan. When they met, he took an immediate liking to him. Like Hager, Lloyd was hand-picked for the job because of his previous performance in the field. He'd been an agent in Charlotte before he was selected by the director to work in the unit.

Originally from Shelby, North Carolina, which is west of Charlotte, Lloyd was typically southern. At age 55, he was nine years older than Hager and only had a few years until he could retire. He was a short, stocky man with large hands. Hager remembered the first time he met Lloyd and shook his hand, which swallowed his like his father's did when he was six. Not only were his hands large, but they had the grip comparable to a vise being tightened and crushed on the knuckles. Lloyd's hair was completely white but it was evident it had been black in his younger days. His skin was rough and he wore gold wire-framed glasses concealing his gentle blue eyes. A recovering alcoholic and a chronic tobacco chewer, his voice was raspy and he had a uniquely southern accent, sounding more like he was from Alabama than North Carolina. His rough personality and demeanor, however, seemed to make a perfect combination with Hager's serious and deliberate persona. Lloyd's whimsical vulgarity and lack of subtlety gave him the appearance of being crude; but he was actually a very shrewd investigator who was always an effective complement to the sedate Hager.

A year later, misfortune once again invaded Hager's life. After four years showing no symptoms of the disease, Kelly's seemingly dormant cancer reared its ugly head swiftly like a tornado appearing on the horizon just before it destroyed a neighborhood. Although she appeared to be the same vibrant, energetic woman she'd been all of her life, she'd been feeling the effects of perpetual fatigue, even from the simplest of movements. Another examination revealed the disease had returned, invading her entire body, and the doctors informed them her health could deteriorate quickly.

As expected, Kelly took the news as an obstacle, but not one that was insurmountable. She resumed the chemotherapy treatments, but during the ensuing month, her health declined swiftly, inducing her hospitalization. Sensing the forthcoming tribulation, Hager took a leave of absence from work to stay by his wife's side during her final weeks. Kelly appeared to have lost her will to live. Painfully refusing any further treatments, Kelly desired only alleviation from the suffering which so quickly devoured her perseverance.

Hager could see it in her eyes. An indication of submission. Hager worried the end may be imminent, and prepared himself to be strong for Elizabeth. His daughter was hit the hardest by far in this tragic episode. Elizabeth would be losing not only her mother and best friend, but in her eyes, the paragon of womanhood to which she vowed to mirror. At fifteen, it was a period of life which shaped a young girl's entire future, and a mother's presence during that time was vital for her.

Clark Hager was losing something very special at the same time. He'd known Kelly since their days in college, and they had been together for almost twenty years. Kelly was the completion of Clark Hager, and he was of her. In Kelly, Hager had found the deep internal love every person wishes to experience. A love which hurt deep in the chest at any moment of insecurity. His wife was the strength Hager needed when he was vulnerable and depressed and she would somehow be strong enough for the both of them during times of impending disaster. Hager knew it was Elizabeth's time to be vulnerable, and his to be strong, not only for her, but for himself.

Kelly died two days later. Hager and Elizabeth mourned quietly and privately with the support of relatives and friends. Having been absent from work for about a month, Hager considered leaving the SBI to be more available to Elizabeth during her adolescent years. Having seen enough violence and death, the meaning of it brought on a new poignancy to Hager.

But a renewed purpose emerged in his mind that influenced Hager to remain and dedicate himself to the job he was tasked to do. And for the past five years since her death, Hager did just that. And he did it well.

Hager picked up the phone after he finished his bagel and coffee and dialed the number for the Hertford County Sheriff. As the phone was ringing he thought about his parents. Walter and Virginia Hager had been living in Ahoskie for thirteen years. As they both turned seventy, and even though they were very healthy, he'd just recently realized their mortality and decided he would visit them more often than he'd done in previous years.

His parents lived on the golf course at Beechwood Country Club where their house stood adjacent to the third fairway. Hager's father Walter was an avid golfer and played almost daily. Hager's mother Virginia spent most of her time reading books, taking care of flowers, and playing bridge with several bridge clubs. Hager's only sister Rebecca also lived in Ahoskie with her husband Colt and their four children. Hager had an older brother Stan, a retired police officer who worked for an investment firm in Hager's hometown of Arlington, Virginia. Stan was married and had two children.

"Hertford County Sheriff, can I help you?" a woman's voice answered.

"Yes, this is Agent Hager of the SBI. Is Sheriff McAdoo in please?"

"Yes he is. I'll put you right through, sir."

Hager sat at his desk and endured the thirty seconds of country music until a man with a deep voice like it came from a drum picked up the phone.

"This is McAdoo."

"Sheriff McAdoo, this is Clark Hager with the SBI. Bob Maxwell asked me to give you a call. Something about a body you found?"

"Yes sir, Mr.—" he stammered, "what you say your name was?"

"Hager. Clark Hager."

"Oh, Mr. Hager, I'm so glad you called. I think we got us a mess down here. Early Saturday mornin', some hunters found the body of a white female, age twenty to twenty-five. She was naked, lying in a wooded area next to Highway 11. Found no clothes, no property. Nothin'. The medical examiner said it looked like she was strangled."

"Do you have any idea who she is? Have you gotten any reports of missing girls there?"

"Naw sir, we haven't gotten any reports yet. I don't know if she's from around here or not."

"Well, Sheriff, if she's not been reported missing yet, she probably will be in the next couple of days. Did you contact the television stations there to see if they can help?"

"No. Not yet."

"They're usually very helpful when you find a body like that. Just give them a description of her and they'll put it on the news. Someone will probably call about it."

"Oh. Mr. Hager, we thought you'd might be interested in helping us, ya know, 'cause we don't get too many of those types of murders here. Just the usual ones. Husbands and wives. Friends and relatives. That sort of thing."

Hager was doodling stars on a pad.

"Sheriff, I don't know if I could be much help to you right now. It looks like you've already done all that can be done. Once you find out who she is, it'll probably all come together for you."

"Yeah, I guess. I've just got a bad feeling about this girl is all."

"Don't worry. If you don't get any response from the news, enter her into NCIC as Unidentified Dead with all physical descriptions you got. You might get a hit from the missing person files. If you still haven't had any luck after about a week or so, give me a call back, okay."

"All right, Mr. Hager. I appreciate your help."

"Sure. Hey! where did you find the body anyway?" Hager asked.

"Oh, over off of Highway 11. Near Ahoskie."

"Near Ahoskie?"

Hager was getting more curious.

"Yeah, Highway 11 runs a stretch between Ahoskie and Murfreesboro. And about half way between, there's this creek that runs across it. The Potecasi Creek. She was found near the bridge that crosses the Potecasi Creek."

Hager leaned forward in the chair and his jaw fell almost to the floor. The Potecasi Creek bridge was about a mile from where his parents lived. He was surprised they had not called yet, but they may not have known. Hager's curiosity was getting the best of him; and yet, he felt like this was an interesting case so far. He tried to picture the locale in his mind. Many times over the years, he'd driven across the small bridge on the way to his folks' home.

"Sheriff, are any of your people going to Chapel Hill for the autopsy?"

"Yes sir, I called this morning and they said it would be done sometime today and we could come tomorrow to talk to the medical examiner."

"Hmm. I guess I could meet you there, you know. To look at your file. Did you get some Polaroid photos?"

"That's great. Yes, we got a couple of shots of the girl, but the rest were done by your people from the lab."

"Good. I guess I'll see you tomorrow morning, Sheriff."

"Sure thing, Mr. Hager. I look forward to it."

The next morning, Hager briefed Lloyd and told him they were going to Chapel Hill to meet with McAdoo. On Hager's desk were two thick, legal-size envelopes bound with a rubber band. The bundle was addressed to the SBI, Investigative Support Unit; the return address was from Wilmington. He immediately recognized it as being the murder case he was waiting to receive for profiling.

As Hager picked up the heavy package, he knew he and his partner would be spending long hours sifting through reports, photographs and sketches, all in preparing a criminal offender profile on the case. He would once again be trying to enter the mind of the killer.

4

LIKE A DRUG it gnaws at your mind constantly wanting more. An addiction perhaps, but more than a simple addiction. A visceral urge that compels a killer to such things. Once you have tasted the sweet fruit of death and all its power, your body is invaded by an unrecoverable obsession no drug can match.

A killer's life depends on being able to conduct his "business" without being detected and one would think he would need to lay low for a while so as not to run a bigger risk of being caught. But the urge grows stronger and stronger after each time.

Then I'll tell the whole world when it's over! It's like being on drugs. I'm addicted to the power of life and death!

He cannot fight it for very long. Not that he wants to stop. But in this business it takes time to find the right target—one who fits the mold for the fantasy. The killer bites his lip, trying to ebb the flow of desire.

Erase it from your mind. It's too soon for another.

The animal craving has enveloped him—overwhelmed his being. A primal urge to satisfy a unquenchable thirst for death.

Being a highly-intelligent man, the killer tries to understand himself. He knows what he is doing is wrong in one sense. But in the other, he is ridding the world and mankind of the most dangerous creature. The manipulative monster whose quest is to destroy all his dreams and aspirations. She nearly achieved her goal years ago, but he rebounded and arose from the ashes of despair with a resurgent power for retribution. Now it is his time to play. A very dangerous game.

He takes a deep breath and the music overhead soothes his nerves. His lust swells as he watches them walk by at the mall with their high-heeled shoes and long legs. A volcanic heat wave erupts in his groin, flashing up to his chest and down to his feet as he sees one he likes. He shudders off the impulse and takes another deep breath which stems the tide of his addiction for now. But soon it will be time. Time to seek out another object of fulfillment.

*   *   *

HAGER WALKED out of his office and saw Lloyd in the corridor where he was talking to the unit secretary, Judy Carroll. Lloyd was sitting on the edge of her desk and talking while gesturing with his large hands. It looked like he was telling a joke, and she chuckled and shook her head when his voice rose to tell the punch line. Lloyd looked up laughing and saw his partner walking toward him smiling. Hager's eyes moved to Judy, who shook her head in friendly disapproval of the joke Lloyd had told her.

"Are you ready?" Hager asked him.

"Yep."

Lloyd got up from the edge of the desk.

"See you later, Judy."

Lloyd walked with Hager toward the door.

"What did you tell her? The one about the kinky man in the bar."

"Yeah. I don't think she liked it too much though."

Holding the door for him, "Lloyd, it might be because she's got a dog."

Lloyd's face wrinkled. He covered his mouth, embarrassed at his joke. He chuckled under his breath.

"OOPS."

Hager smiled and remembered the joke and shook his head at Lloyd's warped sense of humor.

"Awww," Lloyd groaned. "She's a good sport."

The two agents walked down the gravel drive and through the parking lot toward their cars. Rows of layered clouds dominated the sky. Glimmers of sunlight peaked through the clouds foreshadowing a rise in temperature. The asphalt was still wet with small puddles from last night's rain. Tiny droplets of water clung to the blades of grass surrounding the buildings.

"I'll look at this on the way." Hager said holding up the thick package.

"What's that?" Lloyd asked as he pulled out a pouch of Red Man chewing tobacco from his pocket.

"It's the murder case from Wilmington we're profiling."

"Oh, yeah. The one that detective told you about during the seminar last month?"

"One and the same, my friend. You gonna drive?"

Lloyd nodded as he stuffed the bundle of brown leaves in his cheek.

As soon as the car started moving, Hager opened up one envelope and pulled out a stack of 8X10 photographs. In the other, were papers, reports, and a driver's license. Hager skimmed over the pages and made descriptive comments to Lloyd about the case during the twenty-five minute ride along I-40 to Chapel Hill.

Hager made no predictions or hypotheses. It wouldn't be possible until they had spent hours analyzing and discussing the evidence they had before them. Hager used the duration of the trip as an opportunity to get a head start on the profile in familiarizing themselves with the case.

Hager and Lloyd arrived in Chapel Hill and made their way onto the campus of the University of North Carolina. The State Medical Examiner's Office was located at the university and Hager visited the campus frequently since he was assigned in Raleigh, and most of his cases involved murders. Most autopsies were performed inChapel Hill; therefore, he was able to return to the place where he admitted had been the best time of his life.

College was a wonderful experience for Hager. Not only the education he received, but the training for life that college offered. The independence, the self-reliance, all the parties, the girls, the friends, and the late night study sessions. Above all, this was the place he met Kelly and fell deeply in love.

When he first arrived in 1969, he admired the beautiful display of the campus with its colonial styled buildings, the red brick walkways with stone formations lining the sides, the stretches of green grass carefully manicured around many oak and elm trees scattered about the campus, giving shade to the buildings. For all the admiration of its serene beauty, Hager never really appreciated it when he was a student. Only when he returned as an adult, an alumnus, did he truly see it for what it really was. It was his second home. Where his life had changed.

As they passed by the buildings, most were present when he was a student, some recently renovated, or newly built, Hager saw a young couple walking together. They held each other's hands, something Hager thought didn't happen enough in today's "too cool" society of teens. He remembered Kelly. For three years, they walked each other to class, holding hands, talking like they had just met. It was easy then. No real responsibilities. No worries other than being drafted into the war in Viet Nam, which consumed the minds of many of his classmates. Luckily for Hager, he was spared the apprehension of being thrown into a bloody conflict he knew nothing about, nor cared to know. It was college. A period of growth, of experience, and it was 1969. It was the year of Woodstock and rock and roll.

His eyes followed the couple as they approached the large building. At the door, they stopped to sneak a kiss before spending the hour of instruction knowing they wouldn't be able to truly touch one another. He and Kelly used to do that, and he imagined the couple being so deeply in love, like they were at that age. It felt like it was a dream back then, and it still did.

The Medical Examiners Office was near the hospital in the Brinkhaus-Bullit Building. Lloyd turned off Columbia Street and parked the car in the parking lot marked with black signs with white letters labeled:

Medical Examiner Vehicles—24 HRS

The two agents walked through the parking lot and climbed up the cement steps to a courtyard with chairs and tables for students taking breaks from classes.

At the top of the stairs, they entered the building through a pair of glass doors. Once inside, the elevator was immediately to their left. The Office of the Chief Medical Examiner was located on the tenth floor. Hager and Lloyd stepped into the elevator after a pretty girl in a white lab jacket eyed them as she disembarked after the door opened. Lloyd pushed the button for "10" and the door closed in front of them.

The agents stepped from the elevator into a small corridor with a green cloth sofa and end tables covered with magazines. A bulletin board was attached to the wall with notices and job listings in the field of forensic medicine. To the right was an office with a receptionist. The heavy set, middle-aged black woman seated behind the desk immediately recognized Hager and Lloyd, and beamed at their presence. There was another woman, about forty, wearing a bright red sweater, seated at a small table behind the reception desk.

"Well, you two. Where ya'll been hidin' yourselves these days?" the black woman said.

"Hi there, Bertha. Did you miss us?" Hager asked.

"We were just talkin' the other day about you two. And how long it's been since we'd seen ya."

"Yeah. How long's it been Clark? Two or three months," Lloyd asked.

"I think it was around Halloween. We came over for that double murder in Kinston."

"Well, it's good to see you. I wish ya'll would come by more often. We girls like handsome men to visit us," Bertha said smiling, and caused her office mate to smile and shake her head.

"Bertha, we were supposed to meet a Sheriff McAdoo from Hertford County. Is he here yet?"

Hager could see Bertha's eyes light up at the mention of McAdoo's name.

"Oh! That big hunk of a man Sheriff McAdoo. Oooh yeah! He's here. He took his fine self upstairs."

"You like him, huh, Bertha?" Lloyd asked, and then joked with her. "You want us to get his number for you?"

Bertha waved her hand at him like she was swatting a fly.

"Oh, stop it," she said, embarrassed. "You know I don't mess around with married men."

"Ohhh," Hager said as he raised his eyebrows at Lloyd. "You already know he's married. Boy Bertha! You don't mess around, do you?"

"Hey, I can see a ring on a man's finger a mile away," she said laughing which caused her chest to bounce. "You tell him I said 'hello' okay?"

"We'll do it, Bertha."

Hager and Lloyd walked up the stairs to the eleventh floor where the autopsies were performed. The agents were led by a pathologist into the observation room which overlooked the examination area. The examination room was a large open area with four tables, two of which were occupied by cadavers.

The bodies were unclothed and lying supine on the table. Along the near wall lay counters with instruments and scales for weighing organs. A pathologist was using a hose to wash off one of the decedents, a black male, who looked to be in his thirties, his chest and head covered in blood. The blood, dried, had to be scrubbed from his body to reveal the inflicted death wounds. On the other table lay a white female who had to weigh at least four hundred pounds. There was no blood on her and she was so large the sides of her body overlapped the edge of the table and one of her arms had fallen, hanging by her side. A female pathologist with a clipboard was writing on a pad as she walked around the body. Hager and Lloyd entered the room and saw a large black man in a brown and tan uniform leaning against a table, and a white man in a coat and tie seated in the chair by the desk.

"Sheriff McAdoo, I'm Clark Hager, and this is my partner, Lloyd Sheridan."

The sheriff shook both their hands and pointed to the other man, who had risen from the chair.

"This is Detective Raeford. He's working the case."

"Raeford, good to meet you."

Raeford shook hands with both of them.

McAdoo said, "They told me Doctor Rinaldi was teaching a class, and he would be here about ten."

Hager looked at his watch and it was 9:50.

"Well, why don't we take a look at those pictures of the girl."

Raeford pulled the three photographs from the folder he was holding and handed them to Hager. The photographs were Polaroids of the victim's face, and the others of two tattoos, apparently on her back and ankle. Although one was of the victim's face, Hager knew it wouldn't be a very good picture to use for an identification. The ones of the tattoos were taken close and were clear.

"Very good artwork." Hager said and handed the pictures to Lloyd, who flipped through them.

"Hmm, a Dolphins fan. I hate the Dolphins," Lloyd said.

Hager's eyes shifted to Lloyd as he looked at the pictures and then to the Hertford contingent to see their reaction. The sheriff's face was blank and Raeford looked at Lloyd with a confused expression. Hager hoped the remark went over their heads and changed the subject.

"Can I look at your file?" Hager asked.

Raeford handed him the manila folder which contained the basic incident report with a brief narrative on the discovery of the body by the hunters. Other than a rough sketch of the scene drawn by Raeford, it was all they had.

"Boy, when you said you had nothing. You really meant it."

The sheriff spoke up.

"Well, we've done some checking on some things, but they aren't in the report. That's just the incident report filed by the patrol deputy."

He gave the folder back to Raeford.

"What else did you find out?"

Raeford answered, "Well, I checked with a lounge that's a dancing place on the weekends to see if anyone had seen her. I showed her picture to the manager and the two bartenders and they didn't recognize her."

"I guess you haven't been notified of any missing persons with her description?"

Raeford shook his head.

"No. Not yet."

"What I would do, Sheriff, is send a DCI message over a fifty mile radius about the body being found. Maybe one of the neighboring departments has a missing person."

Dr. Rinaldi walked into the room and directed them into his office. Rinaldi, the Chief Medical Examiner, performed the autopsy on the victim. The doctor sat at his desk and the four men occupied chairs facing him. Rinaldi wore a white dress shirt, a blue tie and slacks. He was a thin man with a small neck which looked smaller with the snug collar of his shirt. Dark rimmed glasses covered his eyes and he had jet black wavy hair slicked back on his head. Young looking for his sixty years, his face was smooth, and his nose pointed sharply. He had a nasal tone to his voice that was irritating to the ear. But Dr. Rinaldi was unrivaled at his profession.

"You're here on the unidentified female from Hertford County, right?" Rinaldi asked.

The doctor pursed his lips and shuffled through papers and files on the desk. Apparently finding the correct report, his finger moved along the page as he read and turned back to the awaiting lawmen.

"The victim, age approximately twenty to twenty five years of age, died of asphyxiation by what appears to be manual strangulation. The hyoid bone was fractured, and there were petechial hemorrhages in the eyes, which is conclusive evidence of strangulation."

Hager spoke first.

"Doctor, was there any evidence of rape or other sexual activity?"

He looked at the report, again, his finger scanning the page.

"There was what we believe to be semen found in and around the vaginal cavity. A rape kit was done."

"When you say manual strangulation, do you mean with the hands?"

"It was most likely done with the arm as there were no contusions consistent with the hands being the weapon. We did recover traces of skin under the woman's fingernails and they were collected also."

"Were there any other injuries to the victim? On her hands or feet, perhaps?"

Rinaldi scanned the paper again.

"No. No other injuries."

A woman dressed in surgical garb came into the office with a white box, a brown envelope, and a fingerprint card. The white box was the SBI Sexual Assault Evidence Collection kit, which had the semen samples, hair from combing and known hair samples from the victim. In the envelope were two vials of blood taken from the victim and the fingernail scrapings. The victim was also fingerprinted. The woman gave Hager the evidence, and he signed a form for the chain of custody.

After the meeting with the medical examiner, the four men returned to the waiting area.

"Sheriff," Hager said. "I'm going to put a rush on these photographs and I'd like to see where she was found."

McAdoo looked surprised. His eyebrows raised and he looked at Raeford, who smiled.

"Sure, Mr. Hager. We can do that."

"All right. How about on Friday. We've got another thing to do and it will take about two days. Plus, the pictures should be developed by then."

"That's great. We'll look forward to it. Man, we really do appreciate y'all's help on this thing."

When he returned from Chapel Hill, Hager hand-delivered the vials of blood and the rape evidence kit to the Serology Section and the fingerprint card to the Identification Section. The prints would be entered into the Automated Fingerprint Identification System computer. AFIS, the extensive database containing millions of fingerprints, was used to identify persons if their prints were contained within. Hager requested the crime scene photos be developed immediately.

Hager returned to his office, picked up the homicide case to be profiled, and walked across the hall to the conference room. Lloyd returned with the take-out lunch from a nearby fast food restaurant. They ate and discussed who they thought would be in the Super Bowl. Hager knew for the better part of the next two days, he and Lloyd would lock themselves in the room, trying to infiltrate the psyche of a killer.

5

HIS EYES GLANCED at the titles of the magazines on the display. He was looking for a specific magazine, the one that brought all the important news from around the world. He flipped through the rows of magazines on the three shelves, but he couldn't find the one he was hunting. Picking up different ones, he shuffled through them to see if his magazine was possibly hidden behind one of the other chronicles.

He wanted the magazine that was going to make him famous. He was going to create such a story, an exposé into the heart of all evil. A story identifying the true nature of what was wrong with mankind. Once exposed, he was sure its popularity would die, and he would ultimately become famous for saving the world from itself. He envisioned the article winning the cherished Pulitzer Prize for Journalism for a story that changed the world. Frustrated, he escalated his shuffling and tossed the magazines around the display until one hit the floor.

"Excuse me, sir. Is there anything I can help you with?" the woman standing behind the counter said.

The clerk, a wrinkled fortyish woman with straight brown hair, wearing a black sweatshirt with Dale Earnhart's picture on the front, sat on stool behind the counter of the Exxon convenience store. A cigarette burned in an ash tray on the counter beside a *National Enquirer* she was reading.

Looking up, he realized he'd temporarily lost control for a moment. He smiled and walked over to the woman.

"I'm sorry, but I'm looking for *Time* magazine. It doesn't look like you have it."

"Well, if it's not up there, then we don't have it," she said in a nasal voice that, coupled with the deliberate rhythm of her speech, made her appear more backward.

"You don't have *Time?*" he said in a arrogant tone. "That's too bad. 'Cause it is the best selling magazine in the world. And how do you think I know that, huh?"

She looked at him strangely while smoking her cigarette.

"I know this because I work for them. Yeah uh-huh," he nodded his head. "A journalist," the man bellowed proudly sticking out his chest.

"Good for you. And I'm Barbara Walters."

Insulted, the man left the store in a rage. A controlled fury. The type of calculating wrath that was undetectable. The silent furor which could only be seen in the depths of the eyes and evil grin of the man. His fits of rage were becoming increasingly frequent over the preceding weeks, and he felt like he was coming unglued. It only happened when he was drinking and he knew he must keep his composure and maintain his focus—focus on his mission. It was nearly completed. There was just a little more work to do, and then, he was going to save mankind from itself by exposing its true weaknesses. It exhilarated him to think about it and he fantasized about it often. The fame, the fortune, the notoriety, were all things he never had as a child. It was going to be his, but a great deal of work was ahead of him.

The man had digressed in the involvement in searching for the magazine. He temporarily forgot about his guest waiting for him at the hotel. The notion of her being there stimulated him. An hour had passed since he told her he was going out for some beer. He questioned if she would still be there waiting for him. He was confident of her presence and he grinned assuredly knowing she found him provocative.

Knowing little about Greensboro, he found it difficult to locate a store open at 3 a.m., but he'd found the Exxon station just east of Interstate 40 on Wendover Avenue. Not wanting to return to the sarcastic clerk, he drove west on Wendover passing two rows of restaurants on both sides of the road, a Wal-Mart on the right, and a Super Kmart on the left. The street was brightly illuminated by street lights, but all the businesses were dark, except for security lights. Cruising down the almost abandoned street, he cracked the window and the cold air bit into his skin, gently calming his nerves. A Mustang filled with teenagers pulled alongside and revved the engine in an indirect challenge to drag race, but he ignored them.

After passing the Kmart, commercialization ended and the road was bordered with small houses on large chunks of land with tall trees and unpaved driveways. He continued on Wendover for about a mile until he saw the green and yellow sign of a BP station. Finding it still open for business, he walked in the store and was eyed by the man standing behind the counter.

The clerk was middle eastern, with jet black hair combed straight back on his head, a thick black mustache, and he donned a lime green vest with bright yellow trim displaying the BP logo. His hands rested on the counter, curious of the late customer. Hoping to find the magazine, he approached the counter and asked the cashier, "Do you have *Time*?"

The clerk raised his arm and exposed the watch on his hairy wrist and answered in a heavy accent, "It is three fifteen."

The man, realizing the irony of the joke, smiled and shook his head, but then slammed his hand on the counter.

"No, you idiot! Not *the* time! Do you have fucking *Time* magazine!"

The clerk, his eyes wide open, obviously shocked at the man's response, jumped back from the counter.

"Is this a joke? What the fuck is this? Get the fuck out of here. I call the cops," the clerk shouted, and picked up the phone.

The police?

His adrenaline rushed at the sound of the word, but he remained calm and said apologetically, holding his hands up like he was surrendering.

"Look, hey man, I'm sorry. You don't have to call the police. Hey, I'm sorry. I just wanted a magazine and some beer, Okay? Look I, uh, I'll just leave all right."

He back pedaled to the glass door and out into the parking lot.

Ire filled his entire body. He pounded his fist against the steering wheel, slammed the car into gear and stomped on the gas causing the tires to squeal. Circling the parking lot and around to the exit, he caught a glimpse of the clerk at the door with his hands together like he was writing.

"What was he looking at? I hope not the license number of the car. That motherfucker!" he screamed and struck the wheel again.

"That motherfucking camel jockey! I'll get that sonofabitch you just wait!"

He hurried the car back in the direction from where he'd come. The engine roared as the exhaust blew out the emissions from the abrupt acceleration that jerked him back in the seat. The light ahead turned from green to yellow, and then to red. He looked at the speedometer, and it read 75 miles per hour. From the gas pedal to the brake, the car stopped in time for the light without skidding, but the impetus forced the front end of the car to dip to the road. As he waited at the traffic light, he thought about what had just occurred. Foremost on his mind: the police were probably on their way to the store in response to the complaint about him. What he didn't know for certain was whether the clerk at the store copied his license number or not.

"Oh, shit! It's *her* car. Goddamit! It's her fucking car. I gotta call this one off."

The man took a deep breath and talked to himself.

"You gotta calm down. You're driving her car. The Indian got the license number and he's probably gonna give it to the cops. Okay, all right, think."

He put shaking hands over his face.

"Okay, just bring the car back and tell her you have to leave and that'll be it. The cops aren't gonna come looking for her over this," he said, shaking his head. "They're just gonna think I'm some nut or drunk who was trespassing in the store. Shhhst, I'll be long gone before the cops catch on to me."

The light turned green and he gently pressed the accelerator and continued to the hotel, not meeting a single car.

He drove through the parking lot and parked in the same place she'd parked the car before. As he sat behind the wheel watching for the clerk to leave the front counter, reality slapped his face. He wasn't thinking rationally at the store, and something very important about the woman had slipped his mind during the time he was away. Instead of her eagerly awaiting his return, he knew she was there because she was already dead. He'd killed her in the room just before he left to get the beer and magazine. His chest tightened at the comprehension of being seen doing something that could connect him to all of this. There was no way to nullify what had already been done. Consequently, he would have to cover his tracks more efficiently.

When the clerk disappeared from the counter to the back room, he slipped in the doors and tiptoed down the hall to the stairs. The hotel was quiet. He climbed the three flights, and his heart pounded, but not from the exercise. Maybe this is getting to me, he thought. The door opened silently and he stepped inside and quickly closed it behind him. From his spot at the door, he could see her feet dangling from the end of the bed, and as he crept along the carpeted floor, her legs and then, her entire body were visible. She lay on the bed on top of the dark blue comforter.

Her arms were raised haphazardly above her head; her eyes wide open and displaying the horror she'd experienced before her heart stopped beating. The brown leather belt he had used as a garrote was still fastened loosely around her neck and the silver belt buckle had produced an impression in her pink skin.

Hours ago, he told her he would be the best of her life, but little did she know, he would be her last. He sat close to her on the bed and gently brushed the hair from her face. When he touched her cheek, she was still warm. His fingers glided along the skin down her neck to the shoulder, and then to her breast, which felt cooler. He slowly caressed the soft flesh, and imagined her panting in between the words that conveyed she wanted him.

Suddenly, he felt a rush of blood that warmed his entire body. He reminisced in the delight of the power he held over her. How she begged for him to stop, only to ease the pressure just short of unconsciousness, and then to start it over again, with her gagging and coughing and imploring him to spare her. The look on her face was pictured in his mind, full of fear and horror, and he wondered why she didn't fight or struggle, she just cried. The fantasy prompted a smile, but at the same time, he felt remorse for what he'd done to her. Maybe he should have killed her quickly like the others. But the killer wasn't completely satisfied with them. He wanted to gauge the limits of his power.

He rose to his feet, and stood over the lifeless body of the girl and became extremely aroused. An erection surfaced in his pants and in seconds, they had fallen to his ankles. When he touched himself, he thought about her, and the power he possessed over her, and over all of her kind. Closing his eyes, he re-lived the euphoria which embraced his entire being in total recall of her eyes as they silently pleaded for mercy. Her eyes, with tears streaming a path of ruin down her cheeks, somehow telepathically asked the question, "Why?"

The climax he experienced was fierce and ecstatically, he watched his seed discharge on her body as final degradation to his victim.

Invigorated, he quickly refastened his pants, and shifted his thoughts to the clerk at the BP store. Anger engulfed him and he gritted his teeth in contempt for the man. The bastard, he thought, would have given the license plate number to the police, calling him a nut, or a drunk. Concluding even if the clerk got the license number, it couldn't be traced back to him, only to her. He laughed out loud. The police weren't smart enough to connect the complaint about a drunk in a store to the death of the girl. "Ha!" he laughed and thought they would probably discard the information in the trash after determining the frivolity of the complaint.

"They're not smart enough to get me."

The killer cleaned the room and pulled the woman's limp body to the pillows, sweeping the comforter over her head. Not wanting to risk being seen leaving by the front desk clerk, he quietly closed the door, placed the "Do Not Disturb" sign over the handle and sneaked back down the stairs. He made his way down a hallway and out a rear exit door. The strap of the leather duffel bag he carried over his shoulder squeaked as he strolled through the cool night around the hotel. His paranoia made it more audible, and he placed his fingers under the band to quell it. Only the sounds of passing traffic on the interstate could be heard along with the wailing of a distant siren. He lurked in the darkness, protected by the shadows created by the streetlights.

Unnoticed by anyone, he arrived at his car parked adjacent to his victim's black Camaro. From inside the bag, his hand emerged holding a white cloth he used to wipe off the Camaro's interior, windows, and outside the driver's door. Carefully, he erased his identity from the car surfaces with each deliberate stroke of the towel. Satisfied with the job, he locked the door, and silently pushed it shut with his hip.

When he started his car's engine, the warning signal was deafening to his paranoid ears. Relieved, he shifted the car into gear and eased from the driveway. The killer pulled away thinking about the only living witness who could tie his face to the girl's car. In the seat beside him, his hand felt the cold steel of the Colt .45. He gripped the pistol and felt its weight and power. Looking at his reflection in the mirror, a diabolic sneer materialized on his face.

6

T WO DAYS had passed since Hager and Lloyd traveled to Chapel Hill to view the autopsy of the woman found in Ahoskie. The Ahoskie murder, nonetheless, wasn't the only subject of consequence for the Investigative Support Unit. In the meantime, Hager and Lloyd diligently worked on the profile of the Wilmington murder and immersed themselves in the submitted information. For hours the two agents tried to enter the mind of a killer, to pursue his motivations, and reconstruct the events surrounding Heather Kingston's death.

A thorough background check on the victim was crucial to establishing the type of offender involved. In most cases, the victim's behavior and lifestyle contributed somewhat to their deaths.

The SBI requested the submitting agency to refrain from including facts regarding a suspected offender. Expectedly, the reason for sending a case for profile was to classify the crime and provide insight to the makeup of the offender. Based on the data included, the agents were able to determine the type of personality responsible for the act. Histories of similar cases were examined also, and compared to the active one. Relying on all facets, including experience and intuition, the agents would paint a psychological picture of the offender.

For two days, Hager and Lloyd discussed details and theories each had about the case, and came to conclusions they believed were accurate. The final day, they worked well into the evening and the profile, completed, was ready to be typed in the morning.

Hager was exhausted. His head throbbed and his stomach pained from hunger. He rubbed his eyes as he sat at his desk, and they burned from overexertion. Finished with the eyes, his fingers massaged his temples trying to control the spasms in his head. For hours, he'd tried to think like a killer. To put himself in his place, to experience his calculated reasoning, to mimic the thought processes the killer had when he decided to take her life. It was fatiguing work that depleted his energy and his soul; but Hager knew it had to be done. For without it, this monster may continue to prey upon his innocent victims in search of fulfilling his deranged fantasies. Entering the fiend's mind once again, he pictured the girl's face, terrified, she, at the mercy of the mad man.

Horrified, Hager shook himself from the dream, and the image evaporated. Tiny beads of sweat formed on his forehead and he wiped his brow. He took a deep breath. It calmed his nerves, but the headache returned. His stomach growled, calling for replenishment. Hager recollected he'd ignored his belly's initial demands hours ago and concluded hunger might be the primary cause of the headache.

Without warning, a burning sensation shot into his waist. Startled, he jumped in the chair and reached for his pager. He recognized Vanessa's cell phone number on the display and he suddenly recalled the dinner date he had that night. The clock on the wall read 8:37 p.m. Hager knew he was in trouble. Over the phone, the previous night, he told Vanessa he would meet her at Café Americana at 8:00 p.m. He threw his head back. "Shit!"

Hager quickly picked up the phone and dialed. She knew it was him.

"Are you late? or are you just standing me up?"

"I am so sorry Vanessa. I've been tied up with the profile all day, and I completely forgot about our date. I'm leaving my office right now."

Vanessa's sarcasm showed.

"Oh, you forgot, huh? I'm glad I'm so important, you'd rather think like some killer than see me. Okay, I get it now."

He laughed at her wit.

"Come on, give me a break. They've got my mind, but you, you know what you've got."

"I'm sure, Mr. Hager. I used to have that, but, I don't know lately, hmm, maybe I should find me a younger man."

"Oooh, that hurts," he laughed. "Listen, I am sorry and, I promise to make it up to you."

"Promises, schmomises, that's all I hear from you. Are you here yet?"

She sounded tipsy, most likely due to a few glasses of wine while she waited.

"I'll be there in a few minutes," he said.

Almost a week had gone by since he'd last seen Vanessa. That morning, he eagerly anticipated their evening engagement, but his immersion in the project caused him to ignore the plans temporarily. Disgusted by his forgetfulness, Hager resolved to compensate for the *faux pas* and streaked to the nearest grocery store to get a peace offering of flowers along with a package of Hershey's kisses, her favorite candy. Luckily, a dozen red roses, already wrapped, waited in the floral department, the product of a canceled order he learned. On the move again, Hager raced to the restaurant and to his patiently waiting girlfriend.

For the better part of a year, Hager had been involved with Vanessa Roman. They were former co-workers at the SBI when she worked in the DNA Analysis Unit in 1993. Their attraction was instantaneous, but only discreetly acknowledged. Although both were unattached at the time, Hager was still mourning the passing of his wife, and Vanessa, thinking it improper to chase him, kept a friendly distance. However, the two found each other's work intriguing and they enjoyed the discussions which transpired as a result. Soon, they became friends and frequently they both convenienced themselves to drop in on each other, often for trivial matters.

Realizing his vulnerability, Hager resisted the urge to intensify their relationship, keeping it strictly professional. Vanessa was desirous of a romantic involvement with Hager, but she didn't want to push the issue and consequently, waited for him to approach her. During the ensuing year, Hager battled his feelings of doubt over the attraction toward Vanessa. What troubled him particularly was her resemblance to his late wife.

Vanessa was taller, but they shared many physical traits: the shapely figure, brown hair and dark eyes, a voluptuous mouth with perfect teeth that illuminated a room with a single smile. Always the skeptic, Hager reasoned he was converting his love for Kelly to Vanessa in what psychologists termed transferal of displaced affection. In spite of the attraction which existed between he and Vanessa, Hager decided to search for someone who didn't bear resemblance to his parted wife.

Early in 1994, Vanessa achieved a post at Duke University doing genetic research, her expertise. Born and raised in York, Pennsylvania, she earned her Ph.D. in Genetic Engineering from Duke after completing her undergraduate work at the University of Pittsburgh. Sad to depart, they both said their good-byes, but promised to keep in touch due to the proximity of Durham to Raleigh. As both of them buried themselves in their work, the calls gradually declined in frequency.

Although Hager dated other women occasionally, he often pictured Vanessa being with him sometime in the future. On the other hand, Vanessa didn't see anyone romantically for the simple reason she found few people attractively interesting. The intellectual captivation she desired, along with her physical and emotional wantings, was, in her opinion, the third side needed to complete the triangle, and she believed it was the reason she, then 33, had never married.

Two years later on a February evening, their paths crossed once again. They were among the 22,000 or so people attending a basketball game in Chapel Hill between UNC and Duke. While standing in line at a concessions stand, she appeared from the front and lighted the fire that rekindled their feelings for one another. Hager remembered their rivalry at the SBI. She was a staunch Blue Devils fan, and Hager was passionately loyal to his *alma mater*.

The remainder of the game was spent together after Hager invited her to his section. Both of them excitedly involved in the game, they bantered each other when their team made a great play. In the midst of the teasing, it was the touch of her hand on his chest which sent a bolt of lightning through his body making him realize Vanessa was real. And so was his attraction.

The relationship evolved slowly, and time had to be scheduled for rendezvous because of both their demanding jobs. Vanessa had been promoted and was working on The Immune Cell Biology Research Project, where the work was focused primarily on researching the AIDS virus. Almost methodically, their romance developed over the next several months, and Hager was able to see Vanessa's personality and expressions were as similar to Kelly's as their physical appearance.

Although she wasn't as headstrong as Kelly, Vanessa was a very intelligent and passionate woman whose life had been a series of goals and accomplishments. She aspired to contribute something of herself to the world, and hopefully, be a part of some scientific breakthrough that would affect many people.

More reticent than the affable Kelly, Vanessa preferred to conceal her true self until she was comfortable in the setting, relying on her vivid elegance and charm to break the barriers. Persons close to her knew she was witty and charismatic, much like Hager, who could display bouts of impulsiveness. What reminded Hager mostly were the subtle mannerisms which mirrored Kelly. It was the way she picked the lint from his sport coat, or brushed her hair behind her ear; to the way she would draw a heart next to her name when she left him a note, or fold his clothes thrown on the floor. The eeriness of it would send a warm rush through his spine and he would often question if the two were sisters in a previous life. Vanessa soon became close to Hager's daughter, Elizabeth, and she provided the female guidance to the young woman absent since the death of her mother.

Their involvement had struck a plateau recently and it concerned Vanessa. Still in doubt, Hager acknowledged his love for her, but harbored the uncertainty over her resemblance to Kelly. It had engulfed him again, and, as a result, prevented him from progressing the relationship further. Hager didn't conceal his doubt to Vanessa and she appreciated his candor, but at the same time, she felt somewhat threatened by the affinity and contemplated altering her appearance. Before undertaking such a drastic change, she realized the foolishness of it all, and concluded her insecurity was baseless, and his apprehension justifiable.

Vanessa convinced herself there was no need in competing with a memory because it was simply a memory. Presently, Hager was involved with her, and she was deeply in love and desperately wanted it to continue. Instead of fretting about his reluctance to intensify their affair, she delighted in their trysts with the confidence their commitment to each other would eventually grow.

Once inside the door of the restaurant, the hostess smiled at the man carrying the bundle of roses. Hager scanned the tables of patrons until his eyes found the woman with the long brown hair sitting alone daydreaming out of the window. Their eyes met provoking a radiant smile from her mouth. He quickly made his way to the table and fell into her embrace. It was long and firm signifying their absence from each other. The perfume she sprayed on her neck was delicious. They parted and kissed, her warm hands cupping his cheeks. Oblivious of the fact they were not alone, the kiss sustained until they were hit by the realization. Their lips parted and Hager looked around to see the bystanders had noticed the reunion, gleefully smiling at the spectacle. Vanessa was dressed in a pair of black low slung jeans which snugly displayed her curvaceous figure, and a white long sleeved ribbed turtleneck. He gave her the flowers and candy.

"I'm really sorry about being late. Will you forgive me?"

"Oh, Clark, you know you didn't have to do that. You're such a sweetheart. I love the kisses."

On the table were two menus and a half empty glass of Chardonnay in front of Vanessa. Hager sat opposite her at the table.

"You look beautiful, Vanessa."

Her face flushed.

"Thank you, sweetie. You don't look too bad yourself. But you look tired."

"I am. It's been a rough two days."

"I bet. But you know what alleviates stress the most?"

She touched his hand and eyed him seductively.

Hager smiled at the thought.

"Hmm hmm, I know."

The waiter arrived at the table.

"Oh, sir, you finally made it. What can I get you to drink?"

"I'll have an Ice House, please."

"Okay. Would you care for another glass of wine, ma'am?"

The question caught her in the middle of a drink and she nodded.

"All right. I'll get those drinks for you and I'll be back to take your order."

Hager smiled at Vanessa, her eyes glassy from the wine.

"How many glasses have you had?"

"Oh, about an hours' worth," she said with a grin.

"I'm sorry."

"Don't worry. I'll get my payback."

"You will, huh? It looks like you've caught yourself a buzz. I guess I'll just have to drive you home, young lady. For your own safety, of course."

Her face brightened.

"That was my intention, officer. To lure you back to my lair and seduce you."

She grabbed his hand again.

"You know what wine does to me."

"Bartender!" Hager shouted.

They both laughed.

Hager loved the way Vanessa flirted with him. She was so alluring. What made her teasing more provocative was that she backed it up with action. She was the most sexually passionate woman with whom he'd ever been involved, and sometimes she seemed insatiable. Hager's desire of sex was strong, and he felt blessed they were compatible in this regard. Thoughtfully, she attributed her high libido to Hager's magnetism and he fervently strove to satisfy her intense drive for lovemaking.

The waiter returned with the drinks and asked if they were ready to order. Vanessa picked up the menu and scanned it. Hager took a drink of his beer and watched her as she mulled over her selection. As her eyes searched the entrees, she gently placed her finger inside her bottom lip, which reminded Hager of Kelly. Hager's eyes were fixed on her face; he was in a trance.

"Clark? Clark? Hello, earth to Clark," she said waving her hand in his face.

Coming out of the spell, "Oh, I'm sorry, I'll have the mushroom chicken with pasta."

The waiter nodded and walked away.

"What were you thinking about a minute ago?"

"What do you mean?" he said as he swigged the bottle.

"You know, when you were in the clouds. Just a second ago."

"I was just looking at you. You're so beautiful, Vanessa. I was just admiring how gorgeous you are."

"Why thank you, sweetie. That sure was nice. You're not so bad yourself, for a Carolina fan. Hey, that reminds me. Were you able to get the tickets to the game in Chapel Hill?"

"Oh, shit, I forgot to ask when I was there the other day. Oh well, I'll just call him tomorrow."

The he to whom Hager referred, was Thomas O'Brien, the Athletic Director of UNC, and also, Hager's source for tickets to the Carolina basketball and football games. O'Brien went to Carolina the same time as Hager. The two had played baseball together and had remained friends throughout the years. Hager and Vanessa wanted to attend both Carolina/Duke basketball games each year, and the upcoming game in Chapel Hill would be special as they would celebrate the anniversary of their meeting again.

"You were in Chapel Hill? What, for an autopsy?"

"Yeah, a woman was found near Ahoskie Sunday morning. They called and asked me to help them."

"Ahoskie. Oh my goodness! Have you called your parents? I hope they're not worried."

Hager had forgotten all about it. He'd been so involved with work, he hadn't called to see if his parents were okay. Last week, he talked to them on the phone, but he should have called today.

"No, I was just so busy today. Lloyd and I have been working on the murder case in Wilmington. I just forgot. I'll call them tomorrow."

Vanessa was like that. She was thoughtful of people to whom she was close. It came from her family background. Growing up in a small close-knit family made her especially considerate of one with whom she'd a special relationship. The kind of person who always sent Christmas cards every year and "thank you" notes when someone did something exceptional for her.

"Good. I miss them. They're such nice people. Let's go see them soon, sweetie, okay?"

"It looks like I'll be seeing them the day after tomorrow. Lloyd and I are going there to follow up on the homicide they had. Hey, do you think you can get off work for the day?"

She frowned.

"I don't think so, Clark, we're just so shorthanded in the center. Let's plan it for some weekend so we won't be in such a rush."

"Well, I wouldn't be able to do anything other than work anyway."

Vanessa took another drink of the wine and she stared into Hager's eyes. There was silence. She was ogling him alluringly and the smirk on her face conveyed her thoughts like a headline on a newspaper. Words were unnecessary for this particular message. She had dispatched the signal from the moment he sat at the table. The light from the candle shone in her eyes and created a shadow on her cheek. When her eyes shifted from his, Hager turned to see the waiter bringing a platter toward their table.

"All right, the food's here."

The plates were hot, and the food was good. Hager ordered a glass of Sauvignon blanc with his dinner. His entree was a boneless chicken breast covered with a creamy white wine and mushroom sauce. Angel hair pasta layered the plate and the sauce had juicy button mushrooms perfect to be eaten whole. On the side, a medley of garden vegetables: carrots, broccoli, and cauliflower florets grilled in a honey glaze. Vanessa had broiled swordfish marinated in thyme and lemon juice, brown rice with almonds, with brown sugar sprinkled over top. The waiter brought a loaf of fresh wheat and barley bread which tasted extraordinarily good with the mushroom sauce.

The couple ate the meal while making small talk about her work, Elizabeth, and politics. A custom observed by the two of them was to share a morsel of each other's food. Vanessa fed him some of the fish, and he combined a piece of chicken smothered in the sauce and wrapped in the pasta. He put the fork to her mouth and watched her lips surround it. She had the most exquisite mouth. Other than her eyes, it was the most provocative quality of her face. He referred to Vanessa's lips as the "portals of desire." They were perfectly shaped, and when she smiled, they exposed her straight, white, teeth.

It was a modest café, with a simple elegance that appealed to lovers and encouraged their intimacy. The decor was charming and resembled something from a movie set in France during the Second World War. Hager pictured uniformed soldiers whispering to their girls, trying to convince them to accompany them to the states when it was over.

Lending to the atmosphere, the dining area was dimly lit, and lanterns adorned the four corners of the room. Small tables lined three of the walls, and others were situated to provide enough space for privacy, but close enough to be cozy. The tables were covered with white cloths and dressed with napkins folded in the shape of a flower. Every table was dressed with fresh flowers which were changed daily.

A dark brown wood trimmed the walls and ceiling, and a large bay window provided a twinkling panorama of Raleigh's lighted skyline.

The beer had made Hager a little light headed, but once the meal was finished, the lazy feeling subsided. They ordered more wine, and after the food was finished, the waiter cleared the plates. Hager felt warm. Partly from the intoxicating effect of the wine, but mostly he was hypnotized by Vanessa's eyes. They were a soft brown color with extra long lashes that batted unconsciously when she talked. Her eyes were as serene as a summer breeze at the beach, and had a dark, alluring innocence that was seductive at the same time. He could get lost in those eyes. Meekly, she would gaze at him, and the gentleness would captivate his attention in pure obedience. Hager looked at his watch, surprised at the hour.

"Damn, it's nearly midnight."

She rolled her tiny wrist.

"Really? That late?"

Hager turned looking for the waiter to bring the check.

"Clark, I love this place," Vanessa sighed. "I think it's so romantic."

"Yes it is. And the food's good, too."

With the check paid, they strolled hand-in-hand through the parking lot. The sky was clear and some stars were shining. The air was cold, but their togetherness warmed him. At her door, he reached for her arm and their lips met. Tenderly, they kissed, her mouth opened and he gently stroked her tongue. Her lips were so warm and supple and they seemed to match perfectly to his. He felt her hand lightly touch his neck and it made him shiver. Pulling away, she eyed him seductively.

"Don't forget your payback."

"Please be gentle."

7

TARDINESS was a habit Hager tried to avoid. But on this particular morning it was unavoidable. He'd slept over at Vanessa's apartment after the dinner and a prolonged episode of sex. It was nearly three in the morning when his head hit the pillows for sleep, his energy drained from a day's work and the exertion of lovemaking. Sleep must have been instantaneous for Hager since he didn't remember if he'd told her goodnight.

In fact, Vanessa had teased him that seconds after they were finished and they lay in bed holding each other, she heard the rumbling of snoring.

"Typical man," she said.

Hager reasoned it was the soporific effects of making love to her which induced such a sudden unconscious state.

"Hey, you can't help it if you're so good in bed."

The heat between the two of them had simmered the entire evening during dinner and the drive to her apartment in Durham.

Hager endured the trek from the restaurant while she fondled between his legs and nibbled his ear and neck. Once inside her door, the tension boiled over, and they created a trail of clothes leading from the door to the bedroom, their hands and mouths wildly groping and kissing each other. It was right out of an erotic movie and Hager loved it.

Vanessa awakened early to ready herself for work, while she allowed Hager to stay in bed. To wake him, she placed a cup of steaming coffee under his nose. With his eyes barely open, he strained to a seated position on the edge of the bed. He felt like he hadn't been to sleep and whined about it. Although he'd slept for about four hours, it had been such a deep sleep, it made him groggy. After a yawn or two, and a few gulps of the coffee, he was lucid enough to stand. Hager was still nude and he felt the pressure on his bladder. He looked down and saw his morning involuntary state. Embarrassed when Vanessa noticed him in the mirror, he tried to hide it and turned away from her. But she sneaked up behind him and wrapped her arms around his waist. He felt her hands between his legs.

"At least somebody's awake this morning. Are you glad to see me or what?"

She wasn't addressing Hager, but his state of rigor, like it was a sovereign being. Hager blushed, but became aroused at her touch. Vanessa returned to the bathroom to finish getting ready, and Hager looked around the room, trying to remember where his underwear had been tossed by Vanessa in her passionate haste to get to him naked. Vanessa had gathered the clothes on the path left to the door, folded them, and placed them neatly on her dresser. He admired her work.

Women had this uncanny ability to touch something and make it beautiful. Like folding a shirt. A man could imitate the exact method, but for this special reason, the woman's looked much more appealing, and his more like a chimp had done it. The special woman touch emanated from the shirt.

Although he didn't see Vanessa do it, Hager knew that before she placed it on the dresser, she smelled the collar for his cologne. Most women did it. He guessed it was due to their keen sense of smell. Hager knew from his psychology tutelage that olfactory senses trigger memory more effectively than the others.

Vanessa had left her car in the parking lot of the café and she accompanied Hager to his house so he could shower, shave and dress. The hot water of the shower invigorated him, and after getting dressed, he felt normal again. Dropping her at her car, they had a long kiss good-bye and he promised to call her later that night. Hager suggested he cook for them soon, maybe during the coming weekend.

When Hager walked into the office it was nearly 9 a.m. Fortunately, he and Lloyd had no set schedule, but he'd told his partner he would be there at eight. Judy was busy on her computer terminal putting the profile together for return to Wilmington. Lloyd was in his office, and when Hager stood in the doorway, he saw the familiar white paper bag sitting on Lloyd's desk. Two large Styrofoam cups sat in a cardboard holder next to the bag. Lloyd was reading the newspaper when Hager stepped through the door.

"Late night last night?" Lloyd asked without looking from behind the paper.

"Kinda. Vanessa and I had a late dinner."

Lloyd folded the paper and tossed it on the desk. He crossed his arms and rested them on his chest.

"And?"

"And what?"

"You know." He flexed his eyebrows. "You get some poon tang or what?"

Hager laughed at the question and blushed.

"What do you think?"

"You don't have to say a word. I could tell by the look on your face. She's wearing you out, huh?"

"Not even close. I can keep up. I'm not an old man, you know."

"Yeah, right. You come in an hour late with your eyes all puffy, yeah," he nodded. "You're keeping up all right."

"Don't you worry about it, Lloyd. You didn't get to see her this morning."

"Bright eyed and bushy tailed, huh?"

"Yeah. Damnit," Hager confessed.

Lloyd handed one of the coffee cups to him.

"Here, it looks you need this. It's probably cold, though."

"Thanks. I'll heat it up in the microwave."

Hager turned to walk out and stopped.

"She is good, you know?"

"I bet she is. With a body like that. Even if you died in the middle, you'd be in heaven already."

Lloyd gave Hager the paper to read while he ate, and they both waited for Judy to finish typing the profile. When Lloyd came into Hager's office, he was drinking the second cup of coffee and reading the sports section. Hager looked up to his partner, who had some sheets of paper in his hand.

"Here it is."

"Oh, good. Let's take a look." Hager placed the papers on his desk and began to read.

North Carolina State Bureau of Investigation
Criminal Profile
Submitting Agency: Wilmington Police Department
Type of Case: Homicide
Date Submitted: January 8, 1997
Date of offense: July 30, 1996 Date body found: August 2, 1996
Victim: Heather Marie Kingston W/F/4/18/75

The homicide in this case has been determined to be a single homicide. The primary intent of the offender was found to be sexual. There was evidence of sexual activity before the victim was killed, and the evidence indicated there was probably sexual activity after death. The victim was a female college student who worked full-time as an exotic dancer. It is believed this job contributed to her death in some way. Based on facts regarding her occupation and habits, it is believed the victim was a high-risk victim living in an area that was low-risk for violent crimes. The apartment building was one of four of the complex with a racial mixture of 90% white, 5% black, 3% Asian and 2% Hispanic. No other similar crimes had been reported in the victim's apartment complex or any neighboring complexes. It is determined the offender was operating at a high risk because the killer was, at least, an acquaintance of the victim and may have been observed by someone at the victim's work, or at the apartment itself. It is determined the offender was able to gain the trust of the victim, and therefore did not have to escalate to the use of force for victim submission. The evidence suggests the offender has a history of sexual assault or other violent crime and is likely to continue with his crimes until apprehended. Based on the information presented, it is determined the victim was killed on or about Wednesday July 30, 1996; between the hours of 11:30 p.m. and 10:00 a.m. on July 31, 1996. This is consistent with the time period when noises were heard in the apartment from below. It is determined the offender spent more than enough time with the victim to kill her and to have sexual activity with her body after death, which would indicate the killer was comfortable at her apartment and knew he would not be disturbed. The crime occurred at the victim's residence, indicating further the offender was known to a degree by the victim.

Crime Assessment

Based on the examination of the evidence presented, it has been determined that the victim, who worked at the Doll House Club from 3:00 p.m. until 11:00 p.m., was approached by a person known to her or someone with whom she had some familiarity. It is then believed the offender accompanied the victim to her apartment where some alcohol consumption occurred. It is determined the offender had sexual intercourse with the victim apparently without the use of physical force, or possibly with the threat or presence of a weapon. After the sex act was completed, the victim was strangled with a ligature type tool. The photographs from the autopsy are inconclusive in identifying the actual tool; however, it appears it was a tool of small diameter, perhaps a thin belt or article of clothing. After death, the offender appears to have masturbated on the victim due to presence of semen on her chest and shoulder area. The victim's body was placed under the covers of the bed which covered her body up to her head. The body was found nude, and the crime scene photographs indicate little or no struggle was involved, which would again, indicate the victim was acquainted with the offender. The body was then placed in a bed in a sleeping position. Based on the crime assessment, a profile of the offender can be made.

Offender Profile

It is concluded the offender in this case can be classified as an organized type offender. It is believed the offender is a white male; age 20-30 years; of high or above average intelligence; socially and sexually competent; average to above average in appearance and may be described as charming. It is believed the offender has a skilled job, or has worked in a skilled position before; it is also believed the offender may have some background in law enforcement; and he will follow the events in the news. The offender in this case may live with a partner, or may be married; and he has a car in working condition. The type of car he would own would be a sports type car, one befitting his personality. The offender would probably have some criminal record, and may have a history of this type of behavior based on the risk involved. It is believed the offender lives close to the Wilmington area; but it would be within fifty miles. It is believed this offense was planned; and the offender sought out his victim in a place where he was comfortable but would not be recognized. It is believed the offender was known by the victim or was a relative acquaintance. The sexual activity was either a result of manipulation of the victim or the threat of force or a weapon was the means of gaining the victim's submission, and the offender killed as a part of a ritual. The killer collected souvenirs from the crime scene: the victim's clothes and hair from a brush, and those items would be found at his residence in an effort to continue the fantasy. The sexual activity after death indicated death was a part of the offender's plan.

Post-crime Behavior

Based on the crime scene evidence, the offender in this case may have felt some remorse for the victim as suggested by the position of the body after death. In an effort to somehow personalize the victim, the offender placed the body in a position that was not degrading. The condition of the victim's hair is consistent with the presence of a hair brush found on a night stand next to the body. This suggests the killer may have brushed her hair as a part of a ritualistic fantasy. The profilers also noticed a lack of hair in the brush, suggesting the killer took the hair strands as a souvenir of the murder. The offender left the victim's body at her residence where the recovery of it would be within days. This evidence can be helpful in identifying the offender because it suggests the offender was possibly known by the victim, and the killer may seek to interject himself in the investigation of her death.

He finished reading the profile and was satisfied with its contents. With the profile done, a follow-up call to Detective Matlin would be made to answer any questions he may have, and also to inquire about a suspect. After learning about the suspect, Hager could recommend additional investigative steps or interrogation strategies to be used by the detective.

Hager picked up the telephone and dialed.

"You calling them now?" Lloyd asked.

"No. Mom and Dad," he said, shaking his head.

Lloyd left and returned to his office.

"Dad, it's Clark. How are you?"

"Hey, son. Fine, what's happening with you?"

"Oh, you know, the usual madness. How about you all?"

"Just about the same around here. Momma's getting dressed and then we're going to Wal-Mart."

"You played any golf lately?"

"I played yesterday. It was pretty nice here. About fifty degrees. Hey, how's my beautiful granddaughter, Liz. Has she started back to school this semester yet?"

"Yeah, she started on Wednesday. I haven't spoken to her much this week. It's been kinda hectic around the office."

"So, how's the love life? You and Vanessa still together?"

"Yes, it's going pretty good."

"Great. That Vanessa is a good girl. You'd better keep her. You all made any plans yet?"

Hager grinned. It was just like a parent to ask if there would be a wedding soon.

"Yes, she is a good one, but no, we've not talked about anything. Look, Dad, the other reason I called was to ask you if you heard about the woman they found near your place."

"Oh yeah, we heard about it. It was in the newspaper and Becky said the sheriff questioned her and Colt to see if they had seen the woman at the lounge Saturday night."

"Why would they talk to Becky and Colt?" Hager asked, wondering why Sheriff McAdoo would want to talk to his sister and her husband. "Do they still go there?"

"Oh, you didn't know. They both started tending bar there on the weekends to make some extra money."

"Well, I'm sort of working with Sheriff McAdoo on it and I wanted to see if you all had heard anything different there. As a matter of fact, I may be coming there tomorrow to look at where the body was found."

"Really? That's great. You gonna bring your golf clubs?"

"I don't know if there'll be any time to play, but I'll throw them into the trunk."

"Have they found out who she was, Clark? The paper said she hadn't been identified yet."

"No, not yet. Hey, since it will be Friday, maybe Elizabeth and Vanessa can come down on Saturday. You know, make a weekend of it."

"That sounds great. I'm sure Momma will make something special then."

"All right, Dad, I've got some other calls to make. I just wanted to see if you guys were okay. I'll call you tomorrow morning to let you know for sure about this weekend."

"All right, son. You take care. And give our love to Vanessa and Liz. And tell that crazy partner of yours 'hello' for me. Oh! that reminds me. I've got a joke for you to tell him."

Hager's dad always had a joke or two to tell when he called. They were always somewhat dirty, but usually funny. The golf course was a good source of funny stories.

"All right, go ahead."

"Have you heard the one about the man and his wife taking up golf together?"

"No, but go ahead."

"Well, this golfer is having marital problems. So, he and his wife go to a marriage counselor, and find out the root of her problem is he plays golf too often, and doesn't spend enough time with her. Well, the counselor recommends they both participate in activities together and that would resolve the problem. So, the guy decides he'll teach his wife how to play golf and the next day, they go out to the course. On the first tee, he tells her, 'Honey, you just stand there at the lady's tee while I hit my ball, and then I'll help you with yours.'

"Well, the wife goes and stands in the box, and he takes a few practice swings. He sets up and takes a giant swing and the ball hits his wife in the head, Boom! She's out cold. Well, the guy rushes her to the hospital and is sitting in the waiting room when the doctor comes in with a worried look on his face. The doctor tells him his wife's gonna be all right, she just had a concussion, but they found something strange during the examination. 'What was that?' he asks. The doctor says, 'A golf ball was found imbedded in her rectum and we were wondering how the ball got there.'" His dad chuckled. "So the guy says, 'hey, I gotta have my mulligan!'"

Hager laughed.

"That's a good one. Lloyd will like it, too, I'm sure."

After Hager hung up the phone, Lloyd came back into the office and told him the photographs of the crime scene in Ahoskie were ready to be picked up. Lloyd asked how his parents were doing, and Hager relayed the joke told by his father, and they both laughed.

The subject of lunch arose. Lloyd suggested Chinese, and Hager concurred, but told him he wanted to call Wilmington before they went. Lloyd remained in the office and the call was put on the speaker phone so his partner could be involved in the conversation.

"Homicide, Detective Matlin," the voice answered.

"Bill Matlin. Clark Hager."

"Hey, how are you doin'? Had any luck with our case yet?"

"As a matter of fact, Bill, we just finished the profile about a half-hour ago, and I wanted to call you to let you know."

"Great, Clark. I really appreciate it. I hope you guys can help."

"Well, I hope so. It's pretty much up to you from this point. Look, I was wondering about something. You told me before you had a suspect in this. What happened?"

"Well, the girl had a boyfriend and the two of them had just broken up, so we find him in Myrtle Beach. After we get him back to Wilmington, he denies he killed her. Well, we grill him for a long time, and he doesn't budge. We ask him to take a polygraph and give a sample of his blood, and he consents to it. The next day the polygraph is done, and he passed. I said, 'Shit', you know, 'cause I felt we had the right guy."

"Yeah, it sounds like you did."

"Well, even after the polygraph, I still wasn't convinced, but we had to look elsewhere until the DNA test results came back."

"What then?"

The detective told the agents about a man in the club claiming to be a photographer who offered another dancer a modeling contract. Hager started to get curious.

"So, does anyone know who this guy is?"

"No, one of the girls said he had given her a business card with his name on it; but she threw it away. She did say she thought the first name on it was Rick; but she couldn't remember what magazine or anything."

Lloyd interjected, "Did you check any of the other places to see if they recognized a guy like that?"

"Yeah, we went to all of them. Took a couple of days to talk to just about everyone working there, and no one recalls a guy like that."

"What did this guy look like, Bill?" Hager asked.

"Let's see. A white male, about twenty-five maybe older, brown hair, about six feet tall, and around two hundred pounds, well-built guy; nicely dressed, clean shaven. Nothing special about him. They just said he was very good-looking and talked about being a photographer."

"Bill, I'm assuming the DNA test came back negative for the boyfriend?"

"Sure did. After that, we started concentrating more on this photographer guy."

"Any lead to who he is?"

"No. We were hoping you all could help us with that."

Hager nodded to his partner about the similarity to their profile.

"The profile we came up with fits somebody like that. I'd check around the other clubs again to see if a guy like that works or has worked at any of those places. Being well-built like they said, he may be a bouncer. He might even be into body building. Check the local gyms to see if anyone knows someone like that. Did you say this guy was in the bar three days in a row?"

"Yeah, that's what the other dancer said."

"Do you know if they had ever seen him before?" Hager asked.

"The girl we talked to said she'd never seen him before, but, who knows in a place like that. The dancers move around so much."

Lloyd said, "Well, with the way he was spending money on her, it's likely he'd be remembered if he'd been in there before. They remember that shit."

Hager nodded.

"Bill, have there been any similar cases like this? Before or after the murder. A rape or assault, maybe?"

"No. This was the first case like this, and nothing since involving a man like him."

"Okay, your man may live either out of town, or he arrived in Wilmington just before the murder. Find a guy who came into town about mid-July, and you've found your man. If he's gone, you won't have to worry anymore, hopefully."

"All right. We'll check on it."

Hager suddenly realized there were some similarities of the Wilmington murder to the death of the woman in Ahoskie.

"Was it a coincidence?" Hager asked himself.

He looked at Lloyd to see if his partner was struck with the same revelation. Lloyd nodded in agreement.

"If this guy is mobile," Hager whispered to Lloyd, "then he could be responsible for both of these murders."

Lloyd shrugged his shoulders, "It's possible."

"Clark, thanks a lot for your help," Matlin said.

"You're welcome, Bill. Let us know what you find out. You'll be getting the profile in the mail the next day or two. Good luck."

Hager pushed the speaker phone off. Lloyd sat on the edge of a table, his arms folded across his chest.

"What do you think?" Hager asked.

Lloyd shook his head and wrinkled his mouth.

"I don't know. There are some parallels, but, five months apart. I don't know."

"You're right, it's a long cooling off period, but with the organized type offender, his killing is usually precipitated by some stressor."

Lloyd rubbed his chin.

"Yeah, those types can often go months and then kill when something happened to trigger it."

"Hell, he may have waited that long to find just the right victim.

Anyway, we don't know if it's been four months since he's killed. We don't even know if the two of them are related. I guess I'm jumping the gun a little. Let's wait until the other one is identified, then, if it continues to be similar, we'll talk about it then."

"Okay. Let's eat."

8

THE TROUSERS felt tighter around Hager's waist after he gorged himself at the Dragon Garden Chinese buffet. The bounty of rice, chicken, shrimp, and vegetables also produced the dozing as he rode in the car. In addition, the lack of sleep from the night before was catching up to him.

Hager's body jerked when the pager vibrated on his side and Lloyd, who watched his head nod during the ride, laughed at his partner's reaction. Hager always kept his pager in silent mode because he didn't want to attract attention to himself in public. Besides, it was such an annoying sound, and most people let the beeping continue so everyone around them would think they were important.

Lloyd had just turned onto Old Garner Road when the pager went off. Hager looked at the number, recognizing it as the number for his office. The numbers had a "911" next to them indicating an urgent call. They were only about a minute from the office, and Hager decided to wait instead of using the cellular phone.

Both agents hurriedly walked to the building and into the lobby. Judy was on the telephone. She looked up when they emerged through the entrance. A small piece of pink paper was in her extended hand and Hager took it as they walked by.

It was Sheriff McAdoo. Hoping for some progress in the identification of the body, Hager strode through the hall and in a second was at his desk dialing the number for the Hertford County Sheriff.

"Sheriff McAdoo, this is Clark Hager. I just got your message. What'cha got?"

"Well, we've identified the body. She was reported missing from Greenville yesterday."

Hager sat in the chair and turned on the speaker.

"Great. How did you find out about her?"

"Greenville PD called about it and the description matched, so one of their detectives and the girl's mother came here and I-Deed the body at the morgue."

"Who is she?"

"Her name's Tamara Wall. She was twenty-three, lived with her mother."

Hager wrote the name on a legal pad.

"Hmm, when was the last time anyone saw her?"

"I don't know. The mother hadn't seen her in a couple of days, but her car was found in the parking lot of Striker's Plus. That's where she worked."

"Striker's Plus? What's that?"

"Oh, it's one of those all nude clubs. She was a stripper."

A cold chill rushed up Hager's spine. He looked over at Lloyd.

"Are you serious? Damn!"

"Yeah, why?"

Hager stood up and paced the floor in thought.

"Sheriff, is the detective from Greenville still there?"

"No. He and the girl's mother went back so he could follow up on it. What's wrong?"

"Oh, we just finished a profile for a murder in Wilmington that happened five months ago. The victim was strangled and she was a stripper, too."

"Shit. Do you think they're related?"

"I don't know, but we'll surely find out. We have semen from both victims and we'll have them matched. Look, Sheriff, don't mention what I said to anyone until I say so. I don't want the news to start talking about a serial killer until we know for sure."

"You got it, Mr. Hager."

"We're going to go to Greenville instead of coming there. What's the detective's name and phone number?"

"It's Jamison." McAdoo gave Hager the number.

"Thanks, Sheriff. I'll be in touch."

Lloyd was already on the phone when Hager ended the conversation with the sheriff. He picked up a paper and read.

"Yeah, Heather Marie Kingston. The SBI Lab number is R-triple-0-8-1-6-4-5. A Homicide case. A rape kit was done."

Lloyd waited and pulled the receiver below his chin.

"They're trying to find it."

Hager picked up his phone and pressed the speed dial for the Photography section.

"Hey, this is Hager. Can you bring the crime scene pictures from the Hertford County case to my office?"

He heard Lloyd's voice make the request for DNA analysis of the two semen samples.

"We need 'em here right away," Hager said. "Great. Thanks a lot."

Within a half hour, the two agents were on U.S. 264 East heading for Greenville. The trip would take about an ninety minutes. While Lloyd drove, Hager used the time to examine the crime scene photographs, like he did when they went to Chapel Hill. They also conversed in between Lloyd's occasional spitting of tobacco juice into a Styrofoam cup, and over the twangs of country music playing on the radio. What was once an inkling, was now swiftly becoming a reality. The possibility of the murders of two young women being related had been briefly discussed less than two hours prior, and it appeared their supposition was developing into an actuality.

Lloyd tapped his hands on the steering wheel.

"But what about this woman from Greenville?" Lloyd asked. "She was dumped. The other was left at the murder scene."

"I thought about that. He dumped this one's body because either there was no other place to leave it, or, he killed her in a car. With him being in a car, there was nothing else to do but dump her somewhere."

"Yeah, but all the way to Ahoskie? Why go that far north of Greenville? What's Ahoskie have to do with it?"

"I don't know. Maybe he's familiar with the area and knew it was pretty rural. I don't know. There're still a lot of questions to be answered in all of this."

The two agents arrived at the Greenville Police Department and met Detective Jamison. He was dressed sharply, donning a double breasted, black pinstripe suit with a blood red tie, with spots of black and white. Hager thought he looked more like a lawyer than a police detective. Hager liked to see someone professionally dressed; it displayed a bearing of respect and capability. Appearing to be around thirty-five, Hager was surprised to learn Jamison was forty six, Hager's exact age. His green eyes were striking and unusual for a black man, but gave the impression of sincerity.

In his office, the detective took off his jacket and revealed a wiry frame under the white shirt. On his desk lay a Bible and many references to God, and Hager later found out he was a preacher. Jamison spoke eloquently, and it was clear he was a motivational orator, a common trait for a man of God. Hager imagined him standing before a large congregation, at the pulpit firing off a passionate sermon.

"Agent Hager, I've heard a lot about you. I didn't get to the seminar you taught in Wilmington last month. I understand it was really good."

"Thanks. I hope you heard good things about us."

"Most of it was good, but, you know how some rumors get started from agency to agency."

Hager figured Jamison was talking about the rumor that the Investigative Support Unit didn't work with other agencies very well. That falsehood had begun several years ago when a state Senator was killed in Rocky Mount, and Hager's unit was ordered by the Attorney General to handle the investigation. The detectives and police chief in Rocky Mount were highly offended and embittered because the investigation had been taken out of their hands.

Hager understood their resentment of being removed from the case, but the Attorney General had already made up his mind and wanted the SBI to handle the investigation. He later came to understand the AG's decision better when they learned that two Rocky Mount police officers were seen leaving the scene of the murder just after the gunshots were fired. The SBI's probe led to indictments charging the city manager, the police chief, one of his assistants, and two line officers, with murder and conspiracy to commit murder.

Hager believed the resentment came from either the charges filed, or the fact the agents bluntly refused to divulge any information concerning the case to Rocky Mount detectives. In what turned out to be the state's most extensive investigation into government corruption in the 20th century, the agents learned the Senator had been taking bribes from the city's government officials who were associated with organized crime.

"Don't believe all you hear, Jamison. We're not that bad to work with," Lloyd said as he wiped the dirt off his glasses with a handkerchief.

Hager said, "So, Jamison, what do you have on the woman found in Ahoskie?"

Jamison motioned for the two agents to sit in chairs, which were positioned around his desk. Jamison sat on the corner of his desk.

"Tamara Lynnette Wall, twenty-three, current residence on Jonestown Road, Greenville. She lived with her mother and step-father, Barbara and Johnny Lewis, and her seventeen year old sister,

Kim, and her sixteen year old brother, David. She had two prior arrests: one for worthless checks five years ago, and a DWI last year. She grew up here in Greenville. After graduating from D.H. Conley High School, she started waiting tables at Shoney's Restaurant. She worked there until she got a job at First Union Bank here in town, and worked there until May of last year. Dancing at Striker's Plus was her current job and she'd been there about six months."

"Did she have a boyfriend?" Hager asked.

"According to the mother, she didn't. She didn't know for sure, but she guessed Tammy was a lesbian."

Lloyd looked at Hager with one of his grins.

"The mother said she last saw her on Saturday afternoon. Tammy was supposed to work that night until closing. From what she said, Tammy would sometimes spend the night with another girl who worked at the club, a Cissy. She didn't know her last name. The mother said that's why she wasn't alarmed when she didn't come home for a couple of days. She thought she'd stayed with Cissy."

"What did Cissy have to say?"

"I called her and she said she last saw Tammy after work Friday night, early Saturday morning when they went to the Waffle House after work. They didn't talk about much of anything out of the ordinary other than Tammy told her about this guy who was in the club."

"A guy in the club?"

"Right. Tammy told her this guy was a photographer from some swimsuit magazine, and he wanted Tammy to be in it."

Hager looked over at Lloyd in silent acknowledgment of the similarity to the case in Wilmington.

Lloyd asked, "Did Cissy work that Saturday night?"

"No, she was off but she expected Tammy to come over, you know. They had this *thing* going on," Jamison said waiting to see if the agents understood. "Well, at the Waffle House, Cissy tells Tammy to stay away from the guy, that he was just hitting on her. I think Cissy was jealous. That's what I got from her."

Hager was jotting down notes on his legal pad.

"Were any of the dancers working that night of any help?"

"Yesterday afternoon, I talked to a couple of them who said there was this guy in the club Saturday night who was paying Tammy pretty well. All of them remembered him because he was good-looking and was forking out a lot of money on dances."

"Did they say anything about seeing him before?"

"One of them said she'd seen him on Friday night. Said he was well-dressed, and gave her a business card after he told her he was photographer for a swimsuit magazine."

"She still got the card?" Lloyd asked.

"No, I've got it right here."

Jamison opened the folder and pulled out a plastic envelope containing a white business card. The card was stained partially with black fingerprint powder. Jamison handed the envelope to Hager who turned it to see the printing on the front.

"Ronny Cooper, Free-lance photographer, Miami, Florida," Hager said.

He passed it to his partner.

"Did you get any prints from the card?"

"Yeah, there were some partials, and some overlaps. We were going to send them to AFIS, but since you guys are here."

"Yeah, we'll take 'em. Did you check the name through Florida?"

"I tried Florida's DMV files, you know, by name only and got a list of three hundred and seventy some Ronald Coopers."

Jamison held up the computer printout.

"Unless you have a full name and DOB, it's hard to get an exact match."

Hager took the list.

"We'll probably have to call Florida personally and get them to check. I know someone at the FDLE. Maybe he can expedite it."

Jamison took a sip from his coffee cup.

"Ya'll want some coffee?"

"No, thanks," Hager said.

Lloyd shook his head.

"What about the address and phone number in Miami? Have you done anything with them?" Hager asked.

"I was just getting ready to call the number when ya'll got here. Do you want me to call it now?"

Hager looked at Lloyd, who shook his head. Hager rose from the chair.

"Nah, we'll take care of it."

If Hager wasn't convinced of it before, he was now. The Wilmington murder was so very similar to this case; especially now since both victims were last seen with a man who was posing as a photographer. Although not conclusive evidence to connect the cases, all the facts were now lining up in one single row.

"The sheriff mentioned about her car being found in the parking lot of the club?"

"Oh yeah, the mother, after she hadn't heard from Tammy for a couple days, she decides to call the club manager to see if she'd been at work. The manager said she hadn't been seen since closing time late Friday night, but her car was still parked in the parking lot. And this was Tuesday night. That's when she called us to file the missing persons report."

"And you learned about the body being found through the DCI message, right?"

"No. It was strange. Our Crimestoppers line gets a caller saying a body found in Ahoskie might be a missing girl from Greenville."

Hager leaned forward with a curious look on his face.

"Was that all the caller said?"

"I think that was it. Our Crimestoppers coordinator talked to him and took down the information. We asked him about the call after we confirmed it was the girl found in Ahoskie."

"What did he say?"

"Said the guy sounded like he was white, and didn't sound like he was old, just a normal voice."

Hager stood and put his hand to his upper lip thinking.

"Are those lines recorded?"

"No. Calls to Crimestoppers aren't recorded, you know, for confidentiality reasons, unless they come in after hours. Then an answering machine picks up. But the call came in this morning around eight-thirty."

"Did you get anything from her car?"

"Not really, the usual stuff, and an overnight bag with her dancing outfits."

"What about her purse? Was it in there?"

"No. No purse. We've got the car impounded if you want to look at it."

"No. I don't think it's necessary, right now. It looks like whoever she got a ride with, she went voluntarily. I would like to talk to the dancers who worked Saturday night. Especially the one who had this."

Hager put his finger on the plastic envelope containing the business card.

"Okay, I'll call the club to see if she's working."

The Greenville detective was informed Vivian wouldn't be working that night, so Jamison called the woman at home, and she agreed for them to come over.

Vivian McCauley was petite, with short blonde hair, and dashing brown eyes, which was quite the contrast to her former co-worker, Tammy. With her stocking feet curled up under her, she sat on the couch wearing a pair of gray sweatpants and a navy blue sweatshirt displaying the letters and logo of the East Carolina University Pirates. The twenty-four year old looked like she could have been a college student, and without the makeup, she could have passed for seventeen. There was an innocence about her face. It was almost childlike. Hager found it difficult to imagine the young girl seated in front of him, void of all her clothes, dancing seductively in front of a group of screaming men.

While talking with her, they learned that a man fitting the same general description as the one in Wilmington had asked her about posing for a swimsuit magazine. Vivian said the man was in the club on Wednesday, Thursday, and Friday nights, and he'd only talked to her and Tammy. Friday night, the man had apparently made his choice, and paid attention only to Tammy, paying her five hundred dollars to dance for him exclusively.

Hager understood the significance of this fact. If the man posing as a photographer was the killer, and he was sure it was, it took him approximately two nights to procure his intended victim. Hager remembered the Wilmington case. According to several dancers, the same man was at the Doll House on at least two nights in succession before the victim disappeared. In this case, the same man was seen at least three nights in a row at the same club. It was important to know because this killer, it appeared, was taking the time to find the right victim: the one who he could manipulate the most into going along with his scheme.

Hager thought they could use the stripper angle to their advantage in trying to apprehend the killer. If he could prove the two killings were related, Hager could make it known around the state that a killer, posing as a photographer was targeting exotic dancers. He dismissed the thought, however, feeling it might send the killer away from the state and prove to be an ineffective technique. Hager knew the media should be used to pass along information in the public's interests, but he wasn't sure if it would be the right thing to do. All the killer would have to do is to change his method of approaching his victims. Still, Hager would have to prove the two killings were the work of the same person, and this would be proven by the physical evidence recovered from the victims.

Hager asked Vivian if she would assist with a composite drawing of the man who gave her the card. She was a lucky young woman to be alive and consented. He found out no dancer at the club, other than she, and probably Tammy, had gotten a card from the man. The killer had been trying to lure her into his web of death.

Darkness fell quickly, and it turned cold. The sky was clear and stars were shining. The moon was full, and it illuminated the sky as the agents traveled their way back to Raleigh. For the first fifteen minutes of the trip, Hager and Lloyd talked about the cases, and they concluded the killer of the two girls was probably the same person. The call to Crimestoppers concerned Hager. Was it a concerned citizen? Or, was the killer calling to interject himself into the case?

There was no way to know, but Hager predicted the killer of the woman in Wilmington would follow the case in the news, and maybe he craved some publicity. Maybe the killer just wanted Tammy Wall's family to finally know. Several reasons were possible in this case, but Hager believed the call was made by the killer for publicity. To see his deed in the headlines so he could relive the event in his mind.

They discussed the four month cooling off period, and worried they may have to wait another four months to get closer to the killer. If it held true, then the agents had a good deal of time to develop the case and possibly focus it on one person. The time span could be detrimental to the case as well. What concerned the two agents was a person could travel a great distance in four months, and it appeared this killer was very mobile and probably killed Tamara Wall in his car. If the killer had left the state, then most likely the agents would be unaware of any crimes similar unless they notified the FBI.

Hager concluded even with the similarities, the murders weren't positively linked, and before he undertook such measures, he would have to be sure. He theorized the killer had stayed in North Carolina during the time between the two murders, and, therefore, believed he was safe here. With no reason to think his identity would be revealed, he would stay in familiar territory.

A serial killer is like a shark. A predator. He stakes claim to an area where the feeding is good, and remains there until either his food supply is depleted, or he's chased away or killed by another predator. At present, North Carolina was a ripe feeding ground for this killer, and he would stay here until his territory was threatened by another predator: Clark Hager.

Adrenaline had been pumping through his veins since he'd made the connection of the two cases. He felt alive in the possibility of matching wits with this most vile creature, the monster who kills for no apparent reason, preying upon the weak and vulnerable, beguiling them into his lurid fantasies.

Like a game of chess, Hager's strategic objective was to surround his opponent's king until captured, thus, sacrificing some of his pieces along the way. Conversely, his adversary's goal was to use the king's alter ego, the evil queen, to seek out and kill his opponent's pieces, thereby becoming victorious.

If only it was a game, Hager thought, then it would be fun. However, it was far from being fun. Murder wasn't a cheery subject, nor did Hager receive any enjoyment from it. With murder, there were victims. And with a serial murderer, there were multiple victims who somehow fell into a trap of deception and death. And these victims weren't pawns to be sacrificed in the ultimate quest for victory. They were young women who were specially chosen to play a part in the killer's unfolding tragedy. It was Hager's job, therefore, to swiftly bring the game to a conclusion without surrendering any more of his pieces.

Time had taken its toll on Hager's energy. The combination of the heat from the car, and the glaring lights of passing cars made his eyes close. The smooth ride of Lloyd's Caprice had lulled him to sleep.

In what felt like minutes, he felt the tapping of Lloyd's hand causing him to awaken. The glass from the window was cool against his head, and his neck felt stiff. He rotated his head to limber his rigid neck. Blinking his eyes, he realized they were in the parking lot of SBI Headquarters.

"That was quick," he said as he yawned.

Lloyd laughed under his breath, and smirked at his dazed partner. "You'd better get some sleep tonight."

9

INSTEAD OF RETURNING to his office to check the messages on his phone, Hager chose to drive directly home. Despite the hour long nap, Hager was still tired from the previous days of work. It showed on his face. Dark circles had formed under his eyes, bloodshot from stress. The skin on his forehead was greasy, and his fingers glistened when he wiped his brow.

Even though he didn't display it outwardly, he knew Lloyd was fatigued as well, evident of the lack of crude jokes and snide remarks. He could also see it in Lloyd's eyes. The vessels had dilated in his, too, but the weariness was hidden by the glasses he wore. Lloyd's eyes were gentle behind the glasses, but he had seen the tenderness turn into fire when his mood intensified. It would benefit both of them to get a good night's sleep.

Tomorrow the DNA tests would be back, confirming what they both already knew. Well rested, the agents would be ready to tackle the formidable task of hunting a serial killer. Hager knew he would be working arduously on this case until it was solved. During the drive home, the agent thought about the monster roaming around North Carolina.

The pattern of his crimes had moved in a northerly direction from Wilmington to Greenville, and then to Ahoskie, nearing the Virginia border. Maybe the killer crossed into the commonwealth in search of his next victim. Would he have to wait four months until he struck again? Hager hoped he would. In such a period of time, the agents could shrink the gap already existing between them, before another victim was notched on the killer's belt.

Hager decided it would be wise to contact the three states which border North Carolina: Virginia, Tennessee, and South Carolina, for any similar unsolved murders. The information on the business card indicated Florida might be significant to the killer.

Likewise, Hager would run the name of Ronny or Ronald Cooper through the Florida Department of Law Enforcement and ask if they had any similar unsolved cases.

He imagined the description of the man and tried to put a face with it, to no avail. Anyone who had seen him hadn't remembered any distinct quality about him, if he had one. The generic phrase was "he was good-looking, well built, in his twenties, with dark brown hair that was short and wavy, and no appreciable facial hair." But there wasn't enough detail to formulate a picture.

"Maybe the composite drawing will help," he concluded.

He pictured this faceless creature baiting those young women, like a magnet, into trusting him and his bidding; only to be an instrument in his deranged fantasy. Willing players in the drama until its true aim was revealed, but then, once the ruse was exposed, it was too late. They were powerless to stop the fantasy and helpless to prevent him from fulfilling it.

His thoughts turned to his daughter, Elizabeth, who was just about the same age as the two victims of this predator. Feeling neglectful, it dawned on him he hadn't talked to her to see if she was satisfied with the classes for the spring semester of her junior year at UNC-Chapel Hill. They usually talked and saw each other frequently.

This week, however, had been especially busy for them both. She had spent the final week of her Christmas break in Maryland with Kelly's parents, and he remembered the last time he saw her when he picked her up at the airport Sunday night.

It was hard to imagine Elizabeth as a young woman. Only twenty, she had developed into a taller version of her mother at the same age. He had noticed her sleek figure with her dark brown hair and eyes caught the attention of most men. Not wanting to admit it, he really couldn't blame them. Elizabeth's clean, wholesome appearance was attractive and provoked many second and third glances.

Hager then pictured the little girl fifteen years ago in her nightgown sitting in his lap begging him to read her a story about *Snow White and the Seven Dwarfs*. Tucked in her arms was her favorite teddy bear, and a pair of fuzzy slippers covered her feet. At an early age, she learned the art of manipulation, as all children seemed to do. Along with the request came the soft, imploring tone of voice and the innocent smile and twinkling of her eyes that made him crumble like a cookie. He reminisced at the feeling of her hugs. Those tiny arms wrapped tightly around his neck, conveying her unconditional love. And how good it felt knowing this miracle of a life was totally devoted to him. He marveled at watching her, knowing there existed an unbreakable bond between father and daughter. Realizing how a loving little girl could be transformed into such an intelligent and vibrant young woman was beyond his grasp.

It wasn't the mere fact of the evolution, but the rapidity of it taking place before his eyes without even a moment to stop and savor the innocence of childhood. It seemed like only yesterday when he held the little girl, batting those beautiful brown eyes at him, negotiating whether she was staying up past her bedtime to watch her favorite movie.

At the airport he noticed the hugs were not quite the same. Her arms were larger now, but she didn't squeeze like before, when he was her entire life. He understood he was no longer the center of her world, but just a part of it who stood by admiring the final product.

During her childhood he was puddy in her hands, but she was the clay a sculptor molds into a *Venus de Milo*. From birth and since, everything he did for her was with the intention that it would somehow affect her in the future. The punishments, the adulation, and the rewards for performance and behavior were all a part of cutting away at the clay to make a perfect sculpture. Hager felt he'd outdone himself in rearing a daughter, who endured the tragedy of losing her mother at the impressionable age of 15.

From her mother, Elizabeth inherited many personality traits, but one most compelling was her unrelenting passion for life which was evident in everything she touched. In watching her grow, Hager wanted to reach out and hold her so tightly she would never get older. He was uncertain about today's world of which she would be a part, as all parents seem to be. He wanted her to remain the innocent little girl who believed he could protect her from harm.

In an effort to "spread her wings" she started to call herself "Liz" in high school. The requirement of referring to her as "Liz" was mandated to everyone, except her father, who rather stubbornly refused to grant her request and continued to call her by her given name. Hager concluded she let him get away with it because she knew one thing would never change: he was still her daddy, and she was still his little girl.

Another illustration of her desire for independence was her insistence in getting her own apartment with her friend Jen. Elizabeth maintained since the apartment was in Carrboro, which was closer to Chapel Hill, it was more convenient for her to live there instead of remaining at the house with him. After all, she needed her space and privacy for her developing college years.

Hager pulled the car into the driveway at his house. The Hagers had been its only occupants, and every day he went home, it reminded him of Kelly, whose presence was felt there like her ghost levitated throughout. Those memories of Kelly in the house were good ones: taking care of the flowers, and emblazoning her mark on the decor of the house that was, in essence, truly Kelly's.

Hager drove his car up the long asphalt driveway which widened for a basketball goal on the side and ended at the two- car garage. The front yard was large with tall trees lining the front edge concealing most of the house from the road. Azalea bushes lined the drive on both sides; a flower bed stretched across the front of the house covering the length of the massive front porch. The two-story house was red brick with blue shutters and surrounded on both sides by vacant wooded lots. At the rear, the house expanded into a large wooden deck, outfitted with a gas grill and patio furniture with an umbrella.

Hager's favorite room was the spacious kitchen, where he learned the art of gourmet cooking. He was self-taught from books, magazines, and mostly from experimentation. Trial and error went a long way in the kitchen. He prided himself as an excellent chef and provided himself with the finest cookware that could be purchased.

During the drive, Hager seemed to have forgotten about the evil who prowled the night, but as he pulled into his driveway, reality returned and he remembered he had much work to do, but it would wait until tomorrow. Once inside the garage door, he punched the keypad for the alarm system and laid his keys on the counter. The nose of his English Bulldog Roscoe was felt against his slacks, and he reached down to pat his head. The dog snorted at the affection and his toenails clicked against the linoleum floor as he followed Hager through the kitchen.

In the dark, he opened the refrigerator and pulled out an Ice House beer and twisted off the top. The aluminum cap clinked on the counter, and he gulped the beer. How refreshing, he thought—the taste of cold beer at the end of a long day. The darkness in the kitchen prevented him from seeing the two day old dishes in the sink and crumbs of food on the counter. Knowing the mess was there, he ignored it, telling himself what he didn't see, didn't exist. That was Hager's logic when it referred to tidying.

Hager used the kitchen phone to call Elizabeth to see if her classes were to her liking, but she wasn't at her apartment. He left a message on the answering machine telling her he loved her. Wearily,

Hager climbed the stairs. In his bedroom, he turned on the small lamp on the night stand. His bed was unmade, and his clothes, some scattered on the floor, and the others in a disarray atop his dresser. The mixture of socks, T-shirts, and underwear were accompanied by envelopes for bills, bank statements and other assorted papers.

Hager wasn't the tidiest of people, but he was no pig. It was obvious from the look of his bedroom, he lived a life with constraints for time, and frequently thought about hiring a house-keeper to clean the house once a week.

Hanging up his jacket in the closet, Hager removed all of his clothes, and slipped into a pair of shorts and a T-shirt from the dresser. He fell into bed, the bottle still in his grasp. Under the covers, he gulped down the rest of the beer and thirsted for another. If only he hadn't been so tired, he would traipse back down the stairs. In the bed, he was too comfortable to leave, so he opted to call Vanessa for an alternative stimulation to the beer.

A half hour later, he lay in the bed talking to his girlfriend about their previous night and of the day's events. After a little sex talk, reminiscent of the night before, Hager sleepily said goodnight and drifted into dreamland.

* * *

HAGER WALKED INTO THE OFFICE the next morning feel-ing refreshed and invigorated. Having slept peacefully the night before, he awakened with a renewed energy and impetus about working these cases. A holder with two cups of coffee in one hand, a bag of bagels in the other, he strode past Judy's desk. Judy was on the phone, and she motioned with her hand for him to stop. She cupped her hand over the receiver.

"Nancy in the lab wants you to call her right away. She said something about the test results."

Hager was anxiously waiting the results. This was going to connect his cases together. He walked into his office; put down his coffee and bagels, and picked up the phone. His heart thumped as he dialed the number.

"Hello, Nancy. It's Clark Hager. How are you?"

"Hi, Clark. I'm just fine, thanks. Did you get my message?"

"Yeah, Judy told me you had the results from the tests yesterday. I really appreciate you doing them so quickly."

He pulled off the lid of the coffee cup; steam rose upward.

"Oh, it was no problem at all. I gather this is an important case?"

"That depends on what you tell me. What's the news?"

"The semen samples were an exact match. It's definitely the same man who killed the Wilmington girl. I hope that's good news."

A brief smile came to Hager's face, but then he straightened it.

"I don't know whether I'd call it *good*, but I guess it is because we'll only be looking for one killer as opposed to two. Did you have any luck with the DNA database?"

"No. No matches. I'm sorry, Clark."

"Ah, no need for an apology. I wouldn't love this job so much if it were that easy," he joked. "Thanks, Nancy."

Hager put the phone down and looked up to see Lloyd's smiling face in the entrance to the door.

"Did you get some shut-eye last night?" Lloyd asked.

Lloyd's face appeared rested, his tone of voice was cheerier than last evening.

"Yeah, man, I died when my head hit the pillow. All it took was a beer, and some sweet nothings whispered in my ear from Vanessa."

"Again?" he shouted. "You got some puddin' last night, too? You're the man!"

Hager chuckled, and shook his head at Lloyd's excitement.

"No. I just talked to her on the phone," he said, handing the bag of remaining bagels to him.

Lloyd nodded.

"Oh, had some phone sex, huh?"

He leaned toward Hager and whispered. "So, do you get a boner when she's talking to you?"

118

Hager laughed out loud and his face turned red.

"No, Lloyd, it's not like that. She was just talking softly and it made me sleepy," he lied.

"Umm hmm. Sure it was."

Lloyd's inquisitiveness about his sex life amused Hager. The curiosity had no bounds, but Lloyd was careful not to take it beyond the limits of good taste. It was all a part of his bizarre sense of humor and proved to be a source of abundant laughter between the two. From his frequent innuendoes relating to other people's sexual experiences, Hager concluded Lloyd was lacking in sexual activity at home.

He remembered asking Lloyd why he was so interested in everyone else's bedroom highlights. Hager was amazed to learn Lloyd had sex with his wife very often, and he referred to her as a "nymphomaniac".

"Nancy Lapinski called from DNA," Hager said, sipping the coffee. "The two samples were a match."

"All right. Now all we have to do is find this sucker before he gets the chance at someone else."

"Yep, we'll start with a call to Florida. Then, I think we should go to Wilmington. The killings started there, and there may be something the PD missed during their investigation."

Hager opened the folder and pulled out the plastic bag with the business card.

"Identification said the prints from the card were overlaps and didn't think AFIS could do anything with them."

Lloyd washed the last bite of bagel down with the coffee.

"We can't get a break."

Hager studied the black and red letters on the card.

Ronny Cooper, Freelance Photographer
2823 Brickell Key Drive, Suite 102
Miami, Florida 33131
(305) 374-8437

"You think we should let Maxwell know about this?" Lloyd asked.

"About what?"

"About the match of the semen samples. Should we release it to the public?"

"I don't think we need to let the public in just yet, Lloyd. I don't want to frighten them unnecessarily or scare our boy away. What we should do is notify every agency about the murders. That way, we can be informed of any similar cases."

"All right. You think I should write up a statewide DCI message?"

"Not only North Carolina, but all the states in the region."

Hager looked up in thought.

"What are there, six states in our region?" he said, counting on his fingers. "Us, South Carolina, Virginia, Tennessee, West Virginia, and Kentucky. Just tell them about the two murders, the sex of the victims, the method of death, and the occupation of the two victims. Maybe there's another case we don't know about yet."

"I'll do it right now. You gonna call Florida about the name on the card?"

"Yeah. I thought I'd try now."

He reached for his rolodex atop the desk and flipped to the section beginning with the letter "F". Lloyd gently slapped the top of the desk and stood. As he walked through the door, he jingled the change in his pockets and whistled happily.

Hager stopped at the card bearing the name of John Ramos of the Florida Department of Law Enforcement. The FDLE was Florida's equivalent of North Carolina's SBI. It handled the criminal investigations while leaving the traffic control to their highway patrol. Hager had met Ramos a year ago in Charlotte when a fugitive wanted for rape and murder in the Sunshine State was arrested after a tip during the airing of the popular television show *America's Most Wanted*.

The Investigative Support Unit was interested in the Florida man because his method of binding his victims with duct tape was similar to a series of unsolved rapes. The agents traveled to Charlotte after his capture and interviewed him about the rape cases but were not able to obtain a confession from him. Ramos was the lead investigator on the case where the man was wanted in connection with the brutal rape and murder of a prominent businessman's wife.

Ramos closely resembled the Latino police lieutenant portrayed on *Miami Vice* by Edward James Olmos. He had thick jet black hair, a bushy mustache but was without the ruddy complexion of the character.

Ramos was working out of the Tallahassee office in a unit similar to his. The FDLE had formed a major homicide task force since the early eighties when notorious serial killer, Ted Bundy, was active there. It was a very effective tool used in the case of spree murderer Danny Rolling, the man who butchered five college students in Gainesville during the late 1980's. Hager dialed the number and connected to Ramos' answering machine. He recognized his smooth Latin accent and left an urgent message for him to call back.

In the office next to Hager, Lloyd sat at a table opposite a computer screen with green characters. His fingers were slowly striking the keys while his head turned back and forth to look at the paper on the desk to his left and then back to the keyboard. As Hager approached from behind, he could see both his and Lloyd's reflection in the screen.

"How's it coming?"

Lloyd kept his eyes on the keyboard.

"I'm just about finished and it'll be ready to send. Did you have any luck with Florida?"

"Got his answering machine. If he doesn't call back by lunch. I'll try someone else."

While Lloyd typed on the keyboard, Hager looked at the desk to his right. A mounted shelf above the desk held framed pictures and momentos. Inside the frames were pictures of Lloyd holding his grandson Lloyd, III. In another, the boy, a little older, sitting on his grandfather's lap, Lloyd's face, beaming with pride. A gold framed picture of his son Junior, as he was called, in his police uniform standing beside a Charlotte-Mecklenberg police car. Several miniature police cars Lloyd collected, one, a silver and black replica of the North Carolina Highway Patrol. Tacked to the wall and left of the desk, finger-paintings from Lloyd, III to his "Paw-paw." They were colored stick-figures of Lloyd and his grandson holding hands. On his desk the single portrait of he and his wife Martha together.

"Okay." Lloyd said, indicating he was finished with the message. "How does it look?"

Hager read the text on the screen over Lloyd's shoulder.

Attention All Homicide Units: The North Carolina State Bureau of Investigation is investigating two murder cases that were linked to the same person. The first murder occurred in Wilmington in July 1996, and the second, the body of the victim was found in Ahoskie in January 1997. Both victims were white females in their early twenties, and were employed as exotic dancers. The victims were raped and strangled, one manually and the other with a ligature. In both cases, a customer posing as photographer appeared at the dancing establishment and was rumored to have offered the victims modeling contracts. According to information developed throughout the investigation, this customer was at the business with the victim the night she was last seen alive. The suspect was described as a white male, 25-35, 6'1", 200-220, muscular build, dark brown wavy hair, clean shaven, and described as a neat dresser. Any agencies with similar cases, contact the SBI Investigative Support Unit, Raleigh, NC (919) 585-6725. Special Agents– L.A. Sheridan; C.J. Hager.

"Looks good. Send it."

Lloyd pushed the transmit button and the computer sent the message across the region.

In seconds, the computer modem dispersed the information to police and sheriff's departments for hundreds of miles. Every law enforcement agency within the region would be aware of their investigation, and the agents hoped one of them would respond with some helpful information. They both knew the bulletin would prompt calls from the detectives in the three other cities, thus making the case theirs to handle exclusively.

Hager returned to his desk and browsed through the stack of papers already collected in the two murders. It excited Hager when he understood he would be pursuing a serial killer. Although there had been a few cases related to an actual serial murderer, Hager's only previous role in the investigations was "behind the scenes" where he constructed profiles and made recommendations, and frequently conducted interrogations. It was part of the learning process in the study of personalities and behavior. Now he would be participating in the hunt.

Hager preferred the challenge and electricity of the front lines. The leg work, interviews, and watching evidence develop were all aspects of police work Hager missed immensely. He challenged himself in the endeavor and predicted it would come to a successful conclusion.

Almost as apprehensive as he was stimulated, he wondered if he'd become a creature with a warped sense of fulfillment. Thriving on the tragedy of others. Becoming exhilarated only when death and cruelty were in the air. Was he mad? Or was he the typical detective with an extraordinary feeling of wanting to right all the wrongs in the world?

Eagerly, he accepted the hurdle with a vehement resolve to find the truth. In the truth, the answers would be more vivid than before. But now, facts were contained in a murky cloud of questions, like a box, waiting to be opened, but only to discover inside the box, was another, and so on. Within each container, a bit of knowledge revealed its clever head, thus slowly paving a road toward some final destiny. It was often a road with many forks along the way, and occasionally, the detours led to dead ends.

The telephone rang. Hager picked up the receiver.

"SBI, Hager."

It was John Ramos from Florida.

"Thanks for calling, John. How's it going down in wonderland?"

"Pretty good, I guess. Keeping us busy as usual. And you?"

"About the same. That's the reason I called. I'm working on two murders by the same guy, and I need your help. I think he may be from Florida."

"Shit, what else is new. I think we breed 'em down here. What makes you think he's from Florida?"

"Well, our guy has strangled two young women. Both of them were strippers. We think this guy is posing as some kind of photographer in order to get close to them. He dropped a business card on another dancer, and she kept it."

Ramos sounded interested.

"A photographer, huh? Did you say this guy was targeting strippers?"

"So far, both of our victims danced at those high class strip clubs, and he was there the last nights the girls were seen."

Lloyd walked into the office and leaned against a table.

"I'm not familiar with any cases like that here. What's the name on the card?"

Hager looked at the card on his desk.

"Ronny Cooper, Freelance Photographer. Shows an address on Brickell Key Drive in Miami. Also has a phone number with a Miami area code."

"You have a description of him?"

"Yeah, a white male, late twenties or early thirties. Dark brown hair. Around six feet tall, two hundred pounds with a muscular build. We're gonna check our state's computer for the name, but we think it's probably an alias. You might be able to turn up something with the name in your state files."

"Okay. Have you called the number yet? It sounds like a legitimate Miami number."

He smiled remembering calling the number.

"Yeah, when I called it, I got some Japanese Restaurant," he snickered. "When I finally got someone who spoke English, I was told they'd never heard of anyone by the name. I was hoping you could check with the phone company for a history on the number. Maybe it was this guy's old number."

Hager gave Ramos the address and phone number.

"All right. I'll check it out. If I'm not mistaken, there's a Brickell Key Drive there. I'm not sure of the address though. I'll give the phone company a call about the number."

"I appreciate it. By the way, whatever happened to the guy who was caught in Charlotte? The duct tape guy."

Ramos spoke proudly, "He's on death row. Waiting on the electric chair with the rest of 'em in Starke."

"All right! There is some justice after all."

10

HAGER HOPED John Ramos would be able to locate a name on their killer. The information on the business card indicated that Florida was, in some way, significant to the killer, but to what extent, he didn't know.

Experience had taught him that criminals were very good liars. Nevertheless, he knew small threads of truth were always woven somewhere inside the falsehood. A remark to make their fib more plausible, or a trivial fact which was easy to remember if he was questioned about it. Certainly, the killer expected to be asked about the specific area because Miami was an exotic place. Many dancers were from that part of the country. To appear credible, he would have to know somewhat about the area and surroundings.

While they waited for a response from Florida, the agents accessed their PC and entered the name of Ronny Cooper. The agents searched the records of the Division of Motor Vehicles and all other criminal record files for the name of Ron, Ronald and Ronny Cooper. The responses provided the agents with complete names of persons inside and outside North Carolina who had criminal records or had received traffic citations.

After compiling a list and narrowing it for various reasons, Hager and Lloyd had thirty white males between the ages of 20-40 named either Ronald, or Ronny Cooper, or ones who had used it as a previous alias. Those thirty were entered into the computer and after getting the records, both agents examined them for previous arrests or convictions for offenses related to this case. They were looking for violent offenders—rapists, and murderers. Offenders with histories of arson, child abuse, and cruelty to animals were also closely examined. Both agents knew many serial murderers had prior experiences of setting fires and were also prone to have experimented in animal torture during their childhood or adolescent years.

This work was tedious and time consuming. Both Hager and Lloyd believed it would probably produce a dead end; but it had to be done. No stone could be left unturned, and no name could be eliminated until it was investigated. As remote as it was, it was conceivable the killer was using his real name.

It was also possible if Ronny Cooper wasn't the true name of their killer, then it could be an alias he used at one time or another. If the name entered into the computer had ever been used as an alias, the computer would identify it and respond with the person's true name, thus expanding the scope of the search. They could get lucky.

Even though the DCI computer operated very swiftly, it took two hours to finally obtain a working list of possible suspects. Before the agents delved into examining the criminal records, they decided to break for lunch. Lloyd recommended pizza, and Hager agreed, but suggested they call in a delivery order. While Hager was on the phone, he heard Judy summon Lloyd to the lobby. Lloyd returned just as Hager completed his call.

"Clark, Greensboro PD just called about our DCI message. A Detective Madden is holding on the main line."

"Great!"

"You know Madden?"

"No. I don't think he was in Greensboro when I was, but I remember hearing the name before. I think I talked to him at the seminar in December."

Hager turned on the speaker phone.

"Madden? Yeah, this is Hager, you got something for us?"

"Yeah. I don't know if this is related to your cases or not, but a girl was found dead yesterday morning at the Ameri-Suites hotel."

"What else do you have?"

"Well, she was strangled with a belt and left in the room. Turned out she worked at a topless dance club called Tiffany's Cabaret."

Hager looked at Lloyd and nodded.

"Do you have anything to go on yet?"

"Not much really. Her car was found in the parking lot of the motel, locked, and the keys in her purse, which was found in the room. The room was rented to a subject by the name of Steven Landis of New York City. Paid cash for the room, but the clerk gave a description."

"How did you know she was strangled with a belt? From the autopsy?"

"Yes and no. The belt was still tied around her neck when we found her."

"Were you able to get a description of the guy who rented the room?"

"The clerk said he was a white male, about twenty-five to thirty. Six foot or a little better, good build. According to the clerk, he seemed to be a really nice guy."

"Look, it will take us about an hour and a half to get to Greensboro from Raleigh. As soon as we get some lunch, my partner and I will come and look at what you've got. It sure sounds like the same guy we're after."

"All right. I'll be here."

*   *   *

THE AGENTS ARRIVED in Greensboro at about 4:30 p.m. The city brought back fond memories for Hager. He had lived there for fifteen years, working as a police officer and later as a detective. About a year ago, Hager had been back to visit his old partners in the Criminal Investigations Division. He was asked to profile two murder cases detectives thought to have been committed by the same person. Hager had enjoyed sitting around joking with the same guys with whom he used to work, sharing war stories. To Hager, it was as if he'd never left Greensboro. But it had been ten years since he'd taken the job with the SBI and Greensboro had changed, but it had changed for the better.

Hager liked the Triad area. Cities like Greensboro, High Point and Winston-Salem presented a large metropolitan area without some of the big city problems. This area was also in the center of the state, which made travel to either the beach or the mountains easy.

Greensboro was a root of unpleasant thoughts, too. It was when he lived there Kelly was diagnosed with the cancer which ultimately brought her to a premature death. The memory was vivid in Hager's head, as if it just happened.

As their car approached the front of the police department on Washington Street, Hager noticed a sculpture of a policeman talking to a little boy. The bronze monument was centered prominently in the square leading up to the entrance. The statue commemorated the centennial anniversary of the police department. Not a large work of art, only three feet tall, but its meaning emphasized the importance of its erection. On the base was a plaque and the words engraved which honored those officers who lost their lives in the line of duty.

We honor those who have gone before us and challenge those who will come after us to continue the tradition of excellence. Greensboro Police Department—1889-1989

The Criminal Investigations Division was on the first floor. Hager and Lloyd walked into the large squad room filled with tiny cubicles separated by partitions. There were sounds of a busy squad room: telephones ringing; people chattering; police radios squelching; and also the familiar sound of laughter.

It was quite a different atmosphere than working in a quiet office like SBI Headquarters. Hager had become used to the peace and quiet and wasn't sure if he could ever return to working in a loud squad room.

A receptionist was seated at a table just inside the room. Hager identified himself and asked for Detective Madden. As they waited, a couple of veteran detectives including Captain Ron Fitzgerald, came up to Hager, and they reminisced briefly on some past happenings. Lloyd knew some of the detectives in Greensboro, too. He had been stationed in the district as a field agent in the late 1970's and liked the area very much.

Detective Chris Madden came to greet Hager and Lloyd, and after shaking hands with both of them, they walked back to his office. Madden was around thirty-five; he had thick straight hair, brown with a tint of auburn, and a mustache. Hager sat against a table and looked at the walls of the cubicle and on Madden's desk. A person revealed a lot about himself by the pictures and items in his office. An office was a person's intimate space. His domain.

On the walls were pictures of the classic muscle cars of the late 1960's and '70's. He had four lithographs: a 1970 Pontiac GTO; a 1968 Chevrolet Camaro Z28; a 1969 Ford Mustang Cobra Jet; and a 1972 Plymouth Road Runner. All classic cars from an era when it was popular to have big a car that ran like, as it was said in this part of the country, a "scalded dog".

On Madden's desk were pictures of a woman and a young boy and girl together. Hager assumed they were the detective's wife and children. There were other pictures of just the woman, standing by a Century 21 Realty sign; and single shots of the children mixed in with two group shots, apparently a school class picture.

Although he'd just met the man, Hager could already tell Detective Madden was married and his wife was probably a realtor with

Century 21. He had two children who went to Guilford Primary School, and he was obviously proud of them. He could also tell he was a car enthusiast.

Hager was also pleased to see that Madden's desk was organized and neat; another quality revealed by his domain. Neatness and organization told a lot about a man's abilities as an investigator. If his desk and office were organized, then his investigation was thorough. The concept didn't always hold true, because Hager had seen many organized detectives who conducted sloppy investigations and vice versa.

What amazed Hager was in a matter of seconds, he knew much about Madden's personal life. He reflected on a school he attended several years ago about interview and interrogation techniques, and the instructor was commenting on conducting the interview in an office setting. The instructor asked the attendees who were all experienced detectives what they had on their desks or on their walls in their offices. After getting several answers about photos of kids, wife, family dogs, and the like, the instructor became animated, more than Hager had seen him during the entire five-day class.

Yeah, that's right. Everyone of you is proud of your life, and to show your pride, you display your accomplishments, like awards and citations, and your prize possessions, like your wife, kids, dog, and your thirty foot Bass boat. Where else to show off your life? Then your office—your domain.

When you interrogate some criminal, who may be a murderer, a rapist, a child molester, or even a burglar, in your office, you're telling him about your entire personal life without saying a word.

Hager remembered looking around the room at all the faces and saw a shocking realization. He also realized he was guilty of doing the very same thing.

The instructor concluded.

If you think this dirt bag is not paying attention to those pictures on a desk or other things on the wall, you're kidding yourself. We have come to think that we, as police officers, are untouchable. Well, let me tell you, my friends, we're not. Especially when we spoon feed a child molester with a picture of your kid, and the name of the school he or she attends! Yeah, he may not be able to get to you directly, but if you let him, he can get to you by getting to your family.

Hager remembered the school ended on the instructor's last comment, and it had made an indelible impression in his mind. He wondered if Madden interrogated suspects in his cubicle.

The detective sat in his chair and pulled out a manila folder containing reports on the latest murder.

"The woman was found around eleven a.m. yesterday by one of the cleaning ladies. Her name's Kathryn Gerhardt, twenty-two, of Winston-Salem. She'd been working full-time at Tiffany's since August of last year. She worked there last on Wednesday night, and she got off work at midnight Thursday morning. The victim was identified from the driver's license in her purse which was found in the room. She was nude, but her jeans, top, and her shoes and socks were recovered from the floor. Her bra and panties were not, if she was wearing any. There was nothing of any significance in her car, but they found a business card in the console."

Madden handed the card to Hager. It, too, had stains from the black fingerprint powder.

Steven Landis, Photographer
Manhattan Modeling Agency
1133 Broadway, Suite 512
New York, NY 10010
(212) 854-8700

Hager opened his notebook and removed the card from the strip club in Greenville. The cards were placed side by side and he compared them.

"Did you get any useable prints from the card?"

"Didn't look like it. We've got the latents on cards to give you guys."

"It probably won't do us any good to check out the name and phone number on the card, since the last one was a fake," Hager said.

"I checked the phone number. It's bogus. There's no such exchange. There is a Manhattan Modeling Agency though, but they have no photographers by that name."

Hager patted Madden on the back.

"It looks like you've done a pretty thorough job in this case so far."

Madden smiled proudly. Praise coming from someone like Hager, whose reputation preceded him, was gladly accepted.

"Madden, was there any sign of sexual activity?"

"Beside the fact she was found nude, it looked like there was dried semen on her neck and shoulder area. We figured she was raped."

"What did the M.E.'s office say?" Lloyd asked.

"They did a rape kit on her and collected the stains around her shoulders."

"Then you still have what remained of her clothes," Hager asked.

"Yeah. We figured ya'll would carry what we collected back with you to Raleigh. It's all ready for you."

Madden pulled out a sheet of paper from the stack.

"Steven Landis was also the name provided to the hotel. He checked in Monday evening around eight p.m."

Madden handed the paper to Hager. It was a copy of the hotel registration form. On the paper was the name, the address in New York, and the same telephone number.

"Is this all they got from the guy?"

"Yeah, just the basic information. He paid cash for the room. Two hundred fifty five dollars for three days."

"Her car was found in the parking lot, right? Do they know anything about his car?"

Madden shook his head.

"Hers was parked near the front entrance to the hotel. As far as his car goes, I don't know. There's a blank for it on the registration form, but it's not filled out."

"You said you talked to one of the hotel employees. Was he of any help?"

Madden leaned back in his chair, his hands joined behind his head.

"A little. The one I talked to actually checked this guy in on Monday. He remembered him pretty well. I thought we'd go down there and we could go over step by step what's been done. We already released the room to the hotel, but the crime scene sketch was turned into me today, and I can use that."

Hager was pleased. He liked to revisit the crime scenes. By being there, he would be able to visualize more of what he thought had happened. Madden got up and put on his coat.

"You wanna ride together? We can take my car?" He picked up a leather portfolio case and they left the building.

The Ameri-Suites was a mid-priced hotel located on Stanley Drive, just off Wendover Avenue, near the I-40 interchange. Madden's blue Chevrolet Lumina cruised west on Wendover Avenue from Market Street. As they approached Interstate 40, the Greensboro detective pointed to the right at a purple sign with black letters which read Tiffany's Cabaret.

"That's where she worked."

Hager was riding shotgun and looked over to the building.

"What kind of place is it, pretty nice?"

"Yeah. It's probably one of the nicer ones in the city, if you can call it that."

As the car crossed over the I-40 bridge, "Ameri-Suites" in red letters at the top of the building was visible through the tall trees which lined the interstate. A blue sign mounted on a steel pole stood facing the highway with "Ameri-Suites" in white letters. Madden turned onto Stanley Drive and drove down the short, curvy road leading to the hotel. The building was the color of wet sand and had five floors. A blue logo of the hotel chain in the shape of a fancy "A" topped the structure.

The rear of the building faced the highway, and the parking lot encircled the hotel. At the entrance, a canopy overhung the lobby door to protect guests from the weather when loading or unloading. Farther from the door and beside the canopy was an island with a three tiered fountain made of marble, mounted on a blue tile base.

The fountain, with water gently pouring from its holes, sat next to a pole flying the U.S. and North Carolina state flags. The island was grassy, and on either end a large bed of colorful flowers, maroon, green, and white blossoms, were planted in a bed of dark brown mulch. Tiny spruce trees stretched across the island, their leaves bare from the winter. Wrapped around the thin branches, strings of white lights illuminated when darkness fell.

The three men entered through the double glass doors into the lobby. Behind the front counter stood a man and woman attired in navy blazers with the fancy "A" logo in red on the breast pocket. The counter faced a lounge area. Green couches with colorful flowers, a coffee stand, artificial trees in baskets, and coffee tables gave the lobby an air of relaxation.

The male desk clerk recognized Madden and greeted him at the counter. He'd spoken to the detective earlier about the case. Vinny Salerno was short and stocky, with dark wavy hair, and a large nose. Madden introduced Salerno to the SBI agents, and the four of them retreated to a private office behind the counter. Salerno spoke in rapid phrases, a New Yorker accent evident.

"What do you know about the man who rented the room?" Hager asked.

"This guy, he says he's from New York, and I says, 'Hey! That's where I'm from.' You know, I'm from Brooklyn and, well, the guy gets quiet and says, 'Oh, I'm originally from Florida, but I live in Manhattan now.'"

"Did he make a reservation for the room?"

"No, he was a walk-in. Came in around uh, I think, around eight o'clock."

"Why isn't there any car information on the form? Didn't he have a car?"

"I asked him to write down the information about the car, and he says it's a rental and he doesn't know what the plate number is. He said he would come back and put it down later, but I guess he never did."

"Did he make any phone calls while he was here?"

Salerno turned to the computer terminal on the desk and typed in the name Landis. A list appeared and the clerk scanned the green lines.

"No calls. We don't charge for local calls, so if he doesn't call long distance, then none show up."

"Did you see this guy any other time after he checked in?"

"Yeah. Later the same night, he walked through the lobby around ten o'clock. He waved to me when he passed the counter. The next two nights, I saw him leave around the same time—ten o'clock. The last night. On Wednesday, I spoke to him. I said, 'You hittin' the town again?' And he said, 'Yeah, gotta see the sights.'

"I thought about asking him where he was headin', you know, 'cause I get off at eleven. He looked like a partier, but I got the impression he didn't want anyone else around."

"Do you get off every night at eleven?"

"Yeah, every night."

"Who relieves you at eleven?"

"For those three nights, uh, it was Terry Sinclair. She works from eleven to seven."

"Have you talked to her?" Hager asked Madden

"Yeah," he said flipping through his notebook. "She said she only recalled seeing him walk through the lobby around two a.m. Thursday. He was alone and just waved at her when he left."

"Left? If he was by himself, then he must've killed the girl already."

Hager considered the thought for a moment.

"Did Sinclair say he was carrying any bags or luggage?"

Madden shook his head.

"I don't know. I didn't ask her."

"Let's be sure and call her again to see if she remembered anything like that."

Hager returned to Salerno.

"Are there any other entrances to the hotel?"

"No. The only way you can get in is through the lobby. There are other doors, but they are exit doors only. Can't open them from the outside."

"Why wouldn't Sinclair have seen him return with the girl Thursday morning? They had to have come through the lobby. Especially since her car was parked near the entrance."

Salerno shrugged his shoulders.

"Maybe she went in the back office to do some paperwork. That's when it gets done. On third shift, when it's not very busy."

Hager closed his notebook, twisted his pen closed, and slid it into his shirt pocket.

"Lloyd, do have anything to ask?"

Lloyd shook his head. Hager rose from the seat causing the others to join him.

"Well, let's have a look at the room."

Salerno accompanied Madden and the agents to the room where the body was found. From behind the front desk, the four men walked through the lobby to the elevator. Suite 311 was on the third floor. The hotel's decor was charming, and a warmth of hospitality permeated throughout the fixtures and amenities. The suite doors were of a dark wood finish, probably walnut; the walls were covered with a grooved beige wallpaper and trimmed with matching dark wood crown molding. The walk-ways were surfaced with a subtle navy carpet with the hotel's red logo woven at strategically placed junctures along the hall.

All of them stood at the door. Madden briefed the others on what he learned through his investigation.

"Around eleven a.m., the maid goes to the room to clean it, and there's a 'Do Not Disturb' sign on the knob. She knocked on the door, but no one answered. With the sign on the door, she doesn't want to bother anyone, so she called down to the front desk. The clerk at the desk told her that the person in the room should've checked out. The clerk then called the room to see if anyone was asleep inside, but got no answer. The clerk then told the maid to go ahead and enter the room."

Salerno opened the door and they all stepped into the room and the detective continued.

"Once the maid gets here, she saw someone lying in this bed with the sheet over their head."

He walked over to the near bed.

"She called out, but got no response. The maid said she thought the person was asleep and she got ready to leave; but thought it was odd when the person didn't wake up. She said she nudged the form under the sheet and still, no response. She said she had this feeling something was wrong so she went over to the bed and pulled up the sheet and found the woman with her eyes wide open and the belt wrapped around her neck."

"I bet that made her day," Lloyd joked.

"She started screaming, ran over to the phone in the room, and called the desk again. The front desk called the police."

"Did you get any prints from the telephone or any other part of the room?" Hager asked.

"We dusted the phone for prints and were able to lift some, but they're probably the maid's. The room was clean, and no other prints were lifted, even from the bathroom."

Lloyd walked into the bathroom and looked around.

"Did this maid clean the room every day?"

"Well, he requested that the room not be cleaned because he didn't want to be disturbed."

"Hmm, that's odd. Did she see him at all during the time he was here?" Hager asked.

"She thought she saw him one day. She thought it was on Tuesday, but anyway, she said she saw him coming from inside the room and walk by her cleaning cart. She said the guy she remembered seemed very friendly when he said 'hello' to her as he passed. She gave the same description."

"Where's the closest exit?" Lloyd asked.

Salerno pointed in the direction away from the elevator. "Down the hall to the stairs. It'll take you to one of the doors at the rear of the hotel."

Lloyd stood still in thought.

"What are you thinking about, Lloyd?" Hager asked.

"Just about the stairs."

"What about them? The guy was seen leaving the hotel through the lobby at two o'clock. What's the deal with the stairs?"

Lloyd shrugged his shoulders.

"I don't know. Never mind. You're right. He must've left through the lobby."

Hager looked at Lloyd and sensed he wasn't satisfied with the answer. Like Hager, Lloyd was adept at putting himself in the head of a killer, and something about the stairs being accessible to the killer seemed to bother him. He knew Lloyd would come to some conclusion later, and he would remember to ask him about it then.

"Let's go talk to her co-workers," Hager suggested.

The three lawmen piled into Madden's Lumina and, five minutes later they arrived at Tiffany's Cabaret. At the club, the statements made by the other dancers confirmed the many parallels of the murders of the women from Wilmington and Greenville. Several of the dancers had seen a man paying particular attention to "Felicia", Kathryn's stage name, and he spent a vast amount of money on her for dances. They also learned the same man had been in the club the previous two nights, and he was a representative for a modeling agency in New York.

The closeness of the three cases was striking. In each case, the victim was courted by a stranger posing as a modeling agent. The stranger allowed himself three nights to lure the "right" woman into his perilous trap. Hager knew it was the same person. The name on the hotel register and the business card confirmed what the agents had originally thought. An alias was being used by the killer each time.

Hager found out that Tiffany's much like many of the Gentleman's Clubs around North Carolina was a private club, and non-members were only afforded access if they purchased a membership, or if they were a guest of a member. Hager asked to see the new memberships made since Monday. The manager made a fuss about it, but Madden knew him, and he acquiesced, providing the list. There were no memberships under the name of Steven Landis. Hager asked how someone could get into the club without being a member. The manager told him guests from out of state were exempt and could enter the club after paying just the cover charge.

The agents then asked to see the guest register for the week. Hager examined the rows of signatures and found the name of Steven Landis, and it appeared for three consecutive days. With the manager's consent, although reluctantly given, Hager seized the registration form with Landis's signature on it.

Other than corroborating the link of the killer's method of operation in the three cases, the agents learned very little from their visit to Tiffany's. The intelligence they had received up to this point, had been of diminutive quality in identifying the killer, who was now believed to be responsible for the deaths of three young women in five months.

The four month period of "cooling off" sprang into Hager's mind again. He was confused by the time span between the first and second crime. Hager believed the killer had probably killed somewhere else in the meantime.

As they were driving back to the police department, Hager asked Madden if he knew of any other murders similar to this one in the past four months.

Madden thought for a moment.

"I'm not aware of any others around here. Although, I guess it was just a coincidence that High Point had a murder the same night, only about a mile away from where this one happened."

Hager's eyes narrowed.

"Hmm, only a mile away? Where? Was it a girl?"

"No, the clerk at the BP Station there on Wendover just as you get into High Point was shot during a robbery."

"Robbery, huh?"

"Yeah, that's all I heard about it. One of their detectives called and asked about our case to see if it could be related. We told her what we had and that was it."

"That's awful close. I've got a strange feeling. What do you think, Lloyd? You think we should give High Point a call?"

Lloyd leaned forward and crossed his arms across the head rest.

"I guess it wouldn't hurt any to call them."

Darkness had fallen upon the area, and the streets were lit with various colors from the businesses around. The sky was a dark gray, cloaked with clouds, providing insulation from the cold winter air. The three men returned to the squad room. Contrary to the hectic business earlier, the CID office was quiet and deserted, except for the few lingering detectives working overtime on their cases. Hager hurried to Madden's desk and picked up the telephone. Hopefully, the detective investigating the recent murder in the city was working late. Like them, giving long hours to the cause of learning the truth. Madden knew Detective Karen Peterson's direct number and dialed it for Hager.

"Detective Peterson, this is Clark Hager with the SBI. I'm glad I caught you before you went home."

"Yes, the infamous Agent Hager," she joked. "What can I do for you?"

"I'm over here in Greensboro looking into the death of the dancer at the Ameri-Suites. Madden said you called him about the one you all had on the same night."

"Yeah, I thought since the killings were so close to one another. There may have been a connection. Madden told me about his. They weren't even close."

"Hmm, just for the sake of curiosity, what can you tell me so far?"

"About five o'clock Thursday morning, a citizen goes into the store and can't find the clerk. The store was open, but no one was working. He called the police and an officer comes out. The citizen tells him there was no one working, but the door was open. The officer checked around the store and saw the office door partially ajar. When he pushed the door open further, he found the clerk lying on the floor with a gunshot in the head."

His interest diminished.

"Sounds like a robbery. Was all the money taken?"

"About seven hundred in cash along with a video tape from the recorder."

"Took the video tape, too? This one must have known what he was doing."

"Yeah, it looks like I've got pretty much of nothing," she sighed.

"You all had any other robberies similar to that?"

"Not in a couple of years. It's funny. We got a call from the same clerk an hour and a half before. About some drunk in the store."

"Really? What was the deal with that?"

"Well, the same officer who discovered the clerk, ran a disturbance call there about three thirty. He said he got to the store and the clerk told him this drunk guy came in and cussed him out. The clerk gave the officer a license number for the car. The tag came back to a 1993 Chevrolet registered to some woman in Winston-Salem."

"Hmm. Our girl here was from Winston-Salem. What kind of Chevy was it?"

"A Camaro, I think. Uh," she said shuffling through some papers. "Registered to a Kathryn Gerhardt."

Hager thought he'd imagined the detective. He was about to ask another question when the girl's name struck him like a hammer.

"Kathryn Gerhardt? A Camaro?"

The agent sprang from the chair.

"Holy shit! That was her car! Kathryn Gerhardt! That's the victim's name here!"

Hager shook his head in disbelief. He closed his eyes and thought.

"Are you joking?" the detective asked. "You mean Kathryn Jean

Gerhardt from Miller Street in Winston-Salem?"

"One and the same. Her car was found in the parking lot of the hotel."

Hager thumbed through the pages in his folder. He found the form which documented the towing of the victim's car.

"Let's see, uh, a black Camaro. NC license number K-Y-A-5123."

"I don't believe it. But a white male was driving the car that night," she said.

"Do you know if the clerk told the officer the drunk guy was with a woman?"

"I don't know. I'd have to check with him. The same guy who killed her must have killed our guy. Do you think he did it to get rid of a witness?"

"Anything's possible, but if this guy is our killer, he had other reasons. What caliber gun was used in yours?"

"It was a forty-five. Single shot to the head. We recovered one shell casing and the bullet exited the top of his head."

Lloyd and Madden glanced at one another in amazement, both raising their eyebrows at the news. Hager told the High Point detective to hold on and he addressed his colleagues.

"A male driving Gerhardt's car was causing a disturbance at the BP Station about an hour and a half before the clerk there was killed. High Point PD sent a car out there and were given a license number."

"You think our killer did that?" Madden asked Lloyd.

Lloyd shook his head.

"It doesn't make any sense for this bastard. It may just be a coincidence."

Hager hung up the phone and sat back down in the chair. A frown had developed on his face. Deep in thought, he began to shake his head. Trying to understand the recent development was hard. Ideas were flashing around his head, each a question needing to be answered.

Was the killer of the woman in Greensboro—their killer, the same one who shot the clerk? If so, then why kill a third shift cashier at the BP? If he did do the shooting, was the girl with him or already dead? The night clerk at the hotel already told us she'd seen a man leaving the lobby around two o'clock, but he was alone. A drunk in the store. Cussed out the clerk. Just ninety minutes before he was found. It's got to be him, but why?

"Unless," Hager said out loud.

"Unless what, Clark?" Lloyd asked.

Hager hadn't realized he had spoken out loud.

"Oh, I was just mulling over the situation. Trying to figure out if our killer did the shooting in High Point."

"And?"

Hager rose from the chair, and thoughts streamed through his mind.

"If he killed the clerk, which I truly believe he did, he did it for two reasons."

"You think this guy did the one in High Point?" Madden asked.

"Yes, I do. This is the way I think it went down. The clerk at the hotel said she saw him leave around two o'clock, and he was alone. I think he killed the woman before he left at two. For some reason, he takes her car and drives around, maybe looking for something to drink, you know, something to take off the edge. Or maybe he's just riding around, who knows? Anyway, he ended up at the BP and gets into some kind of argument with the cashier. The cashier tells him he's going to call the cops, and he scrams. A patrol car responds to the complaint about a drunk in the store. Now for the reasons he shot him. First, he's pissed off as hell for whatever reason. I think he may have gone in there to buy some beer and it was after hours, and he was refused. Well, the cashier threatens to call the cops, and..." he pointed his finger.

"He may have seen the guy write down the license number and knew it could tie him to the woman's car. If he knows anything about modern convenience stores, then he knows most of them have surveillance cameras that record activities in the store. And thus, the second reason: to eliminate a piece of evidence that could possibly identify him and make off with a few hundred bucks at the same time. That's why the shooter took the video tape from the office."

Lloyd smiled and turned to Madden."Makes sense to me."

11

THREE YOUNG WOMEN had fallen prey at the hands of the same man over the preceding five months. Two of the three had become victims within the span of six days and over an area encompassing in excess of three hundred miles between them. It looked likely that another victim, the third shift cashier at the BP Station, was this killer's fourth, although for what appeared to be different reasons. From the first murder in Wilmington in early August, the killer appeared to be moving northward to Greenville, and then west to the Greensboro area. Would he continue on the westerly path? Or would he change his direction to fool his pursuers? Hager racked his brain trying to enter the killer's mind. To him, it didn't make sense.

His killer was careful, but at the same time, very negligent in his activities. Was this some clever attempt at intentionally leaving some clues behind, but erasing others? Certainly, he was worried about his identity being revealed, but he was either ignorant about the technology available to law enforcement, or he knew he could only be discovered from certain evidence. By appearing at topless dance clubs, hotels, and other places, this monster was careless but assured of his anonymity there.

However, his confidence wasn't displayed with the taking of the video tape from the BP store. This, Hager thought, was interesting because despite his public displays, he felt somehow threatened by the possibility of a video recording of his face existing and resorted to extreme measures to see to its removal. Hager was sure the killer knew he wouldn't be recognized here, but in some other place he certainly would.

That explained the theft of the tape. At present, the only known aspect of the killer was a generic physical description which fit millions of men. Taken from Vivian in Greenville, they had a composite drawing of the man seen with Tamara Wall at the dance club, but the image was computer-generated; those typically didn't resemble the person. The drawing was done at the SBI field office in Greenville, and Detective Jamison told Hager that Vivian had acknowledged it looked like the man. The killer knew if his photograph was placed on national news, someone would recognize him, and his game would be over. This behavior served to substantiate Hager's notion the murderer was from somewhere other than where the crimes occurred. Perhaps Florida or New York.

His thoughts turned to the evidence left behind at his crime scenes. Although he was careful to wipe away any identifiable fingerprints, the killer abandoned proof of his identity in the semen and hair found in and on the victims.

With technology similar to the AFIS computer, DNA was currently being stored in databases around the United States. The killer's DNA, obtained from the semen samples, was entered into the database. The lack of a definite match merely indicated the killer's DNA wasn't stored in the computer. Being a relatively new concept, and only a few years old, DNA from all previous sexual offenders hadn't been entered into the system. Hager was confident the killer had a previous history of some similar crime.

Reluctant to reveal any information about the cases, Hager and Lloyd faced a dilemma when Bob Maxwell informed them a news conference would be held about the serial killer. Both the agents agreed the publicity may bring him into the open but also acknowledged it may serve a purpose in reinforcing the killer's ego.

It was the fame and notoriety many of these killers desired, and it would be playing into his hands by announcing it to the world. Hager believed the *effective* use of the media was a useful tool in a murder investigation. He had to be cautious. Any intelligence not properly safeguarded and leaked to the press could jeopardize the security of the investigation. With the inclusion of the public, it could provoke many erroneous tips, pranks, or other lunatics wanting to wreak havoc on the probe or to gain publicity.

With this fact in mind, there would be no mention of any theories about the killer or any piece of information concerning the killer's M.O. A concise, general statement, reporting the deaths of three young women were connected to the same man. Not completely sure he was involved, Hager decided against mentioning the killer's association with the BP murder in High Point. The description of the man would be divulged, but his targets and their employment would not. The agents had the weekend to construct a press release disclosing the information they wanted to reveal. Meanwhile, DNA tests could be done on the evidence found from Kathryn Gerhardt, and photographs of the Greensboro crime scene could be developed.

On Monday morning the agents met in Maxwell's office to discuss the news conference. Present in the meeting were Hager; Lloyd; Maxwell; Leonard Rosen, the Director of the Department of Crime Control and Public Safety; and David Oliver, the State Attorney General. Before arriving in Maxwell's office, Hager called the DNA Analysis Unit and received the results of the DNA tests done over the weekend. The tests validated the same man was the killer of three women over the past five months.

Both Hager and Lloyd were given a great deal of latitude in mapping out the strategy of the news conference. Maxwell would initially make a brief statement as to the purpose of the announcement, and he would then turn the questions over to Hager and Lloyd. Hager informed the panel he would only release limited information about the cases and would politely avoid more detailed questions from reporters. The briefing concluded and the conference was scheduled at 1:00 p.m. in the press room of the Attorney General's Office downtown.

Although it couldn't be seen, Hager was nervous as he sat in a chair between Bob Maxwell and his partner. Having taken part in these spectacles before on several occasions, he knew it would go according to plan. The statement, the questions and answers from the reporters. Knowing this didn't prevent the pre-game jitters, however. Hager felt good that his body still reacted to stress normally. He hadn't become a zombie–oblivious to his surroundings. The agent wasn't particularly worried about the questions lobbed from reporters. They weren't as aggressive as their colleagues in larger cities and wouldn't attack the issues a great deal. But a thought popped into his head during the preliminary briefing which made Hager anxious.

This killer was posing as a photographer to lure his victims, but it was possible he was a real photographer and was using his expertise in the con. It made sense. Was he really a photographer somewhere? He tried to enter the killer's mind again. Reflecting to the profile, he remembered he thought this killer would follow the news reports of the case. Would he be so bold as to appear at the news conference? To look Hager in the eye, and maybe ask a question? It was possible.

"I'm not going to take any chances on this one."

Before the news conference began, he called the SBI lab and asked for one of their crime scene specialists to take pictures of the group of reporters convened. When the specialist arrived, Hager made sure he was advised to shoot the group casually and to appear as if he were taking photos as a matter of routine.

Last week at the funeral for Tamara Wall in Greenville, Hager had arranged the same thing. A SBI crime scene specialist photographed the attendees of the funeral because Hager knew sometimes a killer would show up at the funeral of his victims, either in remorse for his deed or to relive the thrill of being responsible for the gathering.

With this in mind, the funeral of Kathryn Gerhardt in Winston-Salem was also going to be photographed. Her funeral was scheduled for Wednesday. Hager and Lloyd would examine the pictures to see if there were any common faces, especially ones which fit the description of their killer. It was a long shot, but to Hager it was worth the effort.

Not only did taking pictures at the funeral help but after the funeral, surveillance on the grave would be conducted to see if there were any solitary mourner, not wanting to be seen by anyone, or thinking the police had the funeral staked out. Even though it wasn't especially common for this type of organized killer to revisit grave sites, Hager felt it was something he couldn't overlook. There may have been a victim who *meant* more to the killer than the others. One for whom he felt some sense of sorrow for his crime. She may have had some symbolic purpose important only to him that would cause him to visit the grave.

Not only were the regional news stations present, but the national television news agencies, CNN and the networks were represented along with all the print media. Serial murders were big news. It was a fascination that traveled the entire continent. Something a movie or novel could be written about. Hager shook his head at the thought.

At the moment, these cases were boring in the public's eyes. Not the makings of a great novel or exciting movie. No lurid crime scenes. No dismemberment of body parts. No great number of corpses discovered underneath a house. It was just a simple case of a strangler posing as photographer or rep from a modeling agency targeting strippers across the state. With this added, it sounded somewhat interesting, but Hager knew the public wouldn't be aware of those facts until the killer was identified.

He tilted his head and smiled, muttering to himself.

"Now that might make a suspenseful movie or book."

Hager's eyes would be peeled for any unfamiliar faces lurking in the crowd.

Unfamiliar faces? Why only unfamiliar faces? This guy could be my next door neighbor and I wouldn't know it.

This was one of the problems with this type of serial killer. One of many. Beside the fact the killer was probably above average in intelligence, the man appeared as normal-looking as anyone, and according to all the reports, he was very attractive. The same thing was said about Ted Bundy, the law student who worked as a counselor.

Hager recalled Ann Rule's book about Bundy, *The Stranger Beside Me.* How the writer, along with being involved in the investigation of the murders in Seattle, worked alongside Bundy as a counselor, unbeknownst to her he was a vicious killer. She thought he was such a nice boy who wanted to be a lawyer.

Hager knew of only one way to solve this major dilemma. Overlook no one. People who were overlooked because of their seemingly normal lives and appearance sometimes turned out to be the killer all along. Up to this point, they had really no one to overlook, other than the boyfriend of Heather Kingston in Wilmington, but he was cleared early on in the investigation.

Maxwell cleared his throat and spoke into the microphone. The mumbling of voices stopped to listen as the event began.

"Ladies and gentlemen, thank you for coming on such short notice. I'm Bob Maxwell, the Assistant Director of the State Bureau of Investigation. First, I have a brief statement to make, and then questions will be taken. We have called this press conference to announce that the SBI, in cooperation with local authorities, is currently involved in the investigation of the violent deaths of three women since August of last year. It has been determined these three homicides have been committed by the same person. The crimes took place in Wilmington last August; in Hertford County a week ago; and in Greensboro on Thursday. The link to the same person was determined through DNA testing of evidence collected from the three crime scenes.

"Special Agents Clark Hager and Lloyd Sheridan of the SBI Investigative Support Unit are leading the investigation. Agent Hager will take your questions."

Hager looked at Lloyd, who smiled revealing his tobacco-stained teeth. He stood and stepped to the podium eyeing Maxwell. In the audience hands were raised from the twenty-five or so reporters and photographers. To his right, he saw a man focusing his 35mm camera on the spectators. Although dressed in casual apparel, Hager concluded the man was a photographer from the SBI lab, as he was pointing toward the gathering instead of at the podium.

He inhaled deeply to slow his heart, which was pounding in his chest. Suddenly, his mouth went dry and he looked around the table for a glass of water. Not seeing one, he motioned to Lloyd that he needed a drink. The oxygen he inhaled helped to calm his nerves. Looking around the room, he saw the lenses of video and still cameras, the faces of the people behind them hidden, the reporters, some with notebooks in hand, the others, with microphones. No one looked at him abnormally, and everyone gave the appearance of busily doing their job. Not even a blank or interested stare.

Hager saw an attractive blonde raising her hand. It was the familiar face of Carrie Newsome of the local television station WRAL Channel 5. He acknowledged her for a question. She smiled brightly at the agent's recognition.

"Yes, Agent Hager, have you any information regarding a suspect in these cases? And if so, has he been identified yet?"

"We have a general description of a man who was seen with the victims on the nights before they were found dead. No, he's not been identified, yet. But we're exploring information as it arrives."

His eye caught sight of a reporter from the Raleigh *News and*

Observer and Hager pointed to him.

"Agent Hager, what has been determined to be the cause of death in the three cases? Are they all the same?"

"In all three cases, the victims were strangled."

The newspaper reporter added another question.

"Have you been able to determine what, if any, weapon or tool had been used?"

"No. We haven't been able to determine it yet. We're still working with our lab to determine if any weapons or tools were used."

The reporter sat down. Hager thought the reporter had asked a good question. Perhaps a trick into disclosing a weapon used in the murder. Very clever, but Hager was prepared for it. Another face in the audience he recognized. It was Vanessa.

She met his gaze and he froze for a moment, embraced in her smile. It had been four days since he saw her last, and she looked fabulous. Hager's prolonged smile provoked glances from the audience to the rear of the room to see the beautiful brunette who had caught the speaker's attention. She was wearing a winter white pantsuit, her right hand gently inside the pants pocket, and one leg crossed over the other as she stood, leaning against the wall at the back of the room. After a fleeting loss of concentration, he remembered his purpose and acknowledged a female television reporter.

"Patricia Starling, NBC News. Are there any connections to the victims at all? Is the killer targeting a particular kind of woman?"

"Another good question," Hager said to himself. "We're in the process of working with the local police departments in order to ascertain all pertinent background information on the victims. As of right now, I cannot elaborate on any connections made so far. It's very early in the investigation."

She sat down, apparently contented with his answer. He returned to Vanessa, on her face, a mischievous smirk. She straightened from her position on the wall and raised her hand, asking a question simultaneously.

"Agent Hager, do you have any theory as to the duration of this investigation? Is there any time frame you can predict as to when this killer will be caught?"

When she concluded, she had to hold her lips together to keep from bursting into laughter. The question had a hidden meaning. Vanessa was actually asking how long her boyfriend would be busy with the case and away from her. Hager looked over to Lloyd, the only person in the room who knew Vanessa, and his partner smiled and gestured that the question should be answered.

A rare event had occurred. Clark Hager didn't know what to say. He wanted to laugh. To somehow convey to Vanessa that he wanted to sprint to her and place a long passionate kiss on her lips.

"Miss?"

"Roman. Vanessa Roman," she said confidently.

Hager smiled as all eyes shifted back and forth to the both of them.

"Miss Roman, there is no way to speculate as to a specific time it will take for the killer to be apprehended, but I can assure you—meaning all of you," he addressed the room, "will be the first to know."

She smiled, but looked disappointed. Maybe it was because Hager couldn't come up with something a little wittier. Or, because she knew this case would more than likely monopolize his time until it was concluded. She remained at her post against the wall, and Hager frequently glanced her way only to catch her eyes sending him signals of arousal.

Hager fielded several more questions about the mysteries and concluded the press conference, accomplishing what he'd intended: to inform the public about the crimes outside of exposing any significant facts, and to convey a message to the killer the State's elite were on his trail. As the room cleared, Hager made his way to the rear to join the newest member of the media.

Vanessa stood, her arms folded across her chest, lips foreshadowing the rise of a cheerful grin. He dodged the exiting reporters and cameramen and came face to face with her, wanting to sweep her from the floor. Instead, he beamed, his face flushed from his faltered riposte.

"I had you on the ropes, Hager," she asserted.

"I know. I know—" he whined.

"I don't know why I let you off, though. I thought you could do better than that."

She put her hands to her hips and stood erect with her chest out.

"There is no way to speculate," she said, parroting his voice. "And I assure you," her head shook, then she broke out into laughter. "That was bad. I guess I may have felt sorry for you. Poor baby!"

She placed her hand against his cheek.

Hager's bowed his head. He sniffled, like he was weeping.

"I'm sorry. I'll try to do better next time." He looked up and snickered at her. "What are you doing here? Aren't you supposed to be at work?"

"I took off the rest of the day. I missed you, so I called your office and they told me you were here."

Hager's face brightened when he heard the news.

"Hey! That's great! We can have dinner together."

She leaned forward and whispered in his ear, "My place or yours?"

Feeling her breath on his skin, a tingling sensation streaked down his neck. He chuckled again, and bit his lip, seeing she wasn't kidding.

"I have some leftover baked chicken in the fridge."

Vanessa smirked, and her eyes shifted behind her boyfriend. Hager turned to see Lloyd approach. Lloyd put his hand on his partner's shoulder and eyed Vanessa.

"Hey there, beautiful," he said to her. "It's good to see you. Clark, Maxwell wants us to come back to his office to discuss strategies on this."

Hager rolled his eyes and looked at his watch.

"It shouldn't take too long, Vanessa. It's two thirty now. You want to go on ahead, and I'll meet you there later?"

"That sounds good. I've got my key."

She gave Hager a quick kiss and walked out of the room. He watched her walk away, admiring the confident way she strode with her purse flung over her shoulder. His eyes full, he turned to his partner, whose gaze was focused on the same thing. He lightly punched his shoulder.

"What are you looking at?"

Lloyd laughed.

"The same thing you were. She sure's got a great ass."

12

HIS EYES saw the newspaper headline in bold letters.

Suspected Serial Killer Believed Responsible For NC Deaths.

The article underneath consisted of only several paragraphs outlining the three murders. No details. No highlights. A dry synopsis that read much like a police report. Just the facts.

Pride filled his body. He had finally made the newspapers. The public knew he was out there. All of them afraid. Worried that a monster prowled among them, waiting to pounce on unsuspecting innocents. But the story had an air of emptiness to it. It had no identity, no personality. Just the facts.

No wonder the report was so bland. Instead of focusing on the most interesting player in the game, the writer detailed a small glamorous biography on the man in charge of the hunt. The killer sat on the cold wooden floor and studied the article again, talking to himself.

"Clark Hager," he sighed. "Who does he think he is? He had no place in this piece. What did he do to cause this?" He threw the paper down in front of his feet in disgust. "It is *I* who this story's about. *I* should be the focal point! Not him!"

It wasn't fair for the credit to be given to someone else, especially when it was undeserved. It wasn't *his* doing.

He picked up the paper again and reread the story, thinking he may have missed something about himself. It read about the same as before. Duller, actually. What was so good about Clark Hager? He wasn't that smart. Not cunning enough to snare a clever-minded foe.

He skimmed the article a third time. It angered him to see Hager's name in print, and not his. Hager didn't deserve the press. He had nothing to do with all that had occurred. With all *he* had done.

"The brilliant profiler, Special Agent Clark Hager of the Investigative Support Unit is in charge of the investigation," he said mockingly.

"Brilliant? He wouldn't know brilliance if it walked by and kicked him in the ass!"

Angry, he tossed the paper across the room, striking the wall, and it fell lazily to the floor. He stood and chugged the rest of his beer and forcefully winged the empty bottle against the wall, smashing shards of glass all over the room.

"This is my story!" he shouted at the top of his lungs.

His deeds were supposed to make him famous. Fame was a thing he desperately wanted, but it had consequences. With fame, came the knowledge of his true identity, and this was dangerous. How could he expand on his popularity and still remain anonymous at the same time?

Contact. Make contact with someone. Someone important, and he knew just the person. The man who stood between himself and achieving his goal. The one who was the source of that horrible article; who stole away his press, and was currently racking that *brilliant* brain of his trying to unravel the murder mystery he faced.

But before he hastily made a move closer to his pursuer, however, he knew a little checking would be required. In order to approach the man and begin a dialogue with him, he had to dig into his past and flush out all his weaknesses. Ones he could use to propel his plan of terror and destruction. Get to know Special Agent Clark Hager. Personally.

But why only contact? Why not turn the table and supply a judicious amount of fear to his opponent. That would teach him to hinder the evolution of his fame and not to steal the show to advance his own bloated ego. Hager would find out he wasn't the only one considered *brilliant* by his peers. In severe fashion. By way of diabolical terror and manipulation. Hager had never faced someone so clever.

Seated at a table in the library, he typed the letters H-A-G-E-R on the keyboard of the computer. On the screen the word "searching" flashed while the computer searched the database's files. The Stauffer library contained newspapers where searches on names, places, and almost any topic could be made. This particular database contained the Raleigh *News and Observer* and would respond with all references to the name "Hager" in newspapers over the last twenty years.

The newspapers were recorded on microfiche from which copies could be made from a viewer. The PC ended its search and a list of different articles flashed on the screen. There were nine listings under the name.

Seven of them were listed under "Hager, Clark", and two others, listed under "Hager, Kelly" and "Hager, Elizabeth." On a scratch piece of paper, he jotted down the dates of the articles for all nine listings.

From the microfiche cabinet, he pulled the individual slides and went to the viewer to examine the articles. The first listing was in July 1991, a feature on Hager and the formation of the SBI Investigative Support Unit. The killer examined the article, learning that Hager had attended the FBI Academy and worked with the federal agency in profiling. A few others were viewed. They were standard articles about cases Hager had investigated: a murder in Rocky Mount; a government corruption case; and some other crimes in which Hager's name was mentioned.

Hager definitely had the newspapers impressed, but the killer saw through all of Hager's bullshit, with the FBI training, and his extraordinary ability as a profiler and investigator. All the hype was merely a sugar-coated version of the truth. Hager was just an ordinary cop who happened to get lucky a couple of times.

He came to a listing of Kelly Hager. An article mentioning her name appeared in October 1992. It was an obituary.

Kelly Hager, 40, beloved wife of Clark Hager died Thursday, October 17, after months of declining health. Mrs. Hager was survived by her husband and daughter, Elizabeth. Memorials can be made in donations to the Hospice of the Triangle.

"Poor guy," he joked, and he mockingly sniffled.

Next to the obituary was a photograph of Kelly Hager. The woman's smile illuminated the frame, and the killer admitted to himself she was a beautiful woman, despite having been married to a putz like Hager.

The name Elizabeth rang a bell, and he remembered seeing the name on another listing. A June 1995 listing for Elizabeth Hager was a high school graduation announcement. Elizabeth graduated from Cary Academy with honors, and the article stated she intended on going to the University of North Carolina—Chapel Hill.

"Hmm. He's got a daughter, huh? I wonder?"

13

RAIN POUNDED against the windows of Hager's office as sheets of water drenched the ground. It was a harsh storm with what appeared to be buckets of water falling from the sky. The gray clouds, almost black, seemed boundless and still. Only strong gusts of wind reminded him the clouds were moving.

The dark sky was the same for miles. Along the edges of parking lots water rushed into ditches and drains. The water's rapid flowing into concrete drains sounded like a shower with its water streaming down into the tub. For all its gloominess, the rain had a calmingly, peaceful effect. It was a rain which provoked thoughts of sleep, and the longer he watched it, the drowsier he became.

All day Hager had been on the telephone organizing a meeting of the investigators involved in the murders. Assistant Director Maxwell ordered him to formulate a task force to assist in the investigation, and the agent had contacted all the parties to meet at SBI Headquarters on Wednesday. Hager was agreeable with the conglomerate but stressed it was *his* unit who would be in charge.

Hager would utilize the local detectives to follow up on any leads that may arise during the course of their investigation. To interview witnesses again. Talk to victim's family members again. Try to learn some new piece of information they had missed or an answer to a question they had forgotten to ask. Hager and Lloyd would take the pile of amassed papers and photos of the three murders and dissect the files once again, like they had done on the Wilmington case.

Additionally, the task force was responsible for checking on any new leads acquired from the recent press release and news broadcasts. The meeting would serve to establish the roles of the individual investigators and to bring all of them up to date on the progress of the case. Hager hoped Florida would return some helpful information about the name given. Maybe they had a similar case, he hoped. His eyes shifted from the window to the wall where a map of the state hung. Large red pins, four of them, stuck in the cities where the four tragedies occurred. A pin map was a useful tool in some cases. It was used to establish a pattern of movement based on the crimes being committed.

In this case, to the extent they knew, the killings began in Wilmington, then moved north to Greenville; northwest to Greensboro; then just a few miles south in High Point. Hager didn't want to count the murder of the convenience store clerk. Not because it was unimportant, but because he believed it had no bearing on the pattern the killer was using, if any. Could it be a pattern? Or was he randomly finding places with which he was familiar and yet wouldn't be recognized. For all he knew, the killer was heading west and Hager estimated the same path of flight would continue until he reached the borders of the state.

He looked at the map for places west of Greensboro, cities which fit the killer's criteria. The larger cities which had topless or exotic dancing establishments. Winston-Salem, about twenty miles from Greensboro, was a possibility.

Too close, Hager thought, but Statesville and Hickory were places that seemed likely. Those cities were also along Interstate 40, the state's main artery to the west.

He gazed out the window again and noticed the rain had stopped, but the dark clouds, gray with lines of white and darker almost black in the center, remained low in the sky. Just a respite. They were taking a break, weary from all the flushing of moisture during the last few hours.

Lloyd stepped into the room and Hager had barely noticed. In his large hands were the two business cards presented to the victims by the killer. Lloyd spent most of the day in the lab having the cards analyzed to see if any clues were evident. On their faces, the cards were very similar, the coloring, style, and paper. What the lab could provide was more information on the origin of the paper stock and identify the printing method on the cards.

"How'd it go today, Lloyd?"

"All right, I guess. Didn't find out anything we hadn't already assumed. The paper is the usual stock found at any office supply store. According to the lab, the cards are on the same paper, and were printed on the same bubble jet printer. Looks like this guy has a PC somewhere, and he's making his own business cards."

Hager sat in the chair at his desk, his fingers together like he was praying.

"Yeah. You're right. We figured that much. They couldn't tell anything else?"

He shook his head. "No. They did say they could link the printer to the cards if a printer was found."

"That's a relief. I feel closer to nabbing this guy already," he said sarcastically.

Lloyd threw up his hands at the remark.

"Did you get everything set—"

The telephone rang in the middle of the sentence and Hager quickly grabbed the receiver.

"SBI, Hager."

"I know you think you're pretty smart, Agent Hager, but you won't catch me."

The man's voice was smooth and calm.

"What? Who is this?" Hager asked.

"You know who this is. I'm the one you're looking for. I guess you could say I'm responsible for all the press you've been getting lately."

Hager, dismayed at the man's statement, asked again, "Who did you say this is?"

As soon as the words left Hager's mouth, he knew he was talking to the killer. Heat rushed to his head. His hands started to sweat.

"C'mon, Agent Hager. I know you're brighter than that. You're the one who's supposed to be so brilliant."

The agent reached over and turned on a cassette recorder connected to the phone, looked at Lloyd, and pointed to the phone mouthing, *It's him*.

"Oh yeah, now I know," Hager said into the phone. "So, I don't guess you'd like to tell me your name?"

"We won't get into trivial matters just yet. Besides, if I tell you who I am, it might spoil all the fun of finding out for yourself."

"Well, I appreciate your concern for my emotional well-being, but I'd rather know your name."

The man's voice sounded irritated.

"Get over it! Don't you like the challenge of pursuing a mysteriously clever person? Something to motivate you."

"I'd rather you stop the killing. By the way, how do I know you're who you say you are? You could be some—"

"Some nut? Not likely. C'mon, Agent Hager. Where's your sense of adventure?"

"You didn't answer the question. How do I know you're the person I'm looking for?"

"You'll just have to take my word for it. If you're looking for admissions, Agent Hager, you're barking up the wrong tree. I'm an honorable man. I wouldn't lie about that."

Honorable man, my ass.

"Look. In order for us to communicate with each other, we have to be honest. We've gotten calls from all sorts of people claiming to be responsible. None of them were able to tell me something the public doesn't already know. If you are who you say you are, you'll be able to do that."

"Don't push me, Hager. You're not in control of this. I am. You want something, you'll have to find it yourself!"

Hager could tell the man was becoming more agitated and he didn't want to incite him into proving he was the killer by taking another life.

"Okay, I understand. All right, but I don't know what to call you. You haven't even given me a name."

"You won't call me, got it," he snapped. "I'll only call you. Oh, and don't worry about tracing my calls or anything like that. There's no way you can do it to me. It's called cell phone cloning."

"I'm not interested in that right now. I just wanted to know what I should tell the news when I call them and say I was contacted. I guess I'll tell them you were a prank like the others."

"You think you're so fucking clever with that psychological bullshit. It's not the right time yet. The entire world will know who I am eventually. I'll leave the problem of discovering my identity to you. Good-bye, Agent Hager."

The phone disconnected. Hager's heart was racing. A chill crept up his spine. He put the receiver back and turned off the tape recorder. Lloyd was still standing next to the desk, waiting for a response from his partner.

"Well, what did he say?"

Hager sat in the chair, his body trembling from the sudden rush of excitement. He admonished himself for not getting the man to talk more. He thought he was better than that. Perhaps he wasn't as smart as everyone believed.

"No," he said to himself. "I tried to get him to talk, but he refused to give any details."

"Clark, what did he say?" Lloyd asked again.

He turned to face Lloyd, a curious expression on his face.

"Not much. He just said he was the person responsible for the press I'm getting."

The thought of the tape recorder jumped in his mind and he reached for it.

"Here, you can hear it yourself." Hager pushed the rewind button.

Hager's chest pounded again as the two agents listened to the tape. Hager concentrated specifically on the voice. Not a strange sounding voice for an adult male. The medium tone of the caller sounded like he was white, but there was no hint of an accent or drawl. To Hager, the voice was familiar, but he couldn't place anyone he knew with it. It had such a normal tone. He could have heard it anywhere from anyone.

As the dialogue continued, Hager listened for background noises, a clue to indicate his location. Carefully he ignored the smooth inflection of the man stating he was the killer and tried to identify any hint in the background. Nothing. Other than the voices of the two men on the recording, the only other sound he heard was the man breathing into the phone. Hager figured he would hear his own heart pounding as excitement rushed through his body.

"Was he telling the truth? Was he really who he said he was?" he asked himself.

Hager lied when he told the caller they had received calls from others admitting to the crimes. There had been no calls in that regard, nor had there been many calls period, other than from people curious for more details about the suspect. He knew it was him. Calls from anyone other than the true perpetrator were rare. Hager knew from the chill he sensed hearing the voice that he was the killer—despite the limited information in the conversation.

The tape ended and Hager turned off the recorder. Lloyd pulled a chair closer to Hager's desk.

"Do you believe that about the cell phone? Cloning and all."

"I don't think he would've mentioned it if it weren't true. He expects us to check the phone number in any case and trace any future calls. I think he's just telling us what we'll find out later to prove he is clever."

"If it is a cell phone, isn't there a way to trap the signal and lock in on that particular phone?"

"Yeah, caller ID can get the number and there is a way to lock in on the actual cell the phone is using. I don't really know much about it. But, I think if the phone is cloned, it will be almost impossible because the numbers change frequently.

"That might be some angle we can approach it from, Lloyd. If the phone is cloned, our guy is either involved in the cloning or he buys phones to be cloned. Either way, we may have someone who can provide us with some information on anyone buying or cloning phones in the state. We'll check with Intelligence, and see if they're familiar with any known cloning operations. In the meantime, we'll get caller ID for this phone and put a tracer on the line in case he calls again."

14

THE WORD *Registrar* was painted in black letters on the darkened gray plastic window of the office door. Next to the door was a clear glass window with a small hole about the size of a baseball with a little shelf underneath. On the other side, a woman sat behind a desk typing on a keyboard. She didn't notice him walk up to the window, and he watched her busily punching away at the keys. The fingers on her wrinkled hands were moving rapidly, and she glanced up occasionally to observe her work. In her fifties, the woman was frail looking and conservatively dressed in a white long-sleeved blouse with a gray sweater draped around her shoulders. She wore those glasses with the metal chain around her neck.

At the window the man grew impatient at her oblivious attention to his presence. He cleared his throat before he spoke, "Excuse me, ma'am," almost like a question.

Surprised, the woman looked up, seeing him standing at the help window. She sprang from her chair and jumped to the counter.

"Can I help you?"

"Yes ma'am," he said meekly. "Uh, I'm Rick Collier, and I'm a graduate student. I'm working on my master's thesis on the demographics in the UNC system."

She smiled at him in a friendly way.

"I need to get an enrollment list for my research."

The woman wrinkled her brow, and she looked confused.

"What kind of list do you need?"

"You know, a list of the students enrolled this semester. Just the basic information. Name, race, sex, and all that."

He smiled at her, trying to convince her he was on the level.

"Why do you need it again?"

"I'm doing my master's thesis in Sociology, you know, Doctor Wynand?"

The woman nodded, and her eyes had a look of recognition when she heard the name of the Sociology department head.

"Doctor Wynand said an intensive examination on the demographics of the UNC system would be interesting."

By the look on her face, it appeared the woman's wall was coming down.

"I don't know. That information isn't supposed to be given to just anyone, with the names on it and all."

She shook her head in doubt, then a smile appeared on his face.

This isn't going to be as easy as I thought.

The man's face inched close to the glass, and he motioned to her with his hand to come closer. Not knowing what to do, she looked around to see if anyone was watching and put her head near the glass.

"I know it's a lot of trouble," he whispered. "But, you know, I'm getting a really late start on the project, and Doctor Wynand won't accept anything late. I'd really appreciate you doing it for me. You seem like such a nice lady. Can you help out a desperate student?"

He tried to put on his most pitiful face. The droopy eyes, helpless, like a child's and his tone, almost like he was whining. It worked. And he saw it in her smile.

"Oh well, all right. I guess it would be okay. It's not like you're some mass murderer or something like that."

She snickered and covered her mouth. When she spoke, he noticed the woman had the sweetest voice. It was amiable, and relenting.

"Yeah, some mass murderer," he laughed.

He raised his hands above his shoulders and curled his fingers like he was scratching.

"A month-ster!" he said in his best Quasimoto voice.

She cupped her hand over her mouth again to muffle her laughter. It was obvious he'd won her over. What a charmer.

"Look. It will take about fifteen minutes to print this out," she said.

"That's fine. I'll wait here in the hall."

She looked surprised.

"Nonsense! You come in here and sit down."

She walked over to the door and opened it, allowing him to enter.

"Damn, I hope I didn't over do it with her," he said to himself. "Next thing she'll be asking me for a date."

"Can I get you a cup of coffee while you wait?" she asked.

A grin appeared on his face, and he laughed silently.

"No thanks."

He took a seat on a comfortable couch in the waiting area of the office and watched her disappear down the hall.

Faintly, he heard the buzzing sound of the printer working. Other sounds, the sound of country music playing on a clock radio on the woman's desk and those of voices, female ones, were heard in another room. Were they talking about him? Did she go back there to tell them how good-looking he was?

He would certainly know in a few minutes if the others conveniently wandered their way into the front office to catch a glimpse of the man waiting on the couch. Women were sneaky, he knew. If one of them thought he was attractive, the others would make an attempt to check him out. To make themselves seen by him. It was their way to get noticed.

His thoughts drifted from the old ladies in the registrar's office to the young ones nearby. The University of North Carolina, like any other large university, was chock full of beautiful women. A dozen, at least, had crossed his path during the walk from the parking lot beside the sun dial, which stood in front of the university planetarium.

The registrar's office was located in Hanes Hall. It was clear across a grassy park called McCorkle Place, crowded with oak trees and students walking to their classes. Beyond "Silent Sam", the statue commemorating the Confederate soldiers who died during the American Civil War.

The walk from the parking lot off Franklin Street was refreshing in the cool air, but the sky said it would rain again today. He worried he might get drenched during his return to the car.

Despite the allure of the young bodies tucked in their jeans and sweaters, there was only one young woman in his sight. That was his mission now. If he was going to be hunted like an animal, then he would only make it fair and prey upon the hunter. Make him realize his vulnerability, to come to grips with his fears. Show him how it felt to be pursued. Stalked.

His brief fantasy was interrupted by the woman when she entered the room again. The man looked up at her, smiled, showing his white teeth, like they were fangs, hidden in the gums, waiting for the sun to set, to protrude their way down into his mouth.

"Here you are. I hope this is what you wanted."

She offered him the papers. The scent of her perfume was stronger, maybe because she was closer, but probably because she was trying to impress him. "No way," he said to himself. "Maybe twenty years ago, she looked good, but now..."

He stood and shook his head.

"Is that not it?"

The man quickly checked over the pages and saw that the paper was what he'd requested.

"Oh, yes. That's what I need. That's just what I needed."

He turned to her and smiled thankfully.

171

"You don't know how important this list is to me," he said, touching her arm, giving it a gentle squeeze. "Thank you, Miss? I didn't catch your name."

She blushed and turned her head away.

"Mrs. Hamilton."

"Mrs. Hamilton, thank you very much."

"You're quite welcome," she said and gently touched his hand. "Good luck on your paper."

Out the door he walked quickly down the hall, flipping through the pages of the list. His eyes scanned the page with the names beginning with "H". Running his finger down the page, it stopped at the last name of Hager.

"Bingo!" he said as he read.

Hager, Elizabeth N. W/F 11/16/77 Jr. CJ

"Hmm, what's the CJ stand for?"

He walked down the stairs of the building, and turned in the direction of his car. It had started raining lightly, but he was too absorbed in the question of the initials to notice drops of water falling on the paper. He stopped instantly when the answer popped in his head.

"I know. CJ means Criminal Justice. Isn't that sweet. She must be following in daddy's footsteps."

15

THE RAIN CONTINUED off and on for two consecutive days. Hager was relieved it wasn't particularly cold those days, and therefore the hours of wetness were bearable. It was winter and snow would have been much prettier than the gray days of rain, but in North Carolina, the days of ground blanketed in the white wonder were few and far between. Mostly, it was snow flakes that evolved into a storm of ice and sleet, making the entire area's roadways hazardous. Rain was, hence, the lesser of the two evils, and was looked upon as a welcome occurrence to the alternative.

There were no new developments in the case other than John Ramos had called the day before. Through Florida DMV, Ramos located a person named Ronald Cooper in Miami. He fit the age range, but had no criminal record. The address Hager had given him from the card was bogus and Ramos asked if the agent wanted him to follow up on Cooper. Hager was elated at the Florida agent's enthusiasm to help.

He informed Hager it would take a few more days to locate the man, and he would call as soon as he learned anything. The word from Florida wasn't entirely promising. Ramos couldn't find any similar crimes, solved or unsolved in the state. Hager didn't know what this meant in the big scheme of things, but now he knew his killer probably hadn't been active in Florida. Again, Hager realized this wasn't going to be an easy task in identifying the murderer. As if he believed it would be easy.

The assemblage of the investigative task force was scheduled to take place later that day, and Hager was optimistic the meeting would prove to streamline the efforts so the most effective use of the manpower would be utilized. The office of the Investigative Support Unit would serve as the command post or clearing house of all information related to the murders. Task force members, upon completing their assigned duties, would FAX a written report to the SBI so Hager and Lloyd could be notified immediately of any new developments and compare the information to any obtained previously.

During the night of the call from the killer, Hager listened to the voice repeatedly, trying to recognize any peculiarities, quirks or sayings which may be useful to him later. Focusing on the voice, Hager tried to paint a face—the face of a brutal killer, still on the loose waiting for his next victim to emerge. The voice had formed an indelible impression in his mind. The smooth inflection, the simple articulation, the nondescript accent like that of television news anchor, with no indication of the region of the country from where they hailed.

Predicting the meeting would last into the evening, both Hager and Lloyd agreed to meet in the office at 1 p.m. With their colleagues' arrival set for 2 p.m., they used the preceding hour to prepare themselves. Hager sat at his desk, perusing the files and photographs of Kathryn Gerhardt, the woman found in Greensboro. From the pictures it was evident the killer was becoming more brutal in his torture of his victims. There were various injuries on the girl's neck indicating she had undergone a lengthy suffering at the hands of this marauder. Hager tried to picture it in his mind.

The killer, an evil grin riveted to his face, feeling all-powerful. Enjoying the satisfaction of domination, of asserting his strength, his lurid will. The agonizing face of the victim, making feeble attempts to free herself from his snare, the tears streaming down her cheeks with the certain feeling of doom.

Hager shook the image from his head. It disgusted him to have such visions, but he knew he must. He had to *see* it. To see it the way he thought it happened, to relive it the way the killer relives his quest.

Although the purpose wasn't the same, Hager found that imagining the incident unfolding before him was helpful in establishing the killer's motivations. To place himself inside the head of a monster. Not to share his elation of power, but to somehow gain insight into how to catch him. Maybe the knowledge obtained would help him anticipate the killer's next move.

It was Hager's hypothesis the killer would stay in North Carolina. Hager came to the conclusion after the phone call from him. He was enjoying the modest publicity, and it was obvious he was following the progress of his deeds. Maybe he had somehow wanted to establish a rapport, a relationship with Hager. To make it a friendly game of cat and mouse.

Hager predicted the killer would call again. He believed a call would be made in response to every new release of information about the case. Maybe he could make the killer play into his hands. Utilize the media shrewdly to furnish the killer a reason to call.

When the telephone rang, he automatically hoped the killer was calling again. Before picking up the receiver he checked the caller ID readout.

Number Unknown

Hager's chest hammered. He pushed the *record* button on the tape recorder, hoping to flush out more from the monster.

"SBI, Hager."

"Daddy, it's me." Elizabeth sounded excited.

"Hey, sweetheart! How are you doing?"

Hager reached over and turned off the recorder.

"Great. You'll never guess what happened to me today."

Her voice was ecstatic, like she'd won the lottery.

"What? It must be good from the sound of your voice. What happened?"

"Well, today at school, there was this guy. He was a rep from *Playboy* magazine, and he was recruiting for this 'Girls of the ACC' thing. And he said I was a natural model. And I would probably be in the pictorial, and it pays a lot of money. Isn't that great?"

"Whoa, whoa," she'd spoken so fast, Hager only heard part of what she'd said. "You said some guy from *Playboy* magazine offered to put you in the magazine. What guy?"

"There was this man on campus recruiting girls for *Playboy*, and he said I looked like a natural model and should audition. What do you think?"

"Well, that's great, Elizabeth, but did you say this man was at school? On campus?"

"Yeah, Daddy. He said he was recruiting for a pictorial of the 'Girls of the ACC'."

Hager was suspicious. Not particularly because of the case in which he was immersed, but because he wasn't sure of his reaction to Elizabeth being in *Playboy* magazine.

"Did he approach only you, Elizabeth?"

"Oh, no, Daddy. All the girls were signing up. There must have been hundreds in line at the Student Union."

"Oh, this guy was there with the university's permission."

"I guess so. Aren't you happy for me?"

"Yes I'm happy, honey, but are you sure this guy is legit?"

The excitement had evaporated from her tone.

"I can't believe you, Daddy. He had a display set up and everything. There were pictures and forms to fill out. Do you think he would be allowed on campus if he weren't? Can't you just be happy for me? Or is it because you don't approve. Is that it?"

He could tell she was hurt by his incredulous questions.

"No, sweetheart, that's not it. I'm just looking out for your well-being, that's all. I think it's great. Tell me, what's the guy's name?"

"What's his name? God! You're kidding me right? Please tell me you're kidding."

"No, Elizabeth I'm not kidding. I'd like to know what his name is."

"Why do you want to know his name? Daddy, you're so untrusting of people. Do you think some nut would go to all the trouble of being so obvious. That would be stupid!"

"You're right, but I'd like to have the name just the same, please."

The agent knew many rapists and killers had a superiority complex and would take high risks to make their crimes more exciting. Some criminals tried to outwit people, being obvious because they were expected to be underhanded, thus providing the same response as his daughter's 'that would be stupid!'

"I promise. All I'll do is make sure he's a legitimate rep from the magazine, and I won't say anything else about it."

She was shouting now, and it sounded like she was crying.

"You just don't want me to pose do you? You're such a hypocrite, Daddy! All you men look at those magazines and get your jollies, but if your wives or daughters want to be in it, then Noooo! It's trash then."

"That's not it, Elizabeth. You don't understand. I don't have a problem with you posing. I just want to make sure he's not some psychopath—"

"I am twenty years old, Daddy. I can take care of myself!"

Her voice reminded him of her mother. The same passion. The head-strong attitude was slapping his face from inside the phone. If only her mother were here, he thought. She could talk some sense to her. Make her realize he was only trying to protect her from harm. From monsters like the one he was chasing. He thought about his killer's M.O. and how he was posing as a photographer to get close to his victims.

Would *he* be this bold? Up to then, he had been targeting only strippers, not college students.

Hager knew *Playboy* did pictorials of college girls, and they had to go to the campuses to recruit the models. "Where else?" he said to himself. Maybe this case was getting to him more than he wanted to believe. It was making him paranoid of everyone and everything.

Don't take it out on your daughter. She's responsible. You have to trust her.

Hager knew Elizabeth wouldn't consciously put herself in harm's way, but she was still a very young and impressionable woman. The perfect bait for a crafty predator, like the one he was hunting.

"Look, Elizabeth," he was trying to reassure her he wasn't simply mettling but sincerely concerned. "I promise. Just the name of the guy. That's all. Do it for me, please?"

He sensed the relentment when she sighed. It was like she'd waved a white flag surrendering to his parental wisdom.

"Okay, if it'll make you feel better. I wrote his name down. It's Jeremy Foster, Photographer, *Playboy* Enterprises, Chicago, Illinois."

"And the number?"

Elizabeth sighed and gave him the phone number.

Hager wrote the phone number underneath the name.

"How did you get so much information about this guy? Did he give you a business card?"

"He gave one to Missy and I wrote down his information on a piece of paper. I guess my subconscious told me you'd be asking questions like you are."

The card could be important. Hager already had two of the killer's calling cards. If he could get that one, he could have it compared to the other two.

"Does Missy have the card?"

"I guess so. I think she put it in her purse. You don't want to see the card, too, Daddy?

"Well, I'd like to see it. Ask Missy about it, would you?"

"You never quit do you?"

"I'll never quit being your father, Elizabeth. By the way, do you remember what this guy looked like?"

"Oh, he was about thirty, good-looking, nicely dressed. He had short brown hair. I don't know. He looked like a business man, but without the suit. Just a shirt and slacks."

"You said he had forms to fill out there. What did you have to give?"

"Just my name, age, year at school, major, and a phone number, that was it. Oh, he took a picture, too."

"How did you find out about it?"

"Missy told me. She saw this long line of girls at the Student Union and met me after class. That's when she told me."

"All right, Elizabeth. I'll make a few calls and get back to you. Promise me, you won't do anything until I let you know either way."

"Daddy, don't worry so much. You really need a vacation. Why don't you and Vanessa go somewhere for a romantic weekend?"

Don't you worry about me, honey. Just remember what I said, okay?"

"Okay, I will. I love you, Daddy."

Hager hung up the phone and thought his daughter may have been right about his need for a vacation. She also might have been right about the recruiter from *Playboy*. It was a lot to go through.

"This guy's not that bold," he said to himself. "Anyway, it has something to do with strippers, not college students."

179

For a moment, he began to feel better about it and debated calling Chicago. On the phone he must have sounded like the typical over-protective father to Elizabeth. The despot king and Elizabeth was one of his subjects.

Although during her teen years he consistently monitored her activities from a comfortable distance, the woman she was becoming was frequently displaying her independence. He'd never treated her this way when she was a teenager. All the questions, the cynicism flourishing in their context, casting doubt onto the person he loved the most.

Quickly, his thoughts switched to the man responsible for his increasing harborment of mistrust. His adversary was no werewolf with a repulsive appearance, lurking through the night, attacking his victims by surprise. No, Hager's foe was quite the contrary. By the descriptions given, the man was at least normal looking, and, in fact, he was characterized as being good-looking and charming. He had no need to take his victims by sudden surprise.

Like a Venus fly trap, he lured them closer with a benign appearance and a charismatic bait. But once in his clutches, the harmless creature transformed into the monster he really was, and only then, his victims realized their horrible fate. The man's voice played in his head, and he remembered the smoothness of his tone and imagined him seducing his next victim with his words.

"I'm not going to let that happen to her," he told himself. "Not until this monster is put away am I going to let down my guard."

The indecision to check on the recruiter from *Playboy* gave Hager a headache. He rubbed his temples, feeling the pulsations throbbing in his fingertips. He dug his fingers deeper and massaged, temporarily relieving the pounding pain in his head. From the hall, he heard footsteps on the carpeted floor and jingling of change in the pockets. As the sounds grew closer, he knew it was his partner, and farther away, he heard voices from the lobby. Lloyd entered the office as Hager looked at the clock on the wall, realizing it was time for the task force meeting.

"You ready, Clark?" his partner asked. "Everyone's here."

Hager jumped from his seat. His eyes glimpsed the paper on his desk. The man's name written on it. Not forgetting its importance, he picked it up and folded it into his pocket.

"I'll take care of this later."

16

A S EXPECTED, the meeting of the task force members lasted until seven o'clock that evening. A total of eleven detectives and agents were delegated to participate in the investigation: Sheriff McAdoo and Detective Raeford from Hertford County; Detective Matlin, from Wilmington PD; Detective Jamison, from Greenville PD; Detective Madden, from Greensboro PD; and Detective Peterson, from High Point PD. Assisting the detectives were SBI Agents Moss, from Wilmington; Motsinger, from Greenville; and Gregson, from Greensboro.

They all assembled in the conference room. After the introductions, Hager briefly summarized the four murder cases, and updated the group on the most recent information from Florida, the business cards, and lastly, the telephone call from someone claiming to be the killer received two days ago, on Monday.

The entire collection of lawmen listened to the tape recording of the man and all of them agreed the voice was ordinary and unrecognizable.

Detective Jamison was aware of a college student at East Carolina, who had been charged with offenses relating from cellular telephone cloning and computer hacking. He accepted the assignment of locating the student and interviewing him about any of his customers. It could be a good lead, Hager thought, but the likelihood of him revealing any information about his customers was nil. He could get lucky though. The conference ended and both Hager and Lloyd felt positive about the level of cooperation. All of the officers and agents involved gave the impression of enthusiastic resolve to accomplish their goal and flush the killer into the open where he could be trapped and locked away.

With the clouds of two days of rain safely out of the area, the sky was clear and the stars were glistening high in the sky. The moon was full and its light produced shadows from the trees and buildings. Without the blanket of clouds, whatever warm air that had settled on the ground earlier, had now drifted into the atmosphere causing an extreme drop in temperature. Hager shivered when he walked out to his car after adjourning the meeting. From his mouth, the warm air steamed as he exhaled a deep, cold, refreshing breath of the night, invigorating his head.

Hager smiled and felt a warm feeling as he looked forward to Vanessa's company that evening. As he planned, Hager had invited Vanessa over for dinner. With his amateur gourmet skills, he was going to prepare a simple but tasty chicken dish that hopefully would knock her socks off. And maybe more. Everything to cook the meal awaited him patiently at home in his kitchen. All he had to do was get there.

During the drive home, Hager thought again about his daughter's news. He touched his left front pants pocket and the squeezed paper containing the name and phone number of the rep from *Playboy*. Maybe he wouldn't have to call Chicago to confirm the existence of this representative of the magazine. Certainly, if he were an agent of the magazine, his name would appear in the credits of all issues and the site of the name Elizabeth gave him would surely erase some doubt in his mind. To his left, Hager saw the lights of a Circle K store and decided to grab a copy of the current issue. He needed a six-pack of Ice House, too.

Hager pulled his car into a parking space to the left of the front door facing a pay telephone. A kid about Elizabeth's age, was using the phone, seemingly immersed in a meaningful conversation. The only thing which overshadowed his baggy pants, which looked to be twice his size, was the flagrantly bright color of the Tommy Hilfiger jacket he was wearing. Unaware of Hager's presence, the kid continued with his discussion, hugging the phone as Hager walked by.

Hager pushed open the glass door and gave a smiling glance at the clerk, an older black man with salt and pepper hair and gold rimmed glasses. Out of the corner of his eye, he observed another kid, about the same age and manner of dress as the phone hugger, but much taller and bulkier, carefully scanning the cooler where the *expensive* wines, like M-D 20/20, Wild Irish Rose, and Boone's Farm were kept. Not particularly worried about the kid's age, as he could possibly be 21, Hager thought it peculiar that the kid was just standing there mulling over his selection.

"Was he up to something else?" Hager asked himself.

When Hager opened the glass door of the cooler to get the six-pack, he appeared in the kid's peripheral vision and detected the furtive glance of preparation to commit a crime. Hager stood with the cooler door open, cold air flowing from inside, appearing to ponder his selection, like the kid, but looking to meet the kid's eyes, signifying he was being watched. But the kid never looked over, and he rubbed his crew-cut head nervously. Another sign of guilt: the "No-look rule."

Impatient, Hager made his selection, closed the door, and slowly walked to the counter where he was third in line behind a woman with a toddler, and a UPS driver, apparently finished for the day. The clerk was ringing up a credit sale for gas. Hager scanned the magazine rack behind the counter where all the "girlie" magazines were kept out of reach of children. He had temporarily forgotten about the potential shoplifter in the back of the store and concentrated on his place in line. When he remembered, out of the corner of his eye, he saw the kid easing his way along the aisle closest to the exit, heading for the door. A bulge that wasn't present before, now evident in his jacket, indicating he'd finally made his selection.

Standing in line, holding a six-pack of Ice House, eagerly anticipating Vanessa's arrival at his house shortly, Hager battled with his perception of duty. Should he involve himself in a misdemeanor theft at the expense of being late for Vanessa? Or should he do what he was sworn to do? Which was to uphold the law. Hager shook his head when he decided the latter and put his beer on the floor, keeping an eye on the kid, who was now at the door. His heart started to pound.

Hager quickly moved forward and shouted to the clerk.

"You got a shoplifter!"

The kid pushed open the door, cradling the bulge in his jacket. He darted to his right, and Hager, reaching for his badge tucked inside his sport coat, pushed open the door, just in time to grab a firm hold of the right sleeve of the denim jacket. When he latched onto the kid and stood face to face with him, Hager realized the kid had four or five inches on him and outweighed him by forty or so pounds. The kid's strength was unmistakable as he didn't move a lot when Hager's right hand snatched his sleeve.

"Police," Hager said, as he put his badge in the kid's face.

Before he uttered any other words, the kid twisted sharply away.

"What the fuck are you doing?" he clamored, still holding the prize in his jacket.

When he twisted, Hager felt the kid's power, and was pulled forward off balance. Realizing one hand wasn't nearly enough to control him, Hager shoved his badge holder in his pocket and grabbed hold of the denim, pulling him back.

"Stop, you're under arrest," Hager commanded, adrenaline surging through his body.

In a micro-second, the kid turned, facing Hager, and with

one arm, shoved the agent backward, causing one of the bottles of wine to fall intact to the ground. Being forced backward and still holding on, Hager pulled the kid toward him—something he didn't expect and took him off-balance. The second bottle cracked open when it hit the concrete, pouring out the red liquid. Still pulling, Hager gained enough leverage and impetus to execute an improvised judo-type hip throw, sending the big kid crashing to the concrete.

The kid hit the ground hard with a thud and a gasp of air. Luckily, he landed on his back because another bottle of wine remained concealed in his coat and would have smashed had he landed on his chest. Hager dropped to one knee next to the thief. While the kid struggled to catch his breath, the agent scooped up an arm, and pulled it behind the kid's back. Hager reached for the handcuffs tucked in the back of his slacks.

With both the thief's wrists cuffed, Hager looked inside the store at the spectators in shock at what they had witnessed. The clerk was holding the phone to his ear, hopefully making a call to the police, but the bystanders just stood still in silent amazement.

"Appreciate all the help!" Hager said frustratedly, trying to catch his breath.

Hager also saw that the other kid—the phone hugger—had mysteriously disappeared. Was he in on this caper? No one would ever know.

Patrol officers from Raleigh PD arrived minutes later in response to a "fight call" at the store. When they arrived, Hager produced his badge and recounted the events leading to the scuffle. Hager had left the remaining bottle of Wild Irish Rose in the thief's jacket for proof positive of his crime.

Fortunately for Hager, the officers took custody of the 18 year old, and charged him with Misdemeanor Larceny, listing Hager only as a witness. The Raleigh officers told Hager that since he used force to make the arrest, some paperwork would have to be completed on their end. Hager promised them he would send a written memo through his agency about the altercation.

Hager returned inside the store, graciously applauded by the store's clerk. Refusing the clerk's proposal of the beer and magazine "on the house," Hager made his purchase and jotted down the clerk's name and address to use as a witness in his report.

Ten minutes later, Hager arrived home. On the back of a chair in the living room he placed his jacket and tie, his neck feeling free from the constriction of the collar. He felt a burning sensation on his knee and inspected it.

"Damn!" he said, seeing a hole in the wool, and the faint redness of the abrasion. "Those were a hundred dollar pair of slacks!"

It was chilly in the house. A fire was a good thought, but the two days of rain had drenched the wood he stored in the back yard near the storage shed. He would have to settle for Duraflame logs. Just as well, he thought. He didn't have a lot of time to devote to constructing a fire as he wanted to get dinner started before Vanessa's arrival and the logs didn't require much work to ignite.

After putting a match to the paper covering the logs, Hager walked through the living room, picked up the magazine and headed toward the kitchen. Roscoe, his old friend, emerged from the stairs. Evidently, he'd been resting on Hager's bed and snorted a "hello" to his master. Hager crouched to pet the dog and grabbed hold of the loose skin around his face and shook it as a greeting.

Standing up with his mind on dinner, he suddenly stopped as he realized he'd forgotten to put on some music. A need to set a mood, a little ambiance for a romantic evening. He placed his three favorite Jazz CDs in the player: David Sanborn, Chuck Mangione, and Herbie Hancock, and turned the volume up so he could hear it in the kitchen while he worked.

Hager was assembling the elements of his version of an extremely amorous interlude. The components: Jazz playing on the CD player, a fire crackling in the fireplace, a succulent dinner by candlelight, and a good bottle of wine, sharing it all with a special woman. Hager was still not exactly sure if he really loved Vanessa. He did know that although they had been involved with each other for almost a year, he still nervously anticipated her arrival, wanting to see her face, to look into her eyes which seemed to sparkle at the very sight of him. The battle inside his head waged on. He couldn't help but think of he and Kelly spending the same kind of evening together, even after the birth of Elizabeth. Those many nights they had sat by a warm fire, wrapped in a blanket with a glass of brandy, her eyes shining in the light of the flames from the fire. He remembered discussing their most intimate feelings, their troubles and heartaches, joys and happiness, sometimes laughing, sometimes crying, but all the time holding each other, feeling the warmth of their love for one another.

The love he had felt for Kelly ran so deep, he honestly felt he was imagining it. Could anyone be so much in love with a woman as he was with her? How could it be so strong, and not seem to wither as time passed? There was no answer but to feel truly blessed they had found one another and lived in happiness until mortality reared its ugly head.

These feelings were what Hager faced and battled in his mind. With Vanessa, it felt the same as it did with Kelly, and this was the issue of the struggle. Was he truly in love with Vanessa? Or was he actually replacing Kelly with her to use as a "stand-in", continuing to live in a fantasy world of love and jubilation?

If it was, how could he tell? What did it matter? Kelly was gone and Vanessa was there. Did it matter he might be living a dream that never seemed to end? To love someone through another person. What would be so wrong if it was true? Was it fair to Vanessa for Hager to constantly think about his late wife?

For him, it was like he was still with Kelly, and nothing had changed. The dinners, the dancing, the intimate moments they shared, he subconsciously believed it was Kelly and found himself almost calling her name because it sounded so right. Vanessa picked up on the hard sound of the consonant as he stopped before it escaped his mouth, and it seemed to hurt her feelings. Undoubtedly, he understood her pain and he saw it in her eyes, but Vanessa took it in stride—not an obstacle to overcome—but like the weather, it was something she had to accept and hope would improve the next day.

The hypnotic sounds of Sanborn's sax faded in the back of his mind, but grew louder as the images of Kelly disappeared into neverland. Back in reality, there was a meal to be prepared and he was late. He donned his familiar white apron, looking truly like a chef but without the silly hat.

Tonight, he was going to cook a chicken dish from a recipe he'd seen in one of the cooking magazines to which he subscribed. The magazine lay on the counter next to the *Playboy*, and he opened it to the page where the recipe was located. He quickly scanned the list of ingredients and pulled the necessary implements, spices and condiments on the counter and began his preparations. From the refrigerator, he pulled out the platter of boneless chicken breasts along with an Ice House beer. He twisted off the cap, gulped a refreshing amount of the beer, and placed the meat in the skillet with some olive oil. Hager chopped some shallots while the chicken breasts seared in the oil. Their vapor burned his eyes, bringing tears.

While he waited for the chicken to finish its first stage of cooking, he poured a box of long grain and wild rice into a pot of boiling water to steam; and into the vegetable steamer, he lined the stalks of fresh asparagus into neat rows. Another gulp of the beer, he returned to the skillet and removed the meat still sizzling, throwing tiny beads of hot oil onto the aluminum range cover. He scraped the shallots into the skillet, along with some additional olive oil. The aroma was delightful. As they sautéed he finished the beer and opened the *Playboy*.

He flipped through the first few pages until he reached the list of credits. Down the hierarchy of names, his eyes scanned until they found the name of Jeremy Foster. Foster was listed as a contributing photographer. That was odd, he thought. He didn't think photographers recruited the models as well, but Hager wasn't at all familiar with the business of publishing a magazine filled with pictures of beautiful women. Curious, he found himself turning the pages looking for Foster's work.

The first pictorial was an article about a former agent with the CIA who decided to pose nude and tell her story about working as a "spy." The woman was fully clothed, standing in front of the Capitol building. He immediately noticed she resembled Elizabeth. A little older version, but very beautiful.

He thought about Elizabeth being in the magazine and how she would pose. Hager had heard the models were paid according to how much skin they showed, and he didn't know if she planned on posing fully nude if she were selected. He had mixed feelings about the thought of Elizabeth exposing herself to millions of men. But, after all, there should be no shame in the human body in its natural form, and he was proud to have such a beautiful daughter.

Playboy is, above all others, the classiest of the adult male periodicals, and he knew if she did appear, then she would be depicted in a respectable manner—showing only the pure loveliness of her body. At the bottom of the page was the name of Jeremy Foster again, and his mind started to feel assured it was just his paranoia talking to Elizabeth earlier. He paged through the spread of photos of the woman in various dignified positions, but suddenly remembered the shallots in the skillet.

He stirred the shallots, poured in a can of chicken broth, some dry white wine, and waited for the liquid to simmer. The mixture simmering in the skillet emanated an aroma that was better than before, and he inhaled, anticipating the flavor.

He didn't hear the door open, but when Roscoe scampered to the front door after a soft bark, Hager realized Vanessa had arrived. A smile came to his face as he heard the clacking of her heels on the hardwood floors in the foyer, coming closer to him in the kitchen. He closed his eyes and tried to visualize what she was wearing. From the sound of her steps, she'd dressed casually, but elegant.

"Clark?" she said.

"In here. In the kitchen."

He felt her presence as she emerged from the doorway and he turned to see her bright eyes and smile. It melted him to see her. She was so beautiful. He was correct in his assumption of her attire. She wore a red cardigan sweater over a white blouse and black velour leggings.

They fell into each other's arms, and instantly he noticed her opulent perfume. Like her, it was soft, but with a hint of what he thought was chocolate. It was new, he concluded, different from her usual scent. And he liked it. Their lips met in a long passionate kiss, and she squeezed him tightly, as if they hadn't seen each other in weeks instead of days. Her hands cupped his cheeks and she pulled away, her thumbs wiping off the transferred lipstick from his mouth.

"Umm," he said as he inhaled her perfume.

"You smell good. Is it new?"

She smiled at his recognition of the day's purchase.

"Yes it is. Do you really like it? It's called Kashmir. I got it today."

"Oooo," he leaned and kissed her neck. "Yes, I like it. You smell good enough to eat," he laughed and she moaned.

He looked at her hair. It was different. The same style, but something was different about it. There were small hints of blonde perfectly mixed with the chestnut brown color of her hair.

"Did you do something to your hair? God, it looks good."

She blushed and held him tighter, then combed her fingers through it.

"Yeah, I had some highlights added to it. I thought it would brighten my face a little. You like?"

"Brighten that face? It already glows. I think it looks great."

She was radiant at his compliment.

"Speaking of smelling good," she inhaled. "What are you fixing? It smells wonderful."

He turned to the oven and picked up the spoon and stirred the liquid more.

"It's called Tarragon Chicken. Boneless chicken breasts covered with a sauce made with shallots, chicken broth, white wine, Dijon mustard, sour cream, and some tarragon. Doesn't it sound good?"

"Hmm, Hmm," she said eagerly. "And what else?"

He reached for the pot, lifted the lid and steam rushed out.

"Wild rice, courtesy of Uncle Ben. And steamed asparagus. I hope I made enough sauce to spoon over the asparagus, too."

She kissed him again and squeezed him, her chin resting on his shoulder. She noticed the *Playboy* on the counter.

"Clark, I know it's been a couple of days, but I didn't think you'd resort to that."

She pointed to the counter.

His eyes traced the direction of her finger to the magazine.

"Yeah, well, you know, a man can only go for so long," he said, and he held her tighter, pulling her hips closer to his. "But now that you're here."

She slapped him gently on the shoulder.

"Ha, Ha. Very funny."

He kissed her again and he felt her lips, so soft and wet. Her tongue gently moved against his and he loved the way she held his head and rubbed her fingers around his ears and down his neck. A person could really tell how the other felt by the way she kissed him. Like the old song said, *It's in his kiss,* but of course, it was in hers and he hoped she detected the same thing.

"Okay, that's enough," she said, "I'll let you finish dinner." She picked up the magazine and walked into the living room.

"Really, I was just looking at it because—"

"I know. Liz called me and she and I went shopping. She told me all about it. She told me what you said. How you made up some reason to check out this guy because you didn't want her posing nude."

"That's not true, Vanessa. I didn't make up some reason. I have a very good reason to be suspicious. There's a man out there pretending to be a photographer, but he's not shooting anything; he's strangling."

Vanessa didn't respond. She opened the magazine.

"I thought this guy you were looking for was only killing strippers."

Hager stirred the sauce more, then opened the refrigerator door and grabbed another beer. "That's right, but—"

"Clark, it looks like this guy's legit. That's a helluva lot of effort to put—"

"I know. I know. Elizabeth said the same thing. You want a beer?"

She nodded and he opened another bottle and walked into the living room where Vanessa was seated on the couch.

"I guess I worry about her, you know? Anyway, the guy is a photographer for the magazine. He's in the credits and he shot the first pictorial there. The one I was looking at before."

She turned the pages to the article.

"Wow! She's beautiful. Did you see the resemblance? She looks like Liz."

"Yeah, I saw it," he grumbled.

"Clark, how do you really feel about her posing in the magazine?"

"I don't know. I really don't know what to think. You know, she's my daughter!"

"Yes, Clark, but she's a beautiful girl. You should be proud she could be chosen."

"Yeah, I guess so. I just want to make sure this guy is on the level. Other than that, I don't care," he shrugged his shoulders. "She's twenty years old. What am I gonna do, ground her?"

Vanessa smiled and took a drink from the bottle, and Hager walked back into the kitchen to finish the meal.

"Do you need any help?"

"No, you just relax. You've had a hard day, with shopping and getting your hair done and all."

They both laughed.

By candlelight, and with the light sounds of the jazz playing on the stereo, and the fire burning in the fireplace, they ate the meal, drank wine, talked, laughed, drank more wine, and looked into each other's eyes. With every passing minute, their feelings grew stronger, their intimacy deepened.

The food was delicious. With his belly full, the wine made Hager sleepy eyed, and he yawned as he helped Vanessa clear the table.

"You've done enough already, Clark. Why don't you just go in there and relax while I do the dishes."

"I can help. It's no problem. Besides, if I go in there and sit in the recliner, with the way I'm feeling, I'll be asleep before you're through."

"You know the rules, sweetie. You cook. I clean up the mess. It's only fair. Now go make yourself useful. Why don't you check on the fire?"

"I know. I'll go upstairs and take a shower while you do the dishes."

"That sounds good. You get good and clean for me."

He smiled and hugged her from behind as she stood over the sink rinsing the dishes. Gently, he placed a sensual kiss on her throat, and tickled her skin with his tongue. She closed her eyes and trembled. He smelled her new perfume again, and it was so lightly sweet.

"You still smell good enough to eat."

"What do you think we're having for dessert?" she said, her lips together, trying to hold back from laughing.

"Bring on the whipped cream!" he said pressing his crotch against her back side.

His heart was pounding when he got to the top of the stairs and into his bedroom. Part of his excitement was because of the anticipation of *dessert*, but mostly, because he'd sprinted up the stairs like a teenager chasing the telephone. Hager hurriedly disrobed, leaving his clothes in a pile on the floor. As he looked at himself in the mirror, he realized he was still in pretty good shape for a forty six year old man. At six foot and hovering around 200 pounds, he'd proven himself still a worthy opponent that evening with his victory over the double X sized 18 year old.

No great accomplishment, but more of a moral victory than anything else.

It let him know he still had some element of toughness. Being absent from street work for almost fifteen years, Hager couldn't remember the last time he got into a physical altercation with someone. All he knew it was when he worked in Greensboro. Hager relied more on his smarts, not his fists, to gain the advantage over people, and it had become almost a trademark for him.

People told him he looked much younger and he thought it was because his hair had only a tiny bit of gray and his face bore no noticeable wear. In his spare time, what little he had, he tried to utilize the small fitness room he'd built in the basement, but in the past few months since the holidays, he hadn't found much time for it.

The hot shower invigorated him, despite the burning of the abrasion on his knee. He was no longer sleepy. With all the day's dirt washed down the drain he felt clean. The mirror was completely fogged and a cloud of steam floated through the air and drifted out the open door of the bathroom. The air outside the shower was colder, and he covered himself with the towel, his body still faintly dripping with water.

Feeling aroused, he slipped on a pair of silk boxer shorts, one of several given to him by Vanessa for Christmas. It felt good against his rough skin and as his hands slid along the smooth fabric next to his thighs, he felt prickly hairs from his legs protruding through the pores of silk.

From his closet, he retrieved a pair of old blue jeans, as comfortable as they had always been. He sprayed some Armani cologne on his chest and neck and pulled a long-sleeved gray thermal top over his head. He put on a pair of socks, brushed his teeth and hair, completing his repertoire and eagerly walked downstairs with Roscoe at his heels.

Downstairs, he saw Vanessa sitting on the floor in front of the fireplace, looking at the *Playboy* magazine. A wine glass was in her right hand and she used her left hand to stabilize herself as she scanned the pages.

Seeing her there stopped Hager in his tracks. In the light and from that particular angle, the woman was Kelly. Stunned at the resemblance, he gazed at her. She looked up, realizing he was staring.

"What's wrong, Clark?"

"I was going to get my wine glass from the kitchen."

"I brought it in here, silly man."

He turned back to the living room and saw another glass and a wine bottle sitting on the hearth, the light from the fire shining through the wine giving it a brilliant golden color.

"What 'cha doin, beautiful?"

She took a drink from her glass.

"I'm just reading the article about this woman who was in the CIA. She really does look a lot like Liz."

Hager grabbed the other glass and sat down next to her, his back leaning against the front of the couch.

"I thought we already talked about that. I feel better since I saw his name printed in the magazine."

He was still shocked and could have sworn it was Kelly sitting there. *Maybe it was a ghost.*

"Yeah, but you're not satisfied are you?"

He sat, deep in thought about the ghost.

"Clark?"

"Oh, uh, what, honey?"

"You're not satisfied, are you?"

He drank from his glass.

"About what?

She was frustrated and she sighed.

"About the *Playboy* guy. You're not satisfied, are you?"

"I guess I feel better, but something's just not right. I can't put my finger on it though."

He took another sip of wine, laid his head back and closed his eyes. He could feel the heat of the fire on his body and he heard the tones of Mangione's flugelhorn from the speakers.

It had to have been a ghost.

"Hmmm," she moaned nuzzling his chest. "You smell good. Is that the Armani I gave you for Christmas?"

"Yep," he said as she climbed onto his lap.

She wrapped her arms around his neck and kissed him.

"Forget about the photographer and kiss me."

Their lips met for a long tender kiss which seemed to drain everything out of him. His tension subsided and his body was overwhelmed with warmth. Their mouths parted and her hand reached under the couch behind his back. She pulled out a can of whipped cream, discharged a little bit and dabbed some on her finger, smiling devilishly. She slowly licked her finger, her eyes never leaving his.

"I'm ready for dessert," she said happily.

17

WHEN HAGER PULLED into the parking lot of SBI Headquarters, it was 10 a.m. Lloyd, who had a doctor's appointment, wouldn't be there until about 10:30. As he passed Judy's desk, she was standing at one of the filing cabinets placing folders that were stacked about a foot high on top of the cabinet. Hager greeted her cheerfully.

"Good morning, Judy," and she quickly hopped over to her desk, pulled a piece of pink message paper from the pad, and handed it to him. He noticed Judy was smiling more than normal and her face gleamed.

"You certainly are the cheerful one today."

She smiled again, looking like she had something to report.

"I have very good reason to be happy, thank you."

"Well, what's the news?"

Judy closed the drawer and turned to Hager, her face bright with excitement.

"I'm going to be a grandmother!"

"Are you serious? Hey, Judy, that's wonderful!"

Hager leaned over and gave her a friendly hug.

"Is it Kevin or Nina?"

Judy had both a son and a daughter who were married.

"Nina," she said proudly. "I am so thrilled. This is my first, you know."

Hager smiled, glad for her good fortune. It was especially fortuitous for Judy since she hadn't had much to be happy about since her husband passed away two years ago. Her two children, both of whom lived in the Raleigh area, were her only family, and she was very close to them.

"Hey! Let's have a celebration. We'll take you out to lunch. Anywhere you choose."

Judy grinned happily.

"That sounds great, but you don't have to do that."

"Of course we do! Don't be silly. This is a special day for you. You should be treated to something good."

After finishing the congratulations to Judy, Hager walked back to his office feeling good about the day. He was truly glad for his secretary. It had been months since he last saw her face smile so brightly. Her only solace after the passing of her husband from cancer was the two children. Undoubtedly, she was extremely proud of both of them with the number of pictures and momentos surrounding her desk. Her eldest Kevin was a Raleigh police officer, and her daughter Nina owned her own flower shop.

Hager's message was from John Ramos asking him to call *ASAP* but the number wasn't the same number he'd called before. He recognized the area code 305 as being from Miami. As he sat down, his heart beat faster in anticipation of a break in the case. Maybe the name on the card somehow provided a true lead, which was something they desperately needed. Hager quickly picked up the phone and dialed the number. He glanced down at the time the message was received; it was 9:45 and he hoped Ramos would still be there.

A man answered in a casual tone, "Florida Department of Law Enforcement, Agent Miller speaking."

"Yes, John Ramos, please."

There was silence. A few seconds later he heard Ramos's Latin accent.

"This is Ramos."

"John, this is Clark Hager. I got your message. What's up?"

"Hey, Clark, good, I'm glad you called back so quickly. I've got some good news. I'm down here in the Miami office with Ronny Cooper. We found him at his studio this morning. He is a photographer. And guess what? He knows someone from North Carolina. And it gets better. The guy he knows is also a photographer."

"What's his name? Where does he live?"

"The guy's name is Mark Kellogg. He lives in Wilmington. They met at some photography convention in Atlanta last year so I asked him what Kellogg looks like, and he said he was kind of short and stocky, wore glasses and had black hair but was partially bald. I knew that didn't sound like your guy, but he said there were a bunch of photographers at the convention. This guy Kellogg may know who your killer is."

Hager was disappointed with the description of Kellogg. It was, however, the first good lead they had gotten since the case began.

"What about Cooper? What's he look like?"

"Not even close. He's confined to a wheel chair. Wounded in Viet Nam."

"Oh well. I tried. He doesn't know anyone else who might fit the description, from Florida perhaps?"

"I asked him if he knew of anyone else like that and he said he knew a lot of people who fit the description of your guy, but none of them were photographers."

"How about any killers?" Hager joked. "Does he have an address or phone number for Kellogg?"

"Yeah, you ready?"

Hager wrote down the information Ramos gave him, which were the phone numbers and addresses for both Cooper and Kellogg, and ended the conversation, thanking the Florida agent for his help. He decided to call Bill Matlin in Wilmington to relay the new piece of information for him to check out. He looked at the clock, seeing it was 10:45, 9:45 Chicago time and decided to call there first to check on the name of the photographer from *Playboy.*

The number he called connected him to the switchboard of *Playboy* Enterprises Incorporated and the voice of an attractive sounding woman played on the automated connector. Hager hated the automated switchboards. He preferred to talk to the operator, so instead of miring through all the departments, he pushed "0" for the operator. After asking for Jeremy Foster, he was transferred, and he listened to soft music playing in the background of an advertisement for the business and the sensual voice of a woman talking. The commercial quickly ended and a man picked up the line.

"Photography," the man said.

"Yes, Jeremy Foster, please."

"Jeremy Foster? He's on assignment. Can I help you with something?"

"This is Special Agent Clark Hager of the North Carolina State Bureau of Investigation. Can you tell me what kind of assignment Mr. Foster is on?"

"North Carolina State Bureau of Investigation?" the man asked surprisedly. "I'm sorry, sir, but I can't release that kind of information," he said in a snotty tone.

Hager would try to be nice. "Then can you put me through to someone who can. It's important."

The man sighed in the same brusque tone. "Sir, you don't understand. That information cannot be released to anyone. Not even the FBI."

Hager was losing his patience.

"I'm not the FBI, sir, but if you like, I can call some of their agents and they can come and visit you personally. Just let me talk to someone who's in charge there. You've got to have a boss."

"You don't have to be rude," the man sniveled. "I'll switch you to Leslie Monroe, the photography director."

"Thank you," Hager said emphatically with a glimmer of sarcasm. "You think I'm rude? I should've let my partner deal with you," he muttered as the music returned.

A woman picked up and Hager asked for Leslie Monroe. "This is she. How can I help you?"

"Ms. Monroe, I'm Special Agent Clark Hager with the North Carolina State Bureau of Investigation. I'm investigating a series of murders here, and I was wondering if you could give me some information on one of your photographers."

"Murders? Where did you say you were calling from?"

"North Carolina, I'm an agent with the SBI."

"Whoa! We don't get too many calls from you folks."

Her voice was strong and professional, befitting her title, unlike the snotty asshole he talked to before.

"We can't release a lot of information about our employees. I hope you understand. But I'll try to help you as much as I can. What's the photographer's name?"

Hager temporarily breathed a sigh of relief, assuming she was willing to help.

"It's Jeremy Foster."

"Jeremy? Yes Jeremy Foster works for the magazine. He's one of our best photographers. What would he have to do with a murder case?"

"I don't know that, ma'am. That's what I'm trying to figure out. You see, I was told he's on assignment, but the guy before I spoke to you said he couldn't say what kind of assignment he is on."

"That's true, Agent Hager. He can't. But that still doesn't answer my question of what Jeremy would have to do with a murder case."

Okay, lady. You don't answer my questions. I won't answer yours.

"Ms. Monroe, I can't elaborate on any of the details of my investigation. All I'm asking for is your help in telling me what kind of assignment he's on. If you can't tell me that, can you tell me what kind of assignment he's *not* on?"

She hesitated.

"I guess so."

"Is his assignment recruiting girls at college campuses here for a 'Girls of the ACC' pictorial?"

Hager waited and heard the woman shuffling papers on her desk.

"No, that's not it. We're not scheduled for another college issue until the fall. No, Jeremy is out of the country doing a photo shoot." Her voice grew more curious.

"Where did you say this was happening?"

Hager's heart was pounding and his palms started sweating.

"In Chapel Hill, North Carolina. There is someone there posing as Jeremy Foster and recruiting girls at the University of North Carolina."

"Agent Hager, I'd like to find out more about this. This is very serious!"

He wanted to get off the phone, the thumping in his chest became stronger and his hands started trembling.

Warn Elizabeth! was his only thought.

"I know that, but I've got to make some calls. I promise to get back to you."

"Sir. Agent Hag—"

He hung up the phone, his hands continued to tremble, his palms sweating, his heart racing. Quickly, he picked up the phone and looked at his clock on the wall. It was 10:55. Elizabeth would probably be in class.

"Lloyd!" he shouted as he dialed the number.

Lloyd ran back to the office after hearing Hager's urgent summon.

"Clark, what is it?"

Hager waited as the phone rang, ignoring Lloyd's question. He nervously tapped his fingers on the desk as the answering machine picked up the phone. He slammed the receiver down.

"Damn! She's not there! She must be in class!"

Lloyd had a worried look on his face and Judy peeked her head in behind Lloyd.

"Clark, what the Hell's the matter?" Lloyd asked.

Trying to think, Hager jumped from the chair and began to pace the floor of his office.

"The photographer, you know, the one from *Playboy*."

Lloyd nodded.

"He's bogus. A fake."

Lloyd raised his eyebrows in shock.

"You're kidding?"

"Oh dear," Judy whispered.

"Hell no, I'm not kidding! I called *Playboy*. The *real* Jeremy Foster is on assignment somewhere else."

Hager's face was red, and he frantically stalked around the room, trying to figure out what to do.

"Lloyd, we gotta go to Chapel Hill and warn Elizabeth."

"Look Clark. I'll go to Chapel Hill. You keep trying to reach Elizabeth on the phone."

Lloyd spun around and almost toppled over Judy, who was still standing behind him. Hager felt hot, and his tie started constricting around his neck. He unbuttoned his collar and yanked loose the knot. Hager picked up the phone again and pushed the redial button.

The phone rang and Hager whispered, "Come on. Pick up, pick up. Someone please pick up."

He cursed the fact that Elizabeth wouldn't carry the pager he'd bought for her. She told him she didn't wear it because she didn't want to be bothered while she was in class; but Hager believed she thought her dad had gotten it just to keep up with her.

The answering machine came on again and he heard the voices of his daughter and her roommate Jen wording a simultaneous greeting with some unrecognizable music playing in the background.

Hi, Liz and Jen can't come to the phone right now. Leave your name and number after the beep and we'll get back to you as soon as we can. Thanks and have a great day!

He implored into the phone, "Elizabeth? Jen? Pick up if you're there. It's Dad."

Hager waited for a few seconds, then put down the phone.

"What the Hell am I thinking? I didn't leave a message."

He pushed the redial again, this time it rang longer and he guessed it was because the answering machine tape had to recycle. The recorded message came on again and after the tone Hager started, "Elizabeth, this is dad—"

"Hello? Hello? Mr. Hager, hold on, I have to turn off the machine."

It was Jen's voice. Hager breathed a sigh of relief.

"Go ahead, Mr. Hager."

She sounded sleepy.

"Jen, is Elizabeth there?"

She yawned, "No, Mr. Hager. She had a ten o'clock class and then she said something about meeting this guy from *Playboy* for lunch at eleven. She said she was one of the girls selected to be in the magazine. Isn't that great?"

Hager seemed to die at that moment, although his heart was still beating, and he was still breathing, but he felt like he was going to die. The clock on the wall read 11:00 and he could hear his heart pounding like a bass drum in his chest. To calm his nerves, he took a deep breath.

"Jen, it's very important," he tried to sound calm. "Tell me exactly where she was supposed to meet him."

"She said they were going to go to the Wicked Burrito on Franklin Street. To talk about some preliminary photos. Why? What's wrong? Is she in some kind of trouble?"

"I can't go into it right now, Jen, but if you hear from her, tell her to stay *away* from him. He's not from *Playboy*. Have her page me right away. Got it?"

"Yes, sir. Bye," she said in a worried tone.

Hager ended the call without returning the receiver and quickly dialed Lloyd's cellular phone. The Wicked Burrito was a Mexican restaurant on Franklin Street near the campus. Lloyd picked up on the first ring as if he were expecting Hager to call.

"Lloyd, get to the Wicked Burrito on Franklin Street. She's supposed to meet him there. You remember where it is?"

"Yeah, I remember when we met Liz there last fall."

"Where are you?"

Hager could hear the siren in the background.

"I'm almost to 54. About twenty minutes away."

"Floor it, Lloyd. You do what you gotta do. I think this may be our boy. That's my baby, Lloyd. I'm gonna call Chapel Hill PD to see if they have anyone close. Then I'll be on my way."

"You got it, Clark. You can count on me."

Again, Hager disconnected the phone while keeping hold of the receiver, and he pushed his speed dial for the Chapel Hill Police Department. As the phone rang, Hager heard the other line ring but he knew Judy would pick it up.

"Don't talk too fast," he ordered himself. "You've got to stay in control. Everything's gonna be all right."

When the dispatcher picked up Hager identified himself and said it was an emergency. He asked for the closest police car to respond to the Wicked Burrito on Franklin Street to locate his daughter. He gave the dispatcher a description of Elizabeth and her car, and then told them she may be with a white male, who was a suspect in multiple homicides. Judy appeared at the door to Hager's office. She had a terrified look on her face.

"What is it?" he shouted.

She pointed at the phone. Her hand was trembling.

"You have a call. I think you'd better take it."

Her voice was shaky and her mouth quivered.

Hager still had the dispatcher on the line, who was trying to ask him a question. Seeing the look on her face, he couldn't become any more fearful, but a feeling of dread overwhelmed his body.

"Who is it?"

"The man said it was concerning your daughter."

She cupped her hands over her mouth and her eyes began to tear.

Hager's heart stopped beating, but he spoke into the phone in a stoic tone.

"Right. Get them there as quickly as possible."

He returned the phone and saw the red light flashing on the

display, indicating a call holding. Not wanting to pick it up, he wiped the perspiration from his upper lip and wiped his sweaty hands on his pants. He had a sickening feeling. He knew who was calling. He had heard the smooth voice before. It was ingrained in his mind after listening to it over and over and over. Decisively, he picked up the phone.

Nothing. Only a dial tone. He looked to the other lines and they were all off.

"Where did he go? He's not there. What did he say?"

Judy could see the frightened look of despair on Hager's face.

"All he said was that he needed to speak to you and it was about your daughter."

Hager closed his eyes and covered them with his hands. Judy crept closer and placed her shaky hand on his shoulder.

Suddenly, his hands left his face.

"Did he say who he was?"

"I asked him and he said you would know."

"Shit!"

Hager spun around and snatched his car keys off the desk.

"If he calls aga—"

The phone rang again and Hager jumped and picked it up before the first ring ended.

"Hager!" he shouted.

"She's coming to see me, Hager. Did you know that?"

It was him. There was no mistaking the smooth inflection, but this time it was breathier. Hager heard some music in the background.

He tried to say something, but his mouth went dry, like he'd swallowed sand causing his throat to swell.

Finally, he blurted, "You sonofabitch! You lay one hand on her—"

"Clark!" the man shouted and then he said matter-of-factly, "I hope you told her you loved her the last time you talked to her."

The phone clicked and the line disconnected.

"What!"

Realizing he'd hung up, he slammed the phone down and shouted, "Fuck!" and sprinted past Judy, out of the office, the door slamming as he ran through it.

Panting and out of breath from the run, Hager reached his Crown Victoria and screeched out of the parking lot. With his blue strobe light on the dash, he flicked the siren switch and stomped on the accelerator down Old Garner Road and onto Interstate 40, heading west, driving like a maniac.

Maneuvering in and out of traffic on the highway, Hager shouted obscenities at the cars who wouldn't give right of way to him. At a hectic pace, he weaved the car in between the other motorists, and out of the congested area, and into more open road. Staying in the far left lane, Hager looked down at his speedometer and the needle was stationary at 125 miles per hour. Due to his speed, the white lane dividers looked like one continuous white line, and the trees streaked by in his peripheral vision.

Oblivious to the sound of his siren and only to what was ahead of him, he noticed a State Highway Patrol car in his rearview mirror. The familiar low profile blue light bar on the roof was flashing. His gas pedal was crammed to the floor, and Hager was sweating profusely soaking the back of his shirt. When the trooper flashed his headlights, Hager concluded it may be an escort for him to Chapel Hill, and he pulled to the right to let the trooper pass. The car pulled aside Hager's car, and the trooper eagerly waved for him to follow. Hager moved back into the left lane after the black and silver car passed and continued on his journey.

"Judy must have called them," Hager said.

The two cars speeded onto NC 54. The cars they neared moved over obediently at the looming lights and siren display. Although not as fast as he was going on the interstate, Hager's speedometer stayed around 90 for most of the way, except for navigating the curves and the temporary slowing to avoid other traffic.

His thoughts turned to Elizabeth. Vivid images of her streaked through his mind. She sitting on his lap, telling her stories, kissing her goodnight, the hugs, the kisses, the pouty grins, the first steps, her first words, the pictures she drew from nursery school, the Easter dress she wore, her first skinned knee, her first bee sting, the first time she found a caterpillar, her first day of school, her first report card, the first time she came home crying because someone called her an ugly name, her first school performance, her first crush on a boy, her first honor roll, her first game as a cheerleader, her first phone call from a boy, her first real date, her first heartbreak, her first basketball game, all the phone calls, the boys, the girlfriends who called incessantly to talk about boys, the way she handled her mother dying, the way she cried for her when she was lonely and needed a mother to comfort her, like only a mother could, her induction to the honor society, her prom, her graduation, her decision to follow her parents to UNC, and finally, the last time he hugged her and it felt so different than it had before. Like she'd grown out of her love for her daddy.

His eyes burned from the impending tears and he thought about the letter Kelly wrote to him the day she died.

Kelly's last measure of energy was used to write a simple letter to her family, one filled with emotion and despair. The letter filled only one page, but the sentiments shared could have completed volumes. Hager discovered it on the table beside her hospital bed the day she died, its paper spotted with tears. The last sentence of the letter was one which Hager would always remember most vividly, and promised himself to uphold her last wish.

Clark, please take care of my baby and let her grow into the wonderful person she has already become, and teach her to make smart decisions, and learn from not only her mistakes, but those of others and most of all to live life completely and to profoundly make an impact on every person she meets. I love you both very much.

Kelly

"Why did she have to die? Why?" he asked himself, trying to hold back the tears. "First, Kelly was gone, now my baby girl may be gone, too. What did I do to deserve this? I loved Kelly so much. We were so happy together. We had so many plans. Now, I'm failing in my promise. I promised Kelly I would protect her, keep her from harm. How can I face myself?"

18

L LOYD TURNED onto Franklin Street and accelerated his car toward the Wicked Burrito, which was only three or four blocks away. With his siren blaring and blue lights flashing, he went through intersections against red lights, nearly colliding with a car, and close to running down a pedestrian.

Ahead of him, he saw the yellow awning of the restaurant and two police cars parked in the street in front of the Hardees across from it, their light bars revolving, flashing white and blue lights. Lloyd screeched to a stop, left his car along the curb in front of the restaurant, and turned off his siren.

A crowd of students had gathered, apparently wondering about the police presence. They were standing around looking and pointing, all of them carrying backpacks. Lloyd jumped from the car and ran over to the side entrance of the Mexican restaurant. In the parking lot, he saw Elizabeth's car, a red Plymouth Neon, parked in front of a hair salon in a small strip center adjacent to the restaurant. He recognized the bumper sticker on the back window.

Support Your Local Police–Date A Cop!

A university police car was also parked in the parking lot. From the building, three uniformed officers, two from Chapel Hill PD, and the other, a university officer, emerged and Lloyd approached them showing them his badge.

"Did you find her?"

The taller of the two Chapel Hill officers shook his head.

"No. There's no one in there who matches her description."

Lloyd pointed to her car and turned to the officers.

"There's her car right over there. She's gotta be around here somewhere."

The campus officer shrugged his shoulders and held up his hands.

"I don't know. Where else would she be?"

Lloyd turned his head and scanned the group of students assembled on the sidewalk. Certainly if Elizabeth was in the crowd, she would see him, and say something. Seeing no familiar faces, Lloyd pushed aside the officers and entered the restaurant. He looked at his watch and it was 11:20. Hurriedly, he elbowed his way past the group of young people waiting in line, and scanned the dining area. No Elizabeth. Not only was he looking for her, but his eyes were fixed on the image he'd produced for the killer, to see if he was lingering nearby, watching the show. Not about to panic, Lloyd started back out the door and heard shouting from outside.

"Hey, there she is!" a voice declared.

Racing to the parking lot, Lloyd pushed an incoming male student through the door, prompting an "asshole" from the student as his back slammed against the glass. Across the parking lot the uniformed officers from before were standing next to Elizabeth's car talking to the beautiful brunette. She had a look of dismay and embarrassment at all the attention she was getting. Lloyd, completely relieved, walked quickly over to her.

"Are you okay?"

"What the Hell's going on, Lloyd? What's the deal with all the cops?"

She looked pissed.

"Jesus Christ, girl. Your dad's worried sick."

She folded her arms waiting for the story, like it were some lecture.

"The photographer, he's a phony. Your dad's been trying to get a hold of you since he found out."

Elizabeth's eyes turned soft, with a look of horror.

"Oh my God!"

"What happened to him? Did you meet him?"

"No. He never showed up. I waited for a couple of minutes then I went over to the bookstore," she pointed to the Carolina blue and white building.

"Thank God you're okay, Liz. We think this guy's the one who's been killing all those girls. I'd better call your dad."

"Oh my God!" She put her hands over her face, her mouth quivering, and began to cry.

19

H AGER WAS LOST in thought as the Ford rocketed its way down NC 54, the Highway Patrol car leading the way. So caught up in reflection, he didn't hear the ringing of his cellular phone beside him. His emotions were shot. Null. He didn't know how he felt, other than the numbness of his entire body. The thoughts and images of Elizabeth being taken away from him by that monster had created a benign stillness about him. He was beyond emotion, beyond anger, beyond hatred. Stoic like the uneasy feeling of air as its pressure rises just before a violent thunderstorm, only to come crashing down without other warning to wreak havoc on any who dared to venture out in the storm.

The ringing continued until Hager regained his sense of reality and picked up the handset.

"Hager," he said coarsely, without feeling.

"Clark?"

He recognized the raspy voice of his partner and it had a

glimmering tone to it. Hager turned off the siren to hear his partner's words, hopefully words of encouragement.

"Lloyd, did you find her? Is she okay?"

Part of him didn't want to know, but most of him had to know.

"Clark, we found her. She's fine. She's right here with me."

Lloyd's voice was as smooth and assuring as the voice of a mother telling her baby it was going to be okay.

"She's okay? She's there?"

Hager's eyes began to fill with tears and his vision soon blurred. He released the pressure on the gas pedal, and his nose burned as he tried to hold back his emotions, drops of water trickling down his cheeks. He laughed and sniffled, wiping his eyes.

"She's okay!" he told himself, "She's okay."

He tried to hold back his emotional outburst and flicked his headlights at the trooper ahead, signaling for him to slow down. The phone was still at his ear and Lloyd was silent.

"Lloyd?" he sniffled. "Thanks."

Like the pressure of water exerting its force on a dam, Hager's emotions were about to unravel. He pulled the car over to the shoulder and stopped just in time for the dam to break. At the side of the road, Clark Hager wept intensely, all of his emotions unloading in a single episode, released like air in a balloon, bursting at its seams until the fibers gave way. Tears streamed down his face, and he realized he hadn't wept this strongly even when Kelly died. Were all his pent-up emotions coming to an explosive boil?

Wanting to be strong for Elizabeth, Hager kept all of his emotions bottled up inside to be the pillar of strength for his daughter. For ten minutes, he wept continuously by the side of the road, cars passing by, unconscious of the trauma he'd suffered that day, and for the five years since Kelly's death.

When his tear ducts were finally empty, Hager felt as if all his blood had been siphoned from his body, his bones removed, filleted into a giant piece of meat, leaving him with just muscles and no support or strength to stand. If he wasn't sitting in the car, he thought he would surely have collapsed from the strain.

Sniffling and blowing his nose, Hager wiped away the tears from his face and composed himself enough to drive the rest of the way to Chapel Hill, although at not such a frantic pace.

Hager turned his car onto Franklin Street and he made his way along the busy street scattered with cars, bicycles, and pedestrians. He, too, saw the familiar yellow awning of the Wicked Burrito and knew he would see his daughter very soon. To the right, he wheeled the car into the parking lot and saw her sitting in Lloyd's Caprice.

She looked up at him through the glass and pushed open the door. Hager leapt from the car and sprinted toward his priceless gem. In the middle of the parking lot, they met in a long, emotional embrace. He picked her up and squeezed her hard, not wanting to let go. The hug felt like a hug from his daughter, strong and loving, like it used to. When her feet touched the ground, he looked at her face, tears rolling down her cheeks, her mascara bleeding around her eyes, and he felt his nose burn again, his throat swelled, and his eyes began to water.

"I'm so sorry, Daddy. I should have listened to you."

Trying to hold it back, his mouth began to tremble and he wiped away her tears, his own falling down his face.

He tightened his lips and took a deep breath.

"I love you, Elizabeth."

20

CLARK HAGER thought his world was coming to an abrupt end. During the frantic trek to Chapel Hill, he had lost all faith, all hope, all belief his daughter was going to escape and survive the trap of the monster he was pursuing. He truly feared she was lost, falling prey to this vicious killer and his sadistic fantasies. There was only a glimmer of hope at the time. But for some mysterious reason, the killer chose to torment Hager instead, by leading him to *believe* she had fallen into his trap rather than actually killing her.

Was the horror of anticipating the result more terrorizing than the outcome itself? Was this his game now? To terrorize Hager to the point of breakdown, to cut him deep from the inside of his chest and through to his brain. Slowly, but so very surely eating away at his mind and his will to fight so the monster could continue his enterprise of bloodshed without interference from Hager.

Or was this a personal vendetta? Someone from the past with a grudge, a violent obsession with retribution for some wrong conjured by his psychotic mind. Regardless of whatever purpose—as inconceivable as it was—Hager decided it was time to take the offensive. Hager no longer had merely a professional interest in catching this killer. It was personal.

Hager's mind drifted back from his thoughts of the killer to those of holding his beautiful daughter so tightly in his arms. He stroked her brown hair, her head braced against his chest like she did as a little girl when she would fall asleep in his lap.

Everything was okay now. Elizabeth was safe with him. Nothing could harm her now, and nothing ever would, he promised himself. Her body stiffened suddenly, and she pulled away, a look of horror on her face.

"I've got to warn Missy!"

Her cheeks were still wet, black streaks of eye makeup outlining the path of tears as they leaked from her eyes. Hager led her to his car and the cellular phone. The phone connected and Elizabeth asked for Missy. It was evident in her eyes. The look of horror and her mouth opened, her lower lip trembled, and the tears filled her eyes once again.

"Oh my God!" she screamed and dropped the phone to the pavement.

Elizabeth turned and covered her face with her hands while she sobbed. Hager quickly bent over and picked up the phone she'd dropped. Hager thought she'd just had a relapse of emotion and realized once again in what peril she'd placed herself.

"Hello, hello?"

"Yes, is this Mr. Hager?" the girl asked.

"Yes, it is. Elizabeth wanted to warn Missy about the man from *Playboy*. He's not who he claims to be. Truthfully, he's probably a killer. Where is she?"

"I was trying to tell her when she dropped the phone. Missy was supposed to meet the man from the magazine for an interview at ten this morning."

Now Hager wanted to drop the phone and bury his face in his hands. He looked at his watch and it was almost noon.

"Where?" he asked quickly. "Where was she going to meet him?" "She said she was going to where he was staying. At the Hampton Inn on 501. Oh no!" she screamed, suddenly realizing her friend's probable fate.

"Please don't let anything happen to her! Oh, please!" she cried.

Hager disconnected the call and yelled to Lloyd.

"We need to get over to the Hampton Inn. Right now!"

Lloyd nodded and jumped back into his Caprice, the engine still running.

"Elizabeth?" Hager said, touching her shoulder.

She continued to cry, her hands still covered her face, her head jerking with every sob.

"Elizabeth, honey. Come on. Get in the car," he said softly.

He held her arm and pulled her away from the back door of his car, opened the door, and placed her into the back seat.

Lloyd pulled away and turned out of the parking lot onto Franklin Street with Hager closely behind. The two Chapel Hill Police cars followed. Although Hager didn't want to expose Elizabeth to any more of the horrors for which the killer was responsible, he didn't want her out of his sight for one minute until he got her safely to his house and under guard.

When the caravan of police cars arrived at the Hampton Inn, Hager instructed Elizabeth to stay in the car even though she insisted on accompanying him to find Missy. One of the Chapel Hill officers stayed behind to look after Elizabeth while the others stormed the motel office. Safe with the knowledge that she knew what the killer looked like, Hager wasn't leery of the officer being alone with his daughter.

Hager quickly approached the front desk, and a little Middle Eastern man who looked like Ghandi with hair appeared from a back office. He was dressed in a bronze colored silk or satin gown that hung down below his knees, and the hairs on his chest overlapped the v-neck collar. Hager expected the little man's speech to be broken, but he spoke quite eloquently, with only a slight accent, and he uttered his words so softly it was difficult to hear him if one didn't listen closely.

Frankly, Hager thought, the man looked like a monk that had been locked away in a monastery for years.

"Can I help you?" the little man asked.

Hager produced his badge from his pocket.

"It's an emergency. We're trying to find one of your guests. A Jeremy Foster? What room is he in?"

The little man smiled and shook his head.

"I am sorry, but I cannot release that information without permission from the guest. Those are the rules," he said and smiled again.

Before Hager could exert himself, Lloyd reached over the counter and grabbed the collar of the gown, and undoubtedly, a few of the little man's chest hairs. Lloyd shoved his badge in the little man's face.

"I don't think you understood what this means. He wasn't *asking*! I think he told you to give it to him!"

Hager saw Lloyd's lips move, but his teeth were clenched together for maximum effect. And it worked. The little man just closed his eyes and grimaced, expecting Lloyd to mash his face. Lloyd pulled the little man as he stomped around the counter. Hager maneuvered around the desk to get a glimpse of the motel's register.

Next to the number 143, Hager saw the name of Foster, and he quickly turned to the clerk who stood helplessly watching while his partner towered over him, ready to grab his chest hairs again.

"Where do you keep the spare keys? Hurry!"

The little man had a blank look on his face and Hager looked to Lloyd, who glared threateningly at the little man. His hand trembling, he pointed his index finger toward the office. On a wooden pegboard were the keys to all the rooms.

Hager grabbed the key for 143 and started for the door with the Chapel Hill officer close behind. He heard Lloyd's raspy voice thanking the little man for his cooperation, in a way only his partner was capable.

220

Walking hurriedly to the room, Hager knew if Missy made it here, she was most likely already dead, and the killer had somehow planned for Hager personally to *see* the results of his work. To compound the shocking effect of his will.

As the adrenaline pumped his heart faster, Hager's pace increased to a slow run through the asphalt parking lot. The door was the first one around the corner of the building and it couldn't be seen from the office. As they got to the edge of the building, Hager stopped, minding the officer survival training tactic of not passing a corner of a building until the other side was cleared of anyone.

Quickly, the agent peered around the edge of the concrete. Seeing no one there, he stepped around the corner, stopping at the perimeter of the door. With the officer still behind, Hager turned his head to whisper to him.

"Most doors open to the inside so I'll cross over and you stay on this side. Here," he said handing the key to him. "The handle is on your side."

The officer nodded nervously. Hager didn't know if he, himself exhibited his tension outwardly, but he felt his heart pounding. He crossed the entrance of the door, resting against the building just short of the large picture window of the room. The window's drapes completely covered any view of the interior. He saw a red Toyota Corolla parked directly in front of the door. On the rear windshield, he could see a "Carolina" sticker in the familiar blue color. He didn't know for certain, but he thought the car belonged to Missy. There were no other cars around the Corolla for several parking spaces.

From the corner of his eye, Hager saw Lloyd's frame at the corner of the building, and Hager nodded he was ready to make entry. Hager turned to the officer.

"We'll knock first and then if no one answers, we'll use the key."

The officer nodded and his Adam's apple jumped when he swallowed his fear. Hager pulled his Beretta from its holster. He looked over to the Chapel Hill officer who responded in kind, his pistol clutched in both hands, pointing directly at the ground.

Hager faced the building and with his left hand, he knocked loudly on the door. Seconds elapsed and he knocked again. The second time, he shouted.

"SBI! Open the door!"

Still no response at the door, Hager nodded to the officer to use the key. With a trembling hand, he inserted the key and turned the handle. Hager used his left hand to help the officer push open the heavy door. Hager's shoulder caught the impetus of the rebounding door and it shoved him stumbling to the left and inside, his Beretta trained on the center of the room, looking for movement of any kind. The officer followed closely behind.

On the bed lay the ghastly figure of a woman, the sheets underneath her body soaked red with blood. The unclothed woman lay sprawled on her back, her eyes wide open signifying the horror of death. No time to think about her yet. There still may have been a killer hiding in the room, ready to launch an attack from seclusion.

There were two beds in the room. The other was left undisturbed. The bathroom door was shut. Hager motioned for the officer to approach it. Lloyd made his appearance in the room and quickly moved to the bathroom door, leaving Hager to stand next to a table and two chairs while his partner and the officer cleared the bathroom.

Only the body of Missy remained. Holstering his Beretta, Hager closed his eyes and shook his head at the grisly spectacle *he* had arranged. The large red stain of blood seemed to surround the young woman's torso, and he could see thin cuts with streaks of red flaring from her chest, indicative of multiple stab wounds. Her legs were spread widely, exposing her genitals to further degrade her and to shock people who discovered her. Hager walked over to the bed and felt her skin. It was still warm. He grabbed her wrist and felt for a pulse. Nothing. There was no movement in her chest to indicate breathing at all. Hager looked deep in her eyes. Like a mirror, they reflected the horror she'd endured before she died.

Lloyd and the officer emerged from the bathroom.

"Clark," Lloyd said calmly, "I think you'd better take a look at this in the bathroom."

Hager's eyes remained fixed on Missy's body and suddenly, he felt responsible for her fate. It was because of him that this monster did this. To prove something. To exert his power and influence. To show Hager he was a worthy foe. Was all of this about him, or did the killer decide to make Hager part of the plot to garner more interest in his deeds?

Hearing his partner's words, Hager entered the bathroom. His image was reflected in the large mirror, but the thin streaks of red distorted the otherwise clear impression. A tube of lipstick lay on the lavatory. Nothing else. The words written in the lipstick were clearly a message to Hager from the killer.

The power of life and death is so exhilarating.
I can get to you if I want.

21

ALTHOUGH HAGER had never been introduced to his daughter's friend from school, tears collected in his eyes when he looked at Missy on the bed. Not because of the sight of the body—he'd seen thousands, it seemed. But Hager cried at the thought it very well could have been Elizabeth on the bed in front of him. If not for the killer's sick ploy of terrorizing his pursuer, Elizabeth could have been the one lying in all the blood with all the cuts in her body. Hager thought about the message.

"I can get to you if I want," he said to himself. "Could he really get to me? Is that what he wants? Or is he just enjoying the satisfaction of putting me through hell with his phone calls and his taunting messages. Who is he?"

As other police, crime lab people, and the Chapel Hill brass started to arrive, Hager sat with his face in his hands. The day had been an exhausting one with the frantic ride from Raleigh, believing his daughter was in the grips of a monster; the joyous reunion with her after she was found unharmed; to the lurid finding of Missy's body and the message from *him*.

He looked up, thinking he should be doing something and met his partner's gaze. Lloyd shook his head, telling Hager all that could be done was being done without him.

Thoughts of Elizabeth resurfaced and Hager realized no one had told her of her friend's fate. He walked to the door and passed lab techs with cameras, people with small brushes dusting for finger-prints, and another pulling open drawers in search of evidence.

Lloyd was outside in an animated discussion with a police cap-tain. Lloyd was red-faced as the captain was reprimanding him. The captain wore a police hat with the bill tucked down to his eyes. He had a pointed nose, and under it, a long black and gray mustache which covered his entire mouth. Unless someone heard his voice, it was impossible to tell if he was talking. The captain looked like he should have been wearing a Civil War uniform instead of a police uniform, and he played J.E.B. Stuart.

He overheard his partner explain why entry into the motel room was made by them instead of calling their SWAT Team.

"There was no time," he heard Lloyd growl, his voice now more gruff from all the stress of the day, "We thought she may still be alive. Fuck you and your SWAT Team! If you don't like it, then call the Attorney General."

Lloyd was really giving it to the captain, Hager thought as he sneaked through the parking lot eyeing his Ford parked in front of the office. A Chapel Hill officer stood beside the car smoking a cigarette, but Hager didn't see Elizabeth. Worried, he quickened his pace until he reached the car. The officer, seeing Hager approach, met him at the rear of the car.

"Where's Elizabeth?"

Before the officer responded, Hager saw her lying in the back seat, her eyes closed in peaceful sleep. Hager smiled at the innocence of sleep. She was still a child in his eyes. Lying there curled up in a ball, she looked like the naive little girl he would watch when she slept after he read her a bedtime story.

Not wanting to disturb her, Hager looked through the big window of the office and saw the little man who looked like Ghandi, standing at the front desk next to a woman. He was pointing at him, apparently telling the woman he was one of the men who bullied him around earlier. When Hager saw the man grab his own shirt collar, he knew what he was doing. An explanation was in order, and who else better to do it. Special Agent Clark Hager. The peacemaker. He laughed at his own sense of himself, but felt sorry for the way the man was treated. At the same time, Hager knew it had to be done that way sometimes.

This was why Lloyd was such a good partner. While Hager displayed the cool demeanor of the cerebral investigator, Lloyd compensated for Hager by being somewhat intense and straightforward, but he also knew Lloyd enjoyed being the heavy most of the time. During interrogations, they both would utilize the "good cop-bad cop" technique, and most of the time, Hager was the "good cop." It was time to be the "good cop" again and smooth things over with Ghandi.

Not only was Hager concerned about manhandling the little man, but the entry into the motel room could be construed as illegal search and seizure. Hager presumed they were operating under the protection of life rule, and they had exigent circumstances to make entry into the motel room without a warrant. But a cooperative motel clerk would give consent, thus covering themselves on both sides of the issue.

When Hager entered the lobby, he could see the man wasn't angry, but fearful from his ordeal with Lloyd. Hager smiled at him and explained the urgency of their purpose. They had found a body in the room. Hager apologized for the rough treatment, but said they didn't have time to explain to him in detail because they felt the girl's life could have been saved.

With the explanations and apologies out of the way, Mr. Azad opened up his books and produced the registration forms for Room 143. There was nothing terribly enlightening about the forms or the interview with Azad about the tenant. The story was the same. Description and all. A three-day stay. He was supposed to check out that day, but he apparently left without returning the key.

On the registration form, Hager saw different hand-writing. *Red Nissan 300ZX* was written in the space for vehicle information, but didn't include a plate number. Hager asked Mr. Azad about the entry, and he said he'd written down the description after the man had checked in. Noticing the tenant didn't put his own car information on the registration form, Azad had scribbled down the description of the car, but forgot to get a plate number.

It was a glimmer of hope, nonetheless. At least, to Hager, it confirmed another element in his profile of the killer. Hager theorized the type of criminal they pursued would drive a sports car. Hager asked Azad how he knew of such cars. The man told him his cousin had one very similar, except it was black. Knowing the body style had changed a couple of times for that particular model of car, Hager asked Mr. Azad, now a witness, to call his cousin and obtain the year of the Nissan.

"1993," he said. "That is the year of his car."

Even though it was no major breakthrough, Hager saw the car as another piece of the puzzle needed to put an end to this nightmare. If and when a suspect was developed, a known car was helpful in attacking him during interrogation and to link him to the other crimes. With this in mind, Hager made a mental note to pass along the new information to his fellow task force members with instructions to re-interview witnesses who may have seen a red Nissan 300ZX.

Hager was also slightly relieved the tenant was due to check out at 11:00 a.m. that day. Since the killer had already vacated the room, entry into it without a warrant wouldn't have been a violation of his Fourth Amendment rights. Hager thanked Azad and shook his hand.

Hager stood on the landing outside the door of the lobby and watched his little girl deep in placid slumber. He thought about how the killer knew of Elizabeth and where she attended school. Was it some fluke that he stumbled across the name and put them together? Or was it an intentional part of his plan to terrorize him?

Hager believed it was intentional. Despite the fact that Hager had a daughter attending UNC was common knowledge in his circle of associates, it wasn't advertised. How did he know how to get to her?

Hager thought deeply about it.

"I have friends who know. Of course, *her* friends know. People in the SBI know. Some other people in law enforcement know, but that's it. There are no others."

Hager thought hard about all the interviews done with the press about his life, and he didn't remember any instance where he revealed any pertinent information about Elizabeth. He still applied what he'd learned in his training years ago, not broadcasting anything about his family. How then? Was he being followed? If he was, he surely didn't notice, not that he was paying close attention. He shook his head, and it started to throb.

"I'm certainly going to pay more attention now. No more chances. Not even with Vanessa."

As he said her name, he realized she was alone in all of this, not even remotely involved. But this killer didn't care. It seemed he would do anything to get Hager to break under the pressure, including getting to Vanessa. If he was being followed, he would certainly know about her, where she lived, and even where she worked. His paranoia intensified. Was he watching them at the restaurant last week? Did he follow them to her place that night? His mind raced back to the motel room and the words in red, *I can get to you if I want,* and he started to hear the evil voice whispering it into his ear.

"I'd better call Vanessa."

Without detailing the horrific events which unfolded during the day, Hager explained to Vanessa in enough detail what had transpired to convince her that she was in danger. Vanessa, not quite as stubborn as Kelly or Elizabeth, agreed and related she'd experienced an uneasy feeling during the drive to work the day before, but couldn't explain it. She felt she was being watched.

"Stay there until either myself or Lloyd comes to get you. "I'll call Judy and have two field agents stand by until we get there. But *don't* go anywhere with them. I don't trust anyone right now. Their instructions will be to stand by, and nothing else. If one of them does anything different, get to your office and lock the door. Understand?"

"I understand. Clark, how's Liz doing?"

Just like Vanessa, Hager thought.

"She's the one in danger and she asks about Elizabeth," he mumbled to himself. "She's doing all right, I guess. She's asleep right now. I haven't told her about Missy yet."

"Be careful when you tell her, Clark. She's been through a lot today."

Hager hung up the phone and called Judy. While it was ringing, he thought of two agents he trusted mostly, other than Lloyd. There were two drug agents with whom Hager worked on an execution-style style murder of a drug dealer, and they seemed reliable enough. They also knew Vanessa.

Judy answered and at once bombarded him with questions, her voice ringing with concern.

"Yes, Judy, Elizabeth's okay," he assured her, but neglected to tell her about Missy.

After apologizing to her about not being able to celebrate her grandparental news, Hager asked for her to contact Agents Rice and Burns. "Rice and Beans" they were called because of their names and because they worked so well together.

"See if they're not doing anything right now and ask them to go over to Duke and stand by with Vanessa until either Lloyd or I get there to pick her up. Tell them it's important and not to let her out of their sight. Remember, tell them just to stand by until one of us gets there."

Apparently, the voice of her father awoke Elizabeth from her nap, which had lasted the better part of an hour. He heard her moan as she stretched and yawned. In the rearview mirror, he saw her face, and on her left cheek, thin red impressions from the seat were imbedded temporarily in her skin.

"Daddy, what happened? Did you find Missy?"

Hager guessed the look on his face gave it away as she broke down crying again, her forehead on the head rest. Fortunately, he didn't need to explain to Elizabeth what had become of her friend. She made no request to see for herself, to somehow disprove what she already knew was true.

Truthfully, Hager wasn't *positive* the girl found in the motel room was Missy because neither he nor Lloyd had ever met the girl. But the license number on the red Toyota Corolla came back to Missy Campbell of Hickory, North Carolina, and Hager knew she was from that city. If this was a nightmare, Hager thought, when would he ever wake up?

22

THE FANTASY is never fulfilled. Although he made an effort to stage his deeds the way he saw it in the vision, reality was never quite the same. Nowhere close to being as good as the fantasy. Powerful and uncontrollable, the fantasies were overwhelming him now.

"It's always better when they're dead," he said to himself. "Then I can play with them the way I want to."

It's never the same.

But they're dead and it's still not enough.

"I'll find the right one someday—maybe soon. I'll find the one to replace the memory of *her*."

The killer bet Hager was loving this. He'd enjoyed the spectacle on Franklin Street earlier. Discreetly concealed from view while sitting in a booth at Hardees, he watched the frantic search and then the joyous reunion. And little Missy. Poor little Missy. The bitch wanted it. But she didn't know how badly she wanted it. Until she watched him watch her die.

He bet Hager loved the way he posed the ungrateful slut. He left his message knowing Hager would be even more determined to get his man. The message was a challenge—a harbinger of what was to come. Him, the vicious killer versus Hager, the bumbling hero.

Missy was simply a pawn to lure Hager more deeply into his trap. Part of the game. Thinking about her left a bad taste in his mouth. She wasn't even close enough for the fantasy. She was all wrong for him. But perfect for Agent Hager.

* * *

SLEEP SHOULD have been instantaneous with the roller coaster ride of stress and emotions throughout the day. Instead, Hager was restless, and he bounced around on his bed for a couple of hours until he found himself downstairs in the comfort of his recliner. A glass of wine in his hand and the bottle on the table beside the chair, Hager watched the bright colors of the flames burning in the fireplace. He hoped the combination would produce enough endorphins to make him drift off into the coma he desired. Sleep was distant though, and his mind shot flashes like a highlight reel of the day's news.

For what it was worth and despite the tragic circumstances of Missy's death, Hager and Elizabeth had emerged virtually unscathed—physically, at least.

But emotionally, Hager had been put through the ringer, forced to reckon with the notion that his only daughter may have been in the perilous grasp of a killer. Only to learn it was by *his* own choosing Elizabeth didn't perish. It was a part of his torture. The killer was sending a message to Hager. Telling the agent who was in control, and he would call the shots and dictate the movement of the story, like an author plotting the sequence of a novel.

As long as he remained a ghost and moved like the wind, control would be in his possession. Anonymity was the key to his success. Until it transformed into notoriety, the killer was free to roam at will, keeping Hager on the defensive and at bay.

Yet, Hager felt relieved in a sense. Elizabeth and Vanessa were safe and peacefully sleeping upstairs. Two state troopers were stationed in the driveway outside, assigned to Hager's house indefinitely. It was secure at his house, but Hager knew he couldn't lock both Vanessa and Elizabeth inside and protect them until the killer was caught. Vanessa had her job, and Elizabeth still had school to attend.

With Maxwell's consent, Hager assigned two bodyguards to each of them. Vanessa would be guarded by Rice and Burns, and Elizabeth by two state troopers. He knew they both would probably object, claiming interference with their lives, but Hager had a feeling it wouldn't be for very long.

It would come to an end soon. The nightmare would be over and they could return to a state of normalcy. Hager saw the impending denouement, but it was shrouded by uncertainty of the identity of the antagonist.

The killer was becoming more and more desperate, evident of his behavior. Desperate for what? Revenge? Notoriety? Fulfillment of some deranged fantasy? If he only knew what the killer desired, he could bait him and dangle it in front of his face, like a piece of cheese used to catch a rat.

In his desperation, however, the killer was becoming more brutal, and his brutality could escalate. But carelessness was playing right into the hands of Hager. He was becoming more reckless and would soon make a fatal mistake that would reveal his identity and purpose.

But how many people remained to suffer before he made the ultimate mistake? How many others would he use to satisfy his evil fantasy of power and lust?

He poured his glass full with more wine and he leaned back, fully reclined. The fireplace was centered between his feet, and he watched the flames dancing with their brilliant colors of yellow, orange and white. It had a calming effect, almost like he was using it to put himself in a hypnotic trance.

He remembered the last night he and Vanessa had spent together. They made love on the floor in front of the fireplace that night. And after, they both held each other, watching the flames flicker and the wood pop as it burned, their naked bodies together, their skin warm under the blanket. Maybe it was a dream, but it felt like he had stepped out of himself and was seeing them sitting on the floor together. They were drinking wine, too, then, and Hager reflected on how good it felt to be with her and how happy she made him.

He smiled in remembrance of the night and of the other occasions he and Vanessa had shared. But for the first time, Hager didn't have the parallel thought of Kelly and how Vanessa compared with her. It was as if some force of nature created a rebirth of Hager's feelings. Maybe it was like a butterfly escaping the periphery of a cocoon. Hager shed the protective covering of his love for Kelly and emerged with a new love for Vanessa. No more ambivalent likening to his memory of Kelly. Kelly would only be a joyful memory.

It was the episode of intense weeping he attributed to this revelation. The stress of the fear of losing Elizabeth was only the trigger to the outpouring of emotions released in those ten minutes. He realized, then, he truly didn't mourn the death of Kelly. Instead, he stored it inside, and it disguised itself as a source of correlation to any woman with whom Hager was involved, especially Vanessa. But the idea of losing his only living link to Kelly stimulated powerful forces inside him and erupted like a dangerous thunderstorm.

Hager felt that after the storm subsided, an evil spirit had escaped from his body, leaving him with a feeling of peaceful tranquillity inside. He'd been cleaned, in essence. There was no more apprehension. Even though this upheaval of emotions occurred hours ago, it was only then, when Hager visualized he and Vanessa holding each other by the fire, he realized the rejuvenation of his love for her.

Suddenly, he felt the need to be close to her. Quietly, he crept up the stairs and opened the bedroom door slowly. She lay still on the bed, her breathing quiet. Lying on her side, one hand was hidden under the pillow, and the other lay against the comforter. The light from the window shone, illuminating her beautiful face. Even in sleep, she was elegant and ladylike.

Of all the times he'd slept with her, he never actually watched her sleep. It amazed him she could do it so gracefully, as if she had staged herself before she drifted off. Without disturbing her, he sat on the bed and gently touched her cheek. Her skin was soft and smooth. Some strands of hair had fallen over her eyes and he brushed them back with his fingers and stroked her hair. He gathered a handful of her hair and brought it to his nose. It emanated the essence of peaches or some other fruit he didn't specifically recognize, but only that it smelled divinely.

Her mouth was closed and he watched her beautiful lips, ever so slightly open as she breathed. She awakened when he started to trace his fingers around the edge of her lips. When her eyes opened, she looked confused. Her eyes brightened when she realized it was him, and he touched her cheek again. She smiled and dropped her head back down to the pillow and readjusted her position. Again, he leaned over and gently kissed her cheek, still smiling, her eyes opened and then closed again.

"Can't you sleep?" she whispered.

"No, and I wanted to tell you something."

"Hmm," she sighed. "What is it?"

"I love you, Vanessa."

His eyes began to burn.

She smiled without opening her eyes.

"I love you, too, Clark," she whispered and drifted back off to sleep.

He tiptoed to the other side and joined her. He pressed closely against her body, wrapping his arms around her, causing her to grasp his hands. She was warm and he rubbed her feet with his and wrapped his legs around hers. He gently kissed her neck and gave her a hug which seemed to last until morning because when he awakened, she was still in his arms.

*   *   *

WHILE VANESSA took a shower, Hager went downstairs and fixed Belgian waffles and turkey bacon. Combined with the smell of brewing coffee, the kitchen emitted a mouth-watering aroma of waffles and bacon which drifted throughout the entire house.

The appetizing smell had evidently found Elizabeth's room, for minutes after he started cooking, she arrived with a sleepy look on her face and her hair messed. It had been a long time since he'd seen her look so unkempt. Not that she looked bad, but she usually brushed her hair and fixed herself before coming down to see anyone. She was still wearing a T-shirt of Hager's, which was more like a short nightgown to her, and socks on her feet.

After giving him a "good morning" kiss on the cheek, she wearily sat down at the breakfast table. Hager brought her a cup of coffee and placed it on the table in front of her.

"How are you feeling this morning, honey?" Hager asked.

She yawned and shook her head trying to remove the cob webs.

"Okay," she whispered and sniffled.

"Did you sleep well?"

She shrugged her shoulders.

"All right, I guess."

Hager could tell she was still quite upset over the death of her friend and knew to be gentle with her.

"Are you hungry? I made your favorite. Belgian waffles."

She managed a tiny smile and nodded slightly.

"Yes, I'm hungry."

That was a good sign. Eating was the purest sign of health, Hager thought. If someone didn't eat, it wasn't good. At least he wouldn't have to worry about her starving herself in depression over all of this. She stirred the coffee, her eyes fixed on the cup like she were in a trance. He watched her and for at least a minute, her eyes didn't blink, and she had a blank stare on her face. Deep in a trance, she apparently didn't hear Hager's question as to whether she wanted bacon or not, as she didn't respond by moving or saying anything.

"Elizabeth?"

Hager walked over to her and gently touched her shoulder. She flinched at his touch.

"Elizabeth, honey, are you sure you're okay?" he asked and stroked her hair.

He could see her eyes fill with fluid and her lips purse and she sniffled again.

"Why is he doing this, Daddy? Why us? Why Missy?"

Tears streamed down her cheeks.

Hager couldn't answer the question because he had no idea why the killer was terrorizing him and his family. Nor did he have the time to explain to her all the insights to personality profiling to help her possibly understand what went through a serial killer's head. All he could do was try to reassure her she was safe, and the killer wouldn't get close to her again. He promised her that.

Hager returned to the stove and turned the frying bacon. Vanessa came down and gave Hager a great hug and a kiss. She looked over to Elizabeth sitting at the table sniffling.

His eyes met Vanessa's and she smiled in such a way, he supposed, she realized Elizabeth needed a woman with whom to talk. She needed the comfort of her mother.

Fortunately, she and Vanessa had grown very close to one another over the past year, and she could provide the needed strength of a mother.

"You hanging in there, Liz?" she said softly.

Elizabeth nodded and drank from her coffee cup.

"I know what we can do, Liz."

Vanessa smiled and looked up at Hager.

"I'll call in at work, and we'll spend the day together. Go shopping or something. Maybe to the bookstore. Just us girls. How's that sound?"

"Yeah, that sounds good," Elizabeth said, a smile emerging.

Hager brought Vanessa a cup of coffee and Elizabeth a plate with a large waffle on it. He walked back into the kitchen and returned with two plates, one with a waffle for Vanessa, and on the other, the strips of bacon.

"I'm only going to ask for one favor from you all while you go shopping. And that favor is to not get upset at the sight of your bodyguards."

"Bodyguards?" Elizabeth said, astonished. "What do you mean, bodyguards? Who are they?"

"Well, I had two troopers assigned to be with you when you went back to school, and two agent friends will stay with Vanessa."

"Bodyguards at school? No way, Daddy. I'm not going to have two jar heads following me around at school, jacking up every person who gets close to me. No way."

Elizabeth had finally awakened.

"Then I guess you'll not go to school then. Because your're not leaving this house unless I know you're safe. And I've got to leave the house to catch this maniac, so either you let them go to campus with you or you stay here all day. It's your choice."

"But—"

"And by the way, you'll live here at this house with me until we catch him," Hager ordered.

"It's probably for the best until your dad catches this guy, Liz. If you want, I'll trade you for the troopers. I think they're sexy in those gray uniforms. They're certainly better looking than the drug agents your dad's got assigned to me."

Vanessa looked Hager's way and he gave her a jealous glance at the remark. Elizabeth smiled, seeming less depressed. She turned to her father.

"I don't plan on going back to school for awhile anyway. I don't want to be there right now."

"That's fine, Elizabeth. But if you decide to leave, the troopers go with you. Don't worry. They won't be in uniform and they're really not jar heads."

Before their shopping trip, the two ladies would have to go to Elizabeth's apartment in Carrboro in order for Elizabeth to shower and dress, along with packing a bag of clothes for the stay at her father's. They were gone when Hager finished getting dressed. Rice and Burns were tailing Vanessa's car and would be their shadows for the entire day.

23

HAGER ARRIVED at his office around noon. Before he sat down, the agent called Bill Matlin in Wilmington. Mark Kellogg was the name Ramos had given him the day before as possibly being related to this case. What Kellogg knew, or didn't know, could be pivotal in the outcome in the investigation.

From the DMV files, Hager located a Wilmington man with the name of Mark Stanley Kellogg. He had no driver infractions nor a criminal record through DCI and FBI files. In essence, he was as clean as if he'd just come from the shower. Matlin would check his local records, once he was given the name, but Hager was reasonably sure nothing important would be there. Hager already knew Kellogg wasn't his killer based on the description given to Ramos from Ronny Cooper, and also because he felt this killer wouldn't have made such a mindless mistake that led directly to his identity.

But Kellogg was a lead, and every lead had to be checked. Perhaps Kellogg could provide a name of someone he knew in the photography business who was also at the convention in Atlanta. Someone he met there. An associate. If it wasn't such a large convention, Hager could have gotten the registration list of the attendees, but since there were so many people from all over the country, registration wasn't required. The attendees had the option of giving their names to be put on a mailing list for the association who sponsored the convention.

Matlin didn't answer the telephone when Hager called; so, he called Agent Moss at the SBI field office in Wilmington. Moss wasn't there either. Hager looked at the clock seeing it was lunch time and left messages on both answering machines with Kellogg's name and address and the reason for the lead.

Missy's murder had made big news around the region and hit the national wires when it was determined she was the fifth victim of "The Strangler," as he was called now. The Raleigh television station WRAL came up with the name for the series of murders based on the method of killing the victims.

How profound, Hager thought. Although the autopsy was probably being performed as Hager sat in his chair, he knew the cause of death would be a combination of asphyxiation and multiple stab wounds. From his inspection of the crime scene, there just wasn't enough blood in and around the motel room to indicate a struggle resulting in so many stab wounds. Not enough blood for a struggle, but too much blood on the bed to suggest she was dead when he cut into her.

More than likely, she would have been incapacitated somehow before he tore into her so viciously with the knife. But not dead. Hager found it inconceivable she would have simply lain on the bed and surrendered to his puncturing blade, like he was tenderizing meat with a fork.

Hager imagined as he'd done so often in this bizarre case. The killer choking the victim unconscious from behind, and laying her down on the bed, thinking she was dead. Then in a fit of rage, or for special effect, he gashed into her flesh with resounding force. Hager would be surprised at any other conclusion.

241

With the media blitz, Hager knew the killer was relishing in the publicity he'd created for himself. He was sure pleasure filled his entire body when the news came up with "The Strangler" name. With an infamous name, so came the publicity he desired. And the agent knew that notoriety was something for which his ego yearned.

The media had also bombarded Hager's office with calls about the murders, which were efficiently screened by Judy, who read them the prepared press release. The statement was generic, similar to the press conference, but with a small piece of information not revealed before. Hager agreed to disclose the fact that three of the five victims were exotic dancers, and it was believed their occupation had something to do with their deaths.

It was something the public had to be aware of, and Hager admitted the release of such information wouldn't jeopardize their case.

The phone rang and when Hager picked it up, he expected it to be someone other than his partner.

"How's it going?" Lloyd asked.

"All right, I guess. I just left a message for Matlin and Moss to check on the name Ramos gave me yesterday."

"Elizabeth hangin' in there with all that happened?"

"Yeah, she and Vanessa went out shopping after they got some of her things from her apartment. Rice and Burns are covering them."

"You had lunch yet?"

"No, I kinda had a late breakfast. I'm really not hungry."

"Well, why don't you meet me at the bagel shop anyway?"

"For lunch?"

"Yeah, for lunch. They have great sandwiches and soup and shit like that. Come on, meet me."

"All right, all right." Hager sighed. "I'll be there in about ten minutes."

Lloyd's car was already in the parking lot when Hager arrived at the bagel shop. He was sitting in a booth talking to Sam, the owner, when Hager walked through the door. Sam was a good guy and an old friend of Lloyd's. A retired police officer in Raleigh, he'd set up shop after partnering with a woman to buy a store in the Best Bagels In Town chain. Sam always greeted the agents with a wave of his hand and a "hello" from the kitchen when they came into the store each morning. He was also Lloyd's source for most of his crude jokes.

The store was busy with people standing in line waiting to order their food, and Hager was surprised at the business' flow of customers. He guessed no restaurant can be exclusively a "one meal" establishment. Bagels were normally breakfast food, but this place served sandwiches on different types of breads, soups, and salads for the rush of mostly women and yuppie types who also frequented yogurt shops for lunch.

Hager sat down next to Sam. Sam's eyes were red and he looked to have been enduring the wake of a hilarious joke because he was still laughing.

"Say, Clark," Sam said. "Do you know what one lesbian frog said to the other?"

"Oh, boy, this sounds like a good one," Hager chuckled. "No, what did it say?"

Sam's eyes brightened, and he started to laugh before he blurted out the punch line. His eyes started to tear.

"Come on, Sam. Spit it out," Hager ordered and he started to laugh at Sam's behavior, looking over to Lloyd, who only smiled and shook his head, like the joke was no big deal.

Apparently, to Sam, it was one of those jokes that hit a person the right way and made them laugh continuously like he was being tickled. Sam finally calmed down enough to flush the punch line.

"It said, you know we really do taste like chicken."

Sam broke out in laughter again which caused some of his customers to glance suspiciously over at the table. The whole table laughed, and even Lloyd who undoubtedly had heard the joke just seconds before, still laughed, but mostly at Sam's ticklish laughter. The dining area, with all the hilarity, sounded more like a bar than a bagel shop.

Hager scooted over to let Sam, still occasionally chuckling from the joke, out of the booth and he returned to the kitchen. A young girl brought Lloyd's sandwich and a bowl of vegetable soup on a tray. The soup smelled tasty and Hager decided he would try some.

"Maxwell called this morning," Lloyd said. "He asked me if we were planning to photograph Missy's funeral to see if our guy shows. I told him we probably were. He recommended this kid who works out of the Greenville office. A crime scene specialist. He said he'd videoed the funeral of the girl in Greenville as well as processed the scene where her body was found in Hertford County. Also did the photographs for the press conference last week. Moffitt, I think he said was his name. Apparently, this guy's been bucking for criminal agent and wants to brown nose Maxwell by volunteering."

"I remember the name. He worked with the Steelman girl. They did a good job on the scene in Ahoskie for what they had to work with. It doesn't matter to me as long as it gets done."

"I'll call him when I get back to the office. Listen, are you sure Liz is okay? She looked pretty shook up yesterday. Frankly, I don't blame her though. Her friend gets whacked like that."

"She'll be all right in a few days. Like me, I think she's just grateful it wasn't her."

"Oh, that asshole captain from Chapel Hill complained on me to Maxwell as well. That was the primary reason for him calling anyway. Said the captain told him I cussed him out in front of his own men. That I embarrassed him."

"What did you say?"

"I told him the truth. I told him that I told the captain to fuck off and if he had a problem with that, then he could call the Attorney General."

Hager snickered at his partner's cavalier attitude toward getting into hot water. "I guess you got what you asked for."

"Fuck that sonofabitch! He had no right coming in there barking orders at me and telling me I should have waited. That sonofabitch can go to hell for all I care. I wouldn't piss on him if he was on fire."

"Tell us how you really feel about him, Lloyd."

Hager smiled and Lloyd chuckled.

Lloyd finished his lunch and Hager ate the soup. It smelled better than it tasted. It was bland. Too much water, he thought. Or maybe they didn't stir it before they spooned it out for him.

They both returned to the office after lunch and there were two messages waiting for Hager. One of them was from Matlin acknowledging receipt of his message earlier; the other message was from the medical examiner's office. Hager assumed they had called with the results of the autopsy on Missy. He sat at his desk and called Chapel Hill and spoke with Dr. Brookings, the pathologist who performed the examination.

As expected, the cause of death was determined to be a combination of asphyxiation and multiple trauma to the thorax from the stab wounds. There was evidence of sexual activity, and the doctor concluded it was probably done before her death, but no traces of semen were found on any part of her body, other than in her vagina. Dr. Brookings also said the lab work on her blood would be done by the day after tomorrow, and complete photographs were taken of the stab wounds.

"No post-death masturbation this time," he said to himself.

Hager guessed either the killer was disgusted by his work with the knife, or was forced to leave in a hurry before Hager arrived. The agent leaned more to the latter.

Hager hung up the phone and wondered if Matlin had located Kellogg yet. The message from him was received about 12:30 p.m. and it was 1:30 at the time. He quickly turned his thoughts to Elizabeth and Vanessa and reached to dial Vanessa's cell phone, but the phone rang instead.

"SBI, Hager."

"The Strangler is a very catchy name. Don't you think?"

Hager recognized the voice. He reached over to activate the tape recorder and glanced at the caller ID box.

Number unknown

"I guess it is, but I can't take credit for it. Channel Five made the connection."

"Don't minimize your contribution, Agent Hager. I'm sure you threw in your two cents. I was hoping you all could come up with something a little more original. It seems so ordinary, 'The Strangler'."

Damn, I just said the same thing to myself a little while ago. What, am I beginning to think just like him now?

"Well, we don't have much experience with naming killers anything other than their true names," he said. "Please forgive us. Maybe you have a suggestion? Something you'd prefer to be called?"

"How about *The Invisible Man?*"

The man laughed a wicked low-pitched laugh which sent a chill up Hager's spine.

"No, that just doesn't tell it all, does it? Let me think," the killer pondered.

"I bet we could come up with something better," Hager said. "Why don't you tell me why you're doing all of this, and maybe I can help you with a name."

"Very funny, Agent Hager."

He laughed again and paused like he was waiting for Hager to say something.

"I bet you're wondering why I didn't carve up your little morsel of a girl instead of her friend?"

"It crossed my mind once or twice."

He laughed cheerfully that time, but it was still an evil laugh.

"Hager made a joke. What an event. Is that your first? To tell you the truth," he chuckled again, "I didn't poke holes in the little wench because I didn't want to ruin it for you."

"Ruin it for me? I don't understand. Why are you worried about me?"

"You need the excitement. Besides, I spared her to make it interesting. If I killed her, you would probably be in such a state, they would take you off the case. I don't want that right now. It means too much to me for you to continue."

"Why is that?"

Hager drew a stick man and wrote *The Strangler* above it.

"Oh, you'll find out soon enough. I'll let the resident expert figure it out for himself. I'm gonna beat you, Hager. I'm gonna force you into making a mistake just like you want to do to me. I don't make mistakes like that. There's no pressure on me. I can simply disappear if I want to and no one will ever notice."

"You will. Someday. And you know what? I'll be there waiting for you when you fall on your ass in the gutter, and I'll be there to pick your scumbag body off the ground and drag you into a cage where you belong. Then, after you're tried and convicted, I'd like to be the one to give you the gas."

"Oooh, Hager, you're so violent. Are you sure you're not the real killer instead of me? I have to admit, your daughter. Whoa, she's hot. I would've liked to stuck my—"

"Shut the fuck up!"

Hager's heart pounded and his body surged with adrenaline. He clenched his hand into a tight fist and his knuckles popped under the pressure.

"I wish you'd try to get to her again. Why don't you? You fuck! Are you scared?"

"Like I told you a minute ago, if I killed the little tramp, you'd be eliminated from the equation. And I don't want that. That's also why I didn't try to make it with your lady friend. Man, is that strange. Jeez, Hager, she looks just like you dearly departed wife, Kelly. No wonder you've got the hots for her."

Hager was boiling and he gritted his teeth together, stood up and paced the floor, but he knew he had to continue the conversation with the animal, whatever he said to provoke him.

"What's wrong, Agent Hager? That hit a nerve? I thought it would. You see, you sanctimonious bastard, I *can* get to you! And I'm proving it right now. I know more about you than you think and you don't know shit about me. I've got the upper hand and I'm slapping you in the face with it like you were a little step child."

"You haven't got shit!" the agent yelled. "You don't know how close I am to nailing your ass to the wall! You're nothing but a dog turd I stepped on and can't get off my shoe. Your stink follows me wherever I walk, but after I stomp on your guts, the stench dies and goes away with the rain. That's what you are to me, you fuck!"

Normally a calm, level headed person, Hager was losing control. The killer was getting to him in a way no one had ever been able. "The Strangler" had hit a sensitive nerve like he hit with a hammer. Hager looked down at his pad; next to the stick figure he'd drawn was another one with its arms extended to the other's throat like he was choking it. Above the other stick figure was *Hager*.

"You are the violent one," the man laughed. "And you're easy, too. Easier than I thought. I thought you were more clever than that, Hager. Listen to you. Cussing me out and threatening my life with the tape recorder recording every word you say, when you should really be trying to skillfully pull information out of me that might help you identify me. You really haven't lived up to your billing, Hager. I'm actually disappointed in you. Maybe you're actually the bumbling idiot, and your partner's the smart one. Like that dumb-assed detective from the movies. What was his name? Oh, Inspector Clousseau?"

"Maybe I'm getting a lot of information about you this way. I've managed to keep you on the line longer than before. I found out just what I thought about you. You're nothing but a worthless coward who can't jack his dick or satisfy a real woman. You have to take them by force and once they're dead, you get your jollies beating your meat over them. Yeah, you're a real man."

The phone was silent. All he could hear was breathing, his own and the monster's. He felt his chest pounding and his palms were wet with sweat. Maybe Hager finally struck a blow for the good guys against the devil.

Then suddenly, the man roared into the phone like a lion. It lasted only a few seconds but was deafening. Hager had to push the receiver away from his ear. Hager returned the phone to his ear; there was silence again. Then calmly, like he was before, the killer spoke.

"Good bye, Hager."

The phone disconnected.

Hager took a deep cleansing breath when he hung up the phone. His forehead was beaded with sweat and his shirt was wet and stuck to his skin as he lowered himself into the chair again.

"That guy is fucking nuts!"

24

LLOYD'S EYES BRIGHTENED, "I didn't think you had it in you, Clark," he said after listening to his partner's voice on the audio tape of the phone conversation with the killer. "I guess I've rubbed off on you a little, huh?"

Hager shook his head in frustration partly, but mostly in embarrassment. He was disgusted with himself because he let the killer make him lose control. But for Hager, this case hadn't only become personal, but intimate.

For some reason, at least at this point, part of the killer's motivation had something to do with him. Why else would he want him to stay on the case, other than to torment and terrorize Hager? Was it him all along? Or did the killer channel his activities toward Hager after the release of the story to the press? That was when the calls started. That was what it was, he thought. It became a game when he knew who his opponent was, and Hager was his foe.

"Don't worry about it, Clark. I'd have done the same thing. What do you expect, for chrissake. He stalked your daughter and murdered her friend. I'm sure you wished you could reach through the phone line and rip the guy's throat out."

Hager smiled and looked down at his notepad with his caricature drawing. Was Lloyd clairvoyant? He was no artist, but it wasn't difficult to see Hager's sentiments about what he would like to do to the killer. Lloyd laughed when he saw it.

"If that ain't the truth. Here, draw another one on the other side and put a gun to the guy's head and write my name on top of it. Then we both can have the fun."

They both laughed.

The trace made on the call came back to a number in the 360° Communications system. The number had a 704 area code and Hager, assuming the number was from a cloned cellular phone, called the Charlotte office and asked for them to check on it.

The rest of the day the two agents examined photographs and reports of the four murders, trying to find some hidden clue as to the identity of the killer. Something they had missed earlier. Something not significant at the time, but of importance now. Something Hager may have learned from the telephone conversations with "The Strangler." They didn't know exactly for what they were looking, but they thought it may just pop out at them if it was found. There was some common thread linking the cases together, and it wasn't only the DNA. It was something else; something deftly secluded in the compilation of data, but overlooked.

Like a mist hovering overhead, it wasn't seen until one looked carefully through its murky film and determined exactly what it was. It had to be in the earlier reports, but it was hidden so well. When they found it, they would know who the killer was.

At 4:30 p.m., Hager and Lloyd were still in Hager's office, this time reading bulletins and reports which had come into the office since the release of the case. Each bit of information was taken, stored in a computer file, and a copy of the lead forwarded to Hager. After Hager and Lloyd read the copy, it would be sent by FAX to the task force members closest to the location of the report. Mostly, there were reports of a possible suspect, a crazy relative, or a strange man seen walking in a shopping mall who matched the description of the man in the composite picture now appearing in the newspapers and news broadcasts all over the region. None of them had produced any fruitful line leading to the killer's identity.

Since the release of the picture about a week after the press conference, the office had received more tips and anonymous calls about the killer than before. Hager knew a picture would cause a flood of erroneous information, but it was a tool to be utilized, like the rest of the investigative steps they had taken. It was one that could result in the killer's capture. Again, nothing could be overlooked.

The Charlotte office called with an update on the traced number from "The Strangler's" call. It was a legitimate cellular phone number linked to a woman in Gastonia. The woman couldn't be located at home and Gastonia police had no information on her or record of any calls to her residence. SBI agents were watching her house until someone arrived.

Earlier, Vanessa and Elizabeth called to let him know they had returned from a successful shopping trip to Cameron Village in Raleigh. Vanessa said Elizabeth was in better spirits, but she still appeared nervous and often looked behind herself in search of would-be followers, only to see their two shadows bringing up the rear.

The success to which Vanessa referred was both of them had bought new outfits. Since spring fashions were on display, they apparently couldn't resist the temptation to add to their wardrobe and get a start on looking stylish when the weather turned warmer. With a new ensemble, a new matching pair of shoes was a requisite purchase. After all, a fashionable outfit only looked good with a new pair of shoes.

Hager could hear the cash register ring "cha-ching" when she mentioned the additional shoes, but he was relieved when Vanessa said it was her treat and didn't divulge the cost. Hager did some quick figuring in his head.

"Let's see, Vanessa only shops at the most lavish stores. An outfit from a place like that would cost about a hundred. Shoes, seventy. Then lunch, multiply it by two and add tax you get, damn. About four hundred dollars."

Regardless of the cost of the trip and who paid for it, Hager felt better knowing they were safe and would be there when he arrived home. Hager estimated it would be around 5:30 p.m. Unless Matlin called and made some progress with Mark Kellogg, it would be a short day today.

Vanessa added they also went to the grocery store and picked up some steaks, which were marinating in Teriyaki sauce until he could put them on the grill for dinner. A couple of baked potatoes and a salad would complete the entree for the evening.

Steaks sounded inviting, and they were especially delicious when soaked in the Teriyaki for a couple of hours. The meat melted in your mouth. Hager's mouth watered thinking about it.

Matlin called a little before 5:00. Both agents were anxious to hear if Kellogg was any help at all. Matlin explained the delay in calling was because he couldn't find Kellogg at home or in his studio at first. Later he caught him at his small office in Wrightsville Beach after he'd been out shooting some photos for a company which produced postcards, one of the many jobs for the small-time, but successful photographer.

Matlin didn't have a positive tone in his voice and Hager assumed Kellogg wasn't very helpful. The detective said Kellogg remembered attending the convention in Atlanta last year and related that several photographers from the coastal area went as well. He named several of his colleagues who were in Atlanta, but said neither of them fit the description of "The Strangler."

Matlin referred to a peculiar event which occurred during the interview.

When Kellogg tried to locate a file box containing all the business cards he'd acquired over the years, including Ronny Cooper's, he discovered it was missing. Kellogg said he hadn't used the box in several months because he hadn't taken any out of town trips since the convention and hadn't needed to use it until now.

The interview wasn't totally a bomb as Hager thought it would be when the file box turned up missing. After Kellogg told Matlin about the file box, he remembered the last time he saw it. It was in July when Kellogg looked for the telephone number of a photographer in Indiana. Matlin said Kellogg's face turned white as though he'd seen a ghost, and Kellogg told him about a man who came into the studio looking for work the same day in July.

The stranger had said he was an amateur photographer, but wished to get into it professionally and wanted to intern with him for awhile. When Kellogg told him he didn't have the business nor the money to afford help, the man left. And that was the last time he saw his file box. Kellogg asked to see the drawing of the killer. After looking at it for a few minutes, making a few indecisive faces, he said it was possible "The Strangler" could have been the man who came into his studio that day. He must have taken the file box, Kellogg had concluded.

Did he get a name? No way. Another encouraging lead flushed down the toilet.

Matlin took the names Kellogg had given him of the area photographers to check and would do backgrounds on them when he returned the next day. Probably another waste of time and effort, but as in the others, it had to be done. Overlook no one. Check and eliminate.

Hager drove home that evening after a frustrating couple of hours at work. Would he get lucky at all in this case? He couldn't catch a break anywhere.

"The Strangler" must have had a horseshoe buried up his ass to be so lucky. Or was it the fact he was extraordinarily clever not to leave any clue to his identity? A little of both, Hager reasoned, and turned his thoughts to dinner.

He took a deep breath and imagined the air filled with the smoky aroma of marinated steak cooking over a fire. The smell itself was intoxicating knowing he would take in the air when the steaks sizzled on the grill. Almost as much as he liked the kitchen, Hager loved to cook outside on the grill.

During the summer, Hager would sit outside on the deck, a cold beer in his hand, and the sun still shining until after eight o'clock. He would sit in a lounge chair and slurp beer waiting on the steaks, or chicken, shrimp, or whatever he had over the fire, while listening to some Jimmy Buffett.

Last Fourth of July, he and Vanessa had Lloyd and his wife, along with a couple of other friends over for a cookout. It was a hot day and he remembered sitting by the grill sweating while he cooked up the feast of steak, chicken, and shrimp kabobs all evenly pierced on long metal skewers in between mushrooms, onions and peppers.

Daydreaming of dinner made him hungrier which increased his speed on Interstate 40. Along with the image of food, he also tasted the cold Ice House waiting for him in the refrigerator and he smiled at his good fortune.

At dinner, they discussed nothing about the murders until Elizabeth brought up Missy's funeral. It was in two days at 1:00 p.m. in Hickory, which was about a three and a half hour drive from Raleigh. Of the four women victims of "The Strangler," this would be the first funeral Hager would attend. All of them had been video taped and Hager and Lloyd viewed them to see any common faces. But as of now, they had no connection which pointed to any person. Vanessa wouldn't be going because she had to return to work; therefore, it would be only he and Elizabeth.

Hager thought about Elizabeth being at the funeral. What if *he* did go to the funerals? Would Elizabeth recognize him? Would he be *that* bold, appearing at the funeral knowing she would be there to see him? To pick him out in front of everyone. What a rush it would be for him to be there, standing like a mourner with the others, only not grieving, but replaying the fantasy in his mind, savoring all the details in his lustful memory.

"He's not that stupid," Hager said to himself. "Or is he?"

After dinner, Hager and Vanessa moved to the living room. Elizabeth had some studying to finish, and she retired to her room, leaving Vanessa sitting on the couch reading a book with Hager's head resting comfortably in her lap. The eight beers had made Hager's forehead feel heavy. But the alcohol also made his eyelids feel like they were weighted down, and soon he was snoring.

The next thing he remembered was waking with a full bladder. He was still on the couch, lying under a blanket, and feeling disoriented. Looking around in a daze, he smelled the smoke from the long dwindled fire, but the house was dark. Vanessa had apparently let him remain on the couch and she went upstairs to bed. There was no sign of Roscoe either—his usual bed companion when it wasn't Vanessa.

In the front hall bathroom, he relieved himself. It felt like it took forever. Feeling refreshed and mildly awake, he ventured upstairs anticipating Vanessa was in his bed, warm and ready to snuggle.

The door was closed and he opened it, but there was no one in the bed. Strange, he thought. Vanessa usually slept with him when she visited.

He thought quickly back to the evening and wondered did he say or do anything to ruffle her feathers. He tried to think deeply but he had a massive headache that drove through his temples like a hammer crashing down on a nail. Too much beer, he concluded. No, there was nothing he could remember. Maybe it was his snoring. With a couple of beers and lying on his back, he was sure he'd cut enough timber to make a small house tremble. But his snoring wouldn't have caused her to abandon her sleeping partner for the night. What was it?

Across the hall was the guest room. The door was closed as always, and Hager opened it slowly, not wanting to disturb her sleep.

He wanted to creep over to her and crawl into bed and kiss her and hold her like he did the night before.

When the light from the hall hit the bed, it hadn't been disturbed. What was she playing here? *The Three Bears?*

"Who's been sleeping in my bed? said the papa bear," he said to himself. Where was she?

He stood in the hall, still in his jeans and Carolina sweatshirt, wondering whether he was dreaming or not. He shook his head vigorously to awaken himself. All it did was make him dizzy and contribute to the throbbing in his head. It was no dream.

Maybe the bathroom. She may be taking a bath. Relaxing in the tub with her book and a glass of wine. He imagined a bubble bath and suddenly became aroused, hoping he could join her in the bubbles and warm water. He entered his bedroom again and walked into the master bath with a smile on his face, but the door was open and the light was off. The smile disappeared. No Vanessa.

Before, he was only curious. Now he was worried. Where was Vanessa? He hurriedly walked back through his room and into the hall again, arriving at Elizabeth's door. The door was closed and he didn't want to awaken her.

He tapped lightly on the door. No response. She must be asleep, he thought. Quietly, he turned the knob and pushed the door open. Again, the light from the hall illuminated her bed; it had been slept in, but was empty, too. If he was worried before, he was now panicking.

"What the Hell's going on around here?" he whispered.

No Vanessa. No Elizabeth. He looked around and turned on his bedroom light looking for Roscoe. Not even Roscoe. A feeling of dread fell over him like an avalanche of snow, and it felt just as cold.

"No," he whispered. "No! There's no way in hell that sonofabitch could've gotten to them here. Both of them? No way."

He shook his head.

"No way. Not here."

The sound of the drumming in his chest seemed to resonate throughout the house; he took a deep breath to calm his nerves.

"I'm being silly," he said, trying to assure himself. "They're around here somewhere."

Frantically, he rushed to the window at the end of the hall which overlooked the driveway and saw all the cars. None were missing. What was going on? Did they disappear? Were they hiding, playing some sick joke? No, not them. He shook his head again.

"No way he came here and took them away. No way!"

Certainly, if someone invaded the house, he would awaken or Vanessa would stir or scream or something to get his drunk ass awake. That was it. Maybe it was the beer. He was too drunk to wake up, even when she screamed for help. He just lay there or turned over in slumber land. What a sorry excuse for a man, let alone an agent with the SBI. To sleep through a monster taking away the two most important women in his life.

He was in a frenzy, stomping through the house, turning on all the lights, calling out their names. Was he going mad? Had "The Strangler" hexed him into acting like a lunatic burglar, ransacking his own house in search of his two guests? Or was he still dreaming? He patted his body like he was frisking himself. No, he was there. No dream.

In the kitchen, he opened cabinets and the pantry door. He looked in the garage—nothing. The front porch—no one. He had looked everywhere and still—no one. They had vanished.

He walked back into the place where he'd awakened and smelled the smoky aroma of the fire already dead.

"Don't think dead," he said to himself. "Just out."

He took a deep breath again and he thought he heard the smoke whispering something to him like the wind.

"Man, I am going crazy if the smoke starts talking to me."

The smoke wasn't talking, but he did hear a voice and it prompted him to open the door leading to the back deck. In the darkness, he could make out the form of a person sitting in a lounge chair. He turned on a porch light and found them both sitting in chairs, wrapped in blankets. Roscoe was at Elizabeth's feet and looked up uninterested.

"Well hello, sleepy head," Vanessa said with her gorgeous smile.

Elizabeth looked up, her face partly covered by the blanket.

"Hi Daddy. Did we wake you?"

After all the air was emptied from his lungs, Hager laughed and his knees buckled, but he supported himself at the door.

"Why are you laughing, Daddy?" Elizabeth asked.

"What's so funny, Clark?" Vanessa asked.

Hager continued to laugh and he was giddy with laughter. Vanessa turned to Elizabeth.

"He's still drunk." Elizabeth said.

She shook her head and giggled.

Vanessa had the blanket draped over her head and both of them looked like women from India who draped cloaks over their heads in public. Their noses and cheeks were red from the cold.

"We're sorry we woke you, Clark, but your snoring was shaking the whole house and we couldn't hear each other talk with it going on."

Hager continued to laugh and the two women looked at each other and smiled, each shaking their heads at the confused man standing at the door. The lover to one; the father to the other.

"What are we going to do with him?" Elizabeth asked.

Vanessa rose from her chair and pulled the blanket tightly around her shoulders.

"I'll take care of him. I'll just put him back to bed. He's probably half asleep anyway."

Elizabeth stood and they both came inside.

"What are all these lights doing on, Clark?" Vanessa asked

Hager kept laughing even though he was truly finished, but he figured he would continue with the charade to avoid the embarrassment of his paranoid thoughts. He stayed silent and gave Vanessa a star-gazed stare of drunkenness.

She turned again to Elizabeth who was locking the door.

"Boy, he did tie one on. More than I thought. I guess we better be glad he doesn't grab his gun and walk around like that when he's in this condition."

"God forbid," Elizabeth laughed.

Hager continued to stare into space, continuing his act and Vanessa led him up the stairs and gently put him to bed. When she lay next to him, he turned to his side and cuddled with her.

"Just one big baby," she whispered and stoked his hair.

He was back asleep in seconds.

25

FUNERALS. Hager hated them. From the time he initially went to one as a youngster when his uncle died, and the several in between until present, Hager tried to avoid them. When he was young, he had no idea as to the aversion. But, in college when his grandmother died, he discovered the reason, and it had molded his opinion of them into his adulthood. Five years ago was the last one, for Kelly. The reality of knowing there would probably be more funerals in his lifetime did nothing but add to the antipathy toward them.

It wasn't only the fact it was difficult comforting people in a time of mourning, as he knew all too well, but it was the way the ceremonies were held that bothered him the most. Funerals, in Hager's opinion, were designed to honor the departed love one, and celebrate life and his or her achievements. What other reason or purpose would be for a eulogy?

To eulogize someone, by definition, was to speak favorably about a person or a person's life. What would begin as a eulogy, quite often turned quickly into a sermon on how the death was God's will and there was some special purpose for the deceased in heaven, and God would take care of the decedent's family. Every time he attended a funeral, the same thing occurred.

Whether it was a pastor, preacher, minister or other man of God, the *eulogy* was centered around God, not the departed soul about whom everyone had gathered to honor.

Hager wasn't anti-religion, believing it had its place for others. But not for him. It took only about ten years working in law enforcement to convince Hager that God didn't exist in the sense which Christians believed. Not the Almighty holy spirit who created the Earth and life on it in seven days.

Anthropology classes had taught him about the evolution of man; therefore, Hager wasn't a true Christian believer before he ventured into law enforcement. But a lesson law enforcement had taught him, if there were a God, like Christians believed, then this world would be much different than it was today. Too many bad things happened to too many innocent people, especially children, to make him believe in the Almighty.

Hager took a much more realistic view of religion: If there were a God, he created the Earth, in its simple form of land and water, and allowed nature to cause the evolution of creatures such as man. And he had other ideas on the creation theory as well. Agnostic was probably an accurate description of Hager's perspective on religion.

His faith, or lack thereof, wasn't something Hager bragged about or revealed to just anyone. Only those especially close to Hager knew of his religious beliefs, and he didn't like to talk much about them. Mainly because religion was a subject that sparked heated debates, especially in the South, where the church was a very powerful entity, and because Hager was afraid people would think he was some devil worshipper who wore a black robe and chanted evil songs in the fires from hell. No one needed to know. It wasn't important.

Mother Nature had dealt favorably upon that Friday afternoon in January, producing an unseasonably warm, sunny day to remember the life of Missy Campbell. It was as if she knew to create a day unlike the chilly days of winter, since the death of someone so young and vibrant was to her, an aberration.

In reality, it occurred much too frequently. When a young person died, especially one who was adored by so many people, it was a tragedy which brought a number of people together to comfort the family of the lost little lamb. Her classmates from high school, newly-made college friends, and neighbors of the family made up most of the mass of people crowded in the small chapel in Hickory. Media persons and other interested guests rounded out the gathering; many were forced to stand during the service.

As predicted, the pastor of the small Baptist church began the eulogy talking about how the death of someone so young, with so much left of life, was taken away before it actually began. But God was truly a loving god and must have had a special reason to sweep her away to heaven and away from her family and friends.

"Here we go," Hager muttered to himself shaking his head. "The next thing he'll do is start passing around the collection plate."

Elizabeth sat beside her father and wept silently, sniffling and dabbing her tearing eyes with a tissue.

She wanted to wear a black dress to signify her mourning status, but the only one she had was an elegant frock reserved for formal affairs. Since they were about the same size, Vanessa provided a conservative pants suit in black to wear over a winter white blouse. Hager wrapped his arm around her as she sobbed.

Luckily, the *sermon* lasted for only about 15 minutes and it was all Hager could endure. Maybe the grave site service, which was reserved only to family and close friends, would be better. The Campbell's had asked their daughter's closest friends to speak about Missy at the grave site service. Elizabeth was non-committal at the time, not knowing what they wanted her to say, but she decided to relate a story about Missy's sweet-tempered personality.

As they inched their way like a herd of cattle behind the crowd leaving the church, Hager scanned the sanctuary for the image from the composite picture of "The Strangler." All heads were bowed and faces meshed together into one large generic face. Still holding onto

Elizabeth, Hager approached the exit door and felt the bright light and heat from the sun. It was a glorious day indeed. Too bad they were remembering a fallen member of the flock instead of having a picnic at the lake.

They stood on the landing near the entrance and Hager spotted a surveillance van in a parking space near the walkway close to where they were standing. Inside the van was a crime scene specialist assigned to photograph the attendees of the funeral. Hager remembered one from the Greenville office was doing the photography. Moffitt was his name.

It was odd for Maxwell to get a tech from so far away to do a job like that, but Lloyd had told him before that Moffitt was probably trying to edge his way into the limelight and to a possible promotion to a full-fledged agent. It was the way politics in the SBI worked. Just like in any other governmental agency. Favors were done, resulting in auspicious promotions and transfers for some.

There must have been at least five hundred people at the church service, but only about twenty cars, including the hearse and the black Lincoln following it, lined behind a Hickory Police Department cruiser. The cemetery was only about a mile away, and the police car led the procession with its blue lights flashing and blowing the siren at intersections. Elizabeth sat with her head down in silence, but she had stopped crying temporarily.

The funeral procession pulled slowly into the cemetery and circled around a paved driveway cut between neatly manicured grass beginning to turn a green color of spring from the faded brown color of winter. It was a fairly large grave yard and well-tended with flowers and wreaths straddling the headstones.

The line of cars stopped adjacent to a blue tent standing above unearthed ground. Four rows of chairs sat under the tent next to a pile of earth that remained to cover Missy's casket. The forty or so mourners slowly walked toward the tent and to their seats, waiting patiently for the pall bearers to bring the casket from the hearse.

Missy's pastor addressed the group first.

"Hadn't he said enough about God and Heaven for one day," Hager said to himself.

Thankfully, the minister was brief. Then he informed the group a few friends wanted to say something special about Missy by which to remember her life and how she spirited them to live their lives. Each of them held a white carnation to be placed on her casket after the remarks were made.

In their own right, each of them were obviously heartfelt, but Missy's brother's speech was the most tear jerking, and made Hager's eyes water as he listened. Elizabeth related a story about Missy adopting two kittens. She seemed to be coming out of her grief, at least temporarily, and didn't shed a tear until she placed the flower on the casket, kissed her hand, then placed it on the coffin as one last display of affection toward her friend as she said good-bye.

After all of them spoke, the pastor ended the service with a prayer in hope God would take Missy's soul into heaven, and that she may serve him there instead of here. Hager bowed his head in respect for the family as the pastor addressed the spirits, and he realized he was sweating from the heat and the jacket he was wearing. The pastor finished the prayer and approached Missy's parents to offer last words of comfort.

Hager watched her parents carefully because the moment just before the burial was the most likely for one of them to break down. In the many funerals he'd attended, he'd seen everything from convulsions and fainting to violent outbursts on the part of mourners when it was really time to say good-bye. Her mother looked a little shaky, but her father was holding her supportively as her knees buckled when she placed the flower on the casket. Seeing Missy's father hold onto his wife made him think back to Kelly's funeral when he held onto Elizabeth with such support. He was being strong for her, as Hager was for Elizabeth.

It was about 2:30 p.m. when the service ended. Hager and Elizabeth were invited to the Campbell's house for lunch, but they declined, Hager saying he had to get back to work. In truth, he didn't want to go and face not knowing what to say to them, feeling almost cruel to smile at a time of such sadness. Maybe what bothered him so much about funerals wasn't the fact that pastors preached at them, but that people continued on with their lives immediately after them, like they could be grim for an hour or two, but at the gathering afterwards, they would make jokes or laugh. Was it right? Was grief only reserved for the funeral, and then thrown out the window when the food was served after the service, like it was a Sunday picnic?

When someone died, especially a person so young, Hager believed people should stop with their lives and be sad. To grieve properly. When Hager saw people milling around a table laughing at something else, it made him feel uncomfortable. Maybe it was healthy to act this way.

"Don't take it too seriously, or you'll go crazy," he said to himself.

Did he take it too seriously? He'd been through it before. He knew how it felt to lose someone.

But hunger had already been talking to Hager's stomach and he decided they would stop at a restaurant before getting on the road back to Raleigh. He mentioned it to Elizabeth and she wanted to eat a hamburger so they stopped at a Burger King near the I-40 interchange. After gobbling up two grilled chicken sandwiches, a large order of fries and a Coke, Hager's hunger no longer existed.

Elizabeth ate heartily as well: a hamburger combo with fries and a Coke, and she got a chocolate pie to take with her for dessert. Her appetite at least seemed normal again.

During the drive home, they listened to the radio and talked about her classes for the semester. They also talked about a guy in her Ethics class, whom Elizabeth wanted to date. She said she always tried to sit near him, but he didn't seem to notice her. Strange, Hager thought, because most men certainly noticed Elizabeth and their frozen gazes were an accurate signal of her beauty.

Hager felt peculiar talking to Elizabeth about boys, but he was glad she finally had a romantic interest since her last boyfriend was almost a year ago. As far as he knew, she'd only dated a couple of times since. Maybe she was a lot like Vanessa in her taste in men, very discerning. He thought about the young man who didn't notice his daughter.

"Either he needs his eyes examined, or maybe he plays for the other team," Hager said to himself. "It *is* the nineties, you know."

He decided not to bring up the subject and felt satisfied with saying, "Maybe he's just shy, Elizabeth. Have you thought about saying anything to him?"

What am I doing? I'm telling my daughter to ask a guy on a date. Be quiet!

Fortunately, Elizabeth's response served to reassure Hager she would not, as she said she wouldn't know what to say.

"Now you know what we men have to go through," he said like he was making a point. "It's not as easy as it looks for us guys. We're the ones who have to deal with all the rejections. Not you."

"What do you mean, Daddy? We get rejected all the time. It's not just the guys who have anything to fear."

"*You* get rejected?"

"Well," she grinned mischievously. "Some of us do."

She laughed.

It was the first time in three days he'd heard her laugh. It sounded good to hear her happy again. He'd forgotten or wasn't aware of her laughing at him two days ago when he wandered around the house late that night looking for her and Vanessa. What was better, they were enjoying a conversation together and none of it was about "The Strangler." For Hager, the brief respite from thoughts of the killer who was terrorizing him seemed like a vacation, and the four hours it took to return to Raleigh flew by without them noticing the time.

26

SEDUCTION. What a wonderful word. Not only does the charmer have to be attractive, but also convincing enough to tear down her defensive walls.

"You smooth-talking wretch," he said to himself as he waited for the woman to emerge from her bedroom.

"What kind of suit will she be wearing?" he pondered as he loaded a fresh roll of film in the camera.

Probably something similar to the outfit she wore while she danced the night away. When he saw her walking sensually toward his table, he had a feeling she would be the one.

There was at least one in every place. One who dreamed of making it big, and those dreams blinded her good sense in that she brought him back to her place after just meeting him in the club. "To take some hot shots of your hot body," he had said to her with his confident tone and innocent eyes. How could she not trust him when he seemed so convincing, telling her she could make it big and *he* would be the reason.

For his trouble, all he asked were some favors given. Some good favors to be exact. But did she know what the favors were all about? Did she realize what she was getting herself into? She'd asked him questions earlier about "The Strangler" and whether or not he was the now notorious killer who graced the headlines of the major newspapers in the region.

In the fancy words which flew over her pretty little head, he did all but answer her question. But she was satisfied with his response, as if his words hypnotized her into believing him even when he never denied it. Why deny it when he could simply schmooze his way around the subject, thus making him appear even more believable?

It was an easy ploy. Harder at first, but it grew simpler as he steadily became more familiar and in tune with what *they* wanted to hear. Fame and money were the biggest grabbers. Stardom was big, too. Everyone of them wanted to be a star. They were performers already, but to be a star with their name in lights or their faces on billboards was the ultimate feat.

Inasmuch as they all wanted to be famous models, not *all* of them fell into his trap. Some gave him the suspicious eye and blew him off, calling him a fake. But, again, there was always one who was on the edge, one who lacked the confidence in herself to realize he was putting on a show. A game. A very dangerous game.

It didn't take long for him to find out which one was on the edge. A couple of days in the same place, and quickly the girls who had it together stood out like a pimple on prom night. Leave them alone, he thought. They wouldn't be susceptible to his smooth tongue. The veterans had dealt with many an oily gentleman who had the gift of *savior faire* in his words. They had been through all the marriage proposals, dates, movie contract offers, and, yes, even modeling contracts.

It was the weaker ones—the ones who didn't have enough experience nor insight into the male mind to distinguish fact from fiction. The old vets would school the younger ones and tell them to put up the gauntlet against any man who entered the walls of their business. "They all lied," the women would say.

But not all of them learned very well.

Emily was no old veteran of the business, but she was also not a rookie. She had the personality and demeanor befitting more of teacher than a stripper, but she was naive nonetheless. It didn't take much to get her to bring him back to her place for some sample photographs in her favorite bikini. Just some business cards, a camera, and some fancy words about contracts and agents, and she was sucked in. Spend about a hundred or so for her to dance, and once she saw the roll of cash, her eyes sparkled. In her line of work, the presidents talked a convincing game.

"What the hell," he told himself. "Spot her some cash to spark her interest. I know I'll get it back later—after."

What a powerful ruse it was to tell someone they had the makings of a supermodel and to watch their eyes light up and their faces blush. They were all over him. And his power.

When he heard the door open, his back was facing her and an evil grin emerged on his face like the devil had taken over his psyche. When he turned around, he was more than pleased at the vision before his eyes. Emily had taken off all the makeup that made her eyes so dark and mysterious and put her blonde hair in a beret which fluffed her hair back on her shoulders. She looked like she was actually ready for a trip to the beach. What a transformation.

He could see why this particular bikini was her favorite. The black color of the fabric matched perfectly with her winter tan and the straps were thin and accentuated her breasts. The bottoms were briefs cut up the sides into a thin strap invading the crack of her ass. Between her legs, he could see the outline of the tasty muff of hair, so neatly trimmed to avoid escaping from the edges of the suit.

His smile turned innocent again and she turned around for him to get a complete picture.

"What do you think?" she asked.

"Wow," he said. "That suit really shows off your fabulous body. Where did you get it?"

"I got it from Victoria's Secret. Isn't it great, I can't wait until summer when I can wear it to the beach."

"Why don't we start taking the shots here on the couch. Do you have some music?"

She looked at him strangely.

"You know, some music, to set a mood," he said. "Play something you'd hear at the beach."

She turned on the stereo and tuned it to her favorite radio station. It was a country station and a song by Garth Brooks was playing. Emily returned to the couch and sat down.

"How do you want me to pose?" she asked.

"Just be natural. You can do anything. Sit, or lie down, kick back your feet, anything you want. Just act like you're having fun and remember to smile all the time."

She sat at first, and he snapped a few pictures while he adjusted his focus for close-ups and for longer shots. She was on her stomach with her hands under her chin. Another close-up of her face, and then one a little farther back to show her cleavage.

With every click of the Canon, his lust grew more intense. As she moved around on the couch, he could sense her inhibitions falling. She lay on her side resting her head in her hand as he clicked and focused more.

"Here, sit up and rest your elbows on your knees and put your chin on top of your knuckles, like this."

He positioned her hands and when he touched her she didn't flinch. She was warm, and the heat radiated from her body. He was boiling.

His eyes caught her stare and her eyes asked for him to kiss her.

"You're beautiful," he said and leaned over to meet her lips.

When he bent his head down to her, he saw the look of astonishment on her face, and her head moved swiftly to the side.

"What are you doing?" she asked disgustedly.

She had a sickened look on her face.

"You wanted me to kiss you," he responded confidently.

"No I didn't. What are you talking about?"

She slid over on the couch out of his reach. He took a step to his right and bent over again to her face. She moved again.

"What are you doing?" she shouted, still with the same disgusted look on her face.

"I said you want me to kiss you. Now what's so wrong with that?"

"No, I don't want you to kiss me. Look, you're a nice guy, but I've got a boyfriend. I thought you were going to take some pictures, that's all."

"No, that's not all, Emily."

He took another step to his right and she tried to get up from the couch, but he grabbed her arm and forced her back down. With lightning speed, he pinned her down on the couch; she screamed as he kissed her, holding her arms. The disgusted look on her face was replaced by one of fear. His camera fell from the arm of the couch onto the floor.

"Stop it! You're hurting me!"

He slapped her face.

"Shut up, bitch!"

He ripped at her bikini top. She screamed again and he slapped her again and again, and then his hands were clutching her throat. She could no longer scream and she gasped for air, her fingers digging into his powerful hands. With his hands still clamped on her neck, he sat on top of her, looking at her face, red from the constriction and from fear.

He didn't hear the keys jingle but when the lock ratcheted and the knob turned, he knew he was being interrupted. He released the pressure of his hands, and she screamed again when the door flew open.

It was a woman. A look of shock and surprise flashed on her face when she heard Emily scream; she dropped her purse at the door.

With all the strength remaining in her body, Emily pushed him off and sent him stumbling on the floor. Emily screamed again and the other woman remained speechless; she stood with her mouth opened.

He regained his balance and saw the other woman now coming at him with a canister of pepper spray. He looked for his camera, but he couldn't find it. With the woman getting closer, it was time to cut his losses and get out of the apartment. He pushed by the woman and ducked the stream of spray aimed at his face, dashed out the door, shoving a male teenager apparently coming to their rescue into a wall. Like a cannon shot, he bolted from the building and out into the night.

When he arrived at his car, he was walking, panting, and his chest hurt from the three block run. Not wanting anyone to see him enter a car and take off quickly, he slowed his pace to give the impression of legitimacy. His lungs filled with air as he took a deep breath while he walked toward his car parked on the street. Only the street lights shone on its bright red paint. No one had followed him that he could tell. With the swiftness of his strides, only a sprinter could have kept up with him. Luckily, it was only a cool night—not cold. He'd gotten away, but he left a clue he didn't want to leave. His prize camera. "Damnit!" he shouted, and put the car into gear, and slowly pulled away from the corner.

27

SEVEN DAYS had passed since his conversation with "The Strangler," and Hager worried he may have gone into hiding since the public was informed he was targeting strippers. Or, maybe he was stalking his next victim and it was taking longer than usual. With all the publicity "The Strangler" was receiving, Hager was sure he was loving it, but hating it just the same because it was hopefully making every woman even more leery of any strangers.

During the week after Missy Campbell's funeral, Elizabeth returned to class, but she was shadowed by two state troopers wearing civilian clothes. Of course, Elizabeth objected to her bodyguards again, but she recanted when she laid her eyes on the youngest of the two troopers. Both of them were recent graduates of the Highway Patrol School, but the youngest one had icy blue eyes and bright white teeth that glowed when he smiled, gaping at Elizabeth.

From this point on, she made it very easy for the troopers to follow her everywhere she went. They didn't have to follow her; in fact, she walked from each class between the two of them, sometimes arm in arm. They looked like a pair of bookend linebackers from Nebraska. Tall, broad shouldered, and muscular, and with their crew cut heads, the troopers provided a serious deterrent to anyone whom Elizabeth didn't want to get close. She soon became very popular, even more than she was, as young ladies followed the entourage around the scenic Chapel Hill campus. Elizabeth had forgotten about the boy in her Ethics class, and he certainly kept his distance when her two *friends*, as she called them, were around.

Hager and Lloyd kept busy with the investigation, looking at reports, receiving leads on the case, and making telephone contact with each task force member and updating them on any progress made. It didn't take long. There wasn't much of any progress.

Charlotte agents found the Gastonia woman to whom the cellular phone number was connected. Valerie Simpson had just returned from a two-week business trip in Los Angeles. She had her cell phone. And it worked normally.

Hager had managed to skim over some literature on cellular phone cloning after "The Strangler" had mentioned it during his first call. The fact of Simpson's phone still in working order was consistent with a cloning operation. Numbers from phones were captured with a device and subsequently plugged into a stolen phone. The numbers, however, weren't used for a long period of time because the companies were becoming more and more aware of cloning activity. Another dead end.

The video tape of Missy Campbell's funeral was shown over and over, as well as photographs of the other victims' funerals, but there were no common faces in the crowds. Just mourners and family members. Hager knew it would be a long shot for the killer to attend the funeral of the victim; but it was a chance to take. The grave sites were also staked out by local police to see if any *visitors* came to pay their respects in private. No one had shown yet, but the stakeouts continued.

Another weekend approached without any signal the killer was still in their midst. Hager pondered the inevitability that the killings could stop. Could it come to such a dead-end conclusion with no sense of closure for any of the victims or their families? Would there be any finality of it for Hager, who had been affected by the monster almost as much as the victims themselves? He was a victim. A victim of terrorization. The calls, the threats, the stalking of his daughter, almost forcing himself to be removed from the case for her safety. But he was alive, and so was Elizabeth. He was a surviving victim, then, and there weren't any of those around who were involved in this bizarre case.

But could the monster just halt his activities? Could he forego the quest of fulfilling his fantasies so he could remain anonymous? It had happened before, many times before. There were numerous serial killers who escaped the clenches of justice for years before their identity was known; or they were able to avoid capture after it was revealed.

They were mostly the smart ones who were able to control their homicidal rages for some period of time, relying upon the souvenirs they had accumulated to help them delight in the remembrance of their deeds. "The Strangler" took souvenirs, Hager knew. Would he be *playing* with them at the same time Hager sat in the recliner in his living room watching the fire flare and listening to some old Eagles tunes. It made him feel sick to think about it.

Hager was sleeping soundly with Vanessa's arm draped gently over his chest. When the phone rang, it startled him, but he didn't know why he flinched when the sound chimed in his ears. But his heart was beating like thunder in his chest, and he took a deep breath to slow its rate. Was he dreaming when he heard the phone? Dreaming about *him* creeping around the house, or was he venturing on a deep sea fishing expedition in the Caribbean, with the hot sun burning his skin and the smell of salt and tanning oil in the air. Hoping for the latter, there was no way to tell. He didn't remember.

Vanessa stirred and turned over as Hager sat up and reached for the telephone beside the bed.

"Hello?" he mumbled.

"Agent Hager?" a man responded.

"This is Hager. Who's this?"

The voice didn't sound familiar.

"This is Detective Leo Kasparillo with Fayetteville PD. I'm sorry to bother you at the late hour, but I thought you'd want to know as soon as possible."

He looked at the alarm clock next to the phone and it was 3:40 a.m.

"It's okay. What do I want to know?"

"He's struck again. 'The Strangler'. Here in Fayetteville."

He said it with such glee as if he were happy to have a death in his city.

Hager sat completely up and touched his feet on the floor. "Struck again? When did this happen? How do you know it was 'The Strangler'?"

"About an hour ago. We've got an eyewitness."

Again, he sounded like he was proud to have a famous killer grace his city with his presence.

So what. There are a dozen people who can identify him. What's the big deal about an eyewitness?

"Someone saw him kill her?" Hager asked.

"No," he chuckled. "There's been no killing here, but a girl was attacked and she survived."

Still a "so what". It doesn't bring me any closer to identifying this guy.

"Survived? Great! What happened?" Hager asked like he was excited.

"Same thing that's been happening all over. She was a dancer. This guy picked her up at the club after he promised her a modeling contract for some magazine. She took him back to her place and he started taking some shots of her in a bathing suit."

The detective took a deep breath and continued.

"Then, he made the moves on her. Tried to kiss her and told her she wanted him and then, he started to slap her around. The girl said he was so strong and he choked her and she thought she'd passed out, but her roommate came through the door. She said the guy got up off her and took off out the front door. And now comes the best part."

Hager whispered to himself, "Please say you've got him in custody. Please."

Hager waited for the detective to finish, but the Fayetteville cop was emphasizing the drama of his revelation.

"Well, what's the best part?"

"We got his camera," he said proudly.

Kasparillo's tone sounded more like he'd stumbled across the vaccine for smallpox as opposed to recovering a trivial piece of evidence like a camera.

"You have his camera and..."

Hager hoped his dramatic pause would produce something more hopeful.

"That's it. He left it in her apartment. Film's still in it and everything."

"That's *all* you've got?"

Hager's voice described his disappointment.

"It's not much, Detective. What are we supposed to do with a camera?" he said facetiously. "Develop the film to see if he took a picture of himself. Or maybe his name is inscribed on it along with his driver's license number and social security number so we'll know exactly who it belongs to. Or maybe he left his address on the lens cap, too."

Hager realized he was being very rude to his colleague and stopped. There was silence on the other end, only breathing.

"I think it's a good piece of evidence, Agent Hager," he snapped. "There're probably prints on the camera, and yeah, the film can be developed."

Hager could see him nodding over the phone so loudly, it could be heard.

"You never know what may turn up on one of those things. Boy, they were right about you. You are a tight-assed bastard!"

Hager had it coming to him and he accepted it with the knowledge of its meaning.

"Look, Detective, I apologize for what I said. You're right; it is evidence. I'm sorry but I was hoping you had something better than what you told me."

He was talking meekly now.

The detective wasn't finished though.

"What did you think, we had the body here waiting for you? Ha! Ha!" he laughed sarcastically.

"Well, something like that," Hager responded. "Look, I've been absorbed by this case since the first body was found. I've been threatened, my daughter's been stalked, and her friend was killed by this maniac, and we haven't gotten any closer to nailing him than we were when we started. Yeah, I was hoping you had him in custody. For the sake of everyone's sanity, including my own. Is that too much to hope for?"

They were even. The detective was silent for a moment and he cleared his throat.

"Okay, I understand. I'm sorry, too. I guess we're all under a lot of stress here."

You're under stress? You haven't even experienced stress, my friend.

"Yeah, that's the way it is around here too. Look, I'll call my partner and we'll head out there. I guess the girl is all right. She can speak and everything?"

"Yeah, she's gonna be fine. Just shook up is all. She's at the hospital now. She should be ready to make another statement by the time you get here."

"What about the camera?" Hager asked.

"It's been bagged by our lab and ready for you to come and pick it up."

Hager heard a voice in the background yelling Kasparillo's name. "Wait a minute," he said to Hager.

He heard only the muffled sounds of voices. Apparently, Kasparillo had placed his hand over the handset.

"All right, you there? One of our patrolmen got a radio call about a suspicious vehicle three blocks from here. A neighbor said a white male was running down the street coming from the direction of the girl's apartment and got into a red sports car. Said he stopped running just before he got close to the car and then walked the rest of the way, looking around to see if anyone was watching."

"Did they get a license number?"

"Bad news, they didn't. It was too dark, but that seals it, don't it? 'The Strangler' was driving a red Nissan 300 ZX in Chapel Hill, right?"

"You're right."

The information on the car wasn't released to the public, but an "all points bulletin" was dispatched to all agencies across the United States, Puerto Rico, and Canada.

"Detective, I appreciate the call. We'll be there by seven. Should we meet at your office?"

"Yeah, I'll wait for you there. You can talk to the girl when you get here."

28

EVEN THOUGH HAGER'S suspicion of the killer going into hiding was diminished, he didn't feel any more relieved about the call he received from Fayetteville. It only confirmed the likelihood of more deaths occurring if the killer wasn't stopped. "This one was lucky," he said to Lloyd during the trip to Fayetteville. But the overwhelming task of determining the identity of "The Strangler" had been riddled with hopeless leads and infinite dead ends. Still, they tried to move forward, slowly putting pieces of the puzzle together, assembling them into a package that would surely convict the monster and send him to the gas chamber. One piece—the most important one, was still missing, however. And the end didn't seem to be anywhere in sight.

Disappointed as he was, Hager predicted the latest incident to be the "breakthrough" for which he'd been searching. The link to the unknown. The value of X in the algebraic equation resulting in the product—*MURDERER*.

For this woman was the only survivor of an actual attack from the killer, and was therefore a vital component and link to the other murders. She was invaluable as a witness and as a tool to be utilized in breaking down the killer's routine and any quirks she may have noticed. As expected, he would make a mistake. A mistake that would symbolically pull away his mask and reveal his true identity to the entire world. Every question would then be answered.

Was this the fatal mistake? Would leaving behind a camera, such a simple prop in an enormously complex story, be the last piece of the puzzle? Hager doubted it. Nothing was quite as simple as this case had already proven. Something with no direct correlation to its owner, consequently, couldn't reveal the individual in whose possession it was. Not like a car or some other property which linked directly to an individual or entity. If only whoever saw the car could have gotten the license number.

Hager experienced an enlightenment at the idea of numbers. He knew it was a long shot, but he was growing weary of the ordeal, and decided to take a chance at discovering something from the remotest possibility. After all, there was nothing to lose and a colossal answer to gain.

Detective Kasparillo met the two agents in the parking lot of the Fayetteville Police Department. By the detective's last name, Hager presumed Kasparillo was of Italian descent, but surprisedly, he looked neither like an Italian nor Caucasian at all. From his dark brown skin and straight greasy black hair combed back from his receding hair line, Hager realized the detective was Indian or bi-racial. A gray sport coat hung snugly over his stocky features, and Hager looked into his intense eyes when he spotted their car.

Hurriedly, Kasparillo walked over to Lloyd's Caprice like he was bothered by something. He pulled on the locked rear door handle behind Hager's seat.

"Let me in. We need to get over to her apartment."

An agitated look was on his face.

Lloyd looked at Hager and acknowledged the personality description described of the detective during their trip.

"Nice to meet you, too," Lloyd growled.

"What's going on, Kasparillo?" Hager asked.

His face was stern and his dark eyes still intense.

"She got a phone call."

"From him?" Hager asked.

Kasparillo nodded and gritted his teeth. He looked at Lloyd and stared, then returned to Hager.

"Yeah, called about fifteen minutes ago. Said he was coming to get her."

"Have you got people on the way?" Hager asked.

The detective looked at Hager like he was insulted.

"Yes," he snapped, and his eyes burned. "There're two cars there already. I don't think she wants to stay there. You think it's possible to put her somewhere until all of this is over?"

Hager's brow wrinkled as he pondered the question.

"Of course. We'll put her in a hotel or something. Can your people watch over her until I get the okay?"

"I don't foresee a problem with it, but I'll have to clear it through the captain."

His eyes turned softer, his tone, much more agreeable.

Kasparillo navigated the streets for Lloyd. Emily Nye lived in an apartment complex off McPherson Church Road in southwest Fayetteville. The complex was scattered with three-level buildings with four or five apartments per floor. Like many apartments, they were made partially of brick and sided with clapboards. The apartments looked old and a bit run down with some junked cars parked in the parking lot.

The mild weather that graced the region over the past week was quickly disappearing and clouds were moving in from the North along with some blustery cold air. The weather forecast indicated there was a chance of snow, and Hager knew all the grocery stores throughout the state would be packed with customers stocking up on staples of milk, bread and eggs in case they were trapped in a snowstorm.

Two marked police cars were in the parking lot in front of the apartment building. Hager, Lloyd and Kasparillo walked up the concrete stairs to a pair of doors. Hager stepped aside to let Kasparillo lead the way into the door and up a small set of carpeted stairs and down a hall to the woman's apartment.

Emily Nye was blonde, good-looking, and bore a striking resemblance to Heather Kingston, the college girl killed in Wilmington. "The Strangler's" first victim. Two uniformed officers were in the apartment, one sitting at a table, the other standing near the front door. The woman was sitting on a white leather sofa with her head down, but she raised it when the three of them entered the apartment. A blanket was draped around her shoulders and her face was disfigured, especially around her right eye, where it was red and severely swollen.

When she turned her head to them, Hager noticed the red blotches on her throat, an injury from the attempted strangling. She definitely looked like a victim.

Emily related the entire episode from the beginning when she was first approached by the man at Silver Fox Gentlemen's Club to the end, when she was attacked after bringing him back to her apartment. While she described the incident, she was composed and unwavering, but when she arrived at the phone call received a half hour before, she crumbled in her emotions.

In between sobs and sniffles, she tried to recite his exact words over the phone.

"He said he wasn't finished with me and he knew I wanted him to come back. He scared me when he said he wanted to see my eyes looking at him when he killed me. He said it was such a turn-on."

She shook her head and wiped her nose with a tissue.

"Such a sick bastard," she said. "But that wasn't what scared me the most."

"What did he say to do that?" Hager asked.

A look of fear came to her eyes as she recalled his words, and slowly she quoted him.

"He said, 'I'm so close they won't ever find out who I am. Not before we can be together. I'll come back and you'll never expect it.'"

She paused and took a deep breath after she said the words.

"It wasn't what he said that scares me the most. It's how confident and sure of himself he seems. Like he knows he's going to win."

Hager walked over and put his hand on Emily's shoulder.

"Don't worry, Emily. He won't lay another hand on you. I promise."

She smiled and looked up at him with helpless eyes pleading for help when all will to fight was gone.

Leaving the two officers with Emily, Kasparillo guided the two agents back to the police department where they ended up in the detective's office. The only pieces of evidence collected from the scene were some latent prints and the camera left behind by the killer. Hager had asked Emily if her attacker gave his name or a business card. She produced the same business card given to Vivian in Greenville, with the name of Ronny Cooper imprinted on it.

"Why not rely on a sure thing?" Hager asked himself.

The camera was on Kasparillo's desk inside a clear plastic bag. Hager picked it up and examined it. A Canon EOS with a lens which protruded from the camera's base about three inches.

"A damned expensive camera if you have all the lenses and shit," Kasparillo said.

"Do you know much about them?" Hager asked, looking for the serial number.

"No, not much. One of our lab guys said it was a nice camera. One that a pro would use. Worth about seven hundred dollars. More with all the lenses. Ya'll want some coffee?"

Hager looked over to Lloyd, who was sitting on the edge of a desk, and silently affirmed the friendly tone in the detective's voice. "What a schizoid." Hager said to himself.

"No thanks, we have to be getting back to Raleigh and start processing this camera."

Kasparillo looked disappointed.

"Oh, okay. When will you let me know about the hotel for the girl?"

"As soon as I get back to Raleigh. I'll check with my boss and call you. It shouldn't be a problem."

Lloyd walked over to Kasparillo and shook his hand.

"It was nice to meet you, Kasparillo," he said with a tone of sarcasm only Hager detected.

When they stood next to each other, Hager could see they were about the same height, but the detective was thicker and possessed the same large hands as Lloyd.

On the way back to Raleigh, Hager explained his idea to his partner. Cameras had serial numbers and if the camera wasn't in NCIC as stolen, then there was a way to find the owner. Lloyd looked at him with dismay.

"How are you gonna do that?"

"I thought about it. Cameras and other property like TVs and stereos are sent to distributors by the manufacturer. Serial numbers are placed on the item at the manufacturer before they are shipped to the distributor. Just like doing a gun trace; we'll start at the manufacturer and work our way down to the distributor and so on."

Lloyd shook his head.

"But cameras aren't like guns, Clark. They don't have to be recorded when one is sold. It'll be like finding an ant at an anteater convention."

"You're right. It's one chance in hell of finding the owner, but at least we may be able to trace it to the store and then to a city. It might give us a place to start looking for him. And we might get lucky and find the owner."

Lloyd shrugged his shoulders.

"Maybe we'll get some good prints from it and not have to worry about it."

"Yeah, and maybe he took a picture of himself, too."

It was almost noon when Hager and Lloyd arrived at SBI Headquarters. Hager asked Lloyd to make a run to a nearby sub shop and pick up some subs for lunch. While Lloyd was gone, Hager took the camera and fingerprint cards from the crime scene to the Identification Section. He logged them onto a lab request form. Hager was careful to copy correctly the model and serial numbers for the camera and wrote down every piece of information on the identification plate to have it handy if needed:

Elan II
9108586
Made in Japan

All the evidence was transferred to the specialist in the section. Hager requested the camera be processed for prints, and the resulting latents entered into AFIS. He also requested the film inside the camera to be developed immediately and 8X10 prints made from the negatives.

Hager quickly returned to his office. He stepped hurriedly, excited in anticipation of tracing the camera. Although he'd never had much luck with traces on personal property through the manufacturer before, Hager always hoped for the one time he would get lucky. Maybe this was the time.

But first, he checked the camera's serial number through the stolen files in NCIC. If the camera was stolen and the serial number entered, it might make Hager's job a lot easier. At least, with this information, he would know where the killer may have lived. Not much hope there. Most people didn't record the serial number for any of their property which were hot items for theft-televisions, stereos, VCRs, and microwave ovens-much less, cameras. Unless they had a home owner's insurance policy and the agent required serial numbers for the property listed, it was unlikely to have been noted.

Hager accessed DCI on his PC and brought up the query screen for *Articles–Stolen*. He entered the type of article, the brand, and the serial number, and transmitted the request. Within seconds the computer beeped the familiar tone denoting a message was waiting. Hager pushed the button.

No DCI Stolen Record.

The incessant beeping continued and he pushed it again.

No NCIC Stolen Record.

Not getting a "hit" simply meant the camera hadn't been both reported stolen *and* entered into NCIC. Hager wasn't disappointed. He knew if the camera had been stolen, then more than likely, the victim had no idea who committed the crime and could therefore be of very little assistance.

Stolen property could change hands several times over a period. The camera could have been stolen in Kalamazoo, Michigan and taken to New Orleans, Louisiana and sold to a pawn shop and then resold to someone else who transported it to North Carolina and traded it for drugs or gotten it stolen from him or herself. The list of people could be endless.

If the camera was *not* stolen and Hager was able to trace its sale, he might be able to get closer to the killer. Either way, both techniques presented Hager with an infinite number of possibilities, as well as dead ends. It was about as long a shot as there was, but Hager was optimistic.

After leaving DCI, Hager clicked on the *Internet* to see if Canon had a manufacturing plant nearby. The screen appeared with a list of matches. The first one said *Canon, U.S.A., INC.*, and Hager clicked the mouse and entered the web site. A menu on the left side of the screen had different headings running vertically and Hager saw the heading *Manufacturing* and clicked the mouse on it. *Canon, Virginia, Inc.* was one of the headings on the screen. Hager clicked his mouse on the name.

The page for Canon, Virginia came into view. It gave a brief summary of the company's activities. But most importantly, CVI, as it was called, was Canon's primary production facility in the U.S. Hager would start there. The company was located in Newport News, Virginia and it gave a telephone number. He returned to the main page in the web site, and looked at the menu for distributors. None were listed.

Lloyd arrived with lunch, but Hager was too excited to eat. Anticipating long periods of being placed "on hold" over the telephone, he placed the footlong turkey sub on his desk and unwrapped it so he could eat during waiting times. Lloyd took a seat beside his desk and stuffed his sub in his mouth in between taking gulps of a drink and crunching on potato chips. After a few rings, the phone was answered by a woman.

"Canon, Virginia."

"Yes, this is Clark Hager with the North Carolina State Bureau of Investigation—"

"Hold please."

"Damn," he mumbled. "She didn't even ask what I wanted."

Hager waited in silence, thankfully absent of the customary dentist office music. He put down the receiver and turned on the speaker phone. With his hands free, Hager ravenously dug into the sandwich.

A minute elapsed, and Hager grew impatient. No music, no ringing. Only silence and the sound of an occasional belch from Lloyd.

"Who are you holding for?" the woman asked.

Hager quickly snatched the handset.

"Well, I don't know, I just told you who I was and you put me on hold. This is Agent Hager—"

"Oh, the police. Mr. Parnell will be with you in a moment. I'll try his extension again."

"Wait," he said, wanting to catch her before she connected him to a wrong number.

"Shouldn't I tell you what I want, then you can send me to the right person?"

"Okay," she sighed.

"I've recovered a camera in the course of an investigation, and I think it's stolen, but it doesn't come back as stolen. Do you think if I give you the serial number you can find out from where it came? Where it was distributed?"

"Mr. Parnell would handle that, sir. He handles all the calls from y'all," she said with a tone that told him the explanation wasn't necessary, but was politely accepted.

"Okay, thank you."

Silence again. Maybe Hager missed the elevator music.

"This is Mr. Parnell. How can I help you?" a man cheerfully asked.

"Hi, this is Clark Hager of the North Carolina State Bureau of Investigation. I've got a camera I recovered during a case I'm investigating and I think it's stolen, but it didn't come back stolen through our records. I was wondering if it was possible, you know, if I gave you the serial number on the camera, you can tell me where it was distributed to."

"Oh, Mr. Hager, hmm, this is a first for us. We get calls from the police all the time, but I'm afraid I can't help you with this one."

Hager's heart fell in his chest and the man continued.

"We don't make cameras here at Canon, Virginia. We only make the copiers and printers and all. I don't know."

"Is there somewhere else I can try?"

"I'll give you a number for the public relations department at Canon, USA. Maybe they can help. Hold on for a second."

Another minute of silence.

"This is getting old," Hager said to himself. "But at least it's better than those automated phone answering services."

Mr. Parnell returned.

"Okay, you there?"

"Yeah, go ahead."

Hager wrote down the number.

"They should be able to help you," Mr. Parnell said.

"Okay, sir. Thanks." Hager said and he hung up the phone. "More of the corporate bureaucracy," he told himself. Could he expect anything less?

Hager dialed the number and while it was ringing, he looked at the information he'd downloaded from the *Internet* about Canon, USA, Inc. The headquarters was located in Lake Success, NY. The public relations department was undoubtedly located there. The phone continued to ring, and a woman, with an obvious New Yorker accent, answered the phone.

"Canon, USA, can I help you?"

"Here we go again with the introductions," Hager groaned. "Hi, I'm Agent Hager with the North Carolina State Bureau of Investigation and I've got a Canon camera I think is stolen, and I was wondering if I gave you the serial number, could you tell me where it was distributed."

"Wow, that's an unusual request. I don't know. What kind of camera is it?"

Finally, some inkling of hope for success, Hager thought. At least she acted like it was possible.

"It's an Elan two and the serial number is..."

Hager quickly looked at the numbers on the notebook.

"9-1-0-8-5-8-6. It said it was made in Japan, but I thought the parts were just made in Japan and assembled here."

"It's possible," she said. "I don't know if I can get it for you. You're the first person who's ever made this type of request. I'll have to make a few calls and get back to you."

"How long do you think it will be?"

"I have no idea, sir. Could be a few minutes, could be a couple of days. More than likely it shouldn't take but a little while."

"Great, what was your name, ma'am?"

"Cindy Marchella."

"And this is the public relations department?"

"That's right. Now what's your name and phone number?"

Hager gave her the information and after hanging up the phone, he finished his sandwich and drink. Just as he finished the last of the sub, the telephone rang and Identification section was on the line. The caller told Hager the photos from the camera were ready. He asked Lloyd to fetch them so he could wait by the phone for the call from Canon.

Since Cindy Marchella said it might not take her very long to track down his request, Hager didn't want to chance missing this most important call.

About ten minutes later, Lloyd returned carrying a brown letter-sized envelope containing a stack of 8X10 photographs and a chew of tobacco in his mouth.

"Wow, she is a cutie pie!" Lloyd announced and he spat in the Subway cup full of tissue paper. "She sure looked better before he smacked her around."

He handed the stack of prints to Hager.

Of the twelve pictures taken, all twelve were of Emily Nye. He was no expert, but Hager could tell that some of the shots were quality, similar to those he'd seen in magazines. But the others: shots of her breasts, her butt, and her crotch area were zoomed in closely.

She was wearing a black thong bikini and was posing in different positions on the white leather couch, which provided a good back drop in contrast with her tanned body and the color of her suit. The close-up shots focused on the normal erotic areas of the body, but the last picture on the roll was the one of her face only, and it really accentuated the beauty of it.

"She really could be model with her skin," Hager said.

Hager placed the photographs back in the envelope and tossed it on his desk. Lloyd reached over and perused the prints again, getting a close-up view of the pretty girl in her bikini.

"Did they say anything about the prints from the camera or the others?" Hager asked.

Lloyd spoke from behind the pictures.

"Gulfman said there were only smudges on the camera, but he was able to get a really good what looked like a thumb print from the lead of the film. He said he almost forgot about it but remembered that some good prints come from film."

"How ingenious! I wouldn't have thought of that."

Lloyd lowered the photos and Hager could see his face.

"He said it was the best print they had, but it didn't match the ones lifted from the scene. I guess it means the other prints were the girl's."

"Or her roommate's."

"Anyway, they were entering it into AFIS when I left and said the search would be done soon."

"I'll hope, if you'll pray, Lloyd."

The telephone rang again and Hager answered.

"SBI, Hager."

"Clark? It's Gulfman down in I.D. I've got some bad news for you. AFIS just went down right in the middle of entering the thumb print from the film."

"Shit. How long?"

"No idea. It probably went down for maintenance, and it could take a couple of hours up to a day. You know how those big systems are. When it comes back up, it'll have to be re-entered because it didn't take the first time. Sorry, man."

Hager hung up the phone quietly. He didn't rant or rave or throw things. He just sat silently with his hands covering his face.

"When are we ever going to get a break on this?"

*   *   *

"HOT DAMN!" Hager shouted, after he hung up the phone. Cindy Marchella from Canon had called and advised him of the location of the store where the EOS camera was sent. Rather excitedly, he scurried out the door and into the hall toward his partner's office, but upon hearing his exclamation, Lloyd jumped out of his chair and met him just outside the door.

"We got it! We got it!" Hager ranted, and raised his arms over his head like he was signaling a touchdown.

"Got what?"

"The camera. The woman from Canon called back, and told me where it was sent. It was sent to a camera store in...you'll never guess where."

29

"Wilmington."

Hager smiled like he'd just been given the news of an impending birth.

"At a place called Cape Fear Camera on Front Street. They gave me the address and everything. And better yet, the camera was ordered in May of 1996. Bef—"

"Before Heather Kingston's murder," Lloyd finished.

Hager stood there glowing and ready to proceed, like he was as a child with a dollar to spend in the candy store. Lloyd wasn't as enthusiastic.

"Well, are you gonna call them or what?"

Hager saw Lloyd's skeptical look and realized although it was a good lead, it didn't produce the answer for which he was searching. He could be enthusiastic if the store had a record of the sale of the camera, but even then, he still had no definite link to the killer.

"Don't go flying off the handle now, Clark," Lloyd warned, appearing to like the role reversal. "It's only one little piece of information."

"I know, Lloyd, but I've got a feeling this is our big break. It has to be."

"Well, the only way you're gonna find that out is if you call them?"

"They probably won't tell me over the phone, and..."

He stopped, realizing his haste in getting excited over something so trivial. He remembered Kasparillo's hoopla over the discovery of the camera, and how quick he was to shoot him down.

"I think I'll call Matlin and have him go over there, and if they don't come up with anything, we won't waste a trip there for nothing."

"And what if they do?" Lloyd smiled, knowing the answer already.

"You bet your ass we'll be there," Hager said.

Hager phoned Matlin and informed him about the attack in Fayetteville. He explained the recovery of the camera and the subsequent lead at the camera shop. Hager gave the detective instructions to call him as soon as he learned *anything*. When he replaced the handset, he crossed his fingers and if he prayed, he certainly would pray for a miracle.

Bill Maxwell was the second person he called. Hager asked if he would authorize the use of agents to provide protection for Emily Nye at a hotel. Maxwell told him all the agents in the district were tied up with a police shooting in Lumberton. The Assistant Director agreed to call the Fayetteville chief of police and request their assistance in guarding the woman temporarily. Hager looked at the clock and noticed it was getting close to 6 p.m. and wondered if Matlin would get to the camera shop before they closed for the day. He sat at his desk thinking about nothing but the camera.

The thought of his family popped into his head, and he decided to call home and check on Elizabeth and Vanessa. After five rings, Vanessa answered the phone in a sleepy voice.

"Hey, babe. I'm sorry. Did I wake you?"

"Yeah, but I need to get up anyway," she said and yawned. "I came home from work early. I wasn't feeling well. What time is it?"

"It's a little before six o'clock. Not feeling well? What's the matter? You think you're coming down with something?"

"I don't think so," she sighed, her voice still sleepy. "I just had a terrible headache and the three Advil I took didn't touch it."

"Well, I hope you feel better. Is Elizabeth home yet?"

"Yeah, she was in her room studying when I went upstairs about two hours ago. I guess she's still here."

"What about Rice and Burns? Are they still around?"

"They said they were gonna watch some TV while I took a nap. They're probably downstairs. How did it go today? Was it the same guy you're looking for? Was the girl in Fayetteville any help?"

Hager didn't want to sound too excited, but he was sure he would when he told her.

"You remember I told you about the camera the suspect left. Well, I was able to trace the camera by the serial number from the manufacturer to the store where it was sold. Matlin's checking out the store right now. I'm waiting for him to call any minute."

"That's great, Clark! I can tell you're optimistic about it by the sound of your voice. I really hope this will be over soon. All this running around with bodyguards and all. I think I'm beginning to get a little paranoid."

"I know, I know. I hope so, too, Vanessa. But I'm not going to take any chances of him getting to either of you again."

"When are you coming home? Will it be too late?"

Lloyd came through the door of Hager's office.

"Clark, Matlin's on line four."

Hager nodded and waved for his partner to come in.

"I don't know for sure, Vanessa. Look, Lloyd just came in and Matlin's on the other line. I'll call you back when I know for sure."

Hager hung up the phone and pushed the speaker phone button opening line 4. Lloyd took his usual position leaning against the edge of the computer table.

"Well, what's the good news?" Hager asked.

"No good news yet, Clark. The store was closed when we got there. They closed at five-thirty."

Hager made a face and Lloyd shook his head in frustration.

"But we were able to get an emergency contact number for the owner from our communications. I called the number but got no answer. So I ran the owner's name through DMV, and I got an address in Wrightsville Beach. We're on the way there now. I just wanted to let you know what we had so far."

"Good deal," Hager said. "If you make contact with the owner, see if he'll go back to the store with you guys to check his records. I'm gonna go on home. Call me there when you know something more, okay?"

Hager disconnected the call, and he looked at Lloyd, who remained leaning against the table with his arms crossed.

"You want me to call you when I hear from them?" Hager asked Lloyd.

"Does a bear shit in the woods? Of course I do."

On his way home, Hager went to a Chinese take-out place and picked up dinner for himself, Vanessa and Elizabeth. China Garden was located in a strip shopping center on Cary Towne Boulevard and was home to the best Chinese spare ribs Hager had ever tasted. In addition to spare ribs, Hager ordered a large container of *moo goo gai pan* for himself and Vanessa, pepper steak for Elizabeth, along with egg rolls and the staples of white rice and fortune cookies.

At dinner, he worried about something going wrong with the camera shop. Nearly 8 p.m., Hager figured Matlin would have called by then.

"You seem preoccupied about something, Clark," Vanessa said. "What's the matter?"

"Oh, just wondering why Matlin hadn't called yet is all."

He looked down at his plate, scattered with specks of rice. The daydreaming hadn't affected his appetite, which nothing rarely did.

"You haven't opened your fortune cookie yet, Daddy."

Elizabeth handed him the yellow cookie wrapped in plastic.

"Will it tell me I'll soon meet a tall, handsome stranger?" he asked.

"If it does, then send it my way, will you?" Vanessa joked.

Hager gave her a jealous glance.

Not being particularly superstitious, Hager opened the cookie intending to find some eloquent rhetoric about some future goals or achievements. He put a chunk of the crunchy lemon wafer in his mouth and pulled out a white strip of paper. On one side, six numbers, randomly selected for the lottery players who also ate Chinese, and on the other:

After encountering many difficult obstacles, one eventually comes to an open gate.

The irony of the message was clear, and Hager wondered if someone had intentionally sabotaged his fortune cookie as a joke or discreet gesture of encouragement. Dismissing sabotage, Hager read it aloud using his best Confucious impression after Elizabeth predicted it wouldn't come true if he didn't.

How convenient, Hager thought, to stumble upon such a symbolic message, one that reeked of irony and coincidence. Maybe it was an omen.

Elizabeth cleared the table of plates and food containers. Hager and Vanessa snuggled on the couch watching television. When the telephone rang, Hager jumped up quickly and dashed to the kitchen, like he'd been called as a contestant on *The Price is Right*. Bill Matlin was on the phone.

"Bill, what cha got?"

"Clark," the background hissing made it obvious he was on a cellular phone. "This guy hasn't shown up yet. It's been a long day. I'm gonna just leave my card on his door with my home number on it and have him call as soon as he gets home. All right?"

Hager had forgotten Matlin more than likely had been at work since 8 o'clock that morning.

"Of course, Bill. Yeah, leave your card. There's no reason for you to sit and wait all night. I'm sorry you waited this long. No sense wasting too much time on a long shot anyway."

"Well, I figured this guy'd be home by now. He must have gone out somewhere."

"Were there any other names on the contact list you have?"

"Nope, just the one. Nick Liverton. Does it ring a bell?"

Hager shook his head.

"No, never heard of it. How about you?"

"Same here. I'll call you if I hear from him, okay?"

"Sure, Bill. Thanks, good night."

For what seemed to be an eternity, Hager tossed and turned in his bed, unable to get comfortable. Still rapt with eagerness about the lead in Wilmington, sleep would come stubbornly. Not until Vanessa, sensing Hager's stress, put him at complete ease with what started as a back massage, escalating into a quiet, but passionate round of sex. Culminating in the Jacuzzi bathtub and enveloped by the warm bubbly water, Hager thought of nothing but the pleasure of Vanessa's tender kisses and rubs. He was in heaven, and sleep was instantaneous for both of them.

Still no word from Wilmington overnight. Hager drove to the office early the next morning, stopping by the bagel shop for his morning ritual. When he arrived at the office, he picked up the handset of the telephone to check his phone messages. Hearing the static dial tone, he knew there was at least one, and he punched in the code to retrieve it.

The recording said he had one message, received at 7:54 a.m., from an unknown number. The clock on the wall read 7:59.

"I just missed it," he whispered. It was Matlin.

Clark, this is Matlin. Liverton just called me. I told him about the camera and he said he could probably dig up the records of the sale at the store. I'm on the way to meet him now. I tried you at home and your daughter said you were on your way to work. I guess you've not gotten there yet. I'll call back as soon as I hear something.

A triumphant smile emerged. Maybe things would come together this time, he thought. Hager pulled his wallet from his navy sport coat, opened it and pulled out the tiny slip of paper from the fortune cookie he saved from the night before. The words were implanted in his mind. Maybe this was his "open gate." The gate which led to the truth and finally, to the end of all the tragedy and despair. He closed his eyes and uttered, "Please be the one."

Lloyd arrived soon after, and they ate breakfast in Hager's office. Judy peeked her head in with a bright smile on her face.

"Hi, Judy," Hager said.

"You want to see my grandbaby?" Judy asked.

Hager was surprised. Was it only the other day she'd told him her daughter was pregnant? Had nine months streaked by without him realizing it?

"Has it been born already?" Hager asked.

"No, silly!" Judy clamored. "I've got the pictures from the ultrasound."

She held three prints and handed them to Lloyd and Hager rolled over in his chair to look along with him. In a black background, there was a small white form Hager guessed was the fetus. If one didn't know at what they were looking, it would be difficult to discern the object of the picture.

"Do they know if it's going to be a boy or a girl, yet, Judy?" Hager asked.

"No, not yet. They don't want to know. They just want it to be healthy."

"Hey, it's got to be a boy," Lloyd said. "There, look! I can see his wiener!"

He pointed to a white appendage on the photo.

"Wow, he's gonna be a stud!"

Judy rolled her eyes and shook her head. Hager snickered at Lloyd. "You're all class, partner."

Lloyd smiled proudly at his remark.

Hager rolled his chair back over to his desk and picked up the phone and dialed Bob Maxwell's office.

"Good morning, Bob. This is Clark. We may have a good lead on the camera found in Fayetteville the other day. Matlin's checking on it right now to see if he can ID the buyer. We hope it will lead somewhere."

Hager heard some papers shuffling in the background.

"Sounds promising, Clark. You guys have certainly done an outstanding job on this case so far, whatever the outcome."

"Thanks."

"Hey, Clark, is Lloyd around?"

"Lloyd? Yeah, he's right here."

Lloyd looked at Hager upon hearing his name.

"Tell him the U.S. Attorney called and they're gonna need him in court this morning. It's about the bank robbery case he helped the FBI with."

"This morning?" Hager asked. "We're planning to go down to Wilmington when Matlin calls back."

"Well," Maxwell said. "Either wait for Lloyd to get out of court, or go without him. Either way, Lloyd has to be in court. He was subpoenaed."

"Okay, I'll tell him."

Hager sighed and hung up the phone.

Lloyd said only one word when Hager told him the news.

"Shit!" he shouted and blasted the U.S. Attorney's timing.

Realizing he had to go, Lloyd told Hager if Matlin called while he was in court, to go to Wilmington without him. The murder case was too important.

A half hour after Lloyd left for the Federal courthouse in Raleigh, Matlin called with the news.

"He found it!" Matlin exclaimed. "I'm at the camera shop now. We've got a name for the buyer. Her name is Jennifer Riley, and she lives here in Wilmington. She bought the camera on May 17 of '96. I called her at home but she wasn't there. I'm running a records check to see if we can find a business address. Are you coming?"

Hager's heart pounded with excitement.

"I'll leave right now. It should only take me about two hours to get there. So, I'll see you around eleven."

"Okay, I'll be here. Hey, our check came back. Jennifer Riley reported a Larceny in July ninety six. We've got a work number. I'll call to see if she's still employed there."

"Great. I'll be there shortly."

Apparently not paying attention to Matlin's words, he hung up the phone, and then the word *Larceny* hit him.

"Larceny? I hope not a larceny of the camera."

His excitement level dropped a little, and he debated calling Matlin back, but he was probably already on the way back to his office.

"Think positive," he said to himself and walked out of the office, briefcase in hand.

30

JENNIFER RILEY worked as a receptionist for an optician in Wilmington. Dr. Massey's office was located on Market Street about six blocks from Cape Fear Camera, and it only took a few minutes to get there from the police department. Matlin had called her at the office to forewarn her of the visit by the investigators, much to the doctor's chagrin. In order not to disrupt the normal flow of clients, Riley arranged to take a short break when the officers arrived to interview her.

Matlin drove. During the ride from the police department, Hager was apprehensive about the interview. After checking the report filed by Riley, they learned she had reported a Canon EOS camera stolen from her car, on July 12, 1996. There were no suspects or leads. No follow-up investigation had been done on the case, which was normal due to the lack of information. She apparently didn't have the serial number recorded in case of theft.

"What a surprise!" Hager muttered.

It didn't look good.

For Hager, it appeared to be another dead end in a string of endless dead ends. He pulled out the white slip of paper from his wallet and read it again, then crumbled it in his hand.

"Open gate, my ass!" he grumbled and put the small ball of paper in the ashtray filled with cigarette butts.

"What are you talking about?" Matlin asked as he puffed on a cigarette, the smoke covering his face.

"Nothing, just some wishful thinking, that's all."

Matlin grunted and blew smoke out the window.

Matlin pulled in the parking lot of the business, which was part of a mini strip center. The L-shaped building housed an optical center connected to the eye doctor's office; a temporary employment service; and an insurance company. On the phone with Riley, Matlin didn't explain the reason for the visit; or ask any questions about the theft, in case she may try to hide something.

Matlin said she'd asked why they needed to talk to her, and he replied he couldn't say over the phone. She must have been worried to death. A presumably, law-abiding citizen getting a clandestine call from the police saying they needed to talk to her. Talk about the drama of it all.

After introductions, the three of them withdrew to a vacant examination room. Jennifer Riley was around thirty, pretty, with short dark brown hair. She was dressed in a white nursing type outfit, white slacks, a white laboratory jacket over a peach turtleneck. In the room, she sat on a stool while the two men stood over her. It didn't contribute to her comfort, and it was obvious she was nervous.

"I apologize for the secretiveness of the call, ma'am," Hager told her, trying to put her at ease, "I want to assure you, you're not under any investigation whatsoever."

She seemed to breathe a sigh of relief and Hager continued.

"Miss Riley, Detective Matlin and I are investigating a series of murders and it appears your camera was recovered at one of the crime scenes."

"Murders?" she asked. "Oh, no. You said my camera was at one the crime scenes? How do you know it was my camera? It was stolen back in July."

"We checked through the manufacturer, and they sent it to Cape Fear Camera shop here in Wilmington. Their records said they sold it to you. We wanted to talk to you about the theft. Maybe somehow it's linked to the murders."

"Oh. Well, I don't know what help I could be. It was stolen out of my car while it was parked in my own driveway. Can you believe it? I don't know who took it. Probably some crack head."

She shook her head in disgust.

"I was so mad when I found it was gone. That camera cost me six hundred dollars!"

"You didn't have any idea who may have taken it? Could it have been someone you knew?" Hager asked, wanting a miracle of recall.

"I don't think so. I don't know anyone on drugs. Like I said, it was probably some crack head who took it. It happens all the time in my neighborhood. You just can't leave anything of value anywhere without nailing it down," she shook her head again. "I wish I could help you. You said it was found at a murder scene? What did he do, hit her over the head with it?"

"No, it was found at the home where a girl was attacked by our killer. He brought it with him to her apartment. Have you heard anything about the case? He's called 'The Strangler'. He killed a college student here in Wilmington last August?"

Her eyes got wide.

"Oh, yeah. I heard about it! I saw the drawing of the guy on the news the other night. Damn, my camera's being used by 'The Strangler'. I don't want it back now."

Hager took a deep breath of frustration. It *was* a long shot, he thought. A serious long shot. He shook his head at another of a series of disappointments in this case. Once again, Hager would have to wait for another victim. Another casualty in the war against "The Strangler." How many more women were to be sacrificed until he could get the monster in his clutches?

Hager was growing tired of the whole ordeal. He wished it to be over now. He'd been terrorized. His family terrorized. The entire region had been put on alert and women were afraid to leave their homes. All because of one man. A monster.

Was all of this worth it? Was the oath he took years ago worth sacrificing his rationality and sense of justice? Was it worth it to ride like a maniac believing his only daughter was in the evil grasp of a killer, only to learn it was all a part of *his* terror. A part of *his* game. Was it ever worth it?

"The Strangler" would find out how much it was worth when Hager got a hold of him. Listening to Jennifer Riley go on about her camera was beginning to annoy the agent. He was ready to leave.

"Did you say y'all were with the SBI or the FBI?" Jennifer asked.

"The SBI, ma'am. Why?" Hager said walking to the door.

"Oh, you may know my ex-boyfriend. He got a job with y'all a couple of months ago. His name is Tom Moffitt. Do you know him?"

Hager had heard the name before and it stung him like a hornet. *Tom Moffitt?*

A strange feeling of enlightenment strangled Hager's collar. His heart started pounding and Matlin had a strange look on his face.

"Tom Moffitt? Yeah, he's a crime scene specialist. Have you seen him lately?" Hager asked.

"No. We broke up just after he was hired. The last time I talked to him was when he was getting ready to go to the academy in Raleigh. It was in July, right before my camera was stolen."

A look of illumination appeared on her face. Then it turned to horror.

"That's right. We broke up the day before my camera was stolen."

Thinking, she stood and faced the door. Matlin looked at Hager; both of them waited for her to continue. Hager's heart was racing.

"You know," she said, pacing. "I remember Tom and I broke up because he started acting weird. He wanted me to dance for him like a stripper. You know, dress up in a teddy with garter belts and every-thing, and take my clothes off for him. I did it a couple of times, you know, for a change in routine, but he started wanting me to do it all of the time. He got mad when I refused, and that was when..."

Her eyes started to tear and she covered her mouth.

"What?" Hager demanded. "What happened?"

She tried to hold back the tears.

"That was when he hit me."

She broke down and started sobbing.

"I thought he was going to kill me!" she cried. "He started choking me and I screamed. Oh my God! Do you think?"

She looked at Hager for reassurance. For him to tell her she hadn't been involved with a killer. Her eyes pleaded for an answer to ease her fears.

"I don't know," Hager said, his heart pumping ninety miles an hour. "You know what he looks like. Does he look like the picture?"

He handed her a copy of the composite.

The correlation of the name and the picture seemed to click in her mind. Horror was written all over her face. Even though the picture was generic and fit millions of people, she knew it was him. She covered her mouth with her hand and shook her head sobbing, never saying a word. It was unnecessary, Hager knew the answer.

"I never realized how much Tom looked like the picture. All of those girls. If I'd have only said something then. Those girls!" she wept. "If I only knew it was him. Those girls!" she sobbed.

"You can't blame yourself, Jennifer" Hager said, trying to comfort her. "It's not your fault."

She continued to cry for several minutes.

"What was Tom doing before he got hired by the SBI?" Matlin asked.

Jennifer seemed to compose herself instantly for Matlin's question. She wiped her nose and eyes.

"He was a reporter for the *Morning Star* when we met. He worked the crime beat, and he did some photography work for them, too. He always told me he had this big dream of making it big with *Time* magazine. He said he was going to do a piece—an exposé that would make him famous like the guy who broke Watergate."

"Why didn't you suspect Moffitt for taking your camera when it was stolen?" Hager asked.

"I didn't think he would steal anything from me. Besides, he already had a camera of his own. A Nikon. What would he need with another one?"

"Did he take any pictures of you?" Hager asked.

"He took some, but mostly he took landscape stills of the ocean and the beach front. He even developed his own film. Had a lab in the spare bathroom in my house. He always wanted to be a police photographer. That's why he joined the SBI. He got into all that stuff."

Thoughts of all the coincidences, the dead ends and the entire investigation raced through Hager's mind as he stood in the examination room talking to Jennifer Riley. As she described every detail of Tom Moffitt's personality, it answered just about every question of the profile he'd conjured from analyzing the cases. The monster was one of their own.

Some of the things were no coincidence though. They were done with the intent, as Hager thought, to re-live the act and fantasize about his deeds. It all made perfect sense.

Moffitt was one of the crime scene specialists who processed the crime scene in Ahoskie. He'd volunteered to photograph the funeral of Missy Campbell, and he was sure Moffitt was the photographer at the press conference. He was there all the time. Right in front of Hager's face. Instead of looking in the crowd for the answer, all he had to do was to look at the face behind the camera to find his killer.

The interview concluded quickly after the revelation from Riley. Hager was eager to return to Matlin's office and confirm his suspicions of Moffitt. Once he got into the car, Hager immediately fumbled through the ashes and cigarette butts and found the ball of paper he'd placed there earlier. It was stained gray from the ash and singed from a cigarette, but when he unwrapped it, the message was still intact. He blew off the clinging ashes, smoothed the wrinkled paper, and read it again. He kissed it. Matlin peered over at him and shook his head in bewilderment. It *was* an omen.

"So much for superstition," he said with a triumphant smile on his face.

His first call was to Gulfman in Identification.

"Gulfman, this is Hager. I've got no time to explain, but call over to Admin. right now, and have them FAX Tom Moffitt's fingerprint card to you and compare the thumbprint you found on the film to his prints."

"What? Who? Wait a second, you want to compare the print to one of our guys?"

"That's right. Tom Moffitt. He works out of the Greenville office. A crime scene specialist. Do it!" Hager ordered and hung up the phone.

He disconnected and dialed his office. Judy answered in her usual cheery tone.

"State Bureau of Investigation, can I help you?"

"Judy, it's Clark. Call over to Admin. and ask for Tom Moffitt's personnel file to be sent over by courier right away. I'll want to see it when I get back to Raleigh. Make sure they have his photograph attached, okay? And call over to Bob Maxwell's office and tell him I need to see him right away."

"A personnel file? For Tom Moffitt?" she asked shocked. "What's this all about, Clark? because—"

"I don't have time to go into it right now, Judy. Just do as I ask. Has Lloyd gotten back from court yet?"

Silence. It was all Hager heard through the phone, except for Judy's breathing.

"Clark, what's this all about, dear. Why Tom Moffitt's file?"

Her voice sounded worried.

"What was with Judy?" Hager asked himself. She wasn't usually this nosy and he was becoming irritated.

"Judy!" Hager shouted. "Just do as I say. I'll tell you later!"

Hager was ready to hang up the phone, but his secretary's unnecessary curiosity bothered him. Her silence did, too.

"Clark," she bellowed, almost like she was crying. "Tell me why Tom Moffitt. What does this have to do with him?"

This was serious. Judy was deliberately disobeying an order. But why, he asked himself. *This wasn't like her.*

"Judy," he said, "I think Tom Moffitt's 'The Strangler' but I don't want anyone breathing a word of it until I can check a few things, okay?"

She blurted it out in one sentence.

"For God's sake, Clark, Tom Moffitt's with Lloyd, and they went to Fayetteville to guard the woman and Moffitt was visiting the office and Maxwell told him to tag along with Lloyd until you got back and they're on their way there now! OH MY GOD! CLARK!"

Judy said it so fast Hager could only understand Lloyd and Moffitt and the exclamation at the end.

"Wait a second. Lloyd and Moffitt are going where?"

Hager's heart was pounding again.

"Fayetteville called and said they needed our agents to guard the woman there. They didn't have the manpower to spare, so Maxwell came down and told Lloyd to go. Tom Moffitt was visiting the office when Bob came over to tell Lloyd. He asked Moffitt to go with him since you weren't here. Clark, what are you going to do?"

Hager had nothing to say. The only thoughts going through his head were those of why Moffitt, if he were the killer, would go to Fayetteville and come face to face with his last victim. It didn't make sense. He sat at the desk in silence with the phone to his ear, thinking. Suddenly, it came to him. He remembered what the killer told Emily Nye over the phone.

I'm so close they won't ever find out who I am. Not before we can be together. I'll come back and you'll never expect it.

The killer predicted it and had every intention of keeping his promise of returning to her. But why go with Lloyd who would certainly thwart any attack Moffitt would make on her. As soon as she realized it was him, she would certainly scream bloody murder, and Lloyd would take care of it. That wasn't his plan. No, he went with Lloyd for a reason. Once Lloyd's back was turned, Moffitt would pull a gun on him and probably make him watch his torture and then he would kill him. That was his plan.

"Why not me?" Hager asked himself.

Moffitt had been terrorizing him all through this. Why did he choose Lloyd to be a martyr and spare Hager? Hager guessed in order to completely terrorize someone, he had to live to enjoy its effect.

"Not if I can help it!" Hager shouted in the phone to an insistent Judy who had been beckoning a response from him.

"Call SHP, Judy. Get them on the way to Fayetteville to intercept Lloyd's car."

"But what about Lloyd?"

"I'll call him and warn him. You just do what I told you to do, okay. Lloyd's going to be fine."

That was a hard pill to swallow.

"Lloyd's going to be fine," he whispered, trying to convince himself. "How do I warn him without tipping off Moffitt?" he asked himself. "Just tell him to be cool and Moffitt will never know."

Hager picked up the phone again and dialed Lloyd's cellular number.

"Please have it on, Lloyd."

Lloyd answered in his usual short, friendly tone, "Yeah."

"Lloyd, this is Clark. Try to act as calm as you can. I just found out Moffitt is probably our killer. We just talked to his former girlfriend in Wilmington. She was the owner of the camera we recovered in Fayetteville. We're having his prints compared to the thumbprint right now. I'm not positive, but I think he's going with you to kill Emily Nye. Then he's going to kill you."

"Is that right. Well, we knew it was a long shot all along, Clark. That's the way it goes."

"Lloyd," Hager whispered. "Where are you now?"

"Oh, we're on I-40 almost at 95," Lloyd said nonchalantly.

"Try to pull over somewhere and get out of the car. He's probably armed. I'm not sure, but he may not wait until you get to Fayetteville to try to get rid of you. Don't take any chances. Get out of the car. Tell him you have to go to the bathroom. Anything! Just get the hell out of the car!"

"Right, Clark," he said calmly. "You going back to Raleigh now? Okay, I'll see you tomorrow in Fayetteville."

"Lloyd." Hager sighed. "You do what you have to do, you understand?"

31

AGENT SHERIDAN held the cell phone up to his ear, a smirk on his face. It wasn't a smile, but more of a sneer that displayed some unconscious anxiety trying to stay hidden inside his brain.

"Right," he said. "I got it. I'll tell him, Clark."

Sheridan disconnected the phone and Moffitt noticed tiny beads of sweat had materialized on his forehead and upper lip. A minute ago, Sheridan's beady eyes glanced over at him and then quickly looked away.

"What did that asshole Hager say to him?" Moffitt asked himself. "From the looks of him, they must have found out something. I wonder what it was."

"Was that Agent Hager?" Moffitt asked, knowing it was.

"Yeah, he said to tell you 'thanks' for all the help you've been to us with the photographs and all."

"What else did he say?"

The old man shook his head and shrugged his shoulders as if to say Hager had said nothing else. He reached over and turned down the car's heater, and wiped his brow, which was now dripping with sweat.

"Nothing much. He's down in Wilmington following up on the camera they recovered from this girl's apartment. They thought the store who sold camera could track down the buyer, but they didn't have any luck."

Moffitt smiled and placed his hands at the front of his pants, feeling the bulge of the pistol concealed under his jacket.

"Hmm, that's too bad. It doesn't seem like you're getting any breaks on this case."

The old man was sweating and a drop slowly inched its way down the side of his face. He wiped it away and pulled on the shirt collar under his sport coat. Although he couldn't see it, Moffitt assumed Sheridan kept his pistol on his right side, and with his jacket on and seat belt fastened, there was no way he could get to it without a lot of effort.

"Are you hot, Agent Sheridan?"

"Yeah, I'm burning up," he said as he fanned his face.

He unbuttoned his shirt collar and loosened his tie.

"I must be coming down with something. Probably that flu that's going around."

Moffitt knew Sheridan was lying. Sweat only started to appear on his body after the phone call from Hager. Although he was trying to stay calm and appear normal, his physiological responses to stress revealed him as if his fly were open. The old man spat out a chunk of brown tobacco in a Styrofoam cup and rolled down the window, discarding it.

I'm gonna have to do the old man before we get to Fayetteville. He knows something. Maybe everything. Who knows? Hager is pretty smart. Sonofabitch really pulled a rabbit out of his hat to think to run the camera through the manufacturer. Damnit! He's probably gonna try something soon, and I'll bet help's already on the way. I'm gonna have to waste him here on the interstate.

Sheridan wiped his brow again and leaned his face toward the partially open window.

"Whew, I'm gonna pull over at the next turn-off to get something to drink," he said. "You thirsty?"

"Sure," Moffitt answered. "This is it," he said to himself. "The jig is up."

The old man started to whistle. Another sign of stress. Or was it fear? Just like in the movies during a suspenseful scene when all the tension mounted and anxiety was at an all-time fever pitch.

"Where's the scary music?" Moffitt asked himself. A crescendo of deep tones beating faster and faster and faster until...

"You know don't you?" Moffitt said.

"Huh? Know what?" Sheridan said and his Adam's apple moved as he swallowed.

"You know, you lying dumb fuck! You know! Hager told you!"

In an almost eerily calm voice, Sheridan responded, almost like he was oblivious to his own stress.

"What the hell are you talking about, son?"

Sheridan's face tried to sustain a look of surprise, but the sweat continued dripping down his face."

"Look at you," Moffitt snapped, and quickly pulled the pistol from his jacket and pointed it at Sheridan's head. "Hager must have figured it out. That fucking slut Jennifer must have told him all about me! There's no reason to pretend anymore, old man. You know who I am!"

Sheridan's face was dripping. He stared at the gun facing him. Slowly, his right hand crept its way along his thigh toward his coat.

"Put both your hands on the steering wheel and keep them there!" Moffitt ordered and touched the muzzle of the gun to Sheridan's forehead.

Sheridan stared at Moffitt. His blue eyes were full of hatred but at the same time showed his acquiescence.

"Look, Moffitt," Sheridan said calmly. "It doesn't have to go down this way. We can work this out. I'm sure you've got your reasons for what you did."

"Shut up, you old fuck! You wouldn't know shit about my reasons. You sound just like my old man. You don't know shit about me!"

Sheridan turned his head and looked Moffitt directly in his eyes.

"I know you're a fuckin' coward who preys upon helpless women!" he growled.

Moffitt shoved the barrel of the pistol against the side of Sheridan's head and cocked the hammer.

"You want to die right now, you old fuck? Moffitt roared.

Suddenly, Sheridan's right hand bolted from the steering wheel and slammed against Moffitt's arm as he tried to grab the pistol. Sheridan swerved the car sharply to the right, causing the sounds of screeching tires and wailing horns of other cars; Moffitt pulled his gun hand back and crashed the butt against Sheridan's head, creating a deep gash. Blood spewed down the side of Sheridan's face.

Sheridan slammed on brakes and Moffitt, absent a seat belt, slammed into the dash and windshield, the gun still clutched in his hand. Quickly, Sheridan unbuckled his seat belt and opened the door, trying to get out of the car. With his back to Moffitt, Sheridan swept open his sport coat in search of his pistol, but Moffitt grabbed his neck from behind and pulled him violently back into the car. The old man was strong, and he turned over, still reaching for his pistol. Moffitt smashed his gun once again onto Sheridan's head as they struggled in the front seat of the car.

Again and again and again and again, with unrelenting fury and strength, Moffitt's pistol crashed down on Sheridan's head, each time splitting the tight skin of his scalp, now crimson with blood. Moffitt raised his hand once more and saw that Sheridan was still. He looked at the hand holding the gun; blood stained and streaked down his forearm.

Sheridan lay motionless across the front seat of the car, his head resting in Moffitt's lap, his feet sticking out the open door. Moffitt reached inside the agent's coat and pulled the Beretta from its holster. Sheridan had only gotten far enough to unsnap the holster. Close, but not close enough.

The car had come to rest on the right shoulder of the road and cars were passing, unaware of the horrific violence taking place. Moffitt looked at the oncoming traffic and spotted a tractor trailer stopped about one hundred yards behind them. A man was running toward his position and Moffitt quickly jumped out of the car with both guns in his hands, his shirt and trousers stained red with Sheridan's blood. Seeing the bizarre spectacle, the man stopped and glared at Moffitt. Recognizing the pistols in both his hands, he obediently reached for the sky.

"Get the fuck out of here!" Moffitt screamed and fired three shots in the truck driver's direction.

The truck driver, in response to the shots, about faced and took off like he was shot from a cannon.

Moffitt returned to the car and the moaning Sheridan. He thought he'd killed him with the crushing blows of the butt of the pistol, certainly fracturing his skull. The old bastard. He had to give him credit for his will to live. Moffitt tucked the Beretta in his left rear pants pocket and grabbed Sheridan by his white hair, now sticky with drying blood, and jerked him out of the passenger side door. He looked down at his Colt .45 and then his right hand. Both were covered with blood, his left with bloody white hairs stuck to the skin.

When he pulled him from the car, Sheridan's face scraped the pavement and his trunk pounded against the asphalt. He moaned again. He was still alive. Moffitt looked at the battered agent, lying face down on the shoulder.

Moffitt looked to the highway again as a flood of traffic approached. Several more cars had pulled over. The passengers hurried toward him and to whatever trouble had befallen the occupants of the Caprice. A man in a pickup stopped just ahead of them, and had gotten out of his car rushing to help. Moffitt fired four shots at him; the man dived under the truck; one of the bullets crashed into the windshield. Passersby slowed and quickly accelerated, seeing the mad man covered in blood and waving a gun, firing shots.

Moffitt felt the heat of capture burning his skin. They were closing in from both sides. Citizens coming to the rescue.

"Gotta get outa Dodge. Fuck it! He'll never live through the beating I gave him.

Moffitt took Sheridan's handcuffs and badge from his belt and dragged his blood-soaked form into a grassy ditch along the shoulder. He jumped into the Caprice from the passenger side, pulled down the shifter, and squealed tires, accelerating down the interstate, slamming the driver's door closed. In less than a minute, he was at high speed. He saw an exit sign ahead.

"I've got to dump this car right now," he said.

From the exit, he turned to the right and speeded down the road, making several quick turns, stopping along an abandoned road beside a creek.

He looked at his hands. They were sticky, stained with dried blood. Drops of sweat ran down his arms, smearing the crimson blotches.

"Man, I look like I slaughtered a hog! A pig to be exact!" he said and laughed hysterically.

32

ONCE AGAIN, Hager raced down the interstate with an escort from the Highway Patrol. He needed to stop all of this high-speed, high-intensity, high-stress driving. Just a week or so before, he'd tried to beat the odds and save his daughter, but this time, it was to help his partner. But like the time before, Hager was too far away to make any difference in the outcome. Yet he felt compelled to give it his all.

It was about ninety miles from Wilmington to the interchange of I-40 and I-95 and averaging around 100 miles per hour, it would take at the outside, fifty minutes to arrive. By then it would be all over. Either Moffitt was under arrest, or he'd escaped and Lloyd was organizing a search party for the killer. Hager didn't want to think of the other scenarios possible. No bad vibes.

Hager was confident his partner could handle himself, and with his smooth tongue and level head, Lloyd was sure to emerge on top. It all depended on how Lloyd reacted to the news about Tom Moffitt. That sitting next to him was a vicious killer.

As much as he tried to restrain it, a feeling of dread overwhelmed his body. Hager realized Moffitt intended to kill Lloyd anyway, and with the phone call warning, he may have gotten suspicious they were on to him. Was the call to Lloyd a mistake? Did Hager react too quickly? Was his knee-jerk reaction the catalyst which precipitated Moffitt's violent attack?

"No," he answered himself. "I had to warn him."

The trip down the interstate seemed so familiar to Hager. With all its trepidation and stress, Hager felt a comforting sense of security that Lloyd was safe, and he was able to outwit the monster. He knew Lloyd was a warrior—a survivor.

His cellular phone rang. When he heard the ringing sound, he remembered when he heard the comforting, raspy, southern accent of his partner telling him his daughter was safe.

"Please make it be Lloyd," he begged. He answered it, not wanting to say anything.

"This is Hager."

"Clark," it was the sullen voice of Bob Maxwell.

"Yeah. How's Lloyd? What happened?"

The phone was silent and Maxwell sighed and cleared his throat.

"Clark, it's bad."

Maxwell's voice was shaken. Full of despair.

"What do you mean, it's bad? Goddamit, Bob! Tell me what happened!"

"Lloyd's been beaten badly. With a club or something, I don't know. Maybe he was pistol whipped. He's on the way to the hospital now. The paramedics said he probably had a fractured skull. They got a pulse, but it was very faint."

Silence. Utter, pure, untainted, absolute silence. Or should it be shock? He didn't know. Hager's throat constricted and his tongue swelled. His eyes started to burn, along with his nose, and soon his vision blurred with tears. He dropped the phone to the seat and wiped his eyes.

Empty. That was the feeling throughout his body. It was emptiness, like someone sliced open his chest and removed all his guts in one single swoosh of a blade. It took away his spine, too, as he had no feeling whatsoever running along the cord of nerves.

The case had taken Hager to his limit. He was physically exhausted and emotionally drained. Not only had his daughter narrowly escaped the jaws of death, now his best friend was on the brink of death because of this monster.

What else could he endure before being pushed over the edge? Hager couldn't take anymore. Catching Tom Moffitt wasn't worth sacrificing the well being of his family. Stopping him wasn't worth paying the ultimate price—something Lloyd may eventually pay.

What reason could Hager have for continuing? Because a sadistic killer was getting his rocks off tormenting his pursuer? Because a devil in human form wanted to play a game of good against evil? It was simply a game to Moffitt. Just a game where there were no winners.

No, Hager was finished. "Let someone else do it," he said.

Thrust the risk on another brave warrior. It was over.

Hearing Maxwell's pleas for Hager to pick up the phone, he grabbed it and put it to his ear.

"I'm here," he said, his mouth dry from stress. "Where did they find him?"

"SHP found him on the edge of 40, near I-95. Clar—"

"What about his car?" Hager asked.

"It was found abandoned a couple of miles away. No one has any idea where Moffitt is. Clar—"

"Which hospital did they take him to?"

"They're going on to Fayetteville. Look, Clark. I need you to come with me to tell Martha. She'll feel better hearing it from you.

The image of Martha's face appeared in Hager's mind. This was going to be difficult. Hager was silent for a minute.

"Clark, are you still there?"

"Yeah, Bob. I'm here."

"Okay, I'm still at the scene. Just meet me here and we'll drive over together."

"All right. Bob?" he sighed, not wanting to ask the question. "Tell me the truth. You saw him, right? Is he gonna make it?"

"I don't know, Clark. He looked real bad. But his heart was still beating and you know that's a good sign."

Maxwell's voice sounded more reassuring than before. Like he believed Lloyd would survive.

"Clark. Lloyd's a fighter. He won't give up. So don't you give up hope."

"Yeah, I know. I guess I just wanted someone else to say it."

Hager took a deep breath, trying to muster enough courage to continue.

"I'll be there in an hour," Hager said and disconnected.

He was numb still. He felt nothing. No emotions anymore. It was more disbelief than anything. It had to be a nightmare. If only he could just wake up and everything would be okay.

Wake up damnit!

Maxwell needed him to be strong. Lloyd's wife, Martha would only want to hear it from Hager's lips. To provide the comfort and support only a friend of the family could do.

You have to be strong. There's still a killer out there on the loose and only you can catch him! That's why you have to be strong. To do what you're supposed to do. Do your job! Avenge all the wrongs committed by this monster!

As the adrenaline pumped through his body, Hager felt a sudden resurgence of fervor. Lloyd was going to pull through. It was supposed to happen that way. Hager was going to beat Tom Moffitt at his game.

33

TOM MOFFITT had disappeared. A citizen who chanced following Moffitt in Lloyd's Caprice from the interstate phoned in the location of the rural road where it was eventually found. The car had been abandoned in the tiny burg of Macks, home of a post office and a country store along Route 50 about 15 miles east of Buies Creek and 6 miles from where Lloyd was found. The man didn't see Moffitt's escape from the car, as he only followed until he made the last turn. Not wanting to be another victim, the citizen, an unarmed former Marine, kept a safe distance behind the maniac.

Moffitt succeeded in having about a half hour lead on the responding search patrols. Lloyd's car was dumped in a remote area, heavily wooded and lined with small creeks. Some blood-stained clothing was found in a creek parallel to the road, indicating Moffitt was heading north.

Police officers, sheriffs, and state troopers responded from counties away to help in the pursuit. Johnston County Sheriff's deputies with bloodhounds began the tireless search for the fugitive. The Bureau's helicopter dominated the sky, hovering over the area. As the bloodhounds began their incessant wailing in hungry pursuit, Hager realized only a few precious hours of daylight remained.

News of law enforcement officers from around the state combing the area in search of "The Strangler" traveled quickly throughout the small communities in Johnston County. Soon, calls with reports of sightings at different locations were received and served only to confuse the authorities rather than help them.

A white man fitting the description of "The Strangler" was observed at a shopping center in Smithfield. A car in Benson was seen being driven by a male who resembled the composite drawing of the killer. None of the numerous calls received turned out fruitful. Either they were completely unfounded, or the police didn't arrive in time to locate the person.

As Hager neared the scene, he observed the spectacle before him. Eastbound traffic on I-40 was completely blocked, except one lane, causing a bottle neck of epic proportions. Cars from the State Highway Patrol, Johnston County Sheriff, cities of Benson and Smithfield, and various unmarked cars of the SBI and the FBI lined both sides of the highway, all responding to assist one of their own. Vans belonging to local TV stations had arrived. Reporters and camera crews busily prepared for live updates from the crime scene.

Lloyd was found lying in a ditch, unconscious and barely alive. His gun, badge, and handcuffs were missing along with the car. Only bloodstains at the edge of the pavement remained as evidence of the heinous violence which transpired there. It was enough to make Hager nauseous at the mere sight and understanding that his friend had been beaten in such a nightmarishly frightening manner.

Hager parked his car along the shoulder of the highway. A number of plain clothes officers stood near the place where the assault occurred. Hager watched his comrades busily pointing out evidence and making notes in their pads, like it was just another investigation. And Hager realized he was seeing his own reflection in their behavior. There was no emotion. Just the dispassionate laborers of truth, honor, and justice milling about trying to somehow contribute to the cause of a fallen hero. The uninvolved investigator with no personal stake in the loss. They did their jobs with a professional indifference to the horror facing them.

He examined the faces of his colleagues, and underneath the mask of indifference was the pain of loss. The struggle for understanding, the battle against misery, all being successfully waged for the sake of their own sanity. He could see it in their eyes, and in the way they shook their heads in disbelief. No one was smiling. What Hager saw in those faces was what had kept him, and every other person involved in law enforcement, who intimately touched the abominable horrors of police work, and faced the unbelievable limits of man's ability to destroy one another, on the positive side of mental stability. He understood.

Inasmuch as Hager understood his fellow law officer's behavior, he discovered his own understanding in how he must right himself and be strong. For he still had a job to do. He had to be there for Martha who, at present, was unaware of the tragic news lingering on the horizon. The news Hager would have to bring. He also still had a killer to catch. A man to hunt. And if he got the opportunity, a man to destroy.

Hager saw Maxwell. The Assistant Director stood leaning against a Highway Patrol car, a cell phone at his ear. Maxwell gave Hager a look of recognition and waved for him to come over. Maxwell disconnected the phone when Hager neared.

"That was the hospital," Maxwell said. "They're airlifting Lloyd to Duke. Good news, though. He's still alive."

"Great," Hager said. "What have you been told about what happened?"

Maxwell started in the direction of Hager's car. "I'll fill you in on the way to Lloyd's house. Come on. You're driving."

Hager followed. He was soon traveling west on I-40.

"The information we've gotten so far is pretty sketchy. A couple of motorists found Lloyd lying by the road. All we were able to get from them was that they saw a man with blood all over himself. They thought there had been a traffic accident or something and stopped to help. And the bloody guy started shooting at them. No one we've spoken to actually witnessed the beating but it looks like it happened in the front seat of Lloyd's car. The trooper who found the Caprice said there was a lot of blood in there."

Hager shook his head at the image of blood in his mind.

"Did they get anything from the car?" Hager asked.

"The only thing they found was Lloyd's briefcase in the back seat and his glasses on the front floorboard."

Maxwell took a deep breath. "Look Clark, I'm really sorry about sending Moffitt with Lloyd. If I had any idea he was a... you know." Maxwell's face turned solemn.

"I know, Bob. No one's going to blame you."

Hager thought about blame. Was there anyone to blame for this? Could it have been handled another way? Hager drove the rest of the way in silence.

Soon after the assault had taken place, local stations had interrupted their normal programs to provide "special reports" informing viewers that an agent with the SBI had been critically injured near Smithfield. After catching one of the news flashes, Martha had been glued to her seat waiting for her husband to call to let her know he was all right.

Hager and Maxwell arrived at the Sheridan house in Apex, a small town southwest of Raleigh. Martha appeared at the front door. She knew it was Lloyd who had been injured. Seeing Hager and Maxwell, the looks of apprehension on their faces confirmed her worst fears. Her eyes swelled and she sank to her knees, muttering only the words, "No, no, no, no, please God, no, no."

By the time they reached the hospital, Lloyd had already been taken into surgery. It was a waiting game now and Hager remained with Martha until her son arrived from Charlotte. During the wait, Hager phoned Vanessa, breaking the terrible news about Lloyd. He also called Elizabeth.

Six hours later, the surgeon visited Martha.

The search for Moffitt continued despite the darkness and the danger of an armed killer in flight. About two hours into the trail, the bloodhounds stopped in the parking lot of a small shopping center along Route 55, almost in Buies Creek. From all appearances, Moffitt had stolen a car.

Moffitt had all but vanished into thin air. Hager knew it would only be a matter of time before he surfaced again. Probably with the recovery of the stolen car. Weary as he was, Hager drove back to Raleigh after leaving Martha at the hospital. He went straight to his office, where the file on Tom Moffitt awaited him.

Gulfman had confirmed it. He'd made a positive match on Moffitt's thumb print to the one from the camera film. Tom Moffitt was "The Strangler."

Moffitt's picture was released along with the usual cautions of extreme dangerousness and hot-line numbers to call for information and sightings. Maxwell had ordered a surveillance team consisting of SBI and FBI agents, state troopers, and Greenville Police to sit on Moffitt's apartment building. Knowing Moffitt's apartment would be an unlikely place for the killer to go, Hager chose to stay in Raleigh and wait for Moffitt to make his next move.

A press conference was in order, Maxwell told him, but Hager refused to stand in front of the cameras, knowing a killer lurked behind them; he relinquished it to his superior. While Maxwell faced the press corps, Hager studied the file of Tom Moffitt.

Hager sat in his office and flipped through page after page of personal and family history, background investigation results, recommendations and appraisals for the crime scene specialist employed by the state since August 1996.

Although Moffitt wanted to be a full-fledged special agent with the SBI, evident of his application, he settled for a position as a crime scene specialist, in hopes someday, he would reach agent status. Born in San Diego, California, Thomas Ian Moffitt was the adopted and only child to Admiral Richard I. Moffitt, US Navy (Ret.) and Nancy Moffitt.

A graduate of Notre Dame, Tom Moffitt earned a degree in Journalism, hoping someday to be a famous free-lance reporter for magazines with worldwide exposure. His history proved to be uneventful, if not exemplary in some regards. During high school he was an all-star athlete, playing football, baseball, and wrestling. He was an honor student, scoring remarkably high on the SAT, which launched him to Notre Dame seeking a degree. He was the stereotypical "All-American boy". Tall, handsome, and popular, Moffitt was voted Homecoming King and Most Likely to Succeed in his senior year in high school.

One missing factor from Moffitt's life was any mention of military service. Due to his father's rank of Admiral, Moffitt certainly would have been encouraged, at least, to seek a career in the armed forces. The records divulged nothing involving military service, not even ROTC. Hager made note of this. A bit of information like that might provide some understanding of Moffitt's personality.

Admiral and Mrs. Moffitt were currently living in Norfolk, Virginia in their retirement years. With their close proximity to North Carolina, Hager felt they could be of some assistance in locating their son; moreover, a visit with them would give him additional insight into the man known as "The Strangler."

Everything about Moffitt's rearing appeared to be normal. Even his psychological evaluations were normal, indicating no psychoses or neurotic behavior. He scored 140 on an IQ test, which placed him as highly intellectual. But somewhere behind the curtain of normalcy, a sociopathic killer who preyed upon anyone who challenged his purpose lay waiting to erupt like a volcano. What stressor could have caused this sort of behavior?

Obviously, Hager had to believe Moffitt's reasons for killing stemmed from a hidden hatred of his mother. This was a common notion in his psychology and profiling texts. But there was some other avenue to explore relative to Moffitt's signature of his crimes. Only targeting strippers was definitely significant, but it was just an M.O. His signature, the presentation of his persona, his reasons for doing it all, would be revealed in the way he carried out his deeds.

The way he killed the women.

Hager definitely knew strippers were an integral part of the equation; but the way Moffitt entrapped and seduced them was vital in assessing his personality. Relying on his perceived charm with women, he knew how to play their game, to reap the rewards of their company. With that method of seduction, he would only be appreciated by his peers, men. This was important. The ego was important in these crimes, evident of the way Moffitt lured them into his web. It was a man thing to be smooth like silk in his charm. His deeds were done to impress his fellow males. His father was somehow linked to all the madness, and Hager figured it had something to do with the military and living up to his father's expectations.

The answer to the question of the strippers still lingered. Was it because they were so vulnerable to seduction in his plan? Or were women who took off their clothes amid a crowd of screaming men the issue of his hatred? Someone in his past who made an impression. A deeply painful and lasting impression to trigger such incomprehensible violence. The answer awaited in Moffitt's apartment and with his parents. Hager planned to be at both places.

Up to this point, Hager supposed Moffitt's first murder occurred in Wilmington, in July 1996, only a few weeks after Jennifer Riley kicked him out of her house for abusing her. It was certainly a stressor, but Hager sincerely believed a person didn't begin a life of crime initially with the ultimate offense—murder. Some event during his youth sparked the fire; there had to be some unsolved crime, peeping tom, burglary or rape, in which Moffitt was involved. One does not learn how to lure, seduce, and kill effectively and endure months of scrutiny, without previous *experimentation* with other types of crimes. It just didn't happen.

34

MOFFITT'S APARTMENT was on the second floor of a two-story building. The building was a cedar stained, clapboard sided structure holding twelve apartments. Flowing across the front of the second story, a wooden walkway led to a long inverted V-shaped wooden staircase at the center of the building. The apartment manager provided Hager with a key in lieu of forcing open the door. Accompanied by Special Agent Ric Morales of the FBI and SBI Agent Gary Josephson, Hager entered the apartment in obedience to his search warrant.

Hager produced the search warrant, carefully wording all relevant facts which led him to believe Moffitt was the killer, and evidence of his crimes would be found at his place of residence. The completed affidavit for the warrant was ten type-written pages. For what would he be looking?

Clearly Hager and the other agents would be searching for evidence which linked Moffitt to the crimes, but what consisted of evidence? In Hager's opinion, anything remotely connected to the murders: Moffitt's souvenirs like photographs, women's clothing, jewelry, hair, press clippings; or any other property significant to the crimes. Hager also planned to search for trace evidence like Moffitt's own hair or his razor containing DNA, the most vital link. But most of all, Hager would search for some hint or window into Moffitt's personality. A piece of the puzzle which answered the question "Why?" He wanted to find the truth.

Moffitt's apartment was spotless. The front door opened to a small living room with a sofa and a leather recliner, a coffee table, two tall artificial trees, a fish aquarium, and a big screen television. Framed prints hung on the wood paneled walls. One of Michael Jordan slamming home a basketball for the Bulls; Joe Montana giving his trademark touchdown signal with the 49ers; and Mike Piazza of the Los Angeles Dodgers, apparently admiring a recent home run.

To the right of the door was a kitchenette. Two bar stools were placed under a breakfast nook facing the kitchen. The apartment had only one bedroom; a master bath connected to the bedroom, and a half bath off the living room. Small and cozy, the apartment by all appearances was the home of a fastidiously clean person.

Hager searched Moffitt's bedroom first. A bedroom was a person's intimate space, and therefore, his most precious stuff was kept there. The bedroom was large, spacious enough to accommodate a king-sized water bed, dresser, and mirrored chest. The walls could be called "love me" walls. There were photos of Moffitt participating in sports, newspaper clippings, awards, ribbons. A frame containing his varsity letters and pins earned in high school. On another wall, three shelves loaded with trophies from the three-sport star's career. It was plain to see that Tom Moffitt held himself in very high esteem, which didn't make a lot of sense to Hager.

Based on Hager's original profile of the killer and from information given by his former girlfriend, Hager had theorized Moffitt possessed many hang-ups and feelings of inadequacy. As a result, the evolution of his cocky, womanizing personality. Trying to deal with the feelings of ineptitude, Moffitt had created the facade of virility and confidence to fool others around him and also to fool himself. This apartment didn't look like the home of someone befitting Hager's profile. Could Hager have been wrong about Moffitt?

Hager studied the room and noticed something peculiar about the position of the wall momentos. They were arranged unusually high, almost touching the ceiling, leaving a large gap between them and the floor. Normally, a person's articles of achievement were placed at or slightly above eye level, coming to the immediate attention and esteem of anyone who entered the room. But their position minimized the effect.

Was it because he considered himself in such a high regard the reason he placed the achievements so high? Subliminally telling anyone who cared to notice he was above them all, looking down on them? Hager shook his head.

"No, he didn't put them there for that reason. He put them so high because they were out of his reach. A place he'd been before, but would never be able to rise to such a level again. That was the reason. He didn't hold himself above anyone else; he considered himself a failure, still below what was expected of him."

Hager had part of his answer. Some of the truth for which he'd been searching. An insight into the mind of the monster.

On the dresser stood a picture of Moffitt and an older woman, presumably his mother. A frail looking woman, who by the look on her face treasured the young man with his arm around her. Hager looked on the floor next to dresser and saw the back side of a fallen picture frame. It was a photograph of a distinguished looking man decked out in a dress white uniform of the Navy. Hager could tell by the stars on his collar, the man in the picture was Moffitt's father, the Admiral. Why was it on the floor? Had it fallen in some sort of careless rush? Hager looked on the dresser for any settled dust revealing the picture's position. Too clean. Not a speck of dust around.

Hager believed the picture wouldn't have fallen in such haste. Moffitt seemed to be too discriminating to allow a fallen picture to stay on the floor for very long. No, it was placed there intentionally. As some symbol of disregard for his father. Maybe Moffitt couldn't stand to see his father's face, probably imagining the picture barking orders, telling him he was no good. Hager could see it. If Moffitt had *any* stress over the killings, Hager imagined the killer turned the photograph of his father away, fearing reprimand for his deeds. If his picture was face down on the floor, then the Admiral wouldn't witness the crimes of a son gone bad.

Why was his mother's picture still there though? Was she the acquiescent sheep giving in to her son's wants, showing her love, but at the same time, never coming to his defense against his father? Hager guessed Moffitt was showing his mother he was doing something special. It all made sense. In just a few minutes in Moffitt's room, Hager had already ascertained some conclusions about Moffitt's personality. Was he right? There was only one way to find out.

After studying the interior of the bedroom, Hager perused through the huge walk-in closet. Hanging on two door pegs was a large *Hustler* calendar. Surprisingly, Hager resisted glancing at the nude model for January, only catching a glimpse of skin. Like the rest of the apartment, the closet was overly neat. The clothes were arranged in order, dress shirts, casual shirts, jeans, slacks, sport coats. On the closet shelves were dozens of white cardboard shoe boxes stacked neatly on top of each other. On the face of each box, the name of a trading card company and year was printed in black. Hager guessed Moffitt was a sports card collector and a thorough one, too. On the same shelf, were three stacks of magazines. Hager pulled down one and saw it was *Time* magazine's most recent issue. He flipped through the pages, finding nothing important. Pulling down the other piles, Hager discovered Moffitt had accumulated three years of the magazine.

On the floor Moffitt arranged his shoes, neatly paired with their mate. Like the clothes, they were catalogued by style and color. Sneakers, casual browns, blacks, dress browns, blacks. It was eerie. Like he'd walked into a pseudo-Felix Unger's bedroom. In one corner of the closet, a large black trunk with gold trim sat on the floor waiting to be opened. In fact, Hager imagined the trunk talking to him, telling him what he sought was cozily tucked inside. It was locked.

Before he moved it, Hager had a crime scene specialist, ironically, Moffitt's partner, Betsy Steelman, take photographs of the trunk in its original position in case it proved to be of evidentiary value. The padlock securing the hasp was no match for bolt cutters. Hager, Morales, Josephson, and Steelman stood over the trunk anticipating the contents like pirates awaiting buried treasure. When Hager opened it, he found out it was full of treasure. Not full of jewels, doubloons, or ill-gotten booty pillaged by pirates long ago. It was the treasure chest of murder and redemption.

Before Hager rifled through the myriad of clothes, jewelry, shoes, and other souvenirs, Steelman snapped another picture. The contents didn't surprise Hager. Women's lingerie, other clothes, small items of jewelry, shoes, fingernail polish, panties, stockings, and four envelopes containing human hair, labeled with the name of each victim.

Heather; Tamara; Kathryn; Missy.

How bizarre, Hager thought, referring to the hair. He wasn't surprised at Moffitt's attention to organization. The entire apartment reeked of it. Against the edge of the trunk, a manila folder rested, and Hager opened it to find an assemblage of newspaper clippings of the murders. Behind the clippings were photocopies of articles which sent a frigid chill up Hager's spine.

In order, Moffitt had photocopied articles from newspapers about Hager when his unit was formed, his wife Kelly's obituary, and a small blurb about Elizabeth graduating from high school. A thick stack of computer paper with a variety of names on it was stuffed under some clothes. The heading on the paper read:

University of North Carolina-Chapel Hill-Enrollment List Fall–1996

333

The names were listed alphabetically; Hager flipped to the letter "H" where he found Elizabeth's name encircled in ink. "That's how he got to her," he mumbled. Anger and fear poured over Hager's body.

On the very bottom of the trunk was an envelope addressed to Tom Moffitt from "Mom" postmarked July 1996. Inside the envelope was a small newspaper clipping featuring a picture of a pretty young brunette. The headline read:

Reynolds-Mitrani Engaged

Under the caption was a wedding announcement:

Mr. and Mrs. Rudolf Mitrani announce the engagement of their daughter, Molly Ann Mitrani to Steven Reynolds, both formerly of San Diego, California. The couple plan a Christmas wedding in Hawaii.

Hager couldn't tell from which newspaper the clipping came, but he thought either the girl or her intended husband was undoubtedly someone important in Moffitt's life at some time.

"Probably the girl," Hager concluded. "Must be a former girlfriend."

Everything important to Tom Moffitt, a.k.a. "The Strangler" was in the trunk, with one exception, however. Where were the photographs of his victims? Certainly, someone as adept at photography as Moffitt would have snapped a few shots to have a visual link to his fantasy world. Or was his imagination so extraordinarily vivid he had no need for photos to rekindle his lust? Hager refused to believe it.

"There's got to be some photos," he reasoned. "But they're probably stored somewhere else. This trunk was just his prop box. The pictures have got to be around here somewhere."

They looked in drawers, on shelves, under the bed sheets and pillows, literally tearing the place apart, to no avail. Hager stood in the bedroom, and his two partners returned after scrounging the rest of the apartment.

"I found some film developing equipment in a cabinet in the guest bathroom," Josephson said. "He must've developed his pictures in there."

Hager turned to the closet and forcefully opened the door, causing the calendar to fall to the floor. Hager looked at the date keeper and noticed something peculiar about the model's face. He looked closer and to his shock, the faces of Moffitt's victims had been cut from photographs and pasted over the original model's face. And the faces weren't smiling. From their appearance, the pictures were taken after the girls had been killed, their eyes exhibiting the look of death. Why had he not noticed it before? The job was expertly done, and the cut-outs neatly trimmed for a perfect overlay.

Hager felt sick to his stomach; a painful headache emerged. He flipped through the months of nude women until he came to December. To his horror and disbelief, the woman, donning nothing but a Santa hat, had the familiar face of his daughter. She was the only face smiling, and he remembered the Polaroid Elizabeth had given him when Moffitt passed himself off as a rep from *Playboy*. Hager closed his eyes and his body shook in hatred. Still holding the calendar, his hands trembled in a battle with his brain to rip the paper to shreds.

Hager's good sense prevented destruction of the calendar, but he wanted to hold it no longer. He had endured enough.

"You take it before I put a match to it," Hager said, tossing it to Josephson. "I need a drink."

Hager walked out of the apartment.

When Hager returned to his office that evening, he was in an irritable mood. Maxwell had left a voice message about a car having been reported stolen in Buies Creek. It was stolen from the same parking lot where the bloodhounds' trail had ended, and they assumed it was Moffitt's doing. A dark green 1994 Toyota Camry was entered into NCIC as stolen, with all the cautions regarding Moffitt. The car's description was provided to the media as well.

Hager called the hospital for an update on Lloyd. He spoke to Martha. The surgery was a success, but Lloyd was in a coma. Martha sounded exhausted, her voice scratchy. She'd been running on little sleep over the past twenty-four hours. Hager was remorseful for not being at Martha's side while she desperately waited for Lloyd to awaken. He wanted to be there to provide some company in her late-night vigil. But Hager knew he had to maintain the pursuit of Moffitt. He promised Martha he would visit the hospital tomorrow.

That night, Hager slept restlessly again, as he'd done since Lloyd's attack the previous day. Only with the help of copious amounts of alcohol did sleep find him the night before. Vivid images of Elizabeth's face on the monster's wall kept flashing in his head, thinking the unthinkable. Of what Moffitt did with it. What he did with all of them during his fantasies. Whenever he consciously thought about it, his body would clench so tightly, he would shake and his face would turn a bright red. Moffitt had to die.

Hager awoke weary from little rest and from considerable stress of the past two days. Rising early, Hager and Josephson planned to drive to Norfolk and meet with Moffitt's parents. The FBI had his parents' home under surveillance for two days and reported no unusual activity. The visit was no surprise to the Moffitts as their son's picture was plastered on every television screen in the country. In fact, they expected Hager's call to set up the interview with them much sooner. They had no idea of their son's whereabouts, but Hager insisted he needed to talk with them anyway. He wanted to clear up some loose ends. Josephson drove, and Hager managed to doze frequently, only to awaken when his head drooped too far.

Hager recognized both Admiral Moffitt and his wife from their photographs. The Admiral stood proudly in the doorway and afforded the agents entry into their home. Mrs. Moffitt appeared to be older and more frail than in her picture, with graying wiry hair. She wore an amiable smile, quite the contrast to her husband who greeted the agents with indifference.

They faced each other in the Moffitt's living room, both parents seated together on a sofa, while the agents were offered some uncomfortable hard backed chairs. The Admiral sat with his arms crossed, an overbearing look on his face.

"He definitely wore the pants in this family," Hager said to himself. She, on the contrary, kept smiling like a gracious host, treating them like guests instead of law men trying to arrest her son. Hager thought she acted strangely and wondered if maybe she suffered from Alzheimer's disease. Maybe she'd forgotten the news of the past two days but could remember what she did twenty years ago.

Hager's strategy was to get the Moffitts to talk about their son in as much depth as possible. It was important for Hager to comprehend their son's personality from all angles in order to determine reasons for Moffitt's crimes.

"Mr. and Mrs. Moffitt," Hager began. "I assure you we believe you haven't seen Tom. That's not what this interview is about. I'd just like to get answers to some lingering questions about all of this."

Mrs. Moffitt looked at the Admiral for approval, and then started to speak, but was interrupted by her husband.

"Agent Hager," he said in an authoritative voice. "I think I speak for my wife and myself, and we just don't know what help we could be to you."

"Well, Mr. Moffitt—"

"Admiral if you please," he snapped.

"Yes, Admiral. I understand your sense of loyalty to your son but—"

"Oh, it's not because of loyalty, Agent Hager. It's because we don't know what we could possibly say that might help you catch him. No, no."

He shook his head.

"It's definitely *not* loyalty."

"Agent Hager?" Mrs. Moffitt asked, her voice soft and slow. "Are you sure my Tom is guilty of all this? How do you know he killed those girls? I just can't believe my son would do such terrible things." She shook her head in disbelief.

The Admiral rolled his eyes at his wife's comment.

"Nancy, the boy may have killed a cop for God's sake! Of course he killed those girls. I told you Tom needed some help years ago, but you let him go. You just let him keep stalking that poor girl until she threatened to have him arrested. He's no damn angel."

"Oh, Richard, don't swear!" she scolded.

The Admiral huffed and waved his hand at her to push her away.

These two were a pair, Hager thought. They certainly were no Ozzie and Harriet.

"What about Tom stalking a girl? When was this?" Hager asked.

"He wasn't stalking her, Agent Hager," Mrs. Moffitt said. "Tom was just deeply hurt by this...this..."

She tried to think of a polite word which could accurately describe the girl.

"Whore," the Admiral blurted, filling in the blank.

"Richard!" she shouted in disbelief.

"I'm just telling the truth, Nancy," he said. "I call a spade a spade."

"Admiral, who was this girl?" Hager asked.

"Molly Mitrani," she answered out of turn.

Hager recognized the name from the news excerpt found in Moffitt's trunk.

"Molly Mitrani," Hager said. "The one who was going to marry the Reynolds boy."

By the looks on their faces, the Moffitts must have thought Hager to be psychic.

"How did you know that, Mr. Hager?" the Admiral asked.

"Oh, I found a newspaper article in Tom's bedroom closet. A wedding announcement or something?"

"You searched his apartment?" she asked, shocked.

"Yes ma'am, I did. I had a search warrant." Hager replied.

"Of course they searched his apartment," the Admiral snapped. "The boy killed someone. They've got to do their jobs!"

She shuddered and shook her head.

"I just don't think you have the right to look through my son's personal things like he were some criminal."

Hager gasped, and although it wasn't funny, he almost laughed at the woman's absurdity.

The Admiral shook his head violently and rolled his eyes again.

"When are you going to get it through your thick skull? That goddamned kid of ours is a killer! He's not just a criminal; he's a killer!"

Mrs. Moffitt shook her head in silent dismissal and tears welled in her eyes. This wasn't going very well, Hager thought. Mrs. Moffitt excused herself, crying. Hager heard her walk up the stairs, and then a door slammed shut.

"I apologize for her," the Admiral said. "She's in denial as you can see. It's too bad. She loves him so much and wanted him to be perfect. She tried too hard. She thinks it's her fault."

He shook his head and continued.

"He's just a troubled kid, that's all. He was never able to do anything for himself. It was always take, take, take. He never once gave anything to us."

"People make choices, sir," Hager said. "He's definitely troubled, but he chose to do what he did. It had nothing to do with his mother or you. I hope you tell her that."

He nodded.

"You know, Agent Hager, Tom was adopted. Maybe he has some genetic defect, or his natural parents did drugs that caused him to have brain damage. It had to be something like that. He was a good kid growing up, you know. He had everything going for him. Basketball, baseball, football. He could have gone anywhere and played those sports. I pulled a few strings and got him commissioned to attend the Naval Academy, one of the best schools in the country. But no. He wanted to have it his way. He wanted to go to school with that girlfriend of his."

"Tell me about her." Hager said.

"Well, it all started back in San Diego in high school. He and Molly started dating. Her dad was in the Navy, too, a Commander, but he retired and moved back to his hometown in Indiana. Tom had gotten offers to play football and baseball at USC, UCLA, Arizona State, and some other major schools, Notre Dame included. Molly wanted to go to Notre Dame, too. You know, to be near her parents, I guess. So, after I busted my ass to get him into Annapolis, he tells me he's going with her to Notre Dame and play football. I said, what the hell. At least he made up his mind and picked a pretty good school. He got a full ride to play football and blew out his knee the first month of practice. Boom, there goes the scholarship, there goes the career. It blew up right in his face."

He took a breath went on.

"So, I tell him he can still get into Annapolis and make a career like the old man, you know. Hey, it was all right for me. But he wanted to stay with her. Before, he had his sports and her, but now he just had her, and from what we learned later, he smothered her."

"Tell me about her. About Molly," Hager asked.

"Yeah," he said like he'd forgotten the original request. "Well, during college, since Tom had to pay his own way and work while he was at school, Molly started dancing at some topless joint."

He had to pay for college. The kid lost his scholarship because of a football injury, and his own father wouldn't pay for him to continue in school. All because he wouldn't go to his precious Annapolis. What an asshole!

The Admiral continued.

"Tom hated her working there, but since she was making a good hunk of money, she stayed. Well, from what Tom told us, she started hanging around with her dancer friends and started taking drugs. Soon, he told us he'd broken up with her. But a couple of months later, we found out the truth. It was really Molly who'd broken it off with him. She'd gotten involved with some guy who managed the club. She told us Tom showed up at her work every night, harassed all her customers, and threatened them if they looked at her too long. She'd had enough. Finally, he was banned from coming to the club, and soon he started following her, showing up in the parking lot, at her door, leaving her notes, and messages on the phone. He was obsessed. Not until she threatened to put his ass in jail did he stop and finally realize she was just a whore who would screw around on him anyway."

"Was he ever charged with anything?"

"No, he wasn't. We promised her Tom would stop if she didn't. And that was that."

"If Tom had forgotten about her, then why did his mother send him that wedding announcement?" Hager asked.

"Oh, yeah," he said, rolling his eyes. "She always thought Molly was the wrong girl for Tom anyway. You know, the protective mother over her baby boy. She sent it to show him she'd turned out like she'd thought she would. A whore."

"Admiral, when's the last time you saw Tom?"

The Admiral put his hand to his face and thought for a minute. He returned his eyes to Hager.

"Tom visited us unexpectedly. I believe the first weekend after New Years. Came late at night. Woke us both up. I think it was either the third or the fourth of January, but it was late on a Friday, I believe."

"What did he say was the reason for the visit?"

"He never did, which I thought to be odd," the Admiral said with a confused look on his face. "He had to leave several hours later when he was paged to respond on a call. Something about a murder."

That was it, Hager thought. Another answer to a lagging question posed from the beginning.

Why Ahoskie? Why would the killer take a girl from Greenville, kill her, and then dump her body in Ahoskie?

Hager knew. He remembered looking at a road map, seeing that Highway 11 ran with Highway 13, which came from Greenville through Ahoskie. The intersection of Highway 13 and 11 was less than five miles from the Potecasi Creek bridge. Highway 13 continued north in the direction of the Virginia line. Moffitt was already trying to cover his tracks by going to his parents' home in Norfolk. The perfect alibi, just in case.

35

LLOYD SHERIDAN was more than Clark Hager's friend. He was Hager's best friend. The kind of friend who many never get to experience. One to whom he was infinitely close, as if they had a pseudo-marriage of intertwining relationships from confidante to acting like a big brother. A partner at work, but more than just a partner on whom he relied to serve as protector, counselor, and critic, inspiration and support unit when times were low, like when Kelly died. No, not only a best friend or a partner. He loved him.

Hager remembered the pillar of strength Lloyd was five years ago during the months of depression. Lloyd and Martha invited them to their home for dinners, brought gifts of food, and especially during Christmas, they both tried to fill the void evoked by the death of Kelly. Along with other members of both Hager and Kelly's family, the Sheridans endeavored to recreate a sense of normalcy in their lives.

Lloyd was there, and he shared Hager's pain and mourning like it was his own, knowing if the situations were reversed, Hager would do the same thing. Now it was Hager's turn to be there for Martha, and he didn't know if he could do it. He took a deep breath and entered the hospital room.

Lloyd lay still in the bed, deep in the sleep of a coma with tubes coming from more parts of his body than Hager could count. His partner didn't look good. A white bandage covered his head, draping just above his eyes. Lloyd's skin was pale—almost transparent, his lips and eyelids were a bluish color. A life-support machine breathed for him; it groaned with every life-giving pump.

Hager touched Lloyd's hand and although it felt warm, the nails were discolored with the look of death he had seen so many times. Death started at the extremities and slowly worked its way to the soul. The grim reaper was coming.

Hager swallowed his pain and looked at Martha seated beside the bed. He gave her his best look of reassurance. She smiled, a glimmer of hope in her swollen eyes, red from a river of tears.

"Are you all right, Martha? Do you need me to get you something?"

Martha shook her head and smiled faintly.

"No. I'm fine."

"What did the doctor say?"

"The surgeon came in a little while ago and said Lloyd's brain activity is below normal. They gave him some other drug to stimulate brain waves, but they won't know anything for sure until he wakes up. The doctor's not ruling out severe brain damage. He said the coma is the best thing that could happen to him. It allows the brain to recover from the surgery."

She rubbed Lloyd's arm.

"The nurses said Lloyd could hear us. That we should talk to him. Encourage him to fight."

"It's a good idea. I've heard that, too."

"The funny thing is, Clark," Martha's mouth trembled, her eyes watered. "I don't know what to say." She broke into sobs and covered her mouth. Hager went to Martha and put an arm around her shoulder. She nuzzled her face against his hip and wept silently.

343

Composed enough to talk again, Martha raised her head and wiped her nose.

"Lloyd's always been the strong one. Always had an upbeat outlook. I was always the one down. He should be here and I in his place. I'm not any good at this."

"Just tell him you love him, Martha. Say you miss him and want him to come home. Talk to him like you do at the dinner table."

She chuckled. "All I do there is laugh at his crude jokes and stories he picked up during the day."

The image of Lloyd telling a joke flashed in Hager's mind. He saw Lloyd's face, his cheek stretched to hold a wad of tobacco.

Martha held Lloyd's hand and started to cry again.

"He's gonna be fine, Martha. You know Lloyd. He's got a lot of fight in him. It'll just take some time."

Martha turned and looked Hager directly in the eyes.

"Do you really think so?" she asked.

Martha seemed to be looking for an answer. Someone to say her husband would be okay. But up to then, she had only been given a series of "wait and sees." Hager stood silently, gazing into her eyes wanting to reassure her. But deep down, he thought Lloyd wouldn't pull through. He looked too dead. But Martha needed to be lifted onto a plane of optimism. Not only for her sake, but for Lloyd's because if he managed to awaken, it would be due to Martha's words of encouragement.

Martha waited for his answer.

"Yes, I'm sure," he said, giving her arm a squeeze. "Lloyd's gonna be fine. Just keep hoping.

Her eyes gleamed in response. His answer appeared to make a considerable impact because her face brightened and her voice sounded more cheerful. Like Hager was a healer whose word people clung to whenever he made a prediction.

"Say something to him, Clark. You know he wants to hear your voice."

Now Hager was at a loss for words.

"What should I say?"

"Isn't that my line?" she chuckled. "I don't know. Tell him you're here. Tell him he better get well. He'll listen to you."

"Right," Hager said with sarcasm.

Lloyd remained still. No change in the minutes passed since he really looked at him. He didn't look good at all.

Do it for Martha.

He leaned over the bed and massaged Lloyd's shoulder.

"Lloyd, it's Clark," he said softly. "You keep fighting, all right? Don't give up. There's a lot of people depending on you. I've got a new joke from Dad. You're gonna love it. I'll talk to you soon."

Hager straightened, tears welling in his eyes.

"I'll get him, Lloyd," he whispered. "Just like the picture. I'll get him." Hager recalled the stick-figure drawing of "The Strangler."

Hager gave Martha a hug and left the room. He was on the brink of weeping and he clenched his lips together, holding it back.

Keep it inside for now. Save the hate for the monster.

Vanessa and Elizabeth were in the waiting room with the rest of Lloyd's family. Hager entered the room and all talking ceased, somber faces looking to him like he was a bearer of tragic news. Hager smiled in spite of feeling a little uneasy from the morbid glances. Brighter faces responded to his reassuring smile, realizing he brought no terrible news. Looking around the room, a little boy, Lloyd, III sat on the floor in the corner playing with a pile of toys, seemingly oblivious to the tragedy causing the gathering. A television on the wall blinked silently.

He spotted Vanessa and Elizabeth sitting next to an elderly woman. When Hager approached, he immediately noticed the woman shared Lloyd's intense eyes. Lloyd's mother.

Both Vanessa and Elizabeth rose when Hager walked over to them. Vanessa introduced Hager to Lloyd's mother Estelle Sheridan. He offered his hand but she, instead opened her arms and wrapped them around Hager's waist. Hager gave her a hug and when she released him, he looked deep into her eyes. Lloyd had inherited their intense blueness from her. To Hager, it was like seeing Lloyd instead of his mother. Imploringly, her eyes gazed deeply into Hager's,

345

unwavering, while communicating a helpless, yet one of resolved confidence that she was looking at the man who would vindicate her son. He smiled into her eyes, and she smiled back, nodding her head affirming the message had been telepathically delivered.

Bob Maxwell was waiting in the hall outside Lloyd's room. He held his head down. His arms were folded across his chest as his back rested against the wall. Hager turned to Vanessa.

"Wait for me at the elevator. I'll be there in a minute. After I see what Bob's got."

Vanessa nodded. She and Elizabeth continued down the hall after Hager stopped to confer with his boss.

"Bob? What's up?"

"Clark, how you holding up?"

"All right I guess. You got something for me?"

"The stolen Camry turned up. In the parking lot of a bus station in Fayetteville. It had been hot wired."

"Bus station? Did they check to see if Moffitt got on a bus?"

"They checked the name, but no luck. That doesn't mean too much. He could've paid for a ticket in cash and used a fake name. Hell, he's done it before."

"What about his picture? Did they show Moffitt's picture to the clerk to see if he was there?"

Maxwell sighed.

"The clerk at the bus terminal said the car was there when he got to work this morning. There's no telling how long it's been there. They're trying to round up the third shift person right now. But Clark, there's one thing I didn't tell you."

"What's that?" Hager asked worried.

Could it be something else to terrorize him even more?

"He left you a note in the car. The cops in Fayetteville said it looked like it was written in blood."

Wow, this guy is a walking book of cliché. What else is next?

"What did it say?" Hager asked, not wanting to know, but knowing all along what it probably said.

He opened his notebook and flipped through some pages.

"I wrote it down exactly as I was told by the officer. It said, Hager, I'm not finished yet. See you in hell."

Hager continued with his inquiry, appearing unconcerned about the message.

"Did they find anything else in the car?"

Maxwell shook his head.

"No, that's all they said. Just the note."

"I guess that was enough," Hager said and walked away.

Maxwell wrinkled his face at Hager's coarseness.

"Where do you think he'll go?" Maxwell asked, following Hager down the hall. "Do you think he's leaving the state?"

Hager stopped at the elevator. Vanessa smiled and Elizabeth pushed a button. Hager pulled out his car keys.

"Maybe. Maybe not. He may be trying to fool us or send us a message about where he's going. Evidently, there's still some unresolved issues. Make sure those agents in Virginia keep a sharp eye out at his parents' house. He may try to show up there. In the meantime, I'll check on another lead."

The elevator door opened and Hager walked in behind the two women.

"What other lead? What did you find out?"

"I don't know yet. There's just something I have to check. An old friend of Moffitt's."

"An old friend?" Maxwell gasped. "Where?"

"I don't know. That's what I have to check on."

Maxwell looked like he was ready to ask another question but the elevator door closed. He had a suspicious look on his face, like he thought Hager was up to something.

"Don't worry, Bob." Hager shouted through the door. "I won't do anything to blow this. I'm still under control."

"Keep me posted, Clark. Josephson will be available if you need him." Maxwell said as the elevator began its descent.

Even though Hager wasn't contemplating any clandestine assassination to fulfill a primal urge of revenge, the thought had entered his mind. He wanted to rid the world of this monster. But at the time, he had no idea where to start. Plus, in all his hate and anger toward Moffitt, he certainly wouldn't commit premeditated murder.

"Only if I get the chance," he mumbled.

"What did you say, Clark?" Vanessa asked.

"Nothing."

Darkness had fallen. The three endured the long walk to a parking deck where Hager's car awaited. While Hager walked he pondered Moffitt's next move. The answer to the question lay somewhere in the trunk of props belonging to Moffitt. Specifically, the envelope containing the newspaper clipping announcing the engagement of Molly Mitrani. If Moffitt had left town on a bus, then he had three choices: run as far and as fast as his resources would take him; seek refuge with his parents; or locate the root of his problem. The cause of it all, in his mind. Find the woman who stole his heart—Molly Mitrani.

All things equal, Hager chose the first and third alternatives knowing Moffitt was keen enough to assume his parents' house was under surveillance. He may have already called them and been informed of it. Of the final two options, Hager leaned toward trying to find Molly. The words in his message told Hager, clearly, *he* wasn't finished. "I", being singular, Hager thought it meant Moffitt may be finished terrorizing the agent. What a relief, if it were true. The last half of the message: *See you in hell*, told Hager that Moffitt intended whatever he hadn't finished, would signify some sort of finality to it all. More than likely, with his own suicide. His last deed, then, would be a murder/suicide. One so frequently portrayed in real life.

The game wasn't over, yet.

Hager decided to bypass going home. Instead he made a bee-line to his office. He drove in silence, still speculating "The Strangler's" ensuing movements. Moffitt's trunk was secured next to Hager's office in a room used for evidence storage. Hager had brought it there after seizing it from Moffitt's apartment.

With the touch of a few keys on the DCI terminal, Hager could locate Molly Mitrani, who was probably going under her married name of Reynolds, if she'd ever married. It would only take a few minutes to get a driver's license, especially with an unusual name like Mitrani. How many Molly Mitrani Reynolds could there be in the country? California and Indiana would be the first states he would try. After that, if he didn't find her, he would have to search by regions. It could take a while, but he was relying on her being in either of those two states.

Moffitt's parents had told Hager the clipping came from the San Diego *Union-Tribune*, but they didn't know where she lived now. They didn't have the Mitrani's phone number, only their address in Indiana. Hager could probably find them easier, but it would take a few calls to the phone company, and it was Saturday.

Hager pulled into the long entrance to the Highway Patrol Barracks and Training Center and turned left toward the SBI offices. The building was dark except for the parking lot lights and ambient light of the moon visible in the clear sky. Hager parked his car along the gravel drive that ran near the side of the building. Hager promised his ladies it would take only a few minutes for him to get what he needed, and once he retrieved the information, he would do the rest from his phone at home.

With Vanessa and Elizabeth patiently waiting in the car, Hager quickly stepped up the concrete walk and put his key in the door. The lobby was dark, but lit enough for Hager to see without turning on any lights. After all, he'd spent the last seven years following the same path every day. He could find it if he were blind.

As he padded his way down the hall toward his office, he suddenly felt a rush of alarm. His gut twinged from butterflies. Maybe it was the anticipation of finding Molly Mitrani. His mood had enlivened since he theorized Moffitt's next move, and he attributed the feeling to his excitement. Shaking his head in silent dismissal of the unnecessary warning from his body, he continued to his office.

Hager heightened his pace. His office door was open. When he crossed the threshold, the same warning feeling slapped his brain. He flicked on the light and started for his desk but stopped when he saw the object upon it.

A pistol. Not just any pistol, but a Beretta 9mm, stained red with blood. It was Lloyd's gun.

Suddenly, he felt his throat constricting as if someone were strangling him, cutting off his air. For a moment, Hager's heart seemed to stop. He couldn't breathe. He stood still for a few seconds, trying to determine if he were dreaming. Reality then dawned on him. He was in danger. His subconscious alarm was right.

Quickly, Hager looked around the room and backed against the wall. He flipped off the light and reached for his own pistol. Nothing. It wasn't there. He didn't wear it to the hospital and had left it in the car with Vanessa and Elizabeth.

"Shit," he whispered and then looked at the pistol on the desk again. Since he'd switched off the light, he couldn't see the pistol well enough to tell if the magazine was inserted.

"No way," he gasped, not believing his eyes. "There's no way he'd leave me a loaded gun."

Glued to the wall and having a view of the hall, Hager didn't want to leave his position. But Hager was unarmed at the moment, and Lloyd's pistol, so metaphorically placed on his desk, was his only hope of defending himself. But was Moffitt there watching him? Delighting in the observation of Hager's fears? Hager knew he was there. Moffitt's presence was detected by the agent's subconscious the moment he walked through the door.

The telephone. He could call for help and within minutes, dozens of agents would storm the place. His only source of strength lay on his desk. His eyes had adjusted enough to the darkness so he could see the line at the bottom of the pistol grip indicating a seated magazine. But was it loaded? Hager would never know unless he peeled himself away from the wall and picked up the weapon.

With a deep breath he took a long, quiet step over to his desk, picked up the telephone with his left hand, the pistol with his right. The phone was dead. Cradling the handset between his ear and shoulder, he pushed the buttons on the phone. It remained quiet.

"Damn, he killed the phone," he whispered.

Hager put the phone down and pushed the magazine release

button on the Beretta; the magazine dropped. He slowly pulled it out hoping, no praying, to see the brassy color of the shell casings.

Amen. Funny how one got religion in extreme peril.

In the darkness he couldn't make out the number of rounds he had, but it felt heavy like it was full. If it were, he would have 16 rounds with which to defend himself.

"Better see if there's one in the chamber," he told himself. With his right hand, he squeezed, pulling the slide slightly back to reveal the loaded cartridge. The slide clicked softly as he returned it forward, and he looked down at his desk calendar, where the pistol had been placed. On the white paper, written in black marker was a message from Moffitt.

To make it fair.

A cold chill leaped up his spine and his heart continued to pound severely. So much Hager thought he would have a heart attack right there.

"It was a game to him," he said. "Hunter versus prey."

The monster was close. Clutching the Beretta close to his chest, Hager found his place against the wall, overlooking the hall toward the lobby.

"Where is he?" he asked himself.

Even though he asked the question silently, Moffitt must have picked it up telepathically, seemingly on cue, Hager heard his voice.

"This was the only way I could make it just between you and me," Moffitt shouted, his voice coming from the lobby.

"Damn, I walked right by his ass just a minute ago," Hager said softly. "Why didn't he just kill me then?"

"I didn't want you to call for help from your buddies, so I cut the phone lines. I knew you would come here. I know you so well Hager. I want this to be *our* fight."

Moffitt sounded calm. A lot calmer than Hager felt.

Hager felt sweat dripping from his face. He quietly pulled off his sport coat and tossed it on the desk. Hager slid his way to the entrance of the door and quickly out, landing his back against the far wall. The faint outside lights rendered little to illuminate the lobby. In the pitch blackness of the hall, Hager took a deep breath, his chest still thumping, his legs feeling like rubber.

"What a shame it has to end like this," Hager said loudly, trying to make conversation while he inched his way down the hall. "I thought we could talk about why you did this. We could talk about Molly?"

Moffitt laughed sadistically like a devil. Hager listened for any indication of Moffitt's position. But the laugh scared him, and he knew Moffitt was prepared to die. It worried him. Once a person had readied himself for death, he was extremely dangerous because he had no fear.

With the Beretta held at his waist, Hager managed to slide with his back against the wall, almost the entire fifteen feet to the opening of the lobby.

Where would he be able to hide in the lobby?

Images of places sufficient in girth flashed in his head, and he arrived at one conclusion. A bookcase behind Judy's desk stood about six feet tall against the wall. It would provide some good cover. Moffitt was probably there.

"No," Hager said. "Don't feel like talking, huh? Aren't you tired of all the killing, Moffitt?" Hager said in a softer tone, not to telegraph his advanced position.

"Yeah, I'm ready for this to be over, Hager. Didn't you get my message? I'll see you in hell! I want it to end like this. Me and you. Winner take all."

"Haven't you done enough killing? How many has it been? Five?"

"Yeah, and the last one was the best. I got the biggest hard-on after I beat your partner's brains all over the place."

Moffitt laughed violently.

"Well, you didn't succeed with Lloyd. He's still alive. You lost that one, Moffitt."

Moffitt laughed arrogantly again. "That was just a battle. You and me. This is the war."

352

Hager clenched his teeth, his body shaking with anger. He neared the opening to the corridor, and the image of Lloyd's face appeared in his head. He was smiling with a wad of tobacco in his mouth, telling Hager to do it.

"Go ahead, Clark, you can do it," Lloyd's image whispered.

His mind flashed all the horrific images he'd witnessed, the faces of those beautiful women, so callously discarded at the whim of an evil monster.

He saw Moffitt's prop box, with all his souvenirs, the calendar with dead faces, and the face of Elizabeth. The body of poor Missy Campbell, an expendable pawn in Moffitt's game, not only to satisfy his lust, but to further terrorize his relentless opponent.

Hager returned to the image of Lloyd's face, but it slowly changed to the face of Lloyd's mother, with those piercing eyes she'd given to her son, silently giving him encouragement.

Moffitt took everything away from a lot of people. He had to pay.

Hager took a deep breath to quell his rage and muster his courage. He clenched the pistol in his sweaty hand and wiped his brow.

In one move Hager darted from the hall, firing two quick shots at the direction of the book case, hoping to draw Moffitt's fire. He crouched behind a leather chair. Three flashes from the muzzle pinpointed Moffitt's position. Moffitt fired two more times and Hager heard a round strike the chair. His right arm burned. Hager whipped his body around in pain, like he'd been stuck with a hot iron. He was shot.

"Get the hell from behind this chair!" he scolded himself, wincing from the pain, but not *really* feeling it.

Try for the door. It's only a little farther.

Hager peered from behind the chair watching for any movement. Seeing none, he fired three more quick flashes from the Beretta and rushed toward the door.

Like being hit by a car, Moffitt slammed into Hager's body, tackling him to the floor. Hager dropped his pistol. Moffitt's strength was immense as he grappled with Hager on the carpet in a flurry of never-ending punches to Hager's body. Hager felt a brush of air as Moffitt heaved him into the air, crashing him against the near wall. Hager sensed his own strength lessening and he was losing consciousness. He felt like he was going to vomit.

The flurry of punches continued. Hager managed to deflect them with his arms covering his head. Like a vise, Hager felt the sinews of Moffitt's arms around his throat and a rush of adrenaline fireballed through his body. Hager let out a loud cry.

I'm not going to let him win!

Hager pivoted to his right, landing a crushing elbow to Moffitt's head, which sent him toppling into the wall. Hager grabbed Moffitt by the shirt and with all of his strength tossed him like a sack of potatoes smashing against another wall.

Hager's head was spinning. He felt like his head was going to explode. He knew he couldn't stop Moffitt by himself.

The gun. Where is it?

Hager knelt on the floor. His hands combed the surface waiting for the feel of metal. Moffitt was on his knees. Hager was exhausted and about to pass out. Like a gift from above, his fingers touched the grip of the Beretta just as Moffitt staggered to his feet.

Hager couldn't see the monster's face, only his silhouette. But as he rose, the thoughts of all the victims flashed through Hager's head again. When Moffitt took the first step, Hager squeezed the trigger.

He fired three quick bursts. But Moffitt kept coming. Hager fired again and he still advanced. Moffitt's eyes were on fire. He moved in slow motion. Hager continued to pull the trigger. Slowly, Moffitt kept coming, the rounds having no effect. Just as Moffitt's hands reached for Hager, the slide of the Beretta locked back, empty.

Hager looked into the eyes of the devil. The glow was gone from them though. Moffitt's eyes rolled back and the monster fell to the ground, still clutching the agent's shirt with a grip of steel.

Hager used his last bit of energy to release the grasp and shove Moffitt's body to the floor. He collapsed as he heard a loud thud at the door.

354

The lights flicked on. Lying on the floor, Hager saw Vanessa come through the door, Elizabeth close behind her. In Vanessa's hands was his own Beretta he'd left in the car. She held the gun in front of her like she was a pro.

"Clark, oh my God!" she shouted.

"Oh, Daddy!" Elizabeth yelled.

Both of them dashed to him. Vanessa dropped to her knees beside Hager.

"Oh, Clark, what, oh my God! Liz, he's been shot!"

Elizabeth cried and put her hands over her face.

"Check on Moffitt," Hager gasped. "See if he's still alive!"

Vanessa looked at the body lying on the floor and shook her head in disgust and closed her eyes at the horror. Her eyes met Hager's.

"He's dead, Clark. There's no question."

Hager saw Moffitt's face covered with blood.

The game is over.

His right arm throbbed and he grimaced in pain. There was blood on Vanessa's hand.

"Liz, hurry, call an ambulance!" she cried.

Hager groaned as he tried to move. Elizabeth jumped over to Judy's desk and picked up the phone. She tapped on the buttons and sighed desperately.

"It's not working!"

"He cut the phone lines," Hager said, his breathing shallow.

"Get the cell phone in the car! Call 9-1-1!" Vanessa yelled.

Elizabeth darted out of the room. Vanessa held Hager's head in her lap. His arm was burning.

"I can't feel my arm."

Vanessa held him tightly, whispering, "You're okay, you're going to be okay. Just don't move."

She held him tighter.

"You just lie there and be still. You're going to be fine," she whispered, tears rolling down her cheeks.

Hager smiled and realized he was going to survive. His daughter was summoning medical help and the love of his life was holding him, comforting him like the good wife she would make. The love he felt for her at that moment was the feeling for which he passionately longed. The good wife, he imagined.

"What a perfect idea," he said to himself.

"What were you going to do with my gun back there?" he asked her.

"What do you think?" she answered, crying and she smiled seeing the grin on his face.

Hager laughed and smiled again. It was a safe-feeling smile. Like being in his mother's arms again. No one could hurt him now. Hager heard the faint wailing of sirens, then Elizabeth's footsteps as she returned to the office. Hager nodded his head and smiled. A teasing grin emerged on his face.

"You have any more of that whipped cream?"

She broke out laughing but crying, and then laughing again, and still crying. She kissed him and her mouth was wet with tears.

"I love you, Clark Hager."

EPILOGUE

Three hours later

HAGER TIPTOED into Lloyd's room. The room was dark; only the television flickered. A blanket covering her, Martha was asleep in a recliner next to the bed. A book lay unfolded in her lap. When Hager opened the door, light from the hallway cast gothic shadows on the bed and wall.

Hager quietly inched near the bed, not wanting to disturb Martha's sleep. Lloyd was still comatose. An IV bottle dripped overhead and the life support machine hummed.

Hager's entire body ached with pain. It hurt to breathe with the three broken ribs and numerous contusions. The bullet from Moffitt's gun managed to pass cleanly through Hager's arm without inflicting any serious nerve damage. The nurse had given him a pain killer and it made him sleepy. But before he drifted off to sleep, he wanted to talk to his friend.

Hager adjusted the strap of the sling immobilizing his arm. He stood close to Lloyd and touched his shoulder.

"Hey, buddy. It's Clark. How you making it?"

Lloyd remained quiet. Hager took a deep breath and sighed.

"I wanted to tell you, Lloyd. We got Moffitt. It's over. We won. He'll never hurt another person again. All you have to do now is wake up. Come on, man. It's over. Moffitt's dead. Wake up."

Lloyd didn't move. Hager's eyes burned with tears.

"All right, Lloyd. You take your time and get better. We'll be here for you."

Hager squeezed Lloyd's hand and started for the door. A familiar gruff voice followed him.

"I hope you got in a couple of shots for me, partner," Lloyd said, his eyes straining to open.

Hager smiled as a tear ran down his face.